The Rebel Priest

WIM HORNMAN

Translated by
J. MAXWELL BROWNJOHN

COLLINS
St James's Place, London
1971

William Collins Sons & Co. Ltd.
London · Glasgow · Sydney · Auckland
Toronto · Johannesburg

First published in Holland under the title
DE REBEL

© 1969 Uitgeverij J. H. Gottmer, Haarlem

ISBN 0 00 221724 4

Set in Monotype Baskerville

Made and Printed in Great Britain by
William Collins Sons & Co. Ltd., Glasgow

The Rebel Priest

This very moving and dramatic novel is set in Latin America where riches and poverty are to be seen in exceptionally glaring contrast. The hero is a young priest, Antonio, who, moved by the appalling conditions, preaches reform until he realizes that reform will never come.

His decision to join the rebels, which will inevitably involve his being forbidden to continue to function as a priest, rather than to accept the existing situation, is made the more difficult by the fact that his superiors value and admire his courage and offer him various compromises. He refuses and they warn him that, apart from other considerations, he will not come out of his adventure alive, to which he replies: 'What counts is not a man but his ideas.' Not only his Bishop but even the harsh military men try to dissuade him, accusing him of preaching communism. He answers that what he is preaching is Christianity. And, in the event, he goes off to live it. But the cost to him is great; his old friends abandon him and the guerrillas whom he tries to join are highly suspicious of him. They do not trust any priest and one who has been ostensibly thrown out of the priesthood is perhaps still more suspect. Gradually the tension mounts and the story reaches its tragic but inspiring conclusion

To my friend Frans
without whose help this book could
not have been written

Preface by Yves Courrière

Che Guevara is dead. His name is known all over the world as a symbol of the revolt of the oppressed; but it also symbolizes a brand of Latin-American Communism which always gives rise to alarm. The name Che has the sound of a rifle shot reverberating among the harsh mountains where the resistance fighters of South America hide out. The name Camilo Torres, on the other hand, conjures up guitars, velvety eyes, curled lovelocks. The smooth-sounding name of the hero of some romantic operetta.

Yet today the name 'Camilo' is scrawled in tar on the shabby walls which in the suburbs of South American capitals hide the shanty-towns, those hideous cancers of a decaying civilization, from the eyes of tourists dazzled by the beauty of Pizarro's cathedrals.

Today the legend of Camilo Torres, who also died gun in hand, is becoming much more powerful than that of Che. Camilo is a more reassuring figure – because he was a priest. The Colombian oligarchy was absolutely right to see him as its chief opponent. So were the revolutionaries, for today all shades of revolutionary opinion are united behind the name of the rebel priest, from the sons of middle class liberals to the Communist or Castroist resistance fighters in the high mountains or the teeming jungles. Camilo Torres was a Colombian; he lived and fought in Colombia and for Colombia. He died from a Colombian bullet fighting in the Colombian resistance, but the oppressed of the whole South American continent identify with him, and in his name they organize and rebel. Camilo has become for them an international figure.

Wim Hornman tells the story of this extraordinary man's adventure in his novel, *The Rebel Priest*.

Except that, to me, it is not fiction.

There is not a single incident, a single scene described by the Dutch novelist which I have not personally experienced or witnessed or that has not been told to me in the course of my travels in South America. His hero, Father Antonio Valencia, *is* Camilo Torres.

7

Hornman himself says so in his introduction. And I, who met this priest in Bogotá a few weeks before he went over to the revolutionaries – I can vouch for it that the portrait is a true one. In Hornman's hands he lives again, real, sure of himself and of his cause, aligned with the poorest and most wretched, yet constantly battling with himself to overcome his natural and inherent timidity and get through to them. *The Rebel Priest* is also the emotional Camilo Torres, prepared to change his life because of what he felt, because of his need for justice.

Without undue emphasis, and with that simplicity which was one of Camilo's outstanding characteristics, Wim Hornman follows the route which led the heir of a great bourgeois family from his comfortable life in a rich villa in Bogotá to the seminary, then to the Catholic University of Louvain, and finally to the resistance.

Up to now, little is known in Europe of the 'Red Priest' – as his enemies called him – beyond a few papers, interesting enough to sociologists and students of political science, but much too scholarly for the layman. What a pity that a man of such profound humanity is nothing more to us than a somewhat vague and folklorish figure, a revolutionary priest. South America is such a long way off . . .

The publication of *The Rebel Priest* presents a Camilo very much like the one I remember from our first meeting. I can recall his features, his giant's stature, his ironical smile, his characteristic way of leaning back in his armchair. I hear his words, sometimes violent but always deeply imbued with that desire for justice which was his driving force. It is no longer the revolutionary ideologist, but the man. Alive.

It was in 1965 that I spent several weeks travelling in South America. When I arrived my eyes were dazzled with sun and marvels, my head filled with evocative names: Calláo, Marquetalia, Valparaiso, Pernambuco, Rio, Santiago, Bogotá.

From Plaza Bolivar to Plaza de Armas, from the Spanish cathedrals to the tombs of the conquistadors, from the Hilton to the Copacabana Palace, from the Caribbean Beach to the Bay of Rio, a tour of South America is an enchantment. So long as you see only that. So long as you want to see only that.

I had seen and marvelled at these splendours. But I had also seen so many frightful scenes, even atrocities sometimes, that when on 25 February, 1965, I kept the appointment granted me by this Camilo Torres who was talked of so much in Bogotá and whose reputation had even spread to Peru, Venezuela, Chile and Brazil, I was expecting to meet a kind of super-revolutionary parish priest.

One of those priests whom life in the shanty-towns has moved to don their armour and try by every feeble means in their power to attract the attention of the powers that be to those sub-human creatures who constitute one-half of the population of large South American cities; priests who also tried to stir the conscience of the oligarchy who have the money and the land and therefore power. One of those priests who provoke smirks or indignation at parties in Lima, Bogotá or Carácas.

At every stage of my journey – a journey to the lower depths of wretchedness in the most beautiful continent imaginable – I had got to know one of these men. At every stage I had left a friend.

Especially in Peru. A bare two paces from those marvels, the Merced and St Peter, St Augustine and St Dominic, religious masterpieces left like wondrous milestones along the blood-soaked track of Pizarro's men, I had met Father Jean-Marie P. He was living at Canto-Gallo (Cockcrow), a charming name for the most wretched shanty-town in Lima. Around the 'house' where he slept – with a revolver lying for safety on the soap-box which did duty as bedside table and bookcase – 15,000 men, women and children were herded into huts of tin and planks. The whole *barriada* was built on a rubbish-dump levelled by bulldozers. The sun and humidity fermented this vile substructure, and from time to time small craters opened at our feet, emitting a bluish flame and a pestilential stench. After a week I had touched rock-bottom. P showed me everything. Twenty-seven persons crammed into a single hut thirteen by thirteen. Daily incest. Children of eight drinking the terrible *chicha*, made from fermented maize. Little girls pregnant at the age of ten.

'At first I was with my brother, another priest,' he said. 'Seeing these wretched children, we used to take them in our arms to comfort them, show them a little kindness. It was a natural human reaction. We soon realized we must stop it. Among the little girls of eight and nine it led to misunderstanding. They thought we wanted to sleep with them. Not force them – oh no! – because here they're all consenting parties. A girl of that age knows that she exists for men to use and use again . . .'

After a few weeks I thought nothing could surprise me. With my traveller's cheques in my pocket, I could do anything, demand anything. I thought I'd seen and heard it all. But I hadn't yet.

After an evening spent with a compatriot in Parada, Lima's most dangerous quarter, where a man's life isn't worth two dollars and where I had seen young Indian girls forced to prostitute themselves

9

for a shilling, of which they themselves got only a quarter, P told me of the most frightful experience which can ever befall a priest. Even months later, and after witnessing so much daily suffering, he could not forget it.

Jean-Marie P and his brother had rescued an Indian girl who had escaped from the brothel of Parada. She was eighteen years old. Unspeakable terror was in her eyes. The mere presence of a man set her screaming.

'But two priests gave her confidence,' P told me, smiling.

He placed the girl in the care of a woman in the *barriada*. She had a great many children and an extra pair of hands was welcome. For the Indian girl it was a week of happiness. But when the father, who was working some thirty miles away, returned home on the Saturday evening, the storm broke. Screams. Hysteria . . .

The third week the two priests had to accept the evidence. The girl was mad. She needed care in a psychiatric hospital.

So the infernal round began. The hospitals were full. 'Find room for an Indian prostitute? You can't be serious, Father!'

Father P had done everything. He had even applied to the sisters of some order or other, well protected by the shade of the palms in their garden, very much at ease in their roomy consciences. The mother superior had looked at Father P in astonishment. There was a world of suspicion in her gaze. P had not insisted. For two pins he would have hung his head.

The thing became a nightmare. Jean-Marie P described it: 'We couldn't keep her. No one would help. My brother and I took her in our old car, telling her we were going to pick flowers outside Lima. She adored picking flowers. We drew up in the country some twenty miles from the town. The girl followed us. We picked flowers. She wandered a little way off. So my brother and I – priests, you realize – tucked up our soutanes, dashed for the car and left her. Yes, we abandoned her. There's no doubt some ponce or other caught her. She must be back in Parada or somewhere similar. And it was two priests who did that!'

Such incidents leave their mark on a man, despite thirteen years in these *barriadas* on the north bank of the River Rimac, which serves as water-supply, sewer and cemetery. And on the opposite bank, a stone's throw away, is the Lima of the rich. The old colonial city with its sumptuous palaces and the new town with its buildings for millionaires.

'Of course I've tried to revolt,' Jean-Marie told me. 'Once, on the radio, I even spoke of heads rolling, said that the rich let all this go on without taking into account that one day their heads would roll; but . . .'

'But what?'

'My brother, who didn't just say it but wrote it, has been driven out. We were accused of Communism . . . So I don't say anything in public any more, I don't want to be expelled. I stay underground. It's better to keep quiet and be able to go on helping these poor people. Besides, the day may come . . .'

Oh yes, the cardinal came down to the *barriadas*. Once. With a television crew. Children were to run down the hill and fling themselves on him, crying 'Little Father! . . . Little Father!' The cameraman gave the signal, the camera began to turn, the cardinal stepped majestically from his air-conditioned Mercedes and opened his arms, – and the children ran down the slope and surrounded Jean-Marie as usual, crying 'Little Father! . . . Little Father!' They didn't know the cardinal, they had never seen him before. P made himself a real enemy that day. Since then, the oily monsignori from the episcopal palace keep an eye on him.

This is what was going through my mind on that 25 February, 1965, at the corner of *carreras* 6 and 7 in Bogotá, whose rectangles of streets are set out with American-style buildings. Camilo Torres would be just another Jean-Marie P who was going to war. But what could he achieve, subject as he was to the orders of a hierarchy whose interests were identified with those of the Colombian oligarchy, those 180 families who owned most of the land?

I was to learn that Camilo was as far removed from folklore as from good works. He homed on the vital issue at once.

'In our country,' he told me at our first meeting, 'governmental decisions are produced by pressure groups. They will always come down on the side of their own selfish interests rather than the general good. So we have to change this power structure. And nothing can alter unless the members of these pressure groups are thoroughly frightened!'

It was the first time a man, a priest from the best section of the bourgeoisie, a doctor in sociology, a university professor, had calmly preached revolution to my face.

'What matters,' he went on, 'is that the revolution could be peaceful if the capitalists and the ruling classes began to be frightened and to make concessions, but there's no sign of that for the moment.'

'What about the Church in Colombia?'

'It is closely linked to the political and economic establishment.

11

So to square its conscience it goes in for a nice little paternalistic job of good works. But good works are a distorted form of charity.'

Camilo was sitting in a big armchair, and he pounded the arms to emphasize his points.

'True charity—'

He thumped the chair.

'True charity means seeking an effective way of doing good. In practice, our situation can be improved only by revolution. So revolution becomes true charity.'

'And what happens when you expound this view to some of the rulers of your country, to the representatives of the big landowners, to your own archbishops?'

'What indeed! They say I'm a Communist, that claims like these must be quashed at once. That I may be right, but that it's very dangerous to say such things.'

Of course it's dangerous. For them!

Matters didn't rest there. A week later Camilo published his *Socio-Economic Platform*. In March the youth of Medellin gave him an enthusiastic welcome. But the Catholic hierarchy accused him of 'active political participation', an extremely serious fault which warranted his dismissal. Camilo retorted by asking for his own immediate suspension. 'I'll say Mass again,' he declared, 'when the people have a voice at last and are no longer dying of hunger.'

It was too much. What follows is well known. Sickened by the mounting opposition which his action aroused, and with prison walls closing round him, Camilo Torres joined the resistance, after a long propaganda tour in the south-west of the country, in the course of which he repeated that slogan which was to become the watch-word of the most radical section of the popular movement:

'With or without Camilo, we'll have a revolution.'

This is the remarkable man whom Wim Hornman has undertaken to recreate before our eyes, displaying a knowledge of men and events which make his novel at once the most remarkable and the most realistic of the documents available on everyday life in this fierce, shameful, marvellous land which is Latin America.

A continent peopled by tens of thousands of sub-human creatures who are born, live, love and die amid general indifference in the most frightful conditions imaginable.

A vast, illimitable continent, the breeder of remarkable men who will some day rouse it from its lethargy.

Camilo is dead because 'the chief priests and scribes sought how they might take him by craft, and put him to death.'

Today his name is scrawled on the walls of the *ranchitos*, the *barriadas*, the *mocambos* and the *favelas*. His prediction, 'I shall be more use dead than alive' has come to pass.

The revolution knows how to recognize its most valiant sons.

Foreword

On 15 February, 1966, in the small Colombian village of Patio Cemento, the ex-priest Camilo Torres was shot by government troops during a clash between the guerrilla unit to which he was attached and a patrol of the Fifth Brigade.

His death provoked violent repercussions, particularly among the students, workers and peasants of Colombia, because he had for years been an ardent champion of improved social conditions and had also, as a priest, advocated a dialogue with the Marxists.

I have dedicated my book to this unusual figure in tribute to all those Latin Americans who have the courage to devote themselves, heart and soul, to the cause of the oppressed peoples in this part of the Third World. I have given Camilo Torres the name Antonio Valencia and surrounded him with a number of characters who are, except where I allude to actual occurrences, fictional. Nevertheless, the germ of the plot is based on historical events which are intimately connected with Camilo Torres and his time. Part of this book has an entirely independent dramatic content in which the reader will be able to recognize more than one person or country. Be that as it may, the character of Antonio Valencia is intended as an expression of my admiration for men like Camilo Torres, and I trust that his shade will forgive me for having recreated him with the aid of my imagination. It was he who galvanized the thoughts and ideas which, as I have discovered in many years of travelling throughout Latin America, can be found among a progressive minority of priests and laymen. These priests and laymen are in revolt against the blatant injustice that is being perpetrated on countless millions of Latin Americans who are only now awakening to a sense of their own value and human dignity.

Camilo Torres had the courage to preach open revolution. Having been debarred from pursuing his vocation and unjustly accused of the most heinous crimes, he realized that force was the only way out. He duly joined the guerrilleros and died in action against the army. His body was never released, nor were his mother and other relatives permitted to visit his grave. Even now they have no idea where he lies buried, a subject on which the authorities remain silent to this day.

Armed police forcibly dispersed church-goers when a requiem mass was eventually held for Torres in Bogotá, but students from the National University burst through every cordon and marched to the National Cemetery, where they paid symbolic homage to their former teacher over an imaginary grave.

People have debated whether Camilo Torres chose the right course and will no doubt continue to do so after reading this book. The fact remains, however, that he was not alone in resorting to violence. The same may be said of those who killed him and did not deign to grant him a Christian burial.

Oscar Maldonado writes from Colombia: 'Torres is dead, but his death does not absolve the new forces in Latin America from devising a new policy, nor does it absolve other nations from their duty to render assistance. Torres did not die for the sake of dying. We must not use his death as an alibi.'

Anyone who has followed the life-story of Camilo Torres will rediscover him in Antonio Valencia. I chose a fictitious name because it gave me, as an author, a chance to invest my principal character with even greater dimensions than the facts sometimes warranted. I have also set the scene in an imaginary country so as to shed light on conditions elsewhere in Latin America. This has transformed my characters into people, not of a single country but of an entire continent which I admire for the ardour with which progressive elements strive to assert their yearning for social justice, often at the risk of their own lives. It is to them that I erect this memorial in the hope that the world will awake to the awakening of Latin America.

Wim Hornman

I

The log cabin stood in the heart of the jungle several hundred kilometres from Cielo, the capital. It was built of dark tree-trunks so that it could not be seen from the air. Silence reigned there except when the wind swept through the leaves of the jungle, stirring them like the breath of some terrible god. There was almost no wind now. The leaves rustled gently as twilight descended on the forest.

Rodriguez Tobar was lying in a hammock outside his hut, smoking a cigarette. He looked grim, and the lips above his thick beard were tightly compressed. On a stool beside him sat Geraldo, another guerrilla leader. Geraldo, who was short and thick-set, wore ankle-boots and a black sombrero. His long pock-marked face, squinting eyes and brace of pistols made him look like a villain in a strip cartoon.

'You're a fool, Rodriguez.' Geraldo spat into the tall grass.

Tobar shrugged.

'What do you mean, *amigo*? Did you come here to insult me?'

'You know very well what I mean. Stop hedging. Nobody agrees with you.'

'About Antonio Valencia?'

Geraldo gave a contemptuous laugh.

'Who else? Of course I mean Valencia. I'm a Communist, and I say we've no use for mealy-mouthed priests. I'm told you've put our men in Cielo under his command. Have you gone out of your mind?'

Tobar turned to watch some heavily armed guerilleros who were coming along the path towards them, men whom he had trained to kill. They were dressed in green uniforms captured from the army and wore their beards clipped, Castro-fashion. Not one of them would have hesitated to mow down any government soldier sent against them.

'You really expect me to take orders from a priest?' Geraldo persisted.

Tobar puffed at his cigarette.

'We can go on talking inside if you like. Otherwise, better get out of here while the going's good.'

He opened the door of the hut and lit the acetylene lamp, which threw grotesque shadows on the wooden walls. He felt slightly ill at ease in his hide-out. The highlander in him detested the humid jungle valleys.

Geraldo followed him inside.

'Now sit down and stop trying to browbeat me. Want some wine?'

'Who gave you the authority to do this thing?'

Tobar grinned.

'Everyone. Last month we had a meeting, here in this hut. We discussed the matter and took a vote.'

'Why wasn't I invited?'

'Because we couldn't get in touch with you.'

Geraldo swore fluently.

'You're a bunch of imbeciles. Once a priest always a priest. Do you really think he'll co-operate with us for ever more? I'll tell you how it will be. First we'll pull the chestnuts out of the fire for him by fighting like madmen. We'll slaughter priests and string up capitalists, and when we've won he and his Catholic cronies will say *muchas gracias* and put us behind bars. That's how it will be, my friend.'

Rodriguez Tobar drained his glass, staring up at the bat that dangled from the roof of the hut. He could not dismiss what Geraldo had said. His own opinion of priests in general was much the same. The *cura* in his native village had ruled the place like a feudal prince. On Sundays he said Mass in the family chapel of the *haciendero*, the local landowner, and never reached the parish church before midday. His mouth was always full of God and heaven but he had never ventured to appeal to the landowner's conscience because he paid his *campesinos* an inadequate wage. Thanks were always offered to God and the *haciendero*, never to the workers. They were merely slaves of the ruling class.

'I have never met a priest like him before,' Tobar said, refilling their glasses.

Geraldo intently followed the progress of a large cockroach and then squashed it with the heel of his boot.

'Priests are swindlers,' he replied deliberately. 'Profiteers, that's what they are. They exploit the good faith of the poor so that the rich can fill their pockets. They claim to be sent by God, but the story doesn't hold water any more, not with me.'

18

'You've never seen him, have you?' There was something in Tobar's voice which made the other man look up.

'He certainly impressed you, from the sound of it,' Geraldo retorted sarcastically.

Tobar ignored the remark.

'I'm a simple man, Geraldo, even if I am in command of a whole province. I know how to run a guerrilla war. We operate in small groups. We teach our men never to play the hero and withdraw quickly when the job is done. There's nothing heroic about a guerrilla operation. We ambush men and shoot them down without warning. We have to be quick and elusive. We have to know the terrain – every stone and rock, every tree, twig and mountain path. We kill our enemies and take their weapons. We trust nobody and nobody trusts us. We're assassins, unseen and unwanted buriers of our fellow-men. Cowardice, that's our strong point – cowardice and the courage to admit to cowardice because we're not after medals or promotion, simply the death of our enemies.'

Tobar sensed that he had drunk too quickly. The other man's face looked blurred, but the wine was making him more articulate than usual.

'Have you ever met someone you admired?' he asked.

Geraldo shook his head.

'Why should I admire anyone? Admiration is unhealthy and dangerous, *amigo*. I'm a simple man too, but I have a certain amount of power and I plan to use it. If the army gets in my way, I fight. Nobody betrays us because we leave the *campesinos* in peace and make them presents of land. But as for admiring someone . . .'

Outside, someone was picking out a melancholy tune on the guitar and the men were singing to it in rough, hoarse voices. Moths flew into the lamp, scorched their wings and fell to the floor.

'I first got to know Antonio Valencia properly in Cielo. Believe me, Geraldo, it was dangerous there, but he didn't turn a hair. We met in one of the shanty-towns on the outskirts and talked together. There was something in his eyes which reminded me of a child. I'm not sure, but I think it was love.'

'Love?' Geraldo's hand did not waver as he refilled the glasses. 'Love? It doesn't exist, my friend! Love is a pretty word used to betray us. Anyone who starts a revolution has to hate, otherwise he's dead before the first gun goes off. Love is for the *curas* in their pulpits. They've used it to keep us docile for as long as I can remember, docile and content to rot in squalor.'

19

Tobar shook his head.

'You don't understand, Geraldo. Either that or you don't want to. Perhaps I should have called it kindness or a wish to help other people. That man is consumed by a sort of fire – you can see it in his eyes.'

'Idealists are dangerous, Rodriguez. We need leaders, not prophets.'

Tobar gave up. There was no point in explaining to Geraldo what he thought of Valencia or in trying to convey what had obsessed him ever since his return from Cielo.

'We're both tough, Rodriguez,' Geraldo said. 'You're as tough as I am but easier to influence – easier than me.'

'So you won't co-operate?'

Geraldo hesitated. He knew that to refuse would isolate him completely. His authority would dwindle without further supplies of arms and ammunition. He knew Tobar well enough to realize that revenge was inevitable.

'Well,' Tobar said, 'why don't you answer?'

Geraldo fixed him with his squinting gaze.

'What can I say? It's all settled. You've taken the best organized guerrilla outfit in Latin America and handed it over to a novice who doesn't even know how we operate, what we do, what our plans are. We may be assassins, Rodriguez, but you're a gullible fool.'

The last word was still unspoken when he felt a bony fist crash into his jaw. He toppled over backwards and lay there glaring up at Tobar, who stood over him with a face like thunder.

'Say that again and I'll fill you full of holes. Now get up and talk sense.'

Getting slowly to his feet, Geraldo saw two of Tobar's men in the doorway. Their guns were trained on him with silent menace. Tobar made a curt gesture of dismissal and poured some more wine.

'Are you ready to talk now, Geraldo?'

The squint in Geraldo's eyes seemed to vanish momentarily.

'I suppose that's how you deal with all your enemies. You drink a glass of wine with them. They say something you don't like, and *pum!* – you blow their heads off. What do you propose to do, force me to accept this *cura* of yours?'

For a moment the silence was so complete that they could hear the leaves rustle in the evening breeze.

Then Tobar said, harshly: 'Yes.'

Geraldo shrugged.

'Very well, who am I to argue with our *generalísimo*? Your word is law, but I tell you one thing: Christian charity sits strangely on a man who has chopped off scores of heads with a machete – or is it hundreds now?'

'Shut up, you fool!'

The wine mounted to Geraldo's head, blinding him to the need for caution.

'You call us bandits, brigands and criminals but you're the biggest of the lot. Aren't you proud of that, Rodriguez, or has the *cura* converted you already? Are we all suddenly to become meek as lambs, the way we used to be in the old days, when we let ourselves be dictated to by those bastard bishops in their palaces?'

'I told you to shut your mouth. Shut it or I'll shut it for you, understand?'

But Geraldo refused to be intimidated.

'You may not want to know, Rodriguez, but I'll tell you all the same. Every *cura* is the son of a whore to me, whether his name is Antonio Valencia or something else. The Church has been here for centuries, and what has it ever done for us? Come on, tell me, if you want me to take orders from a priest.'

Tobar's anger evaporated. Geraldo had a point. What right had he to reproach the man when he had never seen or spoken to Valencia? He and Geraldo had been allies ever since the civil war began. They had both suffered from the tyranny of landowners and the priests' lofty indifference to human misery. What would he have done in Geraldo's place? Would he have welcomed subordination to a *cura*?

'*Bueno, bueno* . . . We won't talk about it any more, Geraldo. Let's assume you're with us and leave it at that.'

Geraldo did not reply. Of course he would have to give way, even though a priest might endanger the cause they fought for.

'But Rodriguez, hasn't it occurred to you that our reputation may suffer if we join forces with a *cura*?'

Tobar laughed.

'Who knows how much longer Valencia will wear the soutane?'

A scornful smile still hovered round Geraldo's mouth. Antonio Valencia's pretty speeches would never convince him. His jaw still ached from Tobar's fist. Valencia would pay dearly for that blow one day. He refused to believe that any *cura* could be well disposed towards the guerrilleros and the people. Every priest wore the cloth of his calling for life, like an extra skin. Besides, Valencia came of a wealthy family. He would promise them the earth and then abandon them to their fate. Why should they have truck with a priest? Victory must go to the Communists, not the Church. Down with all *curas*, down with the lackeys of the rich, down with soft-spoken imbeciles in skirts. His day would come.

'All right, I'm with you,' he said aloud. 'I don't have any choice.' Tobar drew a deep breath.

'Sorry I hit you just now. I'm too quick-tempered.'

'Your wine softened the blow. I must go now.'

'I'll have some of my men escort you to the provincial border.'

The narrow path ascended gradually, flanked by dense undergrowth. There was a smell of rotting vegetation, a heavy, penetrating stench which induced sluggishness and fatigue. The jungle was full of nocturnal sounds: the screech of monkeys, the sudden creak of branches, the high-pitched, spine-chilling call of unseen nightbirds.

Tobar sat erect in the saddle, occasionally glancing back at the dim figures behind him. The horses were small but wiry and indefatigable. They trotted with flaring nostrils along the narrow forest track, as alert to sudden danger as their riders. Every man was armed to the teeth because a skirmish with the army could not be ruled out.

The district commander on the government side was Colonel Zambrano. Ably assisted by his U.S. advisers, Zambrano had made an exhaustive study of the guerilleros' way of life. Since then, special units of the national army had been trained in guerrilla tactics, so a ride of this kind could be fatal. In recent months Tobar and his men had been harried by the army like mad dogs. There had already been a number of clashes which had cost him several men and the army some dozens of soldiers.

But Zambrano refused to give up. There were evidently traitors inside the guerrilla organization, renegades who kept Zambrano informed. There had been no instance of treachery for ten years, and Tobar did not like the look of recent developments. It was a fight to the death now. If they ever caught him, which was not beyond the bounds of possibility, he would end his days in the torture-chambers of the secret police, but not before they had squeezed him like a sponge for names of confederates and particulars of the area in which he had been operating.

Tobar felt a twinge of uneasiness which grew stronger with every step his horse took. His carbine lay across the saddle with the safety-catch off. He wondered if he could trust the local *campesinos*. He knew that they never ventured outside at this hour. They lit the oil lamps in their squalid huts and crawled into their hammocks, where they lay apathetically until sunrise. And yet it was for their sake that the war had begun, a perilous war in miniature waged mainly in areas where landowners had exploited their peasant labourers with particular ruthlessness. Tobar knew every highway, track and path in his domain. He also knew the huts of his friends.

He strained his senses to the limit as he rode on. In recent years, all his active life had been spent in darkness. The guerilleros seldom showed themselves by day. Day-time was when they cleaned their weapons or slept.

'We're there,' he said. 'Dismount and follow me on foot.'

He handed his horse to the man who had been riding immediately behind him and set off alone up a narrow muddy mountain path which led to a hut about fifty yards off the track. As soon as the main force had eliminated all traces of their previous encampment, they would follow.

He was alone now, armed with a rifle, a pistol and a razor-edged machete. Being alone did not worry him. He knew exactly how many turns the path took before it reached the hut. Round the hut stood four trees. Beyond it was a paddock containing a few emaciated cows, and fifty yards beyond that was a stream which splashed and gurgled so loudly that no footfall could be heard. There was only the one path, which petered out immediately in front of the hut.

Colonel Zambrano's troops had never penetrated as far as this. They had once tried to, but ten kilometres short of the place they had run into an ambush. Of the thirty men in the patrol, only two had returned. Zambrano at once dispatched another unit, but they found the area completely deserted. Even the *campesinos* had abandoned their huts, so there was nothing left for the soldiers to loot in their customary way.

That was the army's weak point, Tobar reflected as he cautiously advanced up the path. Their discipline wasn't as good. His men didn't loot, and if they did he shot them on the spot.

'Halt!' The voice was calm, its owner nowhere to be seen.

Tobar recognized the voice but froze for safety's sake.

'It's me, Tobar,' he said, and waited for permission to proceed.

'Password?'

'Mexico.'

'*Bueno, Capitán*, proceed. And welcome!'

There was no irony in the salutation. The man meant it. His

23

home was here in the midst of jungle and mountains, a natural stronghold in the wilderness.

Raoul Castillo, Tobar's second-in-command, greeted him with an embrace. He was a heavily built, muscular man of about fifty. Tobar was acquainted with his past history. His family had been almost entirely wiped out by the army while he was away from home, a coincidence to which he owed his life. Castillo had no sympathy with any member of the ruling parties, liberal or conservative. To him, all landowners and government officials were fools possessed by the devil, and he exterminated them in cold blood. This set him apart from many of the others, who had begun by asking themselves whether violence was justified and ended by joining the guerilleros with a heavy heart, aware that there was no turning back. Castillo cleared a place at the table and poured Tobar a glass of wine. There was curiosity in his yellow face with its heavy pouches below the eyes.

'Well, *Capitán*?'

'I've decided to transfer base camp. This will be our new headquarters. How are things here?'

Castillo glanced round at his men.

'The waiting is beginning to tell on them, *Capitán*. They want arms, wine, better food, women.'

'What about ammunition?'

'More than enough.'

'Your objective is still the same?'

'Yes, the army post at Talmac.'

'How many men are based there?'

'Thirty or more.'

'Well armed?'

'To the teeth.'

'Do you have a plan?'

Castillo smiled. He knew Tobar and his aversion to running risks. Nothing must be left to chance. Every detail had to be settled in advance, every step worked out on paper beforehand.

'I will show you the plan tomorrow morning, *Capitán*. I think we should get some sleep now.'

'Have you posted sentries?'

'Of course.'

Tobar nodded. He stubbed out his cigarette, pulled off his boots and climbed into the hammock.

'Raoul,' he said after a minute or two.

'Yes, *Capitán*?'

24

'Do you ever have premonitions?'

'Plenty. If they had all come true I would be dead ten times over.'

'And homesickness? Are you ever homesick, Raoul?'

The man in the neighbouring hammock sighed. He slapped at a mosquito which was whining round his head.

'We Conciencians are always sad, *Capitán,* even when we're happy.'

'Perhaps because nothing ever changes.'

'There have been many changes already.'

They could distinctly hear the breathing of the men in the next room.

Tobar wondered what had changed. Very little, in reality. The rich still rode rough-shod over the poor. Children still died in droves from malnutrition and average life-expectancy was abysmally low.

'Are you satisfied, Raoul?' he asked. 'Are you content to live like this, hounded from one hiding-place to the next?'

'It has to be, *Capitán.*'

'Why does it have to be?'

His lieutenant sighed again but did not reply. He lit a cigarette and the flare of the match briefly illuminated the wooden walls, the floor, the whole bleak discomfort of the hut where they lay. They heard one of the men give a dry cough. Meditatively, Castillo said:

'That man in there probably has tuberculosis. I often heard them cough like that in my own village. They all died young, and no one mourned them but us. No doctor came, the priest earned his burial fee, and the landowner engaged another field-hand. That is why it has to be, *Capitán.*'

'Do you have anything to drink?'

'Yes, here.'

Tobar drank from the bottle which Castillo handed him. He felt the *aguardiente* forge a fiery path through his entrails and wiped his mouth on the back of his hand.

'What do you think of when you kill a man, Raoul?'

'I don't think at all, not then.'

'Don't you feel hatred or contempt?'

There was a long silence from the other hammock as Castillo searched for a satisfactory answer.

'No,' he replied, 'neither one thing nor the other – nothing at all. I kill so that others can live. You understand?'

Tobar took another swig and handed the bottle back.

'Has it ever occurred to you that you may kill out of love?'

'I can't say that it has.'

'Do you know what I've done, Raoul?'

'No.'

'I've placed us all under the command of Antonio Valencia. Politically, that is.'

'Why, *Capitán*?'

'Because I've never met such a man before – a priest who wants revolution. You know something about him?'

'Yes, the men have been talking.'

'Do you hate all *curas*?'

'They belong to the rich, *Capitán*.'

'This one doesn't. Give me that bottle again.'

A night like a thousand others, thought Tobar. Nothing ever changed. In a few days or weeks they would raid an army post and seize fresh supplies of arms and ammunition. The whole thing would be over in minutes. Attack like lightning, strip the dead of weapons, then withdraw at top speed. Then more waiting, more inactivity. That was the way it had been for years. It was a reign of terror, he knew that, but Castillo was right. It had to be.

'What do you think of Antonio Valencia, Raoul?' he asked.

He got no answer. His lieutenant was already asleep.

Campesinos came to see Tobar daily in the weeks that followed, trotting past the sentries on their skinny little horses. They looked unkempt and poverty-stricken in their ragged clothes, sombrero on head and the inevitable machete at their belt. Their faith in Tobar was touching and their loyalty unbounded. They risked their lives every day to bring him the latest information about the new army outpost. Every detail of their reports was promptly noted down by Castillo, who built up a comprehensive picture of the enemy's routine activities. Tobar learned that the officer in command of the post was a cruel and arrogant man, that he had already slept with several of the village girls and wore gleaming boots whose shine was carefully renewed every few hours. The sergeant was a tough brute who inspired fear in his own men as well as the villagers. The front of the post was guarded by a sentry whose machine-gun commanded almost the entire length of the street. Anyone who entered the building where the soldiers were quartered would find the captain's room on the right and the sergeant's on the left. The soldiers slept in three separate rooms, and behind them was the ammunition store. Posted there was another sentry who could sweep the rear approaches to the building, also with a machine-gun. The men were drawn from specially trained units which had been drilled in guerrilla warfare by U.S. advisers. They received plenty to eat and drink and most of them went to Mass on Sundays. They took their weapons, with the result that the little church looked as if it were under military occupation.

The village itself had grown up along a single main street. There was no sanitation, no piped water, no electricity. Drinking-water had to be fetched from the river a kilometre away, normally by the womenfolk. Almost every man in the village worked on the vast sugar plantation owned by Don Henrico Mendoza, who, backed by the military and his own private army, treated his workers like slaves.

Tobar devoted the next morning to drawing a map. Strategically, as he remarked to Castillo, the army post was badly sited. Opposite it was a narrow track which disappeared obliquely into the mountains. Not far away was another seldom-used track. Every passer-by had to run the gauntlet of three sentries before entering the village. A post manned by the same number of soldiers guarded its egress, so it was impossible to take a single step down the long street without being seen. Across the street from the post was a small café with a bar and a few wooden benches where the villagers could get drunk on cheap cane spirit. Beyond the soldiers' billet was an expanse of sun-scorched country-side, and not far away lay a dense belt of forest. The track that led through it was also closely guarded.

Tobar realized that he had the advantage of his enemy in many respects. To begin with, he could call on his guerrilla-*campesinos*, ordinary agricultural labourers clad in the anonymous uniform of poverty: ragged trousers, tattered shirts, raffia shoes, broad-brimmed straw hats, the *ruana*, a length of woollen cloth draped over the right shoulder, and the long machete from which no *campesino* was ever parted.

They were his best helpers, not only because they hid the arms which he captured but because they took part in almost every raid conducted by his group. They were seldom prompted to join him by political conviction, their usual motive being a desire for revenge inspired by the often inhuman behaviour of government troops.

Tobar and his men dressed like the *campesinos* except during raids, when they wore military uniforms.

The guerrilla units had their own laws. Traitors were shot and their bodies buried in secret. No one who joined a group could ever opt out, and any attempt to desert was automatically punishable by death. Still more important was the fact that no tell-tale traces must be left behind to show where guerilleros had camped. The

27

ashes of their small fires, their cigarette-butts – everything was eliminated with the utmost care because they knew only too well that all who fell into government hands were irretrievably lost. Prisoners were interrogated and then executed, and press reports made it appear that they had been shot while attempting to escape. Tobar could quote countless instances of this. Two of his student contacts at a hospital had recently been killed by the army in this way.

While Tobar was pursuing his own thoughts, Castillo entered the hut.

'There's a man outside, *Capitán*. He wants to speak to you urgently.'

'Who is he?'

'A *campesino* from Taloma.'

'But that's forty kilometres from here.'

'He spent the whole of last week looking for you.'

'What does he want?'

'His two daughters were raped.'

'What am I supposed to do about it?'

'He says it was Guillermo de la Cruz and his men.'

'How does he know?'

'He saw it with his own eyes.'

'What happened then?'

'Guillermo got away.'

'How old were the girls?'

'Fifteen and seventeen.'

'Very well, send him in.'

The *campesino* seemed frightened, pitiably frightened, and Tobar guessed that he must still covertly regard him as the leader of a gang of outlaws, not a rebel commander. He was a small man, weather-beaten, emaciated, and probably consumptive. Tobar put an arm round his shoulders and invited him to sit down. The *campesino's* face brightened at once. Gingerly, he laid his straw hat across his knees and waited for Tobar to question him. It was the habit of a lifetime, and even now he did not venture to speak first.

But Tobar had not been expecting what was to come. Even as he watched, he saw the man's impassive face become transformed into a mask of fury. Suddenly, it was as if he could see himself mirrored in the eyes of the timid little *campesino*, as if that incident in his own past had come to life once more. He looked at the man's small-boned hands and felt the ropes bite into his own wrists as he was tied to a tree and forced to watch a squad of policemen violate his wife and daughter before his very eyes. He heard their despairing screams, felt his gorge rise, spat as the mucus gathered in his mouth.

'Do you know for certain that it was Guillermo de la Cruz?' he asked.

The *campesino* nodded eagerly.

'How do you know?'

'I saw him in the village, several times. Everyone knew that he was the leader of the local guerilleros.'

'Was he alone?'

'No.'

'Who was with him?'

'Two men. Strangers to me.'

'Were you at home when they came?'

'No, I only got there as they were attacking my younger daughter.'

'Did she resist?'

'Yes, *Capitán*.'

'And what did you do?'

'What could I do? They threatened to shoot me if I interfered.'

'Has this sort of thing happened often?'

'I don't know, *Capitán*.'

'Had Guillermo been drinking?'

'Of course.'

'What do you mean, of course? Is he usually like that?'

'Yes, he threatens us with his pistol sometimes, and once he smashed up the café.'

Tobar nodded. He had heard enough. Guillermo de la Cruz was not the only district commander to terrorize the local inhabitants. He had done much the same himself in the old days. Like him, the guerilleros who now operated in the mountains were veterans of the civil war. They fought from motives of hatred, either because they had been personally wronged, or because they were liberals eager to kill conservatives, or because they were conservatives thirsty for the blood of liberals. When the army moved in they had fled to the mountains, where they earned the universally feared name of bandoleros, or bandits. The guerilleros who split off from this group were just as tough, just as dangerous, but idealistic and partly made up of men who opposed the corruption of the feudal ruling class and regarded Marxism as the country's only hope. That meant that they had to win the allegiance of the peasants, because success was impossible without *campesino* auxiliaries. He himself had obliged every literate member of the various groups under his command to read Marx. They called themselves the 'Army of Liberation' or 'National Armed Forces', and defied every danger to bring the reign of oppression to an end. And now Guillermo de la Cruz, an ex-lawyer from Cielo and for many years commander of the Taloma district, had at one stroke destroyed the good reputation which Tobar had built up with so much effort.

'Have you ever worked with the guerilleros?' he asked.

The *campesino* shook his head.

'Do you know how they operate?'

The man smiled and lowered his eyes as if his smile might have betrayed him.

'Listen, *amigo*,' Tobar said, 'ride straight back to Taloma. Take your daughters to the doctor and tell him that I will pay.'

'And . . .'

'Leave the rest to me.'

'What do you mean, *Capitán*?'

'I mean – and you can tell all your friends – that the guerilleros have three laws: no rape, no treachery, no desertion.'

'But . . .'

'All three crimes carry the death penalty.'

The little *campesino* shuffled his feet.

'I fear the revenge of these men, *Capitán*.'

Tobar laughed grimly. 'There will be no one left to take revenge – no one.'

The *campesino* stared at him without expression, turned, and left the hut. Tobar watched him go and then summoned Castillo.

'Raoul, take some men, reliable men, and execute Guillermo and his two lieutenants.'

For the next hour, Tobar listened attentively to what the villagers had to tell him about the army post which was his next objective.

2

The monument to General Lopez, hero of the Conciencian Republic's war of national liberation, was illuminated by a dozen floodlights. Seen by their pale glare, the equestrian statue attracted even more attention than the thirty-storey hotel beyond it, which completely dominated Cielo by day like a huge granite Moloch.

Up in his room, Bruce Cornell tossed the telegram aside, then picked it up again and read it for the second time. *Watch political activities Antonio Valencia stop influence growing stop await first article soonest stop remain Cielo until further notice stop good hunting stop.*

He turned to Esther Graham. 'Esther, you know Conciencia better than I do. Who the hell is Antonio Valencia?'

She took the telegram from him and glanced at it.

'He used to teach at the university here. Professor of sociology.'

'Used to?'

'Yes, they fired him.'

'Why?'

'Various reasons.'

He frowned. 'Why so vague? I don't like guessing games, you ought to know that by now.'

'Ought I?' she retorted, stressing the words, and he knew that he had irritated her. He stood up and walked to the window. Above the city he could see the black crest of the mountains which always inspired him with a vague sense of uneasiness, as though he and a million others were imprisoned by them in this elegant capital with its ugly fringe of slums.

'Sorry, sweetheart, I shouldn't have said that. No reason why I should expect you to be well briefed on my likes and dislikes when we only see each other four or five times a year.'

She laughed.

'I'm to blame too. As soon as you arrive I come running. It's crazy.'

'Why crazy?'

31

'Because I run a bigger risk every time.'

He drew her towards him, but she pushed him away.

'If you don't run risks, Esther, you've no right to be happy.'

'Is that why you're a newspaperman?'

He shook his head.

'Certainly not. I don't think I take enough risks. You expose yourself to danger the whole time, living here in this volcano of a country.'

'Tell you what. Let's go down to the bar. Buy me a drink and I'll brief you on Valencia.'

He put his arm round her shoulders and they rode the lift down to the brightly lit bar. He ordered two dry Martinis and raised his glass.

'*Salud*,' he said. 'Well, what about this mystery man?'

'Antonio Valencia is a priest,' she began.

He choked on his drink and gave a spluttering laugh.

'A priest? God Almighty!'

She lit a cigarette, eyeing him defiantly.

'What do you mean? If you think a priest is unimportant just because . . .'

He smiled.

'No, no, it's just that priests are part of the establishment here. Your ideas on the subject are exactly the same as mine, so don't pretend otherwise.'

'It certainly doesn't apply to Antonio Valencia.'

'Sounds as if you've got a crush on him.'

The public address system crackled and a metallic voice said: 'Telephone call for Señorita Graham.'

Esther was gone for more than ten minutes.

'Important?' he asked, when she returned.

Her face flushed scarlet but she shook her head.

'No, nothing special.' She slowly drained her glass, watching him intently from under her long lashes. Bruce attracted her in spite of herself. It wasn't just his English good looks. There was a vitality about him. His movements conveyed it, but not as strongly as his ability to listen with singleminded concentration.

'This is a dangerous country,' she said quietly. 'The secret police are everywhere – street corners, private parties, even bars like this one.'

He laughed.

'Now you really are exaggerating. What makes you such an expert on the secret police? Anyway, what do they find to do here?'

32

'Their job is to preserve the status quo.'

'Which is?'

'A handful of plutocrats and an army of paupers.'

He shrugged his shoulders contemptuously.

'So that's what you talk about at Cielo University. You forget it applies to all underdeveloped countries.'

'Except that here the situation is perpetuated deliberately.'

He stubbed out his cigarette and leant towards her.

'You were going to tell me about Antonio Valencia, sweetheart.'

'All right. Last week two students were expelled from the University on suspicion of Communist agitation. Our professor of sociology, Antonio Valencia, stood up for them. He said that in a democratic country everyone had a right to his own opinion. What was more, in view of the appalling social conditions in Conciencia a dialogue with Marxism couldn't do any harm. Today the Cardinal had him dismissed.'

'The Cardinal?'

'Yes, Valencia was university chaplain as well as professor of sociology. Apparently, priests mustn't get involved in politics.'

'What about the students? Will they accept his dismissal?'

'I doubt it.'

'So there's going to be trouble here in the next few days?'

'Probably.'

'On account of a priest? I thought Cielo University was a hotbed of nonconformism.'

'It is, but there's nothing conformist about Valencia.'

'What sort of man is he?'

'Young, tall, dark and handsome, an excellent public speaker, upper-class background, originally engaged to be married, then entered the priesthood, studied at Louvain, full of revolutionary ideas, lionized by society, popular with the students, a champion of the poor.'

Bruce smiled.

'In other words, a born martyr.'

She swung round to face him with a glimmer of apprehension in her eyes.

'Say that again.'

'I said, a born martyr.'

She stared at him for a while without moving. If that was a prophecy, what would become of Conciencia? She knew the country better than the United States, where her family came from. She loved the days tremulous with heat, the violent glow that bathed the towering Andes, the people of the villages, the narrow thoroughfares in the heart of Cielo, the University campus which stood like a fortress astride the road to the airport. She also loved the immense vitality of the young people who took such an intense interest in social, political and religious matters. It was no secret to her that the same young people were in a state of revolt, that they were up in arms against their parents, against religion, against the government, against everything. The students were incensed at the misery which existed in their country because the increasingly cosmopolitan nature of society had alerted them to the inhuman conditions which their own fathers had created and which they wished to see changed.

'What are you thinking about?' Bruce asked.

'The young people of this country. I know students who have refused to inherit family fortunes because they regard them as an inexcusable disgrace. I call that magnificent – almost heroic. You wouldn't find that kind of self-sacrifice in Europe or North America. This country has everything, Bruce, every extreme of humanity and inhumanity, nobility and vileness.'

'No need to tell me that.'

'No, but you see it from the outside. I'm in the thick of it.'

'Maybe you're right. Any chance of an interview with Valencia?'

'I don't know. Perhaps you better speak to Francisco Vermeer first. He's a Dutch professor.'

'And a priest?'

'Yes.'

'Why him?'

'Because he's a friend of Valencia's. They say he'll probably succeed him at the faculty.'

'What's he like?'

'Just as progressive.'

'Do you know him well?'

'I've met him socially a couple of times. He's quite as magnetic as Valencia, in his own way.'

'What way is that?'

'Meet him and you'll see.'

Two officers took possession of the bar stools next to them. They looked unfriendly and made no response to Bruce's 'buenas noches' but seemed highly interested in Esther, to judge by their visual reconnaissance of her body. Bruce grimaced with distaste.

'They're mentally undressing you under my nose.'

Esther laughed.

34

'It's an old Latin American custom. You get used to it – in fact it's quite titillating.'

'You need titillation?'

'Maybe so.'

He leant across to her.

'Are they from the secret police?'

She shrugged.

'You never know till they tap you on the shoulder and tell you to come quietly. Sometimes they wear plain clothes, sometimes uniform. They're unidentifiable.'

'What's the general reaction to them?'

'Zero. Keep your mouth shut and never talk openly except among friends, that's the rule.'

'Do you subscribe to it?'

A page appeared and told Esther she was wanted in the foyer. She excused herself again.

The second time that evening, he thought, and still no explanation. She had not told him who had called her. He brooded darkly on the iniquities of a journalist's existence. It was a dog's life, keeping the world supplied with news. News . . . even the word had a sinister sibilance. Scarcely a day passed without his having to write about coups d'état, assassinations and insurrections. The whole of Latin America was in ferment. Sometimes he envied the export salesmen who went round trying to interest jaundiced business men in their products and refusing to take no for an answer. Anyway, what was the matter with Esther? She seemed strung up and nervous, even apprehensive. He surveyed the rest of the bar in the mirror facing him. The array of bottles and glasses in front of it threw off multicoloured splinters of light. The two officers drank in silence while the barman feigned intense activity and the radio oozed soft music interspersed with commercial plugs.

Fifteen minutes passed, and Bruce drank faster than usual. Was it his imagination, or did he really detect a certain tension in the air? His speculations were cut short by the reappearance of Esther. Her cheeks had the same flush as before and she was breathing quickly.

'Popular girl,' he said drily.

She lit a cigarette.

'What do you mean?'

'What I say. A man goes out with a pretty girl and she spends half the evening elsewhere. Is that another local custom?'

'Maybe, but why should you worry? We see each other whenever you come here. The rest of the time we write. My life's my own, Bruce, you know that. We don't have any exclusive claim on each other.'

A man came in and ordered a glass of beer in a quiet voice. He glanced round the bar and the two officers silently disappeared. He was a small, rather forlorn-looking man with large blue eyes, a chin that urgently needed a shave, slender hands and a shabby, crumpled suit.

'A little quiet this evening,' he said affably to Bruce.

Bruce shrugged.

'I don't mind as long as the conversation's good.'

The little man studied Esther appraisingly, with a fixity which made her shrink. His eyes were cold, emotionless, totally indifferent, like the eyes of a homosexual confronted by the opposite sex. This was something else, though – she sensed that immediately. The man reminded her of a predator observing its prey.

'Business man?' he asked Bruce.

'No, journalist.'

The man pursed his lips, but a moment later he was smiling again.

'No shortage of copy in this country, *señor*. You will find plenty to do here. You write political articles?'

Something in his tone made Bruce beware.

'No, archaeology and anthropology are more in my line.'

Three large rings gleamed on the stranger's childish hand. He slid them impatiently back and forth like beads on an abacus.

'Why delve into the past? The present is far more interesting.'

'You think so?' Bruce said.

'But of course.' The little man's voice sounded dreamy. 'We Conciencians have been at daggers drawn for years, *señor*. The outside world fails to find that interesting, but it is. On one side you have the conservatives, on the other the liberals. The conservatives might be generally classified as Catholics whereas the liberals lean to the left. Many liberals are also Catholics but they have a grudge against the clergy. Only a few years ago liberals from one village were attacking conservatives from another and vice versa. The result? Mutual butchery. Hardly a pretty pastime, but there it is. Today they found the body of Carlos Cazuz, a man very well known in Conciencia. He had been garrotted with piano wire. Not pleasant, of course, but that's the way things are round here.'

The man's cold reptilian eyes regarded Bruce intently. His slender fingers drummed on the wooden bar counter.

36

'Well? Don't you, as a journalist, find that all very interesting?'
Bruce shook his head.
'Why should I? Do you find murder interesting? I don't.'
'But your papers do, *señor*.'
His expression remained amiable and he even asked them to have a drink.
'This is the most interesting country in South America,' he went on. 'We speak the best Spanish, as you must have noticed. We have major universities, magnificent churches, huge palaces, and a unique archaeological collection. Our currency is strong, our export trade booming, our coffee among the finest in the world. What is more, our women are noted for their beauty. I wish you much success in Conciencia, *señor. Buenas noches.*'
He rose, bowed, and walked out.
'Who was that, for God's sake?' Bruce asked the barman.
The barman shrugged and went on polishing glasses.
Bruce turned to Esther.
'Why did those officers leave so suddenly?'
'They were scared.'
'Scared?'
'Yes. Are you beginning to understand now?'
'That little man,' Bruce said. 'He was my idea of a professional killer. Did he have a special interest in you?'
'Don't be silly, Bruce. Look, if it's all the same to you I think I'll go now. No need to see me home, my car's outside.'
'Why all the hurry?'
'I'm tired. Just let me go and leave it at that. I'll call you tomorrow.'
He stared at her. She suddenly meant more to him than he had ever been aware.
'Can't you tell me about it, Esther?'
'What am I supposed to tell you?'
'You must know that yourself.'
'I have to go, Bruce – no, don't get up, I'll see myself out. See you tomorrow.'
She was gone before he realized it, leaving him alone. The barman gave him a sympathetic smile.
'A charming young lady, *señor*. She comes here often.'
'Often?'
'Oh yes, very often.'
'Who with?'
The man shook his head.

37

'Different people. I don't know their names.'

'Men?'

'Yes, students, I think.'

She never mentioned them in her letters, Bruce thought. What did she write about, actually? About her father, her sociology course, her girl-friends – never about men. Strange that she shouldn't, really. And why the abrupt departure?

'You live in an interesting country,' he said aloud to the barman.

The coffee-coloured face with the black moustache smiled briefly and then went blank.

'Some people would say too interesting, *señor*. Much too interesting . . .'

'What do you mean?'

The barman concentrated on his glasses. His melancholy features did not change expression and he said no more.

Next evening Bruce Cornell rang the door-bell of Professor Vermeer's apartment. He had made an appointment with him and was expected at about eight o'clock. A tall bespectacled man with iron-grey hair and an uncommonly expressive face opened the door and greeted him with polite interest. The untidy living-room was littered with books and periodicals. On a low table stood a record-player flanked by several records and a bottle of whisky and two glasses. One glass was empty, the other half-full.

Vermeer indicated a comfortable chair and poured Bruce a drink without asking.

'I gather you're a journalist,' he said.

Bruce nodded.

'What was it you wished to speak to me about?'

Bruce fished the telegram out of his pocket and passed it over. Vermeer read it with a frown and handed it back.

'An injudicious telegram to send, by local standards,' he said curtly.

'How do you mean?'

'It's quite simple. A copy of it was on Colonel García's desk before it ever reached you.

'The security chief? You think so?'

'I know so.'

'And now . . .'

Vermeer cut him short. 'And now you want me to give you an introduction to my friend Valencia.'

Bruce shook his head.

'Not exactly, Professor. I wanted to get your views on him. Maybe Valencia's importance has been exaggerated by the local press.'

Vermeer eyed him silently for a moment.

'May I translate your remark, Mr Cornell? You're not keen on this assignment. You hope that Antonio Valencia will turn out to be a dull and insignificant little man. You don't like the atmosphere in Conciencia and you're looking for a pretext to leave at the earliest opportunity – and I'm supposed to salve your journalistic conscience. Well, perhaps I ought to urge you to leave, but I won't. How much do you know about me?'

'Very little, except that you're a friend of Padre Valencia.'

'I'm also a vagabond, Mr Cornell, a vagabond by the grace of God. I'll tell you a few more things about myself. Then you can decide if you want to take another drink off me or cut your losses and go. I'm no stranger to human nature – that's my life in a nutshell, as it were. Do you know what it means when a priest says that? It means sensing that many people can't be other than they are because their personal evolution has propelled them in one direction only. It means an awareness of how many pointless barriers there are in the world, a realization that those who fight each other do so in complete mutual ignorance. It means recognizing the good intentions of those who aspire to do something for others but always base their actions and judgements on their own personal criteria. Do you understand? Do you grasp the immense diversity of human existence? The value of solitude, suffering and boredom? The knowledge that everything has a purpose? The superiority of love to science? The ability of love to comprehend, feel and forgive almost anything under the sun? God's presence in life and his almost total absence in libraries? Have I made sense?'

Bruce drained his glass and said slowly: 'That sounded like a profession of faith.'

Vermeer glanced at him and then chuckled. He refilled his glass.

'You'll do,' he said, almost flippantly. 'I apologize for being so long-winded, but I'm a lecturer by trade.'

'I'm told you're Valencia's probable successor. Any truth in the story?'

'You're well informed.'

'Not well informed enough or I wouldn't be here. Why do you think I received that telegram?'

'Because Valencia is walking around with a political bomb in his pocket. One of these days he'll detonate it.'

39

'What's your verdict on Conciencia, Professor?'

'A magnificent country, rather like a sort of pre-revolutionary Mexico. A clerical country where the bishops are drawn from the highest ranks of society and the priests come from better-class homes. A land of religious faith and contempt for human life, with a God who wields a big stick and a flag inscribed with the word liberty. Is that good enough for you?'

'Is there much unrest?'

'More than enough, but the people had no leader until a short time ago. Are you beginning to grasp something of Antonio Valencia's importance?'

'To be frank, no.'

Vermeer removed his glasses and deposited them on the table beside his half-tumbler of whisky. He closed his eyes. Bruce lit a cigarette and settled himself more comfortably in his chair.

'This is a peculiar country, Mr Cornell, which is why I feel so much at home here in some ways. Peculiar people are drawn to peculiar countries like sailors to the sea. I often feel a sort of claustrophobia in the countries where most of my life has been spent. Too many of the judgements one hears passed there are rooted in modish piety or smug middle-class attitudes. Do you know what I mean?'

Bruce tapped the ash from his cigarette.

'Not entirely, Professor.'

He noted the impatience in Vermeer's eyes with a secret satisfaction which increased as the Dutchman's sentences grew shorter and more succinct, a staccato succession of vowels and consonants, harsh, belligerent and fraught with emotion.

'First you must know something about me, Mr Cornell. Otherwise, strange as it may seem, I shall not be able to tell you anything about Antonio Valencia.'

He paused for a moment and then swung round abruptly.

'Years ago I discovered the Christ of the streets. I also discovered an incredible love for him in people who had received no formal religious instruction. I learned that anyone who wishes to pass judgement on Marx, Lenin and Stalin must take the Christ of the so-called unbelievers as his point of departure because, in the view of the man in the street, Marx and his successors aspired to translate into action what Christ was demanding when he spoke of human misery and oppression. It anguished me to find that these people regarded us priests and practising Christians as unbelievers – not that they used the word – whereas we hung the same label on them.'

Bruce nodded and poured himself another whisky in response to an almost curt gesture of invitation from Vermeer.

'If you were happy working among the poor in Europe,' he said, 'why don't you do the same here?'

Vermeer was unruffled by this barbed question. There was no resentment in his voice when he replied, but he did put his glasses on again and eye Bruce rather more closely.

'I used to be a worker-priest, Mr Cornell, a worker among workers. I learned more from them than you can imagine, but here in this country I quickly realized that it was more important to change the mentality and principles of the ruling class than to pursue my former way of life. I had to belong to the lower orders first, though. I had to be one of them so that I could really speak from experience and steep myself in their needs. Take Cielo University, where I may be given an appointment. Valencia tells me that there are groups of young people there who are jointly trying to evolve a positive attitude towards human existence – trying to discover how to lead a free, active and enjoyable Christian life, unencumbered by the traditional Spanish preoccupation with the world hereafter. I commend their efforts. Do you understand me any better now?'

Bruce evaded the question.

'I'm told you also lectured in Rome and lived in the monastery of your Order. How did that appeal to you? No, no need to answer if you don't want to. You can show me the door if you like.'

Vermeer rose and bent over the record-player. He put a record on and turned to face his visitor in the dim light of the table-lamp.

'So you want to know why a monk should live in a comfortable apartment rather than attend chapel regularly and spend part of his life in a cell. Is that what you mean?'

Bruce nodded without replying.

'In that case I'll give you a straightforward answer. It may be simply a defence of the life I lead. On the other hand, it may prove that you misjudge me. I shall either be doing myself a favour or doing you one.'

'Why are you telling me all this?' Bruce asked.

Vermeer made a curt gesture and sat down again. He leant forwards slightly, fidgeting with his glass.

'You find it strange that I should be so communicative to a casual acquaintance? Well, it isn't because I find you exceptionally interesting or because you know these countries, let alone because you've written about them. It's just that I feel a need to unburden

41

myself at this moment. I should probably do the same if you were a block of wood.'

Bruce grinned. 'Thank you for putting me in my place, Professor,' he said quietly.

'I had no intention of putting you in your place, far less of deliberately humiliating you. What I say is the plain truth.'

'Please go on.'

'Very well. In Rome I had nothing against monks who led a life of contemplation, nothing against people who dwelt in holy simplicity and seclusion, hiding their hands in the scapular, pacing the cloisters, punctually attending chapel and devoting themselves to an ascetic existence which also happened to be refined and aesthetically satisfying. But what in God's name was I to do when they regarded tradition, chapel attendance and punctuality as the essence of religious perfection and had no contact with what was going on in the world? Life in the monastery began at five a.m., Mr Cornell, so I had to attend chapel at that hour. Well, I've nothing against chapel. Even in the slums or the jungle, I read my breviary. But let us assume that someone turns up at a quarter to five and asks to speak to me. I know his history, his personal problems. What am I supposed to tell him when five a.m. approaches – come back tomorrow, I have to go now? The man is in distress. Things may have resolved themselves by tomorrow, but that does not detract from the grief or suffering of the moment. I love such people, I listen to them and give them what advice I have to offer. My fellow-monks in Rome thought I set myself above monastic discipline, but in my view there's a natural priority of values. I sought understanding and failed to find it, so I had to take action myself – assume full responsibility under God. I wanted to make life more tolerable for others even if I made my own life harder in the process. I don't imagine things will be any different here.'

Vermeer paused suddenly and switched off the record-player. The strains of a Mozart symphony drifted through the window.

'Ah,' he said, 'Antonio must be at home.'

'Valencia? Does he live here too?'

'Yes, in the next apartment.'

Bruce got up and paced to and fro. Then he halted in front of Vermeer. 'Was that your life-story,' he asked sharply, 'or Valencia's?'

Vermeer smiled.

'Mine. Why, did you spot some similarities?'

'I wouldn't know, but I suppose there must be some.'

'There are – many, in fact. You must view Valencia against the

42

background of current Catholic thinking, Mr Cornell. Let me start with the Cardinal. Cardinal Medina is the son of a former President and a man who demands unconditional obedience. He believes that the Church is a perfect society of divine origin. In this society, a few men give orders and the majority are in duty bound to obey, not only the Church but the State as well. Discussion is not permitted, still less doubt. Priests are forbidden to concern themselves with politics even when conscience makes it their duty to do so. You have to understand the conditions under which we live here. An immense gulf separates the ruling classes, liberal as well as conservative, from the great mass of the people. The Church towers above everything, as it were, exalted and unassailable in its authority because that authority derives from God and is vested in a trinity consisting of Cardinal, President and employer. You may not believe me, but there are peasants down in the lowlands – even in this twentieth century of grace – who believe that God has entrusted them to their landowner and thank him for his divine and merciful providence in so doing. On the other hand, there is the bandit in the mountains who cares nothing for God and his commandments, the peasant who is starving for want of land, the hopeless poverty of the urban population, the widespread illiteracy, the high infant mortality rate, the forty thousand lepers of which only six thousand are receiving treatment.'

'A volcano, is that what you mean?' asked Bruce.

Vermeer nodded.

'What's worse, an active volcano. Come over to the window for a moment. You see that range of mountains? It runs north and south of here for hundreds of kilometres, dominating most of the cultivated land. Well, those mountains are the home of the bandits – the bandoleros – tough men who have lost faith in politicians and prefer to make their own laws. They're hounded by the army and the secret police but their hiding-places are too well concealed and the peasants are afraid to betray them even under torture. The volcano is already erupting, Mr Cornell. So far, it has cost several hundred thousand lives.'

'Isn't that a shrine up there?'

'Yes, over to the right, where those pin-points of light are. Rich and poor toil up the steps to the church on aching knees, pestered by the most horrifically well organized gang of beggars in the world.'

Vermeer turned back into the room, leaving Bruce alone at the window. Outside, silence had descended. The noise of car-horns had died away and he could hear the isolated steps of passers-by. Iron

43

railings separated the big houses from the outside world and their windows were covered with grilles.

Bruce stood there in silence for some time, peering out. Vermeer did not speak either. Then Bruce said good night and made his way downstairs. A few moments later he was outside in the brilliant starlight, heading for the city centre. One thing had emerged from his conversation with Vermeer: the priest named Antonio Valencia was a revolutionary, a man who wanted to overthrow the established order. In Conciencia, that was bound to be a dangerous undertaking. Bruce doubted if any lone individual could hope to prevail over the politicians, bankers, industrialists, press tycoons, big landowners and ecclesiastical hierarchy, even if he commanded large groups of supporters throughout the country.

He crossed the brightly coloured mosaic paving of the plaza near his hotel, surveying the dark outlines of the cathedral and the cardinal's palace, which stood out sharply against the night sky. The steps were strewn with beggars sleeping on newspaper. He quickened his pace and was happy when he could sink into an arm-chair, order a drink, and ask if there had been any calls for him.

'Yes, Señorita Graham telephoned,' the night porter informed him with the suspicion of a wink. 'She would like you to call her first thing tomorrow.'

Bruce finished his nightcap and took the lift up to his room. He felt tired as he shut the door behind him. Valencia must be a fool, he thought, risking his neck for people who allowed themselves to be exploited in the name of God. He felt a sudden pang of desire for Esther, as though only she could dispel the uneasiness that had settled on him. He undressed and climbed into bed. Then he smiled to himself and sank into a deep and dreamless sleep.

3

The building which housed the Seguridad Nacional or secret police headquarters of Conciencia made a bleak and unattractively barrack-like impression, which was why Colonel Cardoña García preferred to hold his meetings at the Officers' Club, situated in one of the more congenial Cielo suburbs. With its superb grounds, swimming-pools, tennis court, children's playground, stables, snugly appointed bar, and conference rooms adorned with regimental banners and provincial coats of arms, this imposing haunt of the rich was far more to García's taste. He could stroll through the magnificent gardens for hours at a time, deep in thought. He could also repair, when the fancy took him, to the indoor range, there to practise his marksmanship on the life-size dummies which were set up for the purpose. He liked to pass the time of day with Captain Alvarez, the resident instructor. The captain knew who García was but never hinted that he knew his real function in life.

'You ought to try that Israeli Uzi, Colonel – dead accurate and a delight to handle. I've also got an American M14 and a new Browning automatic that might interest you. You only have to hear the rate of fire to imagine how many bandoleros our boys have killed with them, up in the Andes.'

Colonel García eyed Alvarez amiably, and his brow remained unclouded as he replied: 'Yes, Captain, and how many of our boys have been killed by the same guns.'

He had a momentary vision of Rodriguez Tobar, whose photograph adorned his office wall. A man with a big square-cut beard, the curving beak of a hawk, broad shoulders and dark eyes verging on black.

As he aimed at the dummy its blank head suddenly turned into Tobar's face. Without hesitation, García emptied twenty-five rounds into the dummy's cardiac zone. Alvarez studied the target closely and gave an admiring thumbs-up.

'Glad I wasn't standing there, Colonel. I'd be past commenting, to say the least.'

45

The little man with the expressionless eyes nodded.

'I hope you don't think I've spent my whole life firing at dummies, Captain. These machine-pistols are worthy of better things. Until next time.'

García strolled thoughtfully along the broad path and up the red-carpeted steps that led to the Regimental Room, where six men were already waiting for him. The meeting was chaired by André Salazar, the Minister of Justice, who had the face of an examining magistrate. García knew in advance what would happen. First, Salazar would deliver a preamble on the subject of the President, the magnitude and gravity of his problems. Then, after staring into space for a while, he would expound the gravest problem of all. No prizes for guessing what it was: the possibility of a link-up between Antonio Valencia and Rodriguez Tobar, leader of the mountain guerilleros.

García had no worries about Valencia. He was content to keep a careful watch on him and all who came in contact with him. Valencia's phone was tapped, so he had a fair idea of the young priest's activities. García smiled. It was simply a question of contingency planning, of preparing for all eventualities.

Rodriguez Tobar presented far more of a problem. It was alleged that he was working with Valencia, but this could not be proved until he was arrested. So far, nobody knew Tobar's whereabouts because he was so adept at hiding himself in the mountains.

André Salazar shot a glance at García, and García knew that it was time to lend an ear.

'The facts are as follows, *señores*. The man in question is a fine scholar and a brilliant public speaker – an admirable priest, too, fundamentally. You're all acquainted with him, I imagine. He lives with his mother in the Rua Maio. He was brilliant even as a student. He became the centre of a group of young people who styled themselves "*Los Amigos*". Their discussions took place in the attic of his parents' house, and that was where the seeds of his current activities must have been sown. Not entirely, though. He later visited a number of European countries and, according to my information, made a close study of the major papal encyclicals. After his return he worked on a sociological survey of the slums, where he even went to live for a time. The report which he later published was unique in its scope. There is, however, just one snag about Antonio Valencia. He was exposed to Marxist influence while in Europe, and that makes him a danger to this country. We can't take effective action against him at present because it might spark off a nation-

46

wide student rebellion. We must therefore bow to the President's wishes and leave him alone for the time being, particularly as our worst suspicions have yet to be confirmed. Or have you confirmed them, Colonel?'

García made no immediate reply. He gazed round the table, savouring the awareness that he was the only man present who possessed detailed information.

'I reserve judgement, Your Excellency,' he said serenely. 'Antonio Valencia is a discreet man, but that doesn't prevent people from taking an intense interest in him. Consulting my notes, I see, for example, that he telephoned almost every faculty member at Cielo University last week. The calls dealt initially with the proper attitude for him to adopt in the event of government intervention in university affairs. Then, when he had been dismissed from the teaching staff of the University, almost every departmental head phoned him to inquire his future plans. He replied that he was engaged in a study of the social and economic problems of the country. When pressed to be more specific, he replied that this was impossible under prevailing circumstances. He was later telephoned by various students, notably those who sit and vote on the University's administrative committee. He urged them not to strike until he came to a decision himself. I don't know for certain, but I get the impression that he has worked out a plan which he intends to put into effect in due course. His tone is calm and moderate. He speaks of the President with respect. My general feeling is that he knows perfectly well that his phone is being tapped.'

'Many thanks, Colonel. Does anyone else have any comments?'

The military commander of Cielo, General Cuerva, raised his hand. He was a tall fair-haired man who might easily have been mistaken for an American.

'Your Excellency,' he said, 'our troops in the Andes are continuing their search for Tobar, so far without success. The peasants who have been interrogated either know nothing or are too frightened to talk. I would not like to make any rash promises about our ability to capture the man. As for a strike at Cielo University, the army is ready and so are the police.'

'Thank you, General. And now a few practical questions. Does anyone here know when the signal for a strike at the University will be given? Will Antonio Valencia give it himself? Is he a subversive? You are Conciencian citizens, gentlemen, just as I am. You know how easy it is to foment violence in this country. Would we not be better advised to detain Valencia?'

47

García shook his head.

'No, Your Excellency. We don't have enough solid proof that he's a danger to the security of the State. We mustn't give the left-wing press a stick to beat us with. If Valencia disappears now, while he enjoys nationwide popularity, it will start a chain reaction, if not a revolution. You know what idealists are. There comes a moment when they throw caution to the winds, and then . . .' He snapped his fingers.

The State Governor of Cielo looked sceptical.

'You exaggerate, Colonel. Why don't we approach the Cardinal and ask him to transfer Valencia? The man would certainly be less of a danger elsewhere. I am responsible for this city, *señores*. I want no disturbances, and disturbances can be avoided if we ensure that this recalcitrant priest leaves the scene as quickly as possible.'

García smiled.

'You would only be postponing the evil day. If Antonio Valencia is transferred he will pursue his activities, but underground. To repeat: if we get rid of him at this stage we risk the prospect of revolution. One should never underrate one's enemy, least of all when his prestige is at its height.'

The minister gave a nod of approval.

'In other words, *señores*, we take the requisite precautionary measures and await developments. I shall report as much to the President, and my own belief is that he will approve. I suggest we all compile as much information about Antonio Valencia as we can, each in our own field and with the specialized resources that are available to us. When we meet here again next week, I shall hope to receive detailed reports which the President can then study. Any further suggestions?'

The civil police commissioner, Hector Garavito, cleared his throat noisily.

'No suggestions, Excellency, just a question. I agree with the Governor. Why should we make so much fuss about a bunch of university professors, no matter who's at the bottom of it all?'

García banged the table with his fist.

'Why don't you study my reports, Commissioner? Antonio Valencia isn't just any old priest, as you'd damn well know if you took the trouble to brief yourself better. He's an extremely able man, and the students would follow him to hell and back. Take care, Commissioner! You wouldn't be the first ill-informed man to fall on his nose.'

The minister cut the squabble short with an incisive gesture. He

48

was no stranger to the rivalry which existed between the two police chiefs. He rose and shook hands with each of them in turn, lingering a little when he came to García.

'I'm counting on you, Colonel,' he said. 'The President sends his regards and wishes me to say that he is particularly satisfied with your work.'

García bowed but made no response. His cold, impenetrable gaze was fixed on the minister's face. The minister could not repress a slight shudder as he left the building. He had seen the same expression once before, when a peasant was attacked by a shoal of carnivorous piranhas in a river on his estate. They had worn precisely the same fixed stare as they tore their prey to shreds.

García noticed the other man's reaction but was not disconcerted by it. He set no store by popularity. In his view, power and popularity were incompatible.

Esther Graham was lounging in an arm-chair in her cool spacious room, thinking about Bruce Cornell. She was aware that her life took a quieter turn during his visits to Conciencia. She had far less time for her student friends and for someone else, someone far more potentially dangerous. Agitation at Cielo University had increased by leaps and bounds in the last few months. Scuffles with the police were a daily occurrence, and the ringleaders almost invariably belonged to the sociological faculty from which Antonio Valencia had just been dismissed. The students often met at her place afterwards to discuss events with intense enthusiasm. But that was not the extent of their activities. For over two months they had lived in one of the slum quarters and studied conditions there, later to write a detailed report on the subject under Valencia's supervision.

Esther's sojourn in the slums had made a lasting impression on her. When she came to summarize her experiences on paper, fierce compassion welled up inside her for these exploited and underprivileged people, and she was filled with shame that such conditions could still exist in her adopted country. The students' joint report did not deny that the government was taking certain steps to mitigate hardship, but it did state that poverty, so far from originating in the slums themselves, was rooted in the attitude of the property-owning class.

Someone knocked at the door, and before Esther had a chance to say anything her father walked in. Graham was a robust-looking man with close-cropped hair, a lean, earnest face and jerky movements. Esther and he had grown much closer in the five years since his wife died. He had seen very little of her before that. As general manager of an American oil company, he was so bound up in his business interests that he had little time even for his late wife. After her death, father and daughter had developed strong ties which they cemented by lively exchanges of ideas and hours of discussion. Esther believed that she was very like her father in character. She had the same direct way of tackling problems. When something had to be done she improvised, swiftly and skilfully, and her numerous interests left her permanently short of time.

'Everything ready for this evening?' he asked.

She nodded.

'Down to the last sordid detail. Your big wheels can irrigate their tonsils all they want. There's every kind of liquor you can think of, and a cold buffet laid out in the garden. I organized half a dozen waiters to hand the stuff round and another two men to open car doors. Okay, chief?'

He chuckled and perched on the arm of her chair.

'Great. One more thing, though. Maybe you'd lay off the social criticism, just for one evening. I know they're a corrupt bunch, not like those dewy-eyed pals of yours, but do me a favour and don't show it. Most of them are business contacts.'

Esther could not help laughing.

'Sure, Daddy, I know. Incidentally, I invited Bruce Cornell. Any objections?'

'You mean that newshound you trail around with from time to time?'

'Yes.'

'Okay by me. It's about time I met him, and I'd sooner you mixed with him than the local coloureds. They aren't to be trusted, not any of them, but you don't need me to tell you that.'

She suppressed the annoyance that rose in her at this remark.

'Why do you always have to ride that old hobby-horse, Daddy? You've lived among these people longer than I have. It doesn't matter what they do, you never have a good word to say for them. They're untrustworthy, they tomcat around, they're uppity, vain and dishonest.'

'Well, isn't it a fact?'

'Of course not. I've met some marvellous people here, and I hate the word coloured. I'd be ashamed to use it.'

He guffawed.

'Well I'm not. You'll be telling me you'd marry one, next.'

50

'Why not? I don't see any difference. There are good and bad ones among them, just as there are everywhere.'

He made a dismissive gesture.

'Don't delude yourself, Esther. You know damn well that isn't your real attitude, not deep down. Sure, you've nothing against them. You don't get the creeps when they touch you – in fact you might even neck with one if it came to it. That's one thing, but marriage is something else. You'll end up marrying a man like Cornell.'

'You don't even know him.'

'I know he's British, so presumably he's white.'

'There are whites here too.'

They could wrangle on this subject for hours without reaching agreement. Esther was consoled by their mutual frankness. Her father never bothered to pull his punches, which was understandable in a man who had come up the hard way, via oil-rigs and pipelines.

'So everything's ready?'

'Yes, Daddy, no need to worry about a thing. You can sit back and wait for your friends with an easy mind – the President, the Cardinal, the bankers and everyone else who has a finger in the local pie.'

There was a knock and Bruce came in. Esther felt as if the room was suddenly filled with him. The two men exchanged a keenly appraising look and seemed relieved at what they saw. Her father was the first to break the silence.

'Good to meet you at last, Cornell. I suggest we have a drink in the garden so Esther can change. That sun-top might tempt the Cardinal into mortal sin, and I wouldn't want her to have that on her conscience.'

Bruce hesitated, but at a wink from Esther he followed Graham to the door, down the long corridor, across the patio, down another corridor and out into the garden. It was quiet there. As with almost all the big houses on the outskirts of Cielo, the garden was separated from the outside world by a high wall topped with spikes.

'Magnificent place you have here,' Bruce said.

Graham shrugged his shoulders.

'A show-place. My wife liked it that way. Status symbols are even more important in this country than they are back home in the States. What brings you here?'

'Antonio Valencia.'

'Come again?'

'Antonio Valencia.'

Graham gave a puzzled frown.

'Oh sure, now you mention it I recall hearing Esther talk about him occasionally. One of the University professors, isn't he? A priest, if I remember rightly.'

'Is that all you know about him?'

'More or less. I've seen his picture in the paper from time to time. Seems he takes an interest in social problems.'

He poured some drinks at the bar and handed one to Bruce.

'That's one of the troubles with Conciencia, Cornell. The social legislation is excellent – on paper – but every employer fires his staff after a year because he'd have to pay them too much otherwise. They take it lying down, and do you know why? Because it's always been like that and probably always will be. No guts, that's their problem. The only time they raise any enthusiasm is when they're in bed – you only have to look at the birth-rate. And here's another thing: an Indian can marry a white woman, sure, but the children inherit the worst characteristics of both parents. Take a look around you. Basically, this country is governed by a handful of white men, and even they don't have what it takes. The only ones that do are foreigners. They need Americans like me, but when we've sunk enough money in the place they try to nationalize us. We set up industries here because they're too lazy to, and all they do is brand us as neo-colonialists. They've got no fibre, Cornell, believe me.'

'Hello,' called a cheerful voice. 'At the bottle already?'

Bruce turned and saw Esther walking across the lawn towards them.

'Isn't it about time you got ready, you two? The first arrivals could be here in half an hour. Bruce, I'll show you to your room.'

They strolled back to the house arm in arm. Bruce noted with satisfaction that his room adjoined Esther's. She closed the door, turned the key in the lock and threw herself into his arms. Their lips met and he felt the warmth of her body through the white silk dress which displayed her tawny colouring to such perfection. Suddenly she broke away.

'Be quick and change, Bruce. We don't have much time.'

She sat down on the bed, following his movements intently.

'How do you find my father?'

'He calls a spade a spade. I like men of his type. They keep their feet on the ground.'

Her face clouded.

'What's that supposed to mean?'

'I don't really know. It's just that the people you've introduced me to these last few days are so wrapped up in their own problems I wonder if they'll ever get anywhere.'

She shook her head.

'You're wrong, Bruce. It's other people's problems they worry about, or hadn't you noticed?'

Carefully, he pulled on a clean white shirt and gave his dark suit a final brush.

Without turning away from the mirror, he said curtly: 'I just don't understand you. You're young and attractive. You could be having a good time instead of running around after a bunch of priests.'

He saw that she was really angry now but ignored the fact. Her secretive behaviour in the hotel bar the previous night had stung him.

'There speaks the infallible voice of the press,' she said bitterly. 'Oh sure, why should you care what happens here? You only came here to write a couple of sensational articles. You couldn't care less if the daily death-rate from malnutrition is a thousand or ten thousand, except that ten thousand means bigger headlines and fatter fees. Don't the conditions here make any impression on you at all?'

He rounded on her, hard-eyed.

'I'm touched by your concern for my spiritual welfare, Esther, but it's misplaced. Do you know why? Because if I let myself be affected by all the horrors I have to cover year after year as a roving correspondent, I'd have been taken to a funny-farm long ago.'

'In other words, you stay on the outside. You're a spiritual outsider.'

He smiled.

'I'll tell you what I'm not. I'm no preacher – no crusader either. I'm the voice of history, if you like. I absorb filth and regurgitate it in capsules. I assemble facts. I make notes and comparisons. I describe people, conditions, situations, wars, revolutions, strikes. That's my job. You and my editor have put me on to a potentially newsworthy individual and I'll do my damnedest to get to know him. He's a Catholic, I'm not. He puts his faith in God, I rely on my own judgement. He prays, I write. He concentrates on poverty, I concentrate on getting my articles written. Are you beginning to get the picture?'

'No.' Her eyes were almost black with fury.

53

'All right,' he said, slowly and deliberately. 'Then I'll try and spell it out for you – telegraphically, journalist-fashion. Country: Conciencia. Capital: Cielo. Geographical features: mountain ranges, rivers, jungle. Population: mestizos, Indians, and a small group of dominant whites. Political parties: liberal and conservative. Present government: conservative. Prosperity: reserved for the handful at the top, the rest almost dying of poverty. Initiatives: plenty on paper, virtually none in practice. Trade unions: some, but corrupt and without influence. Political situation: extremely tense. Guerrillas active in the mountains, students creating hell in the big cities. Pressure-groups: army, landowners, police, secret police. Religion: Catholic by tradition.

'There you have a basis to work on. And now comes the big fight. On my right: the government, the army, the police, the secret police, the bankers, the landowners, the industrialists, the press tycoons and the ecclesiastical authorities. On my left: a small group of students, trade unionists and intellectuals like Antonio Valencia, possibly backed by the Communists, a few thousand guerilleros and nonconformists. Who's on top, who packs the winning punch, the first lot or the second? God in heaven, can't you really see, or are you just a little group of cranky fanatics obsessed with the idea of martyrdom?'

'Don't be so arrogant, Bruce.'

He lit a cigarette and sat down beside her, but when he tried to put an arm round her she angrily drew away.

'All right, I'll be even more blunt. Your father is just about to throw a party. His garden is tastefully floodlit and swarming with servants. There's enough liquor to float a battleship and enough food to keep a couple of mountain villages happy for a month. And who's coming to this bean-feast? Go on, Esther, you tell me.'

'The people you were talking about.'

'Precisely. You're beginning to catch on after all. But this isn't an isolated occasion, sweetheart. These people meet at parties every other day. They've known each other since birth. They're a mutual protection society. They react *en bloc* if someone threatens their status. They're dignified, witty, aristocratic, well read – in fact, they're the flower of Conciencia. You won't find the other lot around. They die off too fast. Not enough fertilizer, you see – they're dead before they start to live. And who's going to do something about it? An unemployed university professor? Don't make me laugh, Esther. They'll hang him from the highest gallows on the highest peak in the Andes!'

54

Esther stood up and faced him, very pale now. For a moment he thought she was going to strike him. Instead, so low that he could barely hear her, she said:

'Didn't you ever hear of the love of God?'

He laughed aloud, suddenly not caring whether he hurt her or not.

'Allow me to repeat that, so you can hear what it sounds like when someone else says it. The love of God? Who's going to get fat on that? I'll tell you who subsists on the love of God. Not the Cardinal, not the bishops and priests, not the rich, but the illiterate who doesn't have anything else, the poor bastard who believes in tales of paradise because they give him something to hope for, the disillusioned worm who doesn't have the drive and energy to turn on the people who use God as a pretext for continuing to wield power in their own sweet way. The hyenas of this country, they're the ones who proclaim the love of God. To them, God is a magic word which silences opposition, and when that doesn't work they can always preach hell-fire to make the love of God seem more attractive.'

She sighed.

'Maybe we're not so different after all. Let's forget it and join the party. Daddy will be wondering what's happened to us.'

They emerged into the garden without exchanging a word, almost like strangers. Graham noticed it at once.

Bruce lingered in the background and watched Esther receiving guests at her father's side. Suddenly a stir ran through the gathering. A tall thin man in a magnificent scarlet robe entered the garden preceded by a gaggle of bishops. Bruce recognized him immediately from press photographs. It was Cardinal Medina, reputedly the most powerful man in Conciencia. Bruce had to concede that he looked an aristocrat even before he heard him speak. Edging forward slightly to get a better view, he saw Esther and her father kneel to kiss the Cardinal's ring. Medina accepted their obeisance with lofty disdain, surveying the garden over their bowed heads.

Bruce heard Graham say 'Welcome, Your Eminence', but the Cardinal had already passed on.

Medina did not remove the white gloves on which his heavy ring sparkled. He seemed bored. From time to time he glanced at the french windows leading into the garden and spoke a few words to the people who clustered round him, but his lack of interest was conspicuous.

Bruce wondered if prejudice had made him condemn the man too hastily. He leant against the trunk of a palm-tree, entirely relaxed and quite unaware that his very relaxation marked him out from the rest of the party. Everyone else made frantic efforts to appear cordial. It was not until half an hour had elapsed that the atmosphere loosened up slightly, and even the Cardinal turned a more receptive eye on his fellow-guests. Graham seized the opportunity to present Bruce.

The Cardinal coolly extended his hand, but instead of kneeling Bruce grasped it and bowed. A momentary look of surprise crossed the Cardinal's face. No doubt about his arrogance, Bruce thought, but he accepted defeat like an aristocrat. The eyes behind the gold-rimmed spectacles were keener than he had imagined, and they radiated authority.

'*Con mucho gusto*,' he said.

The Cardinal inclined his head.

'You speak Spanish, *señor*? Are you here to write about Conciencia?'

Bruce nodded.

'Yes, Your Eminence. With special reference to a certain Padre Antonio Valencia.'

The reaction was over in a flash. A twitch of the eyebrows, a brief dilation of the eyes.

'A brilliant scholar, *señor*. Have you met him yet?'

'No, Your Eminence, not yet, but I plan to be in Conciencia for some time to come.'

The Cardinal's interest seemed to have been aroused at last. He took Bruce by the arm and led him to a group of wrought-iron chairs which stood in a more secluded part of the garden, then sat down with a sigh and stared into space for some moments.

'Crowds are tiring,' he said. 'Besides, one always meets the same people. I have had a strenuous day.'

Bruce sensed that this was a prelude to something more, an impression which was strengthened when he saw Medina impatiently wave away a bishop who was bearing down on them.

'This ecclesiastical province is not an easy one to direct, *señor*,' the Cardinal said, 'especially as the local Church enjoys a privileged legal status which has been granted it by the legislative organs of government. That is why, ever since I attained a position of authority, I have been convinced that we must stand aloof from politics. We are servants of God, and God does not wish us to enter the political arena. Don't you agree?'

The question came so suddenly that it caught Bruce off his guard.

56

'To be honest, no,' he said.

The Cardinal drew himself up as if he had been stung by a bee. 'No?' he repeated, eyeing Bruce in surprise. 'I used to share your view at first, but when one has lived long enough in a country, is familiar with the political situation and realizes what goes on behind the scenes, one thinks differently. It is a question of experience at the highest level.'

Touché, thought Bruce. That put him squarely in his place. How could a journalist, a mere bird of passage, claim to know how the country's problems should be solved? He ought to have guessed that a man like Medina, one of the leading figures in Latin America, would not tolerate contradiction, especially when it verged on criticism and was uttered in such an unvarnished way.

'Forgive me, Your Eminence,' he said.

The Cardinal rose. For the first time, Bruce saw a faint smile hover about his lips.

'*Señor*, it is my duty to provide for the spiritual welfare of my flock, the flock which has been entrusted to my keeping. I believe this to be my primary function and that of my bishops. Our life here on earth is an exceedingly bleak business compared with that which awaits us in heaven. That being so, let governments worry about this life. My concern is with the life hereafter. And now you must excuse me.'

The Cardinal did not extend his hand but turned and made straight for the President, who was chatting with some senior army officers.

A waiter proffered a silver tray and Bruce helped himself to another dry Martini. Esther, who had been observing the conversation from a distance, came over to him. She had known Bruce long enough to realize that he was not a person to make concessions, even for a cardinal's benefit.

'What were you talking about?' she asked, looking into his sombre face.

He gave a short laugh.

'You really want to know? All right, I'll repeat his parting shot: let governments worry about this life – my concern is with the life hereafter. God Almighty, what an attitude! So the politicians can take care of current problems while he gets to grips with eternity. In other words, you keep order in this godforsaken country, Mr President – I'll take care of the celestial side of things. He said it as if he meant it. Nothing could make that man change his mind.'

Esther stared at him gravely.

57

'He's the prisoner of his bishops, Bruce. Medina is a man with a big heart, believe me, but he grew up behind the walls of a palace.'

Bruce nodded grimly.

'Like everyone else here, sweetheart. You only have to cast an eye round this party. Do you really think all these talkative ladies and gentlemen know what's going on in Conciencia? According to you, people are dying of poverty only a few blocks away while they swill champagne and flash their diamonds.'

Suddenly, Bruce noticed a flutter among the guests. He looked for its source and saw a new figure enter the garden, pause and look round. The late-comer was taller than most of the other men present, with keen dark eyes, an aquiline nose and dark wavy hair. He wore a plain lounge suit.

Esther gripped Bruce nervously by the arm.

'So he has come . . .'

'Who?'

'Antonio Valencia.'

'Is that him?'

'Yes, and wearing an ordinary suit, too. I asked him to come, but I didn't know he'd cause a minor sensation.'

'In what way?'

'Can't you see how they're staring at him? They can't believe their eyes. Priests in this country are always obliged to wear the soutane.'

Bruce looked round. Everyone was whispering excitedly and casting covert glances at Valencia, who smilingly made his way through the crowd towards the Cardinal. Having shaken hands with his host, he waited patiently for the grey-haired aristocrat to conclude his conversation with the President. Bruce saw the Cardinal's brow pucker as Valencia knelt and kissed his ring. Then he smiled and said, loudly enough for everyone to hear: 'Antonio, my son, why this style of dress?'

Valencia topped the Cardinal by several inches when he rose to his feet. He looked very earnest.

'I work among the poor, Your Eminence. *Con permiso*, this suit is more appropriate to the slums than the robe I usually wear.'

The Cardinal nodded with a slightly bemused expression on his face. 'Quite so, my son, with my permission . . . You did not seek it, though. One of the pillars of the Church is obedience. To ignore that is to stray from the path of duty.'

'Will you pardon me, Your Eminence?'

Medina eyed him coolly.

'No, my son. A priest who causes his superiors distress cannot be pardoned lightly. And now leave me.'

He dismissed Valencia with a wave of his hand and turned back to the President, whose face had darkened with anger.

'You tolerate such behaviour, Your Eminence?' he demanded indignantly.

The Cardinal showed no sign of resentment. He even permitted himself a faintly ironical smile.

'The Church has always had her rebels,' he replied. 'Sometimes they became her finest champions, sometimes they made things hard for us. However, they made it hardest of all for themselves. The Church has no use for individualists, least of all in Conciencia. I shall have to tell him so very soon, but not in public. He may reconcile himself to the idea in due course.'

'I doubt it, Your Eminence. I received a detailed report on him yesterday. According to my information, his activities border on the subversive.'

The Cardinal patted his red biretta into place.

'You exaggerate, *Señor Presidente*. Men in government always regard those who disagree with them as potential enemies. Your predecessors did not trust you, you do not trust them. The conservatives wield absolute power in the villages, where they form the majority. The liberals do the same elsewhere. But the Church rules everyone in this country, as you would do well to remember. Without the Church and without me, even a gifted young man like Antonio Valencia would have no prospects whatsoever.'

He glanced across at Valencia as he spoke. Esther Graham was just introducing him to Bruce Cornell. Valencia's handshake was firm, his gaze exceptionally direct, his smile open and sincere.

'Professor Vermeer spoke to me about you,' Valencia said. 'I gather there's a certain amount of interest in me abroad.'

Bruce nodded.

'Why do you provoke people?' he asked flatly.

Valencia threw back his head and laughed.

'I suppose you could call it that. It's unusual to see a priest wearing lay dress in the Cardinal's presence, I grant you – in fact it's technically forbidden. However, I have just come from a meeting where people are unaccustomed to the soutane. To be precise, I've just come from a slum quarter where I would be ashamed to walk around dressed as a member of a particular class.'

'Did Esther invite you, Professor?'

Valencia nodded and bowed in her direction.

'Yes. She put it so charmingly that I could hardly refuse.' He turned to Esther.

'Is Mr Cornell in your confidence, *señorita*?'

She nodded. 'Yes, but I ought to warn you. He has a prejudice against priests.'

Valencia laughed again.

'At least we have one thing in common, even if I am one myself.' He lowered his voice. 'Guess who I saw today.'

She looked at him inquiringly, and his voice sank to a whisper. 'Rodriguez Tobar.'

'What?' she exclaimed in horror. 'Here in Cielo, with a price on his head? Why did he come?'

'To get in touch with me. He has heard of my plans and wishes to work with me.'

'Why are you telling us all this?'

'Because I should very much like you and Señor Cornell to meet him. Would it interest you, Cornell?'

'Of course. When?'

'Tonight. He returns to the mountains tomorrow. A car will pick you up at your hotel at nine o'clock precisely. No need to say anything – the driver will be acting on Tobar's instructions.'

'I can hardly wait,' Bruce murmured.

Valencia heard the remark and a trace of anxiety appeared in his face. He looked Bruce full in the eyes.

'Listen, Cornell. To repeat, you were recommended to me by Professor Vermeer. I need publicity in Europe and you can supply it. I trust Vermeer's judgement, therefore I trust you. I came to this party to meet you – that was why I accepted Señorita Graham's invitation. You may think you've walked into a madhouse but you're wrong. In this country, madmen are the rule. Can I take it you'll come tonight?'

'Try and stop me.'

Valencia shook hands and they watched him go in silence.

'You know, Bruce,' Esther said, 'the Conciencians have a lot of fine qualities. They're proud and brave, but sometimes their courage makes them go to extremes. When that happens they're capable of the most incredible brutality. Valencia wants to avert that.'

Antonio Valencia walked briskly across the lawn to the french windows, followed by the eyes of everyone present. Bruce stared after his departing figure with mixed feelings. One of them was very close to fear.

4

Threading his way through the gloom of the shanty-town, Valencia stumbled over a pig. There was a grunt, followed a moment later by the wail of a child. He switched on his torch and recoiled. There was no great difference between the pig and the child. Both were encrusted with filth, both stared at him with unseeing eyes, and both scuttled off in alarm.

When his own eyes had grown accustomed to the darkness he saw, here and there, the supine figures of men sprawled outside the hovels. They were swigging cheap spirit straight from the bottle, lying outside because their huts were crowded and stank. Valencia knew the quarter well. The huts clung to the steep hillside and were perched on stilts, like the Indian huts that bordered the great rivers of the interior. Sewers were as little in evidence as water mains. The children had the sadly bloated faces and distended bellies of nutritional oedema. Because of inadequate hygiene, starvation and worms, the local infant mortality rate ran at over fifty per cent, and more than seventy per cent of those who inhabited this slough of despair were illiterate. Alms in the form of food and clothing were distributed on feast-days, but that was all that was ever done for the slum-dwellers. Their huts presented a dismal appearance. They were built of bamboo, corrugated iron, and tin, and the roofs consisted of cardboard boxes, planks and grimy rags. Nobody stayed dry when it rained, and in fine weather the excrement of man and beast lay roasting in the sun's rays.

Valencia hurried swiftly along the unpaved alley-ways, thinking of the party he had just left. The Cardinal's words still rang in his ears. He felt he would always hear them because they were a foretaste of the difficulties that were so unquestionably in store for him.

He compressed his lips hard. What had the Cardinal said? 'One of the pillars of the Church is obedience. To ignore that is to stray from the path of duty . . . A man who causes his superiors distress cannot be pardoned lightly.' But there was another way of putting it.

'Do superiors deserve forgiveness if they distress their subordinates? Is obedience to the Church more important than obedience to God?'

He felt rage flare up inside him like a searing flame. God . . . In this country God was treated like a broken reed. For centuries he had been represented as a *patrón*, an employer who dispensed favours in return for bribes of money. Those who rebelled against the established order, whether just or inequitable, feared that they were rebelling against God at the same time. The idea had been dinned into them for as long as they could remember. God commanded and their duty was to obey. The Cardinal and the President spoke in his name; ergo, no dialogue was possible. God spoke in monologues, but always through the mouths of the rich. Anyone who dared to differ in the past had been very soon browbeaten into compliance. Valencia was repeatedly struck by this fear of disobedience, even during his nationwide lecture tours. It was not prevalent among university students, of course, but they had no say in politics. The trade union leaders had a voice, but it had taken endless wrangling to persuade them to make a concerted stand. The Communists naturally took a different view. So did their supporters, the guerilleros. They believed that armed revolution was the only way of solving Conciencia's problems. Valencia agreed whole-heartedly. That was why he had established contact with Tobar, who received air-drops of arms and supplies from Cuba.

He paused in front of one of the huts, the only one built of stone. He knocked three times and the door opened at once.

'Come in, Professor. Were you followed?'

'Not as far as I know, Rodriguez. Don't worry, I've been playing this game for years.'

He felt humble in the presence of a guerrilla leader who ventured into the lion's den with so much outward indifference.

Tobar produced a bottle of wine from a cupboard and set it on the table.

'You think it necessary for this journalist to meet me?' he asked.

Valencia remained silent for a while, eyeing the weapons that lay piled in the corner of the room.

'Yes,' he said at length. 'We must let the world know what is happening here. That is why we need people like him. Do you have any objections?'

'No, but a single slip on his part would endanger us all, you and Señorita Graham as well as me. García would give his right arm to capture me.'

Tobar uncorked the bottle and poured four glasses. He put one in front of him and pushed another towards Valencia. The remaining two he deposited in front of the empty chairs that flanked the table.

'*Salud*,' he said, raising his glass. 'To the Revolution!'

Valencia started. It was the first time anyone had impressed on him so bluntly what he was involved in.

'Tell me,' Tobar went on, 'why do you remain a priest when the Church stands idly by and watches people being exploited?'

Valencia had often asked himself the same question without ever really answering it. He was aware, even so, that the fact of his being a priest would give the revolution a prop which nothing else could provide.

'Because people must be made to realize that there are priests who oppose exploitation,' he replied.

'Then it won't be long before they unfrock you.'

It was no question, just a statement of fact.

Valencia glanced at the rifles and machine-guns. They were instruments of death. They would be used some day, and men would die . . . He wondered how many deaths Tobar already had on his conscience, a succession of murders stretching down the years . . .

'I know what's on your mind,' Tobar said, interrupting his train of thought. 'You fear the consequences of revolution. You're wondering if there isn't another way, without guns and bloodshed. Answer me this, then: why is the Holy Virgin an honorary general in the Conciencian army? Why do priests of the Church which displays her image receive the same salary as an army major? Don't the government troops carry guns and fire them, Professor, or do you subscribe to your Cardinal's statement that armed revolution violates the teachings of the Church?'

'No,' Valencia replied, 'of course not, but I still have a conscience.'

Tobar gave a bitter laugh and splashed some more wine into his glass.

'Don't talk to me about conscience! You just walked through this slum, didn't you? Didn't your conscience prick you then? And there are fifty more slums like it, some of them even worse.'

From outside came the sound of footsteps and Esther Graham's voice. Bruce Cornell followed her in. He smiled when he saw the wine-glasses, shook Valencia and Tobar by the hand and sat down.

Tobar's gaze lingered on Esther. His own daughter would have been about her age if she had lived.

'What do you want to know?' he asked Bruce.

'Some idea of your aims,' Bruce said tersely.

Tobar stared straight ahead. His hard face looked like a leather mask set with two eyes which glowed like embers. There was a fiery red mark on his neck, and Bruce could clearly discern the bulge of a pistol under his jacket.

'I speak to you only because the Professor has asked me to, *señor*,' he said at last. 'I am a man of action, not a theorist. How in the name of heaven am I supposed to explain to you what is going on in Conciencia? You are a foreigner, and nobody who was born outside this country can imagine what is happening here. One thing I will say, however. Do you know what hunger is, *señor* – real hunger, not for half an hour, not for a few days, but for a lifetime, year in year out? Do you know what it means when you cannot get medicines? When you are in pain and know very well that there is a cure but have no money to pay for it? When you are forced to watch your children die, one after another? When the police rape your wife and daughter in the name of the law?'

He paused and stared moodily at the peeling walls.

'And you see revolution as the answer?' Bruce asked.

Tobar nodded.

'We must be thorough,' he said. 'Otherwise, everything will remain as it is. Men will die – very well, nothing can prevent that. I have killed many times and will do so again. The government calls me a murderer. It depends on your point of view.'

Bruce could see, by the dim light of the candle which stood on the table, that the grim face of the man beside him brightened a little as he went on:

'We have thirty thousand men in the mountains at this moment, a well trained army which fears nothing and nobody. I am placing this army at Professor Valencia's disposal.'

Bruce turned to Valencia.

'When do you propose to announce your plans?'

'In a few days' time, when the students of Cielo University launch their strike. Please understand, though. This conversation remains confidential. One does not announce a revolution in advance. The formation of a new party is something else.'

'And the Cardinal?'

'He will probably summon me to account for my actions. What happens then is anyone's guess.'

Tobar rose and leant over the table, propping himself on both hands. His face was very close to Bruce's.

'Before you go, *señor*, you must hear me out. Do you know why we

64

guerilleros live in the mountains under primitive, dangerous conditions, constantly harried by the President's soldiers? Because we have a cause worth fighting for. The newspapers call us bandoleros, which is what we call the police and the army. If we take reprisals, we do so against men who have cheated the people of Conciencia out of their fundamental rights for years. Would you like to hear how the average peasant lives in this country? He works all day long for a pittance. When he comes home from the fields he gets drunk because he wants to forget his wretchedness as quickly as possible, and when it gets dark he crawls into bed with his wife and copulates with her. Drink and sex are the peasant's only forms of relaxation, the only things he knows about. Apart from football and a little music, that is the sum total of his existence. I have already taken steps to change things in the area I control. I have set up co-operatives, confiscated land by force and settled small-holders on it. Anyone who opposed me, I have killed. That may sound hard, but how many peasants have been slowly murdered over the years by landowners, physically and mentally? Can you understand what all this means to us?'

Bruce glanced at Valencia's tormented face. It suddenly looked old and shrunken.

'You talk of murder as if it were a hobby.'

Tobar remained impassive.

'Pay a visit to Colonel García's cellars, *señor*. Murder is a trade there, not a hobby.' He turned to Esther. 'Forgive me if I shock you, *señorita*, but this is a fight to the death. Not everyone realizes that. Any one of us could be the next victim.'

'And any one of the other side,' Bruce retorted.

He found the atmosphere in the little hut quite as unreal as he had found Graham's soirée, with its chattering bevy of elegantly dressed people, the aristocratic Cardinal surrounded by his bishops, the President and his côterie of generals.

'Mutual fear,' Valencia said. 'This country is dying of fear.'

'And wealth.'

'And poverty.'

Silence fell. The candle-light threw strange shadows on the walls and danced on the gun-barrels in the corner. The air was treacly and Bruce could smell human sweat. Tobar had returned to his chair and seemed to be lost in contemplation. He was staring into space with his rugged head supported on his big hands and his shoulders slightly hunched. Valencia drew a hand over his eyes and Esther looked at the three men in turn.

'Do you think the army will join you?' Bruce asked.

Valencia sighed.

'We haven't reached that stage yet. First we must build up a united political front.'

'You'll need money from abroad. Where's it to come from?'

'Certainly not from America. The Americans underpin every oligarchy in Latin America.'

'Russia and China, then?'

'Perhaps.'

Bruce had almost run out of questions. He wondered why these people trusted him. They must know how risky it was. Suddenly he thought of Professor Vermeer.

'When does Vermeer start his lectures? I hear he got the appointment.'

'In a few days' time.'

'When the strike begins, you mean?'

'Yes.'

Bruce pondered for a moment. They were determined men, Valencia and Tobar. One had made violence his watchword, the other was adopting it as a last resort. He realized now that they were not alone. Hundreds of thousands of people would follow them, but not necessarily with the same courage or conviction. One thing was certain: he would no longer have to rely on third hand information for his articles – certainly not if he decided to play this dangerous game.

'It's risky,' he said aloud to Esther. 'I don't know if I can afford to get involved.'

She shrugged her shoulders.

'Nobody deserves to be happy unless he takes risks – that's what you told me a few days ago. I thought you meant it.'

He stared at her. Obviously, she was better informed about their plans than he would ever have believed. Her presence there was accepted as a matter of course.

'Where exactly do you come into this?'

Valencia shook his head.

'Don't ask her, *señor*.'

Bruce relapsed into silence. The circle was beginning to close. First Vermeer, then Valencia, then Tobar, and now Esther. He knew that a choice confronted him too. Either he must leave the country immediately or he would be sucked deeper and deeper into a morass of intrigue and the probable result would be expulsion, if not death. Alternatively, the rebels might win, but he had no faith

66

in that possibility despite the arguments of the men who sat facing him.

'All right,' he said, 'just tell me why you're mixed up in this thing.'

Her face glowed with assurance.

'Because I believe in it.'

'As an American?'

'You forget I was born here, Bruce.'

'What if I asked you to get out while there's still time?'

'I wouldn't.'

Bruce looked irresolutely from one to the other, then addressed himself to Tobar.

'Tell me honestly,' he said. 'How great are the risks?'

'This is a matter of life or death, *señor*,' Tobar replied gravely. 'You are at liberty to wash your hands of the whole affair. We cannot.'

Life or death. Bruce looked at Valencia. He put him at thirty-two or three, in the prime of life, too young to be confronted by such a naked choice.

Someone rapped on the door, three times. The man who entered looked like a beggar. He had a wall eye, his shirt was torn, and he wore a decrepit pair of sandals. His trousers were held up by an unravelled skein of rope. Bruce saw, when he spoke, that he did not have a tooth left in his head.

'The secret police are on the way,' he announced calmly. 'We received word.'

'Who from?' snapped Tobar.

'From the University. The cars have to pass that way.'

'Who said they were coming here?'

'Vincente Zabola.'

'How does he know?'

'One of the policemen talked.'

Tobar rose to his feet.

'*Gracias*, Arturo. Get us out of the *barrio* as fast as you can. Tell your men to hide their guns underground – you know where. Be quick!'

By the time the police convoy arrived Tobar, Esther, Valencia and Bruce were well on the way to a friend of Valencia's who lived on the outskirts of town. Nobody would think of looking for them at the house of Hernando Pinto, general manager of one of the largest sugar plantations in Conciencia. Pinto was a sturdy, pugnacious little man – an agnostic or atheist, not even he knew which. He had quarrelled with his parents while still at university because it embittered him that they did nothing with their astronomical wealth to help the country. The quarrel reached such a pitch that he eventually walked out on them and refused to accept another peso from his father.

The police promptly cordoned off the shanty-town. Located at strategic points, spotlights mounted on trucks bathed the wretched poverty of the inhabitants in a pitiless glare. Colonel García, who was in command, had the occupants of each hut questioned in turn and played a personal part in their interrogation.

'Have you seen a tall bearded man in army uniform?'

'No, Excellency, how could I? It was dark, and we have no fine searchlights like the gentlemen of the police.'

'What about you?'

'I saw no one, Excellency, I swear it by the Holy Virgin. I was drunk.'

'You still are,' snapped García. 'Get lost – you stink like a wine-shop.' He turned to the next man.

'What about you?'

The next man had no teeth. He wore sandals and a shred of rope round his waist in place of a belt.

He hesitated.

'Well?' García said impatiently. 'Talk, unless you want to hang by your thumbs.'

The man trembled.

'I was asleep, Excellency. I see nothing when I am asleep. I sleep most of the time, Excellency. It saves me from having to eat.'

'What's your name?'

'Arturo, Excellency.'

'Haven't you seen anyone from outside – no unusual visitors?'

The toothless man nodded eagerly.

'Yes, Excellency. Padre Valencia was here yesterday.'

'What did he want?'

'To talk to the people, Excellency. He also read Mass.'

'Very well. Next!'

None of them knew anything but García sensed that they were lying. His eyes scanned the neighbourhood vainly for suspicious signs. The policemen who searched the huts found nothing of note, and García had the impression that their scarecrow inhabitants were secretly relishing his lack of success.

He summoned a junior officer, a captain with a moustache like a pencil-stroke.

'How long have these huts been here, Captain?'

'Varying lengths of time, Colonel. A couple more go up every day.'

'Where do the people come from?'

'From the mountains, Colonel.'

'And where are the huts which were built this week?'

The captain pointed, and a spotlight followed the direction of his finger.

García drew a deep breath and expelled it through his nose.

'Very well, destroy them.'

'You mean . . .'

'Destroy them, I said, and don't make me repeat myself again.'

The captain issued a string of orders. The policemen piled into their trucks, which started to advance slowly, their headlamps piercing the night like silver lances. An old woman screamed. A coarse-faced Indian woman hurled a stream of imprecations at the policemen and was knocked to the ground. A pig ran squealing from the wheels of the oncoming trucks, and little children were chased inside the huts with curses and threats, only to dart out again like jack-in-the-boxes and dance back and forth in high delight.

A few minutes later the spotlights illuminated a horrifying spectacle: a huge heap of debris on which human ants scurried to and fro, trying to salvage their meagre possessions. The policemen were already starting to grumble over their work, but a flurry of oaths from the captain with the pencil-stroke moustache silenced their protests. García knew precisely what he was doing. The huts had been erected on a piece of land which belonged to the municipality. The site was due for development in a few weeks' time and had been plastered with notice-boards saying 'No Admittance!', but the hut-dwellers had purloined them for use as roofs. They had come from the mountains in the hope of finding a better life in the city. They arrived by night, erected a hut in a matter of hours, hoisted the Conciencian flag, and thereafter regarded the land as their own. It was the same all over the city. The shanty-towns sprang up like mushrooms and became hotbeds of discontent, sanctuaries for all the dissident elements who represented a threat to the President's authority.

García's tip had come from a reliable source, and he was satisfied that Tobar had been in one of the huts until a few minutes before.

Besides, Antonio Valencia visited the place regularly, and his links with left-wing groups were significant enough. Colonel García knew better than anyone that the President was in constant danger. Attempts were made on his life every other week. Men who had nothing to lose but their lives did not hesitate to stake them on a coup d'état. It was García's responsibility to ensure that they failed. He knew who his enemies were and had already eliminated a whole series of them. Others had been deported or had fled before he could arrest them, but the most dangerous of all went to ground in these shanty-towns. No outsider would dream of seeking there. He would see only the tumbledown huts, the dirt, disorder and demoralization, but García knew better. Many of the inhabitants lacked for nothing. Their poverty was camouflage, the best camouflage an agitator could have, nor did they live there all the time. Their job was to influence the illiterates, which was easy enough. Discontent had always been the ideal fuel for revolution, and discontent reigned among the professional idlers and parasites who lived in these hovels and supported themselves by begging, who burgled houses and sent their children to walk the streets, who drank and whored and, because of their poverty, were aided and abetted by insane idealists like Antonio Valencia, who refused to accept that nothing could be done to improve their lot because he regarded their mentality as an effect of destitution rather than its root cause. Much the same went for the students at Cielo University. They became agitators out of boredom. Many of them had fled their natural environment because they would have had to work, because they would have had to shoulder responsibility for the plantations which were the main source of Conciencia's wealth.

Colonel García moved closer to the huts. His mouth twisted in a mirthless smile as he listened to the dull thud of rifle-butts on wood, the clatter of corrugated iron. The next moment his smile vanished. A flying stone struck him on the forehead with such force that the ground seemed to lurch beneath him. He kept his feet, half-stunned, and a searing pain shot through his temples. Exploring the wound with his fingers, he was shocked to feel the sticky wetness of his own blood. His heart suddenly hammered like a mad thing. For an instant he felt consciousness slipping away, but all that possessed him when the moment passed was a cold desire for revenge. Slowly, he walked over to the captain, who was standing beside the command car. The glow from its spotlight illuminated the gash on his forehead and the thin rivulet of blood that was trickling down his face. The taste of blood banished even the modicum of emotion which sometimes got the better of him at rare moments.

'So they're offering resistance?' he said.

The captain nodded.

'Yes, Colonel. They're using the only weapons they have – stones.'

García shook his head.

'Who says they have no weapons? These shanty-towns make perfect rebel arms dumps. House-to-house searches don't work because there aren't any houses. Just mud, filth and open drains, and nobody bothers to look there.'

As he spoke he watched his men demolishing the huts like so many toys. He saw women trying to wrest the rifles from their hands, saw children gleefully joining in the destruction as if they were on the side of the police, and grinned because the sound of splintering wood was music to his ears. Then, suddenly, the picture changed. Everything happened so abruptly that even the colonel was taken by surprise. A shot rang out, a policeman screamed and fell. García swore, drew his own pistol and fired back. More shots followed, then silence. It only lasted for a second, one fearful second in which life seemed to have vanished from the face of the earth. Finally, although there was nothing to be seen, there came the high-pitched, piercing scream of a child in agony.

'Arrest them all,' García said. 'Every last one. I want them behind bars.'

The wounded policeman was borne away and an ambulance summoned by radio. The other policemen temporarily abandoned their work of devastation and sealed off the area hermetically so that no one could escape. Men and women were wrenched apart and the police proceeded to vent their rage on huts and occupants alike.

'Search for weapons,' García snapped. 'Quickly!'

There was no compassion left in the captain's face. The scum had shot one of his men and they were going to suffer for it. García was right – pity was weakness. Anyone who yielded to pity was courting disaster.

'Send for some more transport. Round them up!'

Resistance by the hut-dwellers seemed to have been broken. Anyone who did not surrender at once was beaten unmercifully while armed policemen stood by with their tommy-guns at the ready. The prisoners were propelled along under a hail of kicks and blows. García watched them shuffle past him, licking the blood from his lips. There was not much left of the huts now. He realized that not all their occupants could have been detained. Some of them, probably including the sniper, had fled in the direction of a neighbouring shanty-town. The rest he would deter from any future fun and games in the cellars of the Seguridad Nacional. He could not hold them for longer than a week, but by the time they came out they would finally have learnt the consequences of armed resistance to the police. There was no point in bringing them to court. Trials only provided the Communist newspapers with welcome propaganda. If they got wind of the story despite this, as they probably would, he could always issue a statement to the effect that the police had been fired on while trying to arrest some criminals. It even accorded with the facts – at least partly. Afterwards, when the prisoners were released, they would take care not to open their mouths too wide. Fear would rule their lives from then on.

More transport arrived. García watched his men prod the prisoners into closed vans, which immediately drove off. He took a last look at the desolation, heedless of the children who were wandering aimlessly around, weeping and dazed with shock. Then he climbed into his car, lit a cigarette and sat back. It pleased him to think that yet another hotbed of unrest had been cleared. In a minute he would radio instructions for the neighbouring shanty-town to be thoroughly searched. He was tired, and his wife would be worried about him by now. She knew nothing of his activities, and thought he was an ordinary police officer. Why should he enlighten her? His days were arduous enough as it was. When your job was to protect a head of State, you had to be ruthless with all who cherished designs on his life.

But from another point of view he was highly dissatisfied. Tobar had escaped him once again. Who had tipped him off? Which of his men had been indiscreet? His head still throbbed but the bleeding had stopped. There was nothing more for him to do tonight. His men would take care of the prisoners – in fact he would not be surprised if they beat a couple of them to death. The rest might be more forthcoming after that. The wounded policeman was not in danger, fortunately, but the shooting incident would be enough in itself to convince his friends and colleagues that they were dealing with a gang of criminals who deserved all they got.

Or so García thought. He did not know that the shot came from a man who had seen the police demolish his hut while his two young children were still lying in their beds of rags. He had not meant to pull the trigger but was so overcome with fury that he fired without thinking.

García was equally unaware that one of the huts contained three dead bodies, nor did he hear Arturo's muttered remark to a neighbour in one of the speeding police vans:

'At least we know what sort of men we're up against. Their punishment will be worse than their crime, I swear it by the Holy Virgin.' It was a *promesa*, a vow, and everyone knew how heavily it weighed.

Nor did García overhear the telephone call which Antonio Valencia had just that moment made to one of his many friends, a professor at Cielo University, who told him what had happened and informed him that the students were even more determined to strike in protest against acts of brutality by the police. Valencia turned to Bruce, who was still with him at Pinto's house in the suburbs.

'Did you hear?' he asked.

Bruce nodded. 'What do you propose to do?'

'Take a look.'

'In the middle of the night?'

'Why not?'

'Aren't you afraid they may arrest you?'

'No.'

'I'll come with you.'

'At your own risk. You realize that?'

'Of course. Shall we let Esther know?'

'No.'

'What about Tobar?'

'Leave him out of it. They're both asleep. We'll be back in a couple of hours.'

Cielo seemed deserted, though the lights of the capital glittered like stars. The night was cool and luminous with the glow of a full moon. It was darker inside the car. Valencia spoke as he drove.

'In a few days everyone will know my intentions. If anything happens to me, one of the students will announce my programme instead. I feel as if I had really begun to live for the first time. I have had many doubts, Cornell. There have been days when I suddenly realized that praying is simply talking to God, to a great unknown who only listens, never answers. That's why a man must make his own decisions. Conscience provides him with the answer he needs. The voice of conscience may well be the voice of God.'

A rabbit darted across the road and was almost caught by the wheels of the speeding car.

'I often feel like that,' Valencia said, 'like an animal running for its life. I know I've made many mistakes. It may be that I over-

73

simplify things, but I don't see any other way. Nothing in this country will change unless we act quickly. I sometimes think that if Christ came back to earth nobody would dare to look him in the eye. At other times I ask myself why I concern myself with these things at all. When I was in Europe, South America seemed far away, so infinitely far away that I found it impossible to conceive of it playing a role in the world of today. I know better now. We mean nothing to foreigners because our countries are glorified puppet-shows. Conciencia is still ruled by the same families that ruled it a century ago. It doesn't matter which party they belong to. There are no genuine programmes of reform, merely laws with loopholes so big that an elephant could slip through. The property-owning classes run a mutual protection society while the under-privileged live without protection, without love. The sacred images in our churches look down on some of the worst social injustices in the modern world.'

Bruce stared along the beam of the headlights. Valencia's words carried conviction, and he was starting to shed his original pre-judices against the man. He knew as well as Valencia that the Latin American world was in turmoil. He knew that these Catholic countries were ruled by people who took everything for themselves and gave the masses nothing. He realized that they clung stubbornly to an evil God of their own devising, one who left the rich in peace because they were rich and the poor in peace because they accepted their poverty. He had spoken to too many simple people not to know that they still believed in God, even if he never helped them, never did anything for them, never gave them anything but a taste of the whip. Their God was not self-operative. He was manipulated by the cardinal and bishops, by those in authority over the established Church.

The engine hummed gently. Valencia's mouth was a hard line. The telephone call had been explicit enough. He knew García's methods. The people from the shanty-town would all be in prison now, apart from a few left to mourn the dead.

He drove along the broad avenidas, skirted some workers' settle-ments, and eventually drew up outside the quarter which was known, by some strange irony, as El Futuro. As he got out and slammed the door he wondered if he would be equal to all the burdens that would descend on him. Whether he would withstand the derision, the intimidation and slander. Whether he would be able to endure it if his closest friends deserted him. His background was not working-class. He belonged to one of the country's ruling

74

families. They had not disowned him in spite of his progressive ideas. But what if they did? Where would he get his strength? He would have to pray to the unseen but omnipresent God. He would have to believe even more strongly, but how could he when he preached a policy of violence which conflicted with that of the Church? They would never forgive him for that. Men had to undergo crucifixion in every century, just as Christ had done. But wasn't the Church being inconsistent? How many times had she not reinforced her authority by force of arms? Who had colonized South America, if not ruthless soldiers with missionaries hard on their heels?

Valencia paused at a bend in the narrow lane and clutched Bruce by the arm. He was appalled at what he saw. Trucks with blazing headlights ringed the outer extremity of the shanty-town, or what was left of it. Just rubble, splintered wood, corrugated iron, refuse, children wandering around aimlessly or frolicking with emaciated pigs and dogs. Near the trucks he saw policemen. Cigarette-smoke rose from them as they laughed and chatted.

Bruce glanced at Valencia. Rage seemed to have added another six inches to his height. His fists were clenched and his chest rose and fell quickly. Without a word, he strode down the muddy path that led to the ruined shanty-town. He stumbled a few times and fell, his hands seeking a purchase in the mire. Bruce followed him, sensing that he was impelled by a fury which would stop at nothing.

A spotlight swung in their direction, dazzling them. By its glare, Bruce saw that Valencia's eyes were feverish and his features tense.

'Who the hell are you?' someone called out.

'Antonio Valencia,' the priest called back, and strode on, even though he must have been completely blinded by the light. He took no notice of the spotlights, the police cars, the voices that shouted incomprehensible things at him. He strode towards the frolicking children, who greeted him with shouts of delight. 'Suffer the little children . . .' Bruce thought, and stared round in horror. But Valencia had him firmly by the arm and was pulling him along. None of the policemen barred their path. A bent old man came to meet them and conducted them to the stone hut where they had sat with Tobar only a few hours earlier. He opened the door and pointed to the corner where the arms had been stacked. Bruce recoiled involuntarily when he found himself looking into the lifeless faces of a man, a woman and a child. The hut was thronged with people praying aloud and running their rosaries through their fingers.

75

Valencia advanced a few paces and stared down at the bodies. The faces of the man and woman were still contorted with fear. Only the child seemed to smile, as if it thought the whole thing was a game, something quite different and far more lovely than it had ever known. It was the child's face which moved Valencia most of all. How many of his supporters would treat his programme as a game when he announced it? How many would be left alive by the time it proved to be no game but an undertaking in deadly earnest?

He folded his hands. An agonizing thought struck him. These three people had died in vain. They were no martyrs, no saints, no heroes – nothing at all. His thoughts turned to the meaning of the Mass for the dead, and he said it aloud to himself:

'*I tremble with fear when I think upon the heart-searching there must be, and upon thy wrath let loose upon mankind. When the heavens and the earth are to be shaken to their foundations. A day of wrath must that day be, a day of disillusion and despair; a day to overshadow all other days, and a day of dreadful bitterness . . .*'

He sensed that the men and women in the hut were listening to him. He knew that they were all thinking of the same thing, not of the day of judgement at the end of the world, but of the day of judgement in Conciencia. And suddenly he knew that these three had not died in vain after all. Their names would echo the length and breadth of the country. Their end was a beginning. It would kindle a flame in the hearts of workers, peasants and students alike, and their destroyer would wish bitterly that he could raise them from the dead because their death had sown the seeds of life in others.

Valencia knelt and prayed: '*Eternal rest grant to them, O Lord,*' and the response came in a hoarse mutter: '*And let perpetual light shine upon them.*'

When he got to his feet the men and women clustered round to tell him what had happened. They pressed his hand, weeping, cursing, praying, crying aloud. Bruce could see Valencia's expression change as he stood among them. It was as though the Bible had come alive again. The poor, the oppressed and the hungry had gathered round one man and were entrusting him with their all, their lives and safety. He gave them new strength because he spoke their language and knew their needs. He recognized the dangers inherent in his chosen course but pursued it regardless of the doubts that beset him. Bruce had doubts too, but they were of a different kind. He doubted the value of his own existence. Perhaps it was a sign of advancing age, but he sometimes felt that his life to date had been futile. He was beginning to see that even more clearly in the shadow of this man. What had he ever done except cultivate his powers of observation? Had he created anything? Had he drawn attention to genuine iniquities or attached too much importance to sensationalism? Wasn't life in Latin America sensational enough? Dictators promised the earth and gave nothing. They grasped at power and built themselves Pharaonic monuments in the shape of statues, theatres, airports and skyscrapers, but what did they ever give the people? What had they given the trio whose bodies were laid out in this little stone hut? The two adults never knew they existed. They vegetated from one dreary day to the next, accepting their wretchedness as an act of God, like thunder and lightning. They grew older because age gnawed at the human body, slowly devouring it, making it wearier and less supple. And the child? It had known nothing at all. Perhaps it thought life was a game, that open drains were a delight to the eye, that starvation was a law of Nature. The child had been on the threshold of life. A bullet robbed it of that life because it had nothing more to give. From him that hath not shall be taken away even that which he hath . . .

Bruce emerged from his reverie with a start, to see that Valencia had produced a pad from his pocket and was making some notes. The priest turned to him.

'Are you coming?' he asked. Bruce nodded silently and cast a final glance at the bodies. Strange that they should be lying in that corner. One of Tobar's guns had been used and the police had fired back. All very convenient for García. His prisoners would be worked on until they confirmed the sequence of events.

The people greeted Valencia respectfully as he passed them, but at the edge of the ruins his path was barred by a captain with a moustache that bisected his face like a pencil-stroke. He eyed Valencia and Bruce with disfavour.

'What are you doing here?' he demanded.

Valencia stared back.

'Trying to bring these people spiritual consolation.'

The captain lit a cigarette and blew the smoke in Valencia's direction.

'Your name?'

'Antonio Valencia.'

'And your name, *señor*?'

'Bruce Cornell.'

'Why are you here?'

'I'm a journalist.'

77

The captain wavered. He did not dare to take action against a priest, even though Valencia's name was familiar to him. Bruce wondered if the man had a wife and child. What would he tell his wife when he got home? Would he tell her that he had helped to kill three innocent civilians in the shanty-town of El Futuro because they had tried to defend the shack that was their only possession? And if he said nothing, would she read it in the newspaper tomorrow, and would he excuse himself by saying that the people had opened fire first so he had to fire back in self-defence? A man must always find excuses for his wife's benefit, and that would no doubt be his. Suddenly, and for no very apparent reason, Bruce thought of Esther.

The captain reiterated his question.

'Why did you come here? They're all thieves and Communists, these people.'

Valencia laughed.

'How would you know? Even if they are, what made them so?'

The captain shrugged.

'Oh, go home!' he said brusquely. 'It's late, and I'm not in the mood for a political debate. If you want to know anything, consult Colonel García. He was in charge of the operation.'

Valencia nodded and walked through the blaze of spotlights to the edge of the *barrio*. He did not speak during the return journey. He could not forget the smile on the face of the dead child. All the children in these shanty-towns began life like that, with a smile on their lips. The smile only faded as they grew wiser in the crowded hovels where fathers and mothers, sons and daughters, sons- and daughters-in-law all slept cheek by jowl. Were these animals that climbed on top of one another to satisfy their physical needs, panting and moaning, crying out when the moment of climax came? The children would lie there and listen with their cheeks aflame, and, as they grew older, learn to satisfy themselves until they were capable of doing as the others did. Such was their sexual life – ugly because it lacked intimacy. And that was only one aspect of their poverty. The other was worse still. Wives aged prematurely and husbands sought sexual outlets elsewhere. Incest and adultery were rife, but what could one do when the wife turned into a slattern, an ill-clad and undernourished creature who lay down apathetically when her husband demanded it, could not raise the energy to play her part and felt relieved when the loveless, wordless performance was over? When children arrived, many of them died of neglect and malnutrition, enduring it all with a resignation that was shocking to see. Poverty was the reason why he, a priest, had to take a hand in politics, why he was compelled to preach violence. He saw his country spread out before him like an open book, impossible to read without a fierce pang of shame.

The car turned into the drive of Hernando Pinto's house. Valencia saw Esther run out to meet them as he braked to a halt. She looked puzzled and anxious.

'Tobar has gone,' she said excitedly. 'Nobody knows where he is.'

Valencia smiled.

'I do,' he said. 'He's back in the mountains. His guerilleros need him.'

5

Raoul Castillo considered the assignment which Rodriguez Tobar had given him – the execution of Guillermo de la Cruz and his two lieutenants – to be far more dangerous than the projected raid on the army post. He knew Taloma, where '*El Mariscal*' operated, only too well. It was one of the few areas where the army had never been able to establish itself for any length of time because lack of roads made the rapid movement of troops impossible. This had enabled de la Cruz to set up a sort of miniature republic-within-a-republic. When a half-battalion of government soldiers invaded his territory, he offered no resistance and temporarily withdrew to the remote mountain village of Dorado.

De la Cruz was an ex-lawyer from Cielo who had been one of the most revolutionary student leaders of his day. After gaining a formidable reputation as a fiercely outspoken defence counsel, he eventually incurred the wrath of the ruling class with a public declaration that the aristocracy was totally corrupt and dedicated to its own welfare rather than that of the people. Two unsuccessful attempts on his life ensued. The opposition press splashed both of them under banner headlines, also his threat to dispose of the would-be assassin before he tried a third time. De la Cruz made good his threat. He shot the man in his home and calmly walked out. A warrant was issued for his arrest but he managed to escape at the eleventh hour to Taloma, where he rose to become one of the most dreaded guerrilla leaders in Conciencia. There was a price of fifty thousand pesos on his head, but nobody had summoned up the courage even to think of earning it.

Raoul Castillo had only seen de la Cruz twice, each time during briefing sessions at Tobar's headquarters, but he had a vivid recollection of the tall, powerfully-built man and, above all, of his eyes, which seemed to transfix anyone he looked at.

De la Cruz had objected violently to his territory being placed under the supreme command of Rodriguez Tobar, but submitted with bad grace when he got no support from the other guerrilla leaders.

It was not easy to penetrate de la Cruz's territory. Visitors had to cross the river either by means of a primitive ropeway or by swimming their horses through the fast-flowing water. Guerilleros posted on the far bank questioned all comers and dealt with undesirables. Mules and horses were the only means of transport in Taloma. Even maize, rice and sugar were carried by pack animals because there were no proper roads, let alone bridges. De la Cruz could not be blamed for this. He had contacted the Minister of the Interior via a police inspector on his pay-roll and received a promise to the effect that this intolerable situation would be remedied, but nothing had been done.

In recent years, however, one or two changes seemed to have occurred in Guillermo de la Cruz's territory. It was widely reported that the co-operatives which he had founded were defunct; that the district's one school, where a schoolmistress had taught Marxism, among other subjects, was derelict; and that the peasants were closer to starvation than ever. There were also rumours that de la Cruz was a sick man and had started to drink, though nobody had so far confirmed this except the little *campesino* whose daughters had been raped.

Reluctant as he was to accept Tobar's assignment, Castillo did not show it. He devoted the first few hours to selecting the men who were to accompany him. This was not easy because no guerillero readily lent himself to shooting members of his own side, but after much argument Castillo mustered a party of four.

The first was Emanuel, nicknamed *El Diablo*, a thick-set man with a massive torso supported on disproportionately short legs. His mood was permanently grim. Killing meant nothing to him and had never cost him a night's sleep, but he was an idealist in his own way. He had never been known to strike or abuse a *campesino*, and everyone knew that he could be relied on when it really came to the pinch.

Pedro, known as *El Mono*, the monkey, was in every respect the opposite of Emanuel. Short and slight, never coarse-mannered but habitually arrogant, he had a cold-blooded deliberation about him – especially when stalking the enemy – which even his friends found spine-chilling.

Carlos, who they called *El Gerente*, the manager, was a man who talked of nothing but himself. He had earned his sobriquet by claiming to have been a factory manager, not that anyone believed the story.

Armando's gruesome nickname was *El Esqueleto*, the skeleton. Tall and bony, he adorned his bald cranium with a black beret which he never removed, even at night in his hammock. His general attitude towards the others was one of sombre distaste. Other men swore when a bullet whined too close to their hiding-place; Armando cackled hoarsely, raised his rifle and fired back. He seldom missed, and greeted each addition to his score of victims with a contented smirk. He was the finest marksman in the guerilleros' ranks, which was why Castillo had picked him.

Raoul Castillo disliked the underhand nature of his mission. He was to inform Guillermo de la Cruz that Tobar had appointed him deputy supreme commander of all the provinces and wished to convey the news of his promotion in person. Tobar was counting on the Marshal's vanity, which had presumably driven him to his present rather incongruous way of life. Or was it his marriage? De la Cruz's wife, who came from an upper-class family, had left him after only a year. She despised him because of his ideas, the friends he brought home and his one-man campaign against the establishment.

Perhaps the Marshal's revolutionary sentiments were rooted in this experience, thought Castillo – perhaps that was why he had joined the guerilleros so precipitately. Perhaps he was motivated neither by hatred nor idealism, merely by an emotional trauma which he sought to forget in the jungle. No man of that sort was capable of leading a rebel army to the victory which only relentless and single-minded endeavour could bring.

Once Castillo had reached this conclusion, the Marshal's forthcoming execution ceased to trouble him. He ordered his men to saddle their horses and inspected their weapons. They wore the simple attire of *campesinos* and were instructed, if stopped by soldiers, to behave with suitable humility and pretend that they were going in search of employment.

The horses that had been assigned to them were small and lean, with old saddles, rope bridles and no bits. The five men rode out of Tobar's camp at a brisk trot. They passed bamboo huts beyond which lay plantations of green bananas, the sort that could only be eaten cooked. The banana groves gave way to fields of manioc and potatoes and extensive coffee plantations. The men's saddle-bags contained sticks of unrefined sugar, the iron ration of the guerillero. Trucks passed them from time to time but they barely looked up, never knowing who might be inside. They carried no rifles, only revolvers which could be concealed under their clothing.

Mountains towered above them to the left. To the right, they gazed down many hundreds of feet to where, far below, the tree-tops of the eternal jungle formed a carpet of impenetrable greenery. Reaching a friend's *finca*, they dismounted and tied their horses to the balustrade which ran round the house. They were warmly welcomed and given a meal. For the first time in weeks, they tasted *sancocho* and soup made with yucca, meat and vegetables. They went to bed early because they planned to leave before daybreak so as to reach the borders of Guillermo de la Cruz's territory by noon.

Castillo slept badly that night. He felt chilly, and his stomach hurt him. Sometimes, like now, he wondered if there was any purpose in the hard life he led. Nothing in the country seemed to have changed. The newspapers published glowing reports on industrial progress, the President inaugurated a series of buildings and then attended Mass. The only difference was an occasional picture or article devoted to the priest named Antonio Valencia.

After two sleepless hours he got up and went outside. The night was cool and clear. There was no sound except the sporadic braying of a donkey in the far distance. He eyed the little house with a touch of envy. Up in his mountain hide-out he sometimes dreamed of owning a *finca* himself, of growing his own yucca, maize and coffee, of keeping cows and pigs and chickens. But as long as nothing changed in his native land he had to remain what he was, an outcast who slept in trees or on the hard ground, who trekked from one end of the province to the other, a tough, cruel, fanatical guerillero who had been trained to treat soldiers and landowners as mortal foes.

He returned to the shack, which was stuffy and overcrowded. He could not even raise a chuckle when Pedro said:

'Well, Raoul, how was she?'

At about midday they reached the river and urged their horses through the water to the other bank without using the ropeway. Ten heavily armed *campesinos* were waiting for them on the far side. Grimly, they inquired what brought the party to Taloma.

Undeterred by this hostile reception, Castillo announced that he was the personal representative of Rodriguez Tobar and, as such, entitled to friendlier treatment. He had a message for Guillermo de la Cruz from his commander-in-chief – an urgent message.

It was bluff, he realized that, but it seemed to work. The *campesino* who had been acting as spokesman stepped aside and informed him that the Marshal might be either in Dorado or at Oro, only two hours' ride distant. Castillo's party would in any case have to report to the police inspector at Oro, and the inspector would no doubt tell them where to find de la Cruz.

Relieved, they rode on, but Castillo had an uneasy sensation that they were being followed. Besides, he had seen a horseman gallop off a few minutes before they received permission to proceed. Within an hour or even sooner, Guillermo de la Cruz would know who was on the way to him.

They followed a track which was scarcely deserving of the name. It was no more than a donkey-path, a succession of rocks and pot-holes. Here and there they saw neglected peasant huts. Apathetic women barely paused to watch them as they passed by.

Reaching a clearing, Castillo stopped to hold a council of war. They had not been there more than a minute when twenty horse-men came galloping down on them led by a big well-dressed man with a yellow sombrero and a pistol in his white leather belt. He was mounted on a superb black horse with a *lanero* saddle embroid-ered in silver and carried a carbine in his right hand. He reined to a halt just in front of Castillo.

'If you wish to speak to a friend,' he said without preamble, 'why not come alone?'

'Are you Guillermo de la Cruz?'

'Yes. Who are you?'

'Raoul Castillo, second-in-command to Rodriguez Tobar. These men are called Emanuel, Pedro, Carlos and Armando.'

'You have not answered my question.' The Marshal's voice had a harsh, imperious edge to it.

'A man does not ride alone through this sort of country.'

'No? Why not? It would be safer and less conspicuous. Are you armed?'

'Of course.'

'Why of course? If you travel in the guise of *campesinos* it is safer not to carry weapons.'

'That is a matter of opinion.'

'The only opinion that counts here is mine. Hand over your guns and follow my men. Be quick about it. One false move and you will never see Rodriguez Tobar again.'

Reluctantly, they obeyed. The Marshal wheeled his horse and galloped off without waiting for the others to follow.

Castillo and his companions were surrounded. After an hour they reached the small and dirty village of Oro, where they were marched under escort into one of the larger huts. Inside, seated behind a desk, was Guillermo de la Cruz, and beside him stood a man in the uniform of a police inspector. Evidently, this was his office.

De la Cruz surveyed the prisoners calmly. A minute passed in silence.

Castillo felt a twinge of uncertainty. The man facing him seemed too self-assured to be suffering from a guilty conscience. He did not look like a heavy drinker, far less a degenerate.

'Ever heard of psychological warfare?' The question came so suddenly that Raoul Castillo could only stare at the Marshal in bewilderment.

'What do you mean?'

'What I say. Ever heard of it?'

'No.'

A faint smile passed over the Marshal's face.

'Well, you have now. It almost did for the lot of you, not to mention me.'

'I don't understand.'

'Did you check on the man who denounced me?'

Castillo was taken aback. So, to judge by their expressions, were the rest of his party.

De la Cruz crossed his legs and grinned.

'My friend Rodriguez Tobar swallowed the bait, *amigo*. I don't hold it against him. My only quarrel with him is that he didn't tell you to make sure of your facts before blowing my brains out.'

Castillo feigned incomprehension, but he knew that his act carried little conviction. Pedro stepped forward.

'You're wrong,' he said. 'We came to tell you that Tobar has appointed you second-in-command of the whole area.'

'That's right,' Carlos put in. 'Our orders were to tell you that Tobar wanted to speak to you.'

De la Cruz scrutinized the two men and gave a sudden laugh. He turned to Castillo.

'You picked your men well, Castillo, but stop trying to hoodwink me. You're the ones who have been tricked. A few weeks ago I caught a man who had raped two girls. He wasn't a guerillero, so I had him thrashed and expelled from the district. I was too lenient. It so happened that one of my contacts was watching Colonel Zambrano's headquarters some days later when he saw the same man turn up and request an interview. The man was then trailed to Tobar's camp, where he turned the tables on me and laid the rape at my door.'

'How do you know that?' Castillo demanded swiftly.

'Quite simple. My men jumped him after he left your camp and brought him back here. We worked on him until he confessed. Perhaps you'd like to see him – not that he's a very beautiful sight.'

'You mean . . .'

De la Cruz nodded.

'I mean that Colonel Zambrano's advisers dreamed the whole thing up so as to cast suspicion on me. You know that death is the only penalty for rape among the guerilleros. They have been circulating the foulest rumours about me for months now. That I drink, that I terrorize the whole area, that conditions here are worse than ever. It's their way of demonstrating that Marxism is the wrong answer to the *campesinos'* problems. If you had shot me the story would have been given to the international press as a graphic illustration of what would happen if Conciencia ever underwent a successful revolution. The country would probably have been flooded with foreign correspondents, all sincerely believing that you had done the right thing. In other words, our enemies would have fulfilled their aim, which is to bring discredit on the leadership of our movement. That's what psychological warfare is, my friends, and that's what you nearly fell for.'

One member of the party remained unconvinced. Armando, the Skeleton, raised his hand. He looked bonier than ever, and his lugubrious face was dark with mistrust.

'I have a question,' he said.

'Your name?'

'Armando.'

'Proceed.'

Armando glanced round at his companions, and his eyes dwelt on Castillo as though seeking support.

'How are we to know that what you say is true? You speak of psychological warfare, but those are words which I scarcely understand. I know nothing of such a method or its effects. Shooting is the only thing I do well, and I should no doubt have shot you. You were a lawyer once, Guillermo de la Cruz. Your tongue is more skilful than ours, but how can you prove that we are wrong?'

De la Cruz was still smiling.

'Bravo, Armando. Your words are a tribute to your common sense. I'll introduce you to the man who was at your headquarters.'

He clapped his hands and two guerilleros came in leading a small bent figure. Raoul Castillo could see that the Marshal's men had done their work well. The little man could barely put one foot before the other. His eyes were buried in a mass of puffy flesh and his back bore the weals of a protracted thrashing.

'Tell them how it was,' snapped de la Cruz.

'It was the Colonel's idea,' the *campesino* mumbled. 'I went to him because I had been beaten and wanted revenge. He asked me if I would work for him and earn the reward. With fifty thousand pesos I would be a rich man and have no need to work for the rest of my life. The Colonel told me exactly what to say. I was to blame the Marshal for what I had done and then go. The rest would take care of itself. I never stopped to think that rape was punishable by death among the guerilleros.'

'Then you can think about it now,' roared de la Cruz. 'The same goes for treason. Take him out and shoot him!'

Castillo stared after the unfortunate man as the guerilleros dragged him out.

'Do you believe me now, Armando?' asked de la Cruz. 'It's all so simple. Colonel Zambrano must know that communications are our weakest point. We may fight bravely, we may even be idealists, but we're so ill-informed about the activities of other groups that these slip-ups are bound to occur again and again unless we ensure that things change. They must change – we can't afford another blunder like this. And now listen. I want to visit Rodriguez Tobar before another two weeks go by. We cannot sit back and watch ourselves being systematically branded in the eyes of the world as rabble, as bandits and robbers who have no respect for anyone or anything, ruthless criminals who are leading the people to even greater poverty than they had to endure before. That's why we must get together, Tobar and I. I've given the matter a great deal of thought in the last couple of hours. Psychological trickery of this kind is far more dangerous to our cause than any number of soldiers. I have no need to tell you that slanderous rumours about us are being spread inside the country and abroad. Those of you who can read a newspaper will know what I mean. You planned to kill me, but you have learnt the truth. Well, my friends, I propose to use you as propagandists, but first you must see the difference between fact and fiction for yourselves. Follow me.'

What they saw in the next few hours came as a complete surprise to them. De la Cruz showed them two model villages which he had just built, explained the workings of four efficiently run co-opera-tives, introduced them to a team of medical orderlies, guerilleros like themselves, who spent their whole time touring the area, and conducted them round a small but well equipped field hospital manned by a doctor and four nurses.

Castillo and his men could not refrain from wagging their heads at these wonders. This was a new image of Guillermo de la Cruz, and quite different from the one they had formed on the basis of assiduously fostered rumours. Abruptly, it dawned on them how important propaganda could be. Back in Oro once more, the Marshal returned their weapons and shook hands with each of them in turn.

'And now go back and tell Rodriguez Tobar what you have seen. Colonel Zambrano knows perfectly well what we're doing here, but he has every reason to keep quiet about it. If it weren't so risky I'd invite the national press to take a look – in fact I've been toying with the idea for some time, but I suppose the danger of espionage is too great. *Hasta la vista, camaradas,* and tell Tobar to look before he leaps in future. I'll get some men to escort you as far as the river.'

The party rode off in silence. Just as the village disappeared round a bend in the track they heard three shots ring out in quick succession.

'The price of treachery,' said one of their guides.

Colonel Zambrano's plan had misfired, but the essential thing now was to ensure that they got back safely. If Zambrano had been notified of their coming he would have them trailed to Tobar's hide-out and so kill two birds with one stone. Castillo called a halt and explained the problem to their guides, who were so impressed that they decided to take the party back to de la Cruz rather than risk possible disaster.

The Marshal greeted Castillo and his men with some surprise, but after listening in silence for a while he nodded.

'Your best plan would be to converge on a rendezvous from different directions. Assemble there first before trying to reach your headquarters. In the meantime, I'll spread the word that your attempt has failed and that you yourselves have paid the penalty. Stay here overnight and make an early start tomorrow. Zambrano and his men will probably reach here about midday. One dirty trick deserves another. Besides, I'm all in favour of a little excitement.'

Some hours later two galloping horsemen reached Colonel Zambrano's camp. In a near-by café they loudly related what they had overheard while unloading sugar-cane on the far side of the river. Apparently, five men had been captured by the Marshal and summarily executed. It was rumoured that their orders had been to shoot de la Cruz on the spot. The rumour-mongers then drank up and left, secure in the knowledge that Colonel Zambrano would receive the news within a very short time. They remounted their fast horses and galloped back to the Marshal's territory. It was a relief to them to know that they had been able to carry out his orders at such speed.

Colonel Zambrano, U.S.-trained in the relentless art of guerrilla warfare, combat-toughened in Europe and Korea, and fresh from an extended tour of observation in Vietnam, heard the rumour just as darkness was beginning to fall. Sitting in his office, unadorned save for a large-scale map dotted with flags purporting to indicate major concentrations of guerrilla units, he swore aloud and summoned his adjutant.

'Fetch me the owner of the café. I want a precise description of those men.'

The adjutant saluted and withdrew.

Zambrano reached for the antiquated telephone and dialled a number.

'John? Listen. It didn't work. Get over here quickly. De la Cruz has given us the slip again.'

He heard his American adviser swear volubly in English, grinned, and very deliberately hung up.

6

Antonio Valencia sat alone in his Cielo apartment. His mother had gone to Washington. It was strange how much he missed her. She would have looked at him from the depths of her arm-chair and told him that he was the only member of the party that evening who had the gift of inspiring others. And if he had laughingly protested and told her not to exaggerate, she would have replied that he did not know himself and his own strength of personality.

Surveying the litter of empty glasses now that his guests had departed, he realized that his mother's verdict on him was inaccurate. All she had ever done was deliver him from subservience to the demon doubt. That much she had accomplished, but the sight of her empty chair somehow brought it home to him that her judgement and views no longer ruled his life.

He looked round with deep contentment. This was his world – the works of Augustine, Plato, Hegel, Marx and Kant, the latest papal encyclicals with which he could prove the injustice of what was happening in his native land. Book after book filled with the wisdom of centuries, human lives turned to paper as if they had never been flesh and blood.

The drinks had done him good, stimulated him. Also, the evening had brought another meeting with Esther Graham, who was to become his secretary. At their very first encounter he had sensed that she was as deeply committed as he was himself – no, even more so because she was younger and more uncompromising. He could still recall something she had said to him. 'Peace is for weaklings. You are the exact opposite of peace. You are conflict personified.'

The words sounded a little high-flown and he had laughed at them, but she was right in a way. Force was the only solution now. No more long-winded discussions with vacillating trade union leaders, eternal doubters who hovered between certainty and uncertainty, no more agreements which went by the board as soon as sectional interests were at risk.

No, Esther was right to be so uncompromising.

Esther . . . A partisan, a young and beautiful girl . . . He thrust the thought of her aside, but he knew that it would return to plague him again. He stood up and began to pace up and down. Pausing in front of the wardrobe in his bedroom he opened it and looked inside. Four cassocks hung there, each with a multitude of buttons. He took one out, clasped it to him and mechanically started to count the buttons. He felt an almost touching affinity with the garment. It was his sacrificial robe, a sort of embodiment of his ideals. He was priest and man combined. People might poke fun at the long black robe and call its wearers 'black crows', but the soutane really did embody all that he had sacrificed, all that he had to forget. Women . . . Esther . . .

His pipe was not drawing well. He laid the soutane on the bed and went back to his arm-chair in the living-room. Taking another pipe from the rack, he filled it carefully, lit it and exhaled a cloud of smoke which wreathed his head like a cloud. Esther's face reappeared in it, and immediately afterwards he heard Vermeer's voice: 'Don't pick a quarrel with the Church merely as a pretext for marrying with a good conscience!' He laughed aloud. Esther already had a boy-friend, the journalist Cornell. She was simply an intellectual stimulus. He only saw her face and eyes – or was he deluding himself? Did he visualize her body too? But he had renounced all that. Could he ever convince people? They would say he was mad, pop him in a drawer and stick a label on it. He preached violence but nobody realized that he abhorred it. As a priest he resisted the love of women, but nobody accepted that this love could take possession of a priest without his wanting it. Why did people have to approach everything from one direction? He wanted revolution, true. He advocated force and opposed it at the same time, but when force was the only answer it had to be used for the greater good, willy-nilly.

It dawned on him suddenly that his apartment was a prison. Sitting there alone and without human advisers, he had to find a solution whether he wanted to or not. There was nothing more difficult than answering one's own questions. Here in the utter seclusion of his room, with the murmur of the city as an accompaniment, he had to sit in judgement on himself, and nothing was harder than that. He himself was the question and he himself the answer. He could allow a country to perish or kill men to save it. Which was the lesser evil? You could try to compute it mathematically. Take the average number of people who died annually from poverty and malnutrition, multiply by the years of peace ahead, and compare it with the probable number of people who would die in the course of a revolution. But that was where fear took hold of him, and that was where his mistake lay. Real decision-makers never yielded to fear, always believed in the rightness of their chosen course of action, whatever the consequences.

Sudden consternation seized him as he refilled his glass. The walls of his room melted away, and he realized that he was sitting in the heart of a country which he planned to save because people were dying while he sat there and drank. The wealthy could afford to do that even when they were priests like himself. But didn't the wealthy have a right to happiness? No, none, because they feasted on the blood of the poor. They revelled while the *campesinos* suffered.

He got up and walked into the bedroom. He picked up his soutane, draped it over a hanger and put it back in the wardrobe.

With a final look at the bottles, glasses and brimming ashtrays, he opened the door of his apartment and went downstairs. The cool night air of Cielo flowed over him as he emerged into the street.

He strolled through the sleeping capital. The overhead traffic lights floated like carnival balloons between the dark walls of the sky-scrapers. It was a strange sensation, hearing the crisp sound of his footsteps unswamped by the roar of traffic.

He gave a sudden start. A man had stepped out of a doorway and was barring his path. His clothes were dark and his face was obscured by shadow. The broad avenida was deserted. Only the traffic lights winked conspiratorially at each other from one inter-section to the next.

'Padre Valencia? Kindly come with me.'

The priest shrugged his shoulders.

'Why should I? I don't know you. Going for walks with strangers can be dangerous, *amigo*, especially at night and without witnesses.'

The hand of the unknown man vanished into his pocket.

'No games, Padre. Colonel García wants to see you.'

Valencia laughed, and his laughter broke the tension.

'A strange coincidence. I was just on my way to see him. Do you have a name, *amigo*?'

The man dressed in black preserved a morose silence. His dark jacket and white shirt made him look like a stray penguin.

'My name doesn't matter,' he said eventually.

Valencia sighed. They were all the same, he reflected. No sense of humour – not even sarcasm. High-speed operators of a gigantic sorting-machine. The yeas filtered through, the nays were left behind in the mesh of their displeasure and conveyed to the cellars of the security police for processing.

They passed the cardinal's palace. Constructed of natural stone in the colonial style, it was the most impressive building in the entire plaza. The windows were a peculiar, provocative shade of green, presumably designed so that those inside could see out but not vice versa. At night, this device was superfluous because the interior of the palace was screened from the outside world by heavy curtains. The parliament building formed one side of the rectangular plaza, the cathedral and the cardinal's palace another. Valencia found it strange that, during the Revolution, the mob should have confined their attentions to the cardinal's palace and left the cathedral alone. Since then the palace had risen phoenix-like from the ashes, grander and more lovely than before, the noblest building in the entire city and a monstrous provocation to the poor who passed it every day.

Valencia had a sudden vision of the palace as Communist Party headquarters, and instantly recoiled from the idea.

'Do you always arrest suspects at night?' he asked.

The man turned his head and Valencia saw him full face. He had a low forehead and a wide, loose mouth. His eyes were blank, possibly with fatigue.

'As a rule,' he replied.

'Not very pleasant, is it?'

'No, we don't get enough sleep.'

'For the prisoners, I mean.'

'Oh, them . . .'

The man's voice was flat and indifferent. The fate of detainees evidently held no interest for him.

'They're human beings too,' Valencia said, 'sentient creatures who feel joy and pain like anyone else, most of them poor people – and you deprive them of their freedom.'

'Trying to soften me up, Padre?' The cold eyes regarded him with faint surprise.

Valencia grinned.

'Not much hope of that with you, eh, *amigo*?'

'Listen, I detain people for questioning. If we detain people it means they know something. We get it out of them. Sometimes they co-operate, sometimes they don't.'

'And in the last resort there's always the torture-chamber – or am I exaggerating?'

Their voices reverberated from the granite walls of the cardinal's

93

palace, and Valencia thought of the man who presided there by day.

Medina must be at home and asleep now, in his villa on the out-skirts of the city, but he was more of a prisoner than Valencia him-self. He was the prisoner of his group, his kind, his clan. He peered myopically into an alien world like someone watching a stage pro-duction on a grand scale. Occasionally he met the leading actors. The supporting cast he only saw from a distance or, because of his short-sightedness, not at all. If an actor or a role displeased him he summoned the producer, demanded to see the script and cut passages which did not appeal to him or insisted that the leading roles be re-cast. He never went back-stage because it was too chaotic, the atmosphere too strained and tense. He remained in his box and listened to the actors' voices with his mind on other things. As a result, he seldom grasped the meaning of the play despite the bevy of sociologists and psychologists who put their expert advice and knowledge at his disposal. To what purpose all the sociological research, the surveys and censuses, the congresses, the articles and papers? What did it matter if the problems of the underdeveloped countries were 'psychosomatic' or the shanty-towns 'discontinuous' or 'disintegrated'? Of what use all this verbiage when time sped by and people were abandoned to their fate without any practical attempt to mitigate their sufferings?

'Were you there when they destroyed the huts?' Valencia asked.

'Yes.'

'Did you enjoy it?'

'We were acting under orders.'

There was no change of expression on the man's face. The fact of being under orders absolved him of personal responsibility. They walked on in silence without meeting anyone until they entered a side street and stopped outside a large but nondescript building guarded by a policeman armed with a submachine-gun.

'For the Colonel.' The nameless man might have been delivering a package. The sentry stepped aside with reluctance, seemingly loath to be parted from the patch of concrete where he had been standing.

'You know the way,' he muttered, and kicked the door open with his boot.

Valencia preceded his escort up some stairs. The walls on either side of him were whitewashed like the interior of a cell.

'Turn left at the top,' the man said. 'The last door on the right.'

The passage was dimly lit and the floorboards groaned as Valencia trod them – a dismal, almost human sound which made him feel as

94

if he were trampling the victims of the regime. His escort brushed past him just before he reached the door and knocked. A uniformed police officer opened it at once and silently gestured in the direction of García, who was seated behind a desk.

'You can go,' García said curtly to the other two, and waited until the door had closed behind them.

'We work overtime here, Padre Valencia. An unrewarding profession. Our employers insist on day-and-night service, our customers detest it. However, national security demands certain sacrifices on the part of the individual. That's why you see me here now, even at this hour.'

Valencia interrupted him brusquely. 'Why have you detained those people, Colonel García?'

The colonel spread his hands.

'For interrogation. One of them fired at the police.'

'Wouldn't you be tempted to pull the trigger if somebody tore down your house?'

The answer came back like a pistol-shot.

'No, not if he was acting on behalf of the State.'

Valencia glanced round the room. Four white walls, a desk, a row of filing cabinets.

'You goaded them into it. They were desperate.'

'Don't talk nonsense, Padre, you know better than that. Also, let me make one thing clear. I ask the questions here, not you. Do you know the present whereabouts of Rodriguez Tobar?'

He spoke in the amiable tone of someone inquiring after a mutual friend, but his cold eyes were riveted on Valencia's face. His right hand toyed with a paper-knife which had been honed like a razor.

'I wouldn't tell you if I knew, Colonel.'

'We have numerous ways of extracting information.'

Their eyes met, but that was all. It was as if any movement might have been construed as a sign of weakness.

'If I'm not home in an hour, Colonel García, the students will be informed.'

García laughed contemptuously.

'And they'll come and release you, Padre? Now, in the middle of the night?'

'That remains to be seen.'

'You're very popular with them, aren't you?'

'If you choose to call it that, yes.'

'Powerful men are never popular, Padre. Popular figures are always doomed in the end.'

95

'Is that a threat?'

'If you like. Where were you during the raid on the shanty-town?'

Valencia did not reply at once. He had foreseen this moment. First intimidation, then threats, then blows, perhaps, and finally death. All that surprised him was the speed with which it had happened.

'I'm waiting for an answer.'

Still Valencia did not reply. He stared at the light above his head, a harsh white light.

'Is this a formal interrogation, Colonel?' he asked. 'If so, on whose authority? You may not know it, but I still have some influential friends in this city.'

'Answer my question!'

'I'm sorry. All I can tell you is that I am fighting to obtain a decent life for my fellow-countrymen. You find that reprehensible?'

'It depends on your methods.'

'What about yours, Colonel?'

'I work on behalf of the State. That is sufficient justification.'

'I work on God's behalf.'

'And you think God will protect you if you get into trouble?'

'I hope so, Colonel.'

'So you're presumptuous too.'

'You confuse presumption with faith.'

'You still haven't answered my question.'

'Nor will I.'

Colonel García sighed. Somewhere or other he had a soft spot for courageous people, even if their courage was suicidal. He studied the athletic-looking man opposite him, the energetic square-jawed face, the lofty brow and commanding eyes. He had been authorized to question Valencia on condition that he did him no physical harm. Valencia still wore the armour of his cloth. García was aware of his nationwide popularity and knew that he must tread with care.

He rose and offered Valencia a cigarette. The priest's face relaxed and he settled back in his chair.

'Love always conquers hatred, Colonel, didn't you know that?'

'What in heaven's name is that supposed to mean?'

Valencia smiled.

'There once was a man who claimed to be the son of God. The authorities saw to it that he was put to death, but two thousand years later his doctrine of social justice is more relevant than ever. He died and rose again, and his ideas with him. You and your kind are wrong, Colonel. Nobody ever eradicated true faith by torturing

96

people, imprisoning them – even throwing them to the lions. On the contrary, persecution has been the mainspring of every new movement.'

Colonel García did not reply. Instead, he walked to the window, where the sun was just rising above the black rim of the mountains. He had always known that the mountains were a repository of secrets, but in the past twenty years they had become a mass grave for the hundreds of thousands who had fallen in the fanatical struggle between the two major parties, liberal and conservative. The bloodshed had meant little to him. He was powerful enough to dismiss such slaughter as an aberration and ascribe it to the volatile temperament of a nation incapable of self-restraint. But now he had been drawn into the struggle himself. It was his task to end it. The armed guerilleros had acquired a dangerous political tinge and kidnapped a number of prominent landowners, and their leader in the most important of all the Conciencian provinces was Rodriguez Tobar.

'This new movement of yours,' he said abruptly. 'Any connection with Rodriguez Tobar?'

Valencia stubbed out his cigarette in the ashtray on García's desk. It tasted foul, and he wished he had brought his pipe with him.

'Why do you ask?'

'I know this country, Padre Valencia,' García said, still at the window. 'I know these massacres in the mountains have nothing fundamentally to do with money. This isn't the United States. Tobar's motives aren't financial. He wants revenge and political chaos, revenge on the property-owning class. He also possesses a pathological degree of courage which is destructive rather than constructive. His men are rootless individuals who have lost everything, even the ideals of honour and justice for which they once claimed to be fighting.' He swung round. 'Don't you agree?'

Valencia leant forward and looked García full in the face.

'No, I don't.'

'Why not?'

'Because you ignore the human aspect, Colonel. Let me tell you a story, a true one. Years ago, under a conservative government, the police turned up in a small mountain village. Without rhyme or reason, they murdered two elderly people who were highly respected in the district. The children of the murdered couple were sent for but were refused permission to bury their parents. When they did so despite this, the police put in a second appearance. A fight broke out and the only educated inhabitant of the village, a man named Rodriguez Tobar, was arrested and tied up. His wife and daughter were raped before his eyes and his son was shot during an exchange of fire. Rodriguez Tobar was rescued by the enraged villagers, who fled with him into the mountains. I don't have to tell you how many atrocities have been committed since then, on both sides.'

'And this man is a friend of yours?' Colonel García's eyes shone with anger.

Valencia made no response, but García walked up to him and stood there with his legs splayed.

'Do you know what enables those thugs in the mountains to behave as they do, Padre Valencia? Moral support from the students of Cielo University, egged on by your subversive lectures and published attacks on our system of government.'

Valencia interrupted him with a curt gesture.

'What system is that, Colonel García? The system of obedience to an authority which is abused every minute of the day, as I repeatedly point out in my lectures? Or a system imposed by financial tycoons who think that injections of charity will keep the people of this country comatose for ever? Or perhaps you mean the system prescribed by the security police: silence or imprisonment?

'Do you know the statistics, Colonel? Under your system, 61% of the land belongs to 3.6% of the population whereas 56% of smallholders work only 4.2% of the good soil. Your so-called system gives 4.6% of the population more than 40% of the national income. And you really have the effrontery to defend such a system to a priest who also happens to be a sociologist?'

'What you preach is Communism.'

'No, Colonel, Christianity. A better Christianity than the Church preaches in this country – the only true and equitable form of Christianity. Our own is remote from the world of reality. Conciencian intellectuals read widely on religious topics and the poor collect medallions and pictures of saints. Such is the refined egoism of our upper classes, to which I myself belong, that brotherly love takes the form of good works – a means of enhancing one's social status, obscuring the fact of exploitation, and satisfying one's desire for personal salvation. Think of the common people, who see things in a less ideological light. God and his saints are realities to which they turn for mercy and protection. In other respects, they live as public opinion demands. As realities, God and his saints are stronger than Catholic doctrine, yet the horrors of civil war demonstrate how remote from reality the common people can be. During the atrocities committed here in recent decades, mobs of lynchers summoned priests to the dying or removed crucifixes and pictures of saints from houses before burning them and their occupants to a cinder. Do you see what I mean? What was the Catholic Church to these people, if not a sort of free insurance policy guaranteeing their passage to heaven? The same applies farther up the social ladder too. One last thing, Colonel. I don't dispute the good faith and piety of my average fellow-countryman. His trust in God is impressive in the extreme. I do, however, doubt whether this traditional, safety-first type of Catholicism is capable of galvanizing the country's future development. Do you know what must happen, Colonel? Catholicism in Latin America will have to renew itself inwardly so as to become an all-embracing expression of life. This inward revival is already in progress, not as a stand against traditions established by law but as a clearly perceptible hunger for spiritual sustenance. And this hunger is a concomitant of social and economic revolution based on ideological motives.'

'Communist motives, you mean,' García said acidly. His face had lost the faint air of relaxed condescension which Valencia had noticed at the start of the interview.

'Are you aware that you have just delivered an extremely dangerous lecture, Professor Valencia?' he asked.

'Why dangerous?'

'Because it has been recorded on tape.'

'I can't think why. It's only what I've been saying publicly for months.'

'Well, now we have an official record of your views.'

Valencia was undeterred. He pointed to the window, where a blood-red sun was soaring majestically above the mountains.

'Do you see that, Colonel? Some people might call it a symbol of national awakening. Many people are late sleepers. They miss a great deal.'

'But not you, Padre Valencia.'

'No, not me.'

Colonel García sighed for a second time.

'I think you're a fool, Professor. I admire your courage – in fact I even have a certain admiration for your beliefs. But overstep the mark just once and you'll be brought back here. What's more, you won't leave this building alive. Is that clear?'

Valencia smiled.

'I was expecting that, Colonel, but you're too late. It isn't a man that matters, it's his ideas.'

99

'When do you propose to announce yours?'

'In due course. May I go now?'

'Of course, for the time being. *Hasta la vista*, Padre, and remember that violence breeds violence. Look what happened the other night.'

'Are you going to release them, Colonel?'

'When I think fit. Now go before I change my mind.'

Valencia walked back along the whitewashed corridor. Somewhere in the building a man screamed. He shivered and hurried down the stairs. The sentry at the gate said nothing, merely stood aside to let him pass. It occurred to him that García, whose name inspired such terror throughout the country, had not really interrogated him at all. Wasn't he obliged to submit a report of their conversation? The tape would only have recorded his general ideas. But perhaps García had simply wanted to know his enemy better, learn something more of his personality. Again, perhaps he had meant to impress on him the inevitability of arrest if he persisted in his present course.

Cielo was coming to life again. Crowded buses lurched and swayed through the centre of the city. Beggars took up their favourite positions and shoe-shine boys busied themselves with their first customers of the day. Well-dressed women hurried to early Mass, and here and there bells began to chime.

Outwardly, the capital looked quite as peaceful as it had seemed all those years ago, when an assassin's bullet struck down the leader of the Left and signalled the start of a popular insurrection.

The sun climbed higher, flooding even Colonel García's dingy office with golden light.

'How's the tape, Lieutenant? Everything loud and clear?'

'An excellent recording, Colonel. That was pure and unadulterated subversion.'

García dabbed his forehead with eau-de-Cologne, carefully avoiding the plaster that still adorned it.

'Why do you think he was so outspoken?' García eyed his subordinate calmly. 'Well?'

'Perhaps because he wanted to force your hand.'

'In what way?'

'Compel you to arrest him.'

'And then?'

'Then he could have claimed that it was your fault, not his, if disturbances broke out among the students.'

'I wish it were as simple as that, Lieutenant.'

'But Colonel . . .'

'Listen. I want a couple of people tailed – Esther Graham and the journalist Cornell. You know who I mean?'

The lieutenant nodded.

'Good. I want to know everything about them. Have Professor Vermeer watched too. He's Valencia's successor at the University. Keep them under surveillance at all times and report to me regularly, you understand?'

García stood up. He glanced out of the window once more as he slowly straightened his tie. Then he pulled on his jacket and rang for a car.

He felt jaded. The interview with Valencia had been a waste of time. He had soon realized that his own arguments were insufficient. But what were his arguments? Maintenance of order and obedience to orders. He had killed innumerable times for those very reasons, but wasn't there an even better justification? What would become of the country if the mob seized power? What would become of him personally if they burst into his office? He would be the first victim – and of what? Of ideals cherished by bloodthirsty bandits and hotheaded students? His chiefs were right. It was no good waiting till blood flowed, not in this country, because there was no doubt whose blood it would be. Idealists like Antonio Valencia were too blinded by emotionalism to recognize that. Hence, Valencia and his kind must be exterminated before they could succeed, and extermination was his, García's, trade.

But how?

He was still pondering the question as he drove down the broad avenida, halted at some traffic lights and caught sight of Antonio Valencia. The priest was striding along with the sun gilding his face, eyes and hair, like a young and invincible god. For the first time in many years, Colonel García shivered.

7

Monsignor Ariano Zasi, Bishop of Cielo, was not on amicable terms with the Cardinal. They differed so widely in every respect that an unbridgeable gulf had opened between them in the course of time. This was evident in their respective ways of life. The Cardinal had many years earlier built himself a villa in the most expensive suburb of Cielo, a luxurious establishment whose décor testified to his refined tastes and unerring sense of style – though it had to be conceded that every peso he spent on it came from his own coffers, not those of the Church. Spacious lawns surrounded the house, which stood in the shade of a palm grove, and passers-by would often see the Cardinal strolling there in contemplation of his flowers, for all the world like an elderly monarch who had chosen to spend his declining years at his summer palace. A small staff of well trained servants saw to it that his personal needs were met. Occasionally he would hold a reception for the members of Cielo's social, political and diplomatic upper crust, always raising his first glass to those who were in good standing with Church and State. Every morning at eight o'clock sharp a long shiny limousine which had originally been presented to the Cardinal by an American businessman drew up outside the villa, and his chauffeur-bodyguard stood there at attention, ready to give the old man a helping hand. The car then purred smoothly through the fast-flowing traffic while the Cardinal read his breviary and evinced little interest in what went on around him.

The Cardinal loved Conciencia, even if he did observe life rather like a theatre-goer in a box. He loved Conciencia in his own way just as his father, a former President, had done. He knew how highly cultivated the aristocratic class was and appreciated the potential importance of social changes. But these changes had to spring from the ruling class which had granted the Church its prerogatives.

The bishop, Monsignor Zasi, who had been given full authority by Rome to conduct the affairs of the diocese of Cielo on an independent basis, differed entirely from the Cardinal. He looked like a peasant and was not, unlike his superior, a native of Cielo. Zasi had been a parish priest in Taloma, the district now controlled by Guillermo de la Cruz. His family was quite wealthy enough for him to have afforded a suburban villa like the Cardinal, but no such thought had ever entered his head. Instead, he occupied a modest suite in the archiepiscopal palace, where a few silent nuns did the cleaning and prepared his frugal meals. When he retired to his living-room after a busy day he would don the habit which he was entitled to wear as a member of the Third Order of St Francis.

Monsignor Zasi saw the country's problems quite differently from the Cardinal, as everyone in the Conciencian hierarchy knew. Whatever the prospects of a palace revolution one day, the little bishop was bound to lose. The prevailing attitude was almost unbelievably conservative. Moreover, the horrors of civil war were far too deeply imprinted on the minds of Church elders for them to forget the treasures that had been lost during the great insurrection.

On this particular morning Monsignor Zasi was receiving a delegation of trade union leaders in his simple office. The bishop listened to what they had to say for upwards of an hour. He began by referring them to the Cardinal, but they stubbornly insisted on speaking to him in his capacity as Bishop of Cielo. The men facing him were nervous and unsure of themselves, and Zasi guessed that only bitter necessity had driven them to see him at all. They informed him that they had decided to place their unions under the leadership of Antonio Valencia, whose proposed National Revolutionary Front would offer uncompromising opposition to the government's present policy.

Although he realized that he was secretly in general accord with the men's attitude, Zasi reacted with the caution of a bomb-disposal expert.

'Have you thoroughly considered your decision?' he asked.

The union leaders nodded, and one of them was bold enough to say that he had faith in Antonio Valencia as a priest who was ready to put the papal encyclicals into practice.

Monsignor Zasi subjected the man to a pensive stare and gently replied that other people in Conciencia were trying to do the same. The union leader, who had no wish to be discourteous, did not contradict him.

What Zasi had really wanted to say, with characteristic candour, was: 'You are right. The Conciencian Church has a shocking historical mortgage to redeem. Many priests have stripped Christ's own personality of all dynamism. They have turned him into an apple-cheeked sister of piety and entirely obscured his manly and heroic qualities. That is why I understand you so well. You are rebelling against a colourless and reactionary Christianity. You want to live life to the full. You want to break with the established order. The situation is grave, but crisis is unavoidable. We are faced with a challenge which must be met and overcome. Great things are afoot. We are glad that the security of past centuries is falling away, happy that we are about to brave the storms of the open sea. Unfortunately, many of us lack the courage to take such a plunge. That is the tragedy of our age, a great age but lacking in faith.'

Such, at least, were the words which he had entered in his diary the night before. He dare not utter them aloud because he knew that they would inevitably come to the Cardinal's ears, tomorrow if not today, and it was better for him to remain Bishop of Cielo rather than be replaced by someone who might provoke popular fury and the frightful consequences that were bound to flow from it.

'Are you acquainted with the Cardinal's views?' he asked.

The man who had so far acted as spokesman nodded.

'We are,' he said sullenly. 'I can repeat what he told us last time, word for word. We must preserve the status quo because progress among the ruling classes is slow but sure. Revolutionary movements create chaos and afford no guarantee of future stability.'

A smile crossed the little bishop's face, then vanished abruptly as if he feared that it was an offence against Christian charity.

'You realize, of course, that I shall have to report our conversation to the Cardinal?' he said. He noticed suddenly that he had forgotten to put on his bishop's ring that morning, and wondered vaguely if it was an omen.

The union leaders nodded and took their leave.

Monsignor Zasi sat alone at his massive desk, lost in thought. He sometimes envied the Cardinal his unswerving devotion to the principle of obedience. How easy it must be to think when one's thoughts always followed the same course, without doubts or digressions. How wonderful it must be to ask oneself no questions because they had all been answered beforehand by the omnipotent God in whose name one took all decisions.

Sometimes, as now, Monsignor Zasi wondered if he were really being fair to the Cardinal. Part of Medina's attitude might stem from the fact that the palace in which he used to live – this palace – had been transformed into a blazing inferno by the mob, but that could not be the sole reason. It was more likely that he saw the unconditional obedience on which he insisted as the sole guarantee of security. Obedience in all things and, above all, to him personally. But again, perhaps he had only become what he was in the course of time. He must have nurtured some very progressive ideas in the old days, by all accounts. As a young bishop – far too young for his exalted office – he had wanted to change many things in Conciencia. His confrères had repudiated him, even laughed at him, and derision was the one thing he could not endure. Medina had an innate sense of dignity. In view of his early religious vocation, he had probably been insulated by his family against many things which other boys of his age would have encountered as a matter of course. He had never been told that a man must live with his eyes and ears open and keep his head at the same time. That would have been quite out of keeping with his religious training, which consisted largely of exhortations to avoid opportunities for sin.

Zasi recalled a conversation with Professor Vermeer. The Dutch priest had told him something which rather shocked him but did, on the other hand, open his eyes to the true dimensions of every-day life. One of Vermeer's students had consulted him on a sexual problem. The young man, who came of a wealthy family, confessed that he had embarked on an affair with a maidservant. The girl had grown up in a peasant world where sex held no secrets and inspired little sense of prudery. Having little free time and few opportunities to go out, she found it easiest to satisfy her natural appetites in the house where she worked. But the young man had not confined himself to this one girl. He could not remember how many there had been after her and was still having a succession of affairs. The result was that he felt incapable of genuine love. Everything inside him was overlaid with sexuality to such an extent that he could never remain faithful to one girl. He lost his head again and again. Sexual intercourse had become an obsession with him. What was he to do? Stop altogether and regain his sense of proportion? All very well, but loving one girl did not preclude one from casting an eye at others.

Vermeer could not refrain from laughing as he continued his story. He accompanied the student to a deserted beach, where the young man poured out his heart. They talked for hours, sitting on the white sand. Vermeer spoke of the mentality of the Spaniards and Italians, who, unlike the cooler-blooded Anglo-Saxons, felt titillated whenever they saw a half-naked girl on a bill-board. It was the same in Latin America, he said, where children in upper-class homes were reared with a prudishness and austerity which ran counter to nature. Artificial juvenile 'sanctity' of this kind usually collapsed at the age of sixteen or seventeen like a house of cards. Thereafter, young people rejected their parents' traditional beliefs outright and searched for a theory or ideology which would justify their revolt to themselves. The fault lay with their parents, however, not with them.

Later, after a stroll along the beach, Vermeer stripped off his clothes and went for a swim. The student was shocked, but Vermeer laughed him out of it. 'See what I mean about hypocrisy? You dress up in dark suits and wear ties in a hot climate because convention prescribes it. You even think a man ought to wear bathing-trunks when he goes for a bathe on an empty beach. You're scared to gaze on God's creation as if there were something immoral in it, yet you're quite prepared to go to bed with three different girls in the same week. There's a connection somewhere, can't you see that?'

Zasi tried to picture himself retailing this anecdote to the Cardinal. The old man would fall down in a faint, no doubt. This was the stuff of life, of an existence which became more incredible the more one heard about it, but how much did the Cardinal hear of what really went on round him, despite his great love for the country that had given him birth? He believed in text-books; to him, novels were merely fantasies written by people who occupied a far lower plane than his own. How could one learn anything from such people? In the many years since he became the spiritual leader of Conciencia, it was as if he had built himself a rampart of theory out of the sumptuous volumes in his library, as if he only felt safe within the confines of his intellectual prison.

Zasi could never have followed his example. He had spent too long working among the bandoleros of Taloma, where the most revolting atrocities had occurred and the death-roll had risen to a hundred thousand. Zasi had taken the trouble to investigate these incidents, and over the years a terrible truth had revealed itself to him, so terrible that he now felt able to cope with this fearful, wonderful life in which men scaled the heights of heroism only to descend, a short while later, to the foulest depths of infamy of which humankind was capable. It also became clear to him during those years that far too many priests spent their time lobbying patiently for the life to come – priests who considered their own salvation before that of their flock. He had realized that Christianity, if it was to accomplish its great mission, must begin with man rather than end with him because beginning with man meant that, before one could demand his obedience, one had to listen to him and decide if his complaints were justified. A Christian would seldom attack the basis of his faith. He would never proclaim that love of God and one's neighbour was not the prime requirement, but he might dispute that it was practised by priests and even bishops.

Still pondering, Monsignor Zasi lit a cigarette, a luxury in which he seldom indulged.

Was the Cardinal unaware of all this, and, if so, was he in a position to judge? These were dangerous questions rendered still more dangerous by the fact that obedience was at stake here. Naturally, Zasi himself still cherished hopes of the Conciencian ruling class. The time had come for them to face facts, but would they realize it, would they be willing to invest money and experience in an attempt to redeem their past errors? Zasi recognized that the poor were still incapable of governing. In that case, who was to rule? The circles in which the Cardinal had moved since birth, the foremost aristocrats of the land, who loftily discounted everything which would one day cry out for a remedy?

Monsignor Zasi bowed his head, reached for the telephone and dialled a number known only to a privileged few. He knew that the internal phone on the Cardinal's desk would now be emitting a faint buzz.

He sighed deeply as the receiver at the other end was lifted, feeling as if he were about to betray the men who had just confided in him.

The Cardinal dismissed his secretary with a nod, waited until the door had closed behind him, and then put the receiver to his ear. Zasi's voice came crisply down the line.

'Your Eminence, I have just had an important discussion with the trade union delegation. I should like to talk to you about it. Without delay, if Your Eminence can spare the time.'

The Cardinal frowned. He still found the bishop's Taloma dialect irritating. Besides, it irked him that the request had been phrased so abruptly. Zasi might at least have remembered to inquire after the state of his liver. A moment later, remembering his beloved mother and Presidential father, he chided himself. Not everyone had been born in such fortunate circumstances as he, nor benefited from so careful an upbringing.

'Good of you to call, Monsignor,' he said. 'I appreciate how much you do for the diocese of Cielo. What news of your sisters?'

With a touch of annoyance Monsignor Zasi thanked the Cardinal for his interest and then said, point-blank: 'I have just been informed that the trade unions intend to join the National Revolutionary Front under Padre Valencia's leadership.'

The Cardinal gave an involuntary start. He had read the name a hundred times in the reports and articles that reached his desk, publications which had shaken him to the depths of his being. He knew Antonio Valencia's family. Professor Valencia senior, an eminent surgeon, had operated on him for a serious internal condition. Some years after his death Medina had shown his gratitude by sending Antonio Valencia, then a young priest, to Europe to study at his own expense. And now the dog was biting the hand that had fed it.

He thought swiftly. He had no inclination to discuss Antonio Valencia with Monsignor Zasi. He wondered, too, why the union leaders had not approached him direct. Not that it mattered, of course. He had friends in plenty who could put pressure on the unions to reverse their decision.

'Kindly draft a report on your interview with these people and have it sent to me, Monsignor. I cannot comment until I know what their reasons are.'

He replaced the receiver, picked it up again, and called his nephew the President.

He was put through immediately.

'Medina here, Luiz. How is your wife? Splendid. And the children? Are you still planning to holiday in Europe? Paris? Excellent. You ought to visit Rome sometime. Oh yes, thank you, my liver is dormant at present. No, no pain for several days now. Thank you for inquiring, Luiz. By the way, Zasi informs me that Antonio Valencia has managed to incorporate the unions in his National Revolutionary Front. I thought I ought to let you know. What was that? Yes, that's what I'm wondering too. What am I to do with the boy? I've already had him dismissed from his university appointments, but things are going from bad to worse.'

Invisible at the other end of the line, President Colombo paled perceptibly.

'Could you spare me half an hour this evening, Your Eminence? I wouldn't ask you if I didn't think it vitally important.'

The Cardinal smiled to himself.

'Of course, Luiz. I suggest you come early, in time for an apéritif. Afterwards we can have dinner together.'

'Certainly, Your Eminence. Until this evening, then.'

Medina replaced the receiver carefully, stared into space for a moment or two, and then called Zasi back.

'About your interview with the union leaders, Monsignor. I should greatly appreciate it if you could dictate the details to your secretary right away. How soon can you let me have your report? Two hours? I'm most grateful for all your hard work. I really can't think what I should do without you.'

Nestling in President Colombo's black leather briefcase was the tape which Colonel García had made of his conversation with Antonio Valencia, also reports on him compiled by various government agencies. Colombo wanted advice on what to do with the young man. He had no reservations about Valencia's brilliance – in fact he wished that his own circle included at least one man of comparable intellect. All the more reason for doing something about him. Conciencia had enough problems without Antonio Valencia. For one thing, there was the steady growth of anti-Americanism, mainly among intellectuals and strenuously fostered by the Communists, who always kept to the side-lines but were excellently organized. For another, there was the pressure exerted on him by foreign press correspondents to admit that the U.S. Southern Command had sent him a number of guerrilla warfare experts, a fact which he had always denied hitherto. There was the detention of Gilberto Granada, which he had managed to hush up, and the new technique adopted by the mountain guerilleros, who were beginning to alarm the aristocracy by kidnapping wealthy landowners and ransoming or killing them. There was the inflationary spiral, not the first of its kind, which had defied his efforts to check it and forced him to appoint a new Minister of Finance. And now, with the emergence of Valencia, there was a danger that everything would slip through his fingers. That must be avoided at all costs, he told himself grimly, even at the cost of Valencia's life.

Cardinal Medina's personality had always fascinated the President. He radiated authority even now, as he personally and with immense care filled their glasses. That done, he returned serenely to his capacious arm-chair and watched the President switch on the portable tape-recorder.

He sat back as Colonel García began his interrogation. An occasional smile flitted across his face as if he were entirely at one with the young priest, but in general his expression remained grave and aloof. Occasionally, too, he shot the President a reproving glance which implied that he was to blame for everything.

As he listened, the Cardinal realized that he and Valencia had much in common. Once upon a time, when he was a youthful bishop, he had seen things in much the same light. He could still vividly recall the incident that had prompted him to take such an attitude. He had been visiting a cemetery on a blazing hot day. Afterwards, in a meditative frame of mind, he went for a stroll. The wretched hovels built against the cemetery wall had aroused his curiosity, and he decided on impulse to enter one of them. Its occupants lived there under appalling conditions, but what struck him most of all was that the back wall was streaming with moisture even though it had not rained for weeks. Puzzled, he asked the woman of the house why this was. She merely looked at him in surprise and replied calmly: 'Oh that . . . It comes from the graves on the other side. The bodies rot and the water seeps through.' He remembered that he had not slept for nights after this experience and recounted it at the next episcopal conference. The other bishops were quite as horrified as Medina himself and resolved to make a suitable donation from Church funds, but that was as far as they went.

Meanwhile, Medina was viewing things in a new light. He proposed that a sociological faculty be established for senior clergy, but the then Cardinal had pointed out that the Gospel transcended all programmes of social reform, and that anyone who wanted to pursue the matter could always study the social encyclicals. It was clearly impressed on him that the government disliked bishops who meddled in matters that lay outside their domain. Finally, his friends argued that his duties were onerous enough already. As a bishop and a potential cardinal, he must observe due form.

The harsh, malevolent voice of Colonel García interrupted his train of thought: 'What you preach is Communism.' Then came Valencia's reply, crisp and incisive: 'No, Colonel, Christianity.'

Medina refilled the President's glass, something he only did for very exalted guests. He doubted if he would have had Valencia's effrontery, even in those days. How could he have rebelled against his fellow-bishops, who were all so much older and more experienced than himself? He had respected them. They were strong, devout, resolute men, and under their leadership Conciencia had been one of the most stable countries in Latin America. They represented national culture, spiritual values, and the priests who were subordinate to their authority. What was more, they firmly believed that what they did was for the good of Christendom. It had taken him only a few years to grasp the futility of protest, of formulating new ideas, of being everyone's enemy and no one's friend. Many years had passed since then, and in the course of those years he had seen the cardinal's palace sacked by a furious mob. He had escaped in his night-clothes, in company with the cardinal of the day. He would never forget that humiliation. Since then he had changed. It would not happen again while he remained the country's spiritual leader. He would not give any man a chance to provoke a repetition. He would urge the President to act promptly as he had already done on several occasions in the past, thanks to the army, which had so far remained loyal to the government.

'. . . a clearly perceptible hunger for spiritual sustenance . . .' he heard Valencia say, and then the tape ran out.

President Colombo switched off the machine and sat back, staring at the valuable collection of antique china behind the glass doors of his uncle's big teak display cabinet. Then he said, more loudly than he had intended: 'With your help, Your Eminence, I can easily put a stop to this nonsense.'

The Cardinal glanced at him with a faint air of surprise, as though he had altogether forgotten his presence.

'Can you, Luiz?' he said acidly. 'Are you really in a position to do so, and have you weighed the possible consequences? I have here a statement by the leaders of all the major trade unions. They have informed Monsignor Zasi that they are placing themselves under Valencia's leadership, that they intend to support his ideas from now on and join the National Revolutionary Front.'

He went to a small rosewood desk, removed a sheaf of papers, and read: 'We, the undersigned, are profoundly dissatisfied with the government's legislative policy. The President is well aware that we have repeatedly pressed for an improvement in workers' living conditions. Over twelve months ago he sent for us and we had a friendly exchange of views which led to the appointment of a committee consisting of trade unionists, industrialists and landowners. After numerous sessions we reached general agreement and drafted a report. This report was to be studied by a parliamentary committee whose recommendations were to be communicated to us at the earliest possible moment. The inquiry has lasted for a whole year, cost a great deal of public money, and produced no results whatsoever. For that reason, the trade unions have lost faith in the President and Congress.'

'Is that explicit enough for you, Luiz?' demanded the Cardinal.

The President flushed at his uncle's caustic tone. Nervously, he lit a cigarette and drained his glass at a single gulp.

'Commanding a division is rather different from governing a country,' Medina added with gentle irony.

Colombo's face stiffened. He had been dreading this conversation.

The Cardinal's tongue was razor-edged. Meanwhile, Medina took a sip of whisky and thoughtfully studied the archiepiscopal ring on his shrunken finger.

'Tell me,' he said, 'what have you managed to glean about Antonio Valencia? No, no, not his date of birth, education and so on – I know more about his background than you do. I'm talking about the Antonio Valencia of today.'

The Cardinal studied the President as he put the question. He saw a tall slim man who would have looked better in uniform than the civilian suit he wore. He had to admit, nevertheless, that Colombo made a striking figure with his thick curly hair, long brown face, penetrating eyes and lofty forehead. Outwardly he was an ornament to the family, no doubt about that, but it was a shame about his vanity. Medina knew him well. Luiz Colombo had been vain all his life, but he also had a perseverance and precision of mind that was rare in a Latin American. It was this combination of qualities which had made him the leading light of one of the wealthiest families in Conciencia, and when the conservative party regained power his relatives pressed him to stand for the Presidency.

Colombo felt slightly firmer ground beneath his feet after the veteran churchman's last question.

'I have had Valencia watched,' he said. 'The man can hardly be said to follow a regular daily schedule. He has an incredible number of social contacts at every level. He enjoys his drink, occasionally to excess, tells risqué stories, likes to take off his soutane and dance at parties. He's popular with men as well as women and has an American secretary, Esther Graham, who was born here and is currently having an affair with a British journalist named Cornell.'

'That is immaterial,' Medina observed sharply. 'I want relevant details only.'

The President opened his briefcase. He produced a number of folders, opened one of them and began to read.

'Valencia may be described as the spokesman of a large group of intellectuals, principally teachers and students at the National University, who have for years been holding clandestine meetings at which the theories of Marx, Lenin and Che Guevara are discussed and armed insurrection is advocated as a logical point of departure. This group is in contact with Moscow and Peking as well as Havana. We are almost certain that weapons from Cuba have been parachuted to the guerilleros in the mountains. We are also virtually convinced that Valencia conducts regular meetings with Rodriguez Tobar and that the guerrilla movement has acknowledged him, in principle, as its political leader. The intellectuals all work on the assumption that the Conciencian ruling class is abusing the people just as the United States abuses the Alliance for Progress in order to realize its imperialist aims in our country. They are anti-democratic, anti-American and anti-clerical. They accuse the Church of making common cause with the ruling class and charge the government with taking corrupt and dictatorial measures for the sole benefit of a small oligarchical clique. They further accuse the United States of retaining the special predilection for dictators which it has always shown in the past. They cite names such as Batista of Cuba, Trujillo of the Dominican Republic, François Duvalier, friend of Trujillo and President of Haiti, and General Jorge Obico of Guatemala. Another name which figures in their list is that of President Colombo of Conciencia . . .'

The President paused. 'Is that explicit enough, Your Eminence?'
Medina nodded.

'That is why I welcome your visit this evening, Luiz. I had a talk with the American Ambassador a few days ago. He is equally worried by local developments.'

All trace of irony had vanished from the Cardinal's voice. He knew that he was confronted by the dilemma of a lifetime. A priest was challenging his authority; more than that, he possessed the ability, knowledge and even the power to carry that challenge through. Without fully understanding why, the Cardinal feared for Valencia's life. Colombo, who had presented such a helpless and irresolute picture only a few minutes earlier, suddenly seemed brusquer and more authoritarian. Not even Medina's notorious gift of mockery would be proof against him now.

'May I?' said Colombo, pouring himself another whisky.

The Cardinal sensed that the President had got over his brief spell of weakness. As for the President, all his doubts had evaporated. He knew now that the man facing him was a weary, apprehensive, obstinate septuagenarian whose assessment of Valencia as a potential threat coincided with his own.

'Your Eminence,' he said, and there was no compassion in his keen eyes as he studied the Cardinal's face, 'I am the elected president of this country, like it or not. Valencia is becoming a menace, so I shall have to take action against him. You can rely on me to use every weapon at my command – but only after you have asserted your authority. This is a civilized country. Our administration may work slowly, but we are doing all we can. We have the best education programme in South America, a modern approach to the housing problem, and a number of social reforms under review. Nobody is going to dictate the speed at which I operate, not even Valencia. Apart from that, I have been a soldier. As such, I know that strength is the only thing which an enemy respects. You understand what I mean, Your Eminence?'

Medina understood only too well. All that surprised him was that the President should have forgotten his earlier warning so quickly.

'I'm afraid you're talking wildly, Luiz,' he said, trying to keep the sarcasm out of his voice. 'You are dealing with a scholar, not a soldier. Valencia may be a fanatic but he's also a highly intelligent man, not a fool. There's a difference, my boy. And don't forget how popular he is. Men of that calibre make dangerous enemies.'

The silence which followed his words was broken by the gentle tinkle of glass and china as members of his household staff put the finishing touches to the dining-table next door. Medina sensed that a crisis was imminent. He could infer from all the reports he had received that there was no stopping Valencia now. The man believed heart and soul in what he said and wrote. He was going, open-eyed, to his own destruction. Medina could see no way of dissuading him. Men like Antonio Valencia were not born every year. They were a product of the culture, strength and courage of generations, all distilled into a single person. No, he would not be able to stop him. Worse still, Valencia would not be able to stop himself. He would not be the first young man to plunge into the abyss, strong in the faith, eyes afire with the joy of martyrdom. The only way of saving such people was to shunt them into a siding, divert them by stealth into a backwater where they would be forgotten.

'Why not try to discover Valencia's weaknesses?' he said. 'You have the men to do it. Drink, women, no matter what. I differ from you, Luiz. I want no victims of violence – the Church has more than enough martyrs as it is. I feel drawn to this young man in some ways. On the other hand, remembering Castro's Cuba, I realize that our country cannot be allowed to go the same way.'

A wave of doubt assailed him as he spoke, but he could not help himself. He knew that deep inside him there still burned the flame which he had never quite managed to extinguish during all his years as a prelate. But this flame was overlaid by the other flames that had destroyed the cardinal's palace. They had been a warning to him that the same thing must never recur. Ever since then he had been inhabited by two different men, one of them unknown to another living soul. In his relations with the outside world this second self was obscured by dignity and mockery, pride, self-assurance and authority. But, for all the expedients he had adopted, he knew that the young bishop within him sometimes wept at the decisions taken by the Cardinal and refused to be quelled by the authority that threatened to smother him.

Perhaps it was Monsignor Zasi who most reminded him of his former ideals. Zasi made him secretly nervous because he was too old and weary to study his reflection regularly in the mirror. Sometimes he listened to his own pulse, which raced a little. Sometimes he looked with envy at a young man running swiftly across the road. Sometimes he wished that he were Zasi, who had no need of a cardinal's self-assurance. His office was a crushing responsibility. If he gave Valencia his head he would, in a very few years, have to tread a bloodstained path that would wend its way throughout Conciencia. Oh yes, he knew how Zasi saw him – as authority personified and the custodian of Church property. Where Zasi was concerned, he never gave the young bishop in him a chance. With Zasi he remained the Cardinal. With Zasi he had to play the cool and calmly decisive prince of the Church. Suddenly he shrank. When had he ever given the young bishop a chance, Zasi or no Zasi? Had he not turned him into a prisoner who lay chained in the recesses of his own heart?

'What exactly do you have in mind?' the President asked.

Medina shrugged.

'I don't know yet, Luiz. I only know that time is short. If Valencia makes a public statement in the next few days I shall send for him, though I doubt, knowing him as I do, whether I shall achieve very much. My one incontrovertible certainty is this: I do not want him playing politics in his capacity as a priest. The position is grave enough already, thanks to lack of vocation and the need for a Catholic revival, without clerics dabbling in matters divorced from pure religion.'

The President felt dissatisfied. He had been expecting the Cardinal to give a more conclusive answer. He found it quite impossible to classify a man like Valencia. In the circles where he moved, no priest had ever contradicted him. Priests had never been more than advisers, and then on the purely human plane. They had never meddled in his political activities. They were friendly intellectuals who spoke of their Church, of their congregations, of religious revival and, needless to say, of the funds they needed for various purposes. They acted as confidential intermediaries when he had trouble with members of his family. Any priest who played politics was neglecting his spiritual calling.

The Cardinal cleared his throat as though to remind Colombo of his presence.

'Strange developments have taken place in recent years,' he said. 'There were teachers who thought they could dictate to me. I had them dismissed. What would become of the Church if discipline collapsed and everyone went his own sweet way?'

He faltered, and the President realized that he had gained an ally. At the same moment, the Cardinal shivered at the thought of the loneliness which he had been compelled to accept in order to preserve Christianity in Conciencia. He shivered when he thought what would have become of his native land if the young bishop in him had gained the upper hand. The faithful would be deprived of their mainstay. Materialism would vitiate their faith as it had so patently done elsewhere in the world. Priests would rebel against their bishops and flocks against their priests. Private property would be violated and the authority of Church and State destroyed. Guiding principles would be overruled and the concordat between Church and State abolished. Political leaders of the Left would come forward and be hailed by the people as latter-day prophets. They would act in the name of Marx and Lenin and dismiss Christ as a village idiot. It would be a repetition of Cuba. First jubilant crowds and empty prisons; then a nation in which the human being became a machine and prisons overflowed so that a new dictator could sustain his authority. That was how it would be if Antonio Valencia was given his head.

'Do you have any plans?' he asked the President.

Colombo nodded.

'I shall place the matter entirely in García's hands. He will be given carte blanche. I shall request Ignacio Fierro to launch a campaign against Valencia in his newspapers and periodicals. I shall order my military commanders to take all measures necessary to keep the nine thousand students at Cielo University in check, and I shall maintain a day-and-night watch on Valencia. Then I shall summon the trade union leaders and promise them my fullest co-operation in the immediate future. I shall step up military operations against the guerilleros and double the price on the head of Rodriguez Tobar. Finally, in the event of a students' strike, I shall proclaim a state of national emergency and keep it in force until the situation returns to normal.' He paused. 'Well, Your Eminence, what do you think?'

The Cardinal merely nodded. It was the only solution. The rest would be up to him.

'And if Valencia still refuses . . .' He could not bring himself to finish the sentence.

Colombo spread his hands.

'If so, Colonel García will do his duty and I shall know nothing about the matter until it is resolved. No one is going to stop me from purging this country of agitators. There is nothing I would not do for the sake of Conciencia.'

Medina felt a sudden stab of pain in his back. He said earnestly:

'Did you hear yourself, Luiz? "And the chief priests and scribes sought how they might kill him, for they feared the people." '

Colombo ignored the remark and followed the Cardinal into the dining-room, where the butler was already hovering with a bottle-basket.

'Mouton Rothschild,' Medina said. 'A wine with a memorable bouquet. Did you hear what I said just now, Luiz?'

Colombo raised his glass.

'I propose a toast to Conciencia, Your Eminence, coupled with the hope that the concordat between Church and State will endure for many years to come.'

The threat in his voice was barely disguised.

They drank, and as the Cardinal felt the wine warm on his tongue he knew that the young bishop within him was dead at last.

'We live in a sinful world,' he said, so quietly that the President, who was brooding on what had been said before, scarcely heard him.

8

When Bruce Cornell emerged from his hotel he saw a man get up from one of the benches in the plaza and knew that he was being followed again. It had surprised him to be left in peace for so long, but perhaps Esther was right in surmising that the authorities had no great aversion to his articles about Valencia. They could hardly object if he publicized Valencia's ideas abroad. It would only lend them added justification if they defended themselves against a left-wing priest with dangerous revolutionary views.

Casually, Bruce strolled across the plaza. A young couple were sitting on a bench near an ornamental pond. The boy suddenly stood up and asked him for a light. As he cupped his hands round Bruce's lighter he whispered: 'Four-thirty this afternoon in Professor Vermeer's office, Department of Sociology. Take care, you're being followed. The man in dark glasses.' Then he thanked Bruce, replaced his arm round the girl's shoulders and kissed her, the cigarette dangling from his fingers.

Bruce walked on for a while, thinking. He paused to admire the city's access roads, which were multi-level on the North American pattern. He saw giant bill-boards promising 1 million pesos for a single lottery ticket or bearing advertisements for radio and TV sets or foreign airlines. Sandwiched between modern buildings as though it had strayed there by mistake was an old baroque church of the colonial era. Bruce's gaze lingered for a moment on the hotel where he was staying, a pencil of glass and stone which towered above its neighbours. He had chosen it by design. The *Plaza* was a cosmopolitan rendezvous built with all the refined elegance of Latin American taste and paid for with North American money. If all went well, it would remain a glorious symbol of twenty centuries of Latin civilization; if not, the *Norteamericanos* would naturally take the blame. Even in the hotel's various bars, where Bruce and Esther often met, there was an involuntary tendency to whisper because of the muted murals, old armour and dim lighting.

Inside the hotel Bruce always had the feeling that the entire wealth and cultural assets of a highly developed people, of an ancient civilization like that of the Pharaohs, had been assembled under one roof. Now, as he stood there on the outside, he realized that this monument to refined taste looked like an orchid on a dung-heap. Instead of symbolizing the inevitable contrast between wealth and poverty, it was an edifice which the rich had been able to build because they had sucked their own people dry.

Innumerable encounters with fellow-guests at the *Plaza* had shown him that they regarded the country's poor as flies to be doused with insecticide whenever they became importunate. But the flies always returned, and no amount of personal wealth could banish them from the face of the earth. Consequently, one of the main preoccupations of the Conciencian rich was to keep the flies at bay.

Bruce sighed as he sauntered down the Avenida San Martin, the Bond Street of Cielo. He paused in front of a shop window to check that he was still being followed. He saw the man buying a newspaper and sighed again. It was typical of Latin American dictatorship to stage a performance in which the leading roles were played by charm, smiles and beauty, but in which all who were seduced by them ultimately died or disappeared. To grasp that was to feel a chill of fear. Today's best friend could be tomorrow's assassin, one's mistress the mistress of another man, one's death a mere traffic accident or a felony committed by criminals who happened to belong to the secret police.

Suddenly Bruce stopped. A large and silent crowd had gathered round something on the pavement. He elbowed his way to the front and heard a harsh voice say: 'Why do you sell American cigarettes? You know the law. Stand up!'

The man who had spoken was dressed in civilian clothes, but he was so obviously a policeman that he might as well have been in uniform. The object of his ire was old and feeble and evidently half-blind. He wore torn trousers and a threadbare shirt, and it was many days since his chin had seen a razor.

The old man was squatting on the ground. He looked up at the by-standers as if he expected help, but nobody moved. Nobody spoke either. They all seemed hypnotized by the policeman's surly voice. Without warning, he drew back his foot and kicked the contents of the old man's little wooden tray on to the sidewalk. The crowd drew back as if the cigarette-packets were live grenades, widening the circle. The old man, who had not managed to move his face in time, started to bleed from the nose. He crawled around on all fours, trying to collect his scattered merchandise. 'Please let me keep them, *señor*,' he quavered. 'My family have nothing else to live on.'

Implacably, the policeman picked up the offending articles and bore them off to his car, climbed in and drove away. Once more the old man gazed up at the people round him as if seeking help, but they slowly turned away and dispersed with a few muttered words of indignation. Bruce had been watching their faces as the policeman vented his sadism on the street-vendor. He had read fury in them, but the fury was masked by a fear inherited from centuries of oppression.

As he thoughtfully resumed his stroll he recalled one of his conversations with Vermeer during the past week. The professor had apparently gone to Bishop Zasi and asked him if, as Valencia's successor, he could have some priests to help him with social work among the students. Zasi was enthusiastic about the idea and sent him the senior members of a team which had been commissioned to work out a new spiritual welfare programme for Cielo – 'five extremely worthy men,' Vermeer told him, 'but hide-bound and obsessed with the formal aspect of Catholicism to the exclusion of all else. I did my best to open their eyes. I asked them how it was that people packed the churches on Sundays and lived as though they had absolutely no philosophy of life for the rest of the week. I asked them if they felt equal to conveying the social relevance of Christianity. But what can you expect of priests who have not only been reared in the Spanish contempt for life but grew up in a country where observance of the law is the *ne plus ultra* of moral perfection? That's a legacy of the wars of independence – the freedom fighters of the nineteenth century were lawyers, unfortunately. I've never known a country so dominated by formalism. Conciencia churns out paper like a machine.' Vermeer heaved a sigh and went on: 'I'm afraid the spiritual welfare committee must have greeted my words with considerable scepticism. I do have certain contacts in high places, but there's a widespread dislike of foreigners who create trouble by turning up here with ideas which don't fit into the Conciencian scheme of things. I've known too many foreign clerics who insist on tackling everything in their own particular way – American, French, Spanish, Italian, Dutch or whatever. Every country thinks its own methods are the beginning and end of all wisdom. It's nothing new.'

Vermeer had pursued the subject next evening.

'I couldn't effect an overnight change in the priests sent me by Monsignor Zasi. If they listened to me, it was because they regarded me as the bishop's friend. I made no accusations, merely drew attention to the spiritual hunger which I had found all over Latin America and rediscovered in Conciencia. But my way of talking to laymen in phenomenological terms, full of respect for any honestly held view or conviction, was entirely alien to them. That was why the students would have nothing to do with any priests except Valencia and me. I couldn't tell my five committee members that, of course. They already knew everything and had a private line to Almighty God. They also thought they knew the people – a people which respects and abominates them simultaneously with the sort of double vision for which Conciencians are notorious.

'Well, the five committee members wanted to make a good impression on their superiors, so they decided to initiate a debate with priests from various universities. This seemed to accord with Monsignor Zasi's intentions. About twenty delegates attended the first meeting, which took place in an atmosphere of complete candour. I presented my own analysis of Latin America in a tactful way, but they wanted to know the layman's angle as well. It was decided to invite teachers and students from the various universities to attend future sessions. The first time, one professor and two students turned up. It would have been worth recording their remarks on tape. They spoke freely because they were under the impression that the other priests shared my views *in toto*. Their complaints came straight from the heart. They had several times requested the Cardinal for help in important matters and been fobbed off with lame excuses. His attitude had disillusioned them to such an extent that the professor said bitterly: "I doubt if the Cardinal can still be called a Christian. Everything is politics with him." The priests who heard this presumably regarded it as heresy. To the laymen, discussions with priests were something altogether new, but it soon became evident that, although they had been invited to a frank exchange of views, the clerics said very little. They sat there in a black phalanx reminiscent of the Inquisition. I've no doubt that everything was passed on to the Church authorities, and that I was classified as dangerous from that moment onwards.

'Because the first meeting had taken such an exceptional turn, the second was attended by representatives from all the universities. Charges were levelled at the ecclesiastical administration and the priesthood, and I began to fear the worst. The priests in attendance included an observer sent by the Cardinal. At one point he grew very angry and shouted something about "lay hysteria". The professor who had been speaking was an uncommonly level-headed and intelligent man. "If this is hysteria," he retorted, "we may as well bring this so-called dialogue to an end. Realities are what matter here. If we're mistaken, tell us in what respect. It isn't enough to be right *in abstracto*. We must approach each other with due regard to the actual situation and then see what we can do to remedy it. I may be guilty of exaggeration or bias. If so, put me right." The only reply was a glacial silence.'

Vermeer's account of these meetings so intrigued Bruce that he attended the next one in person. He noticed that the number of teachers and students had swelled whereas the priests' ranks had thinned.

Students at other Conciencian universities had found out what was happening and sent delegates of their own. This was striking enough in itself, and Bruce waited eagerly to see what would come out of the meeting. He was disappointed. The Church representatives now formed an inquisitorial bloc whose members were convinced that they alone had grasped the real meaning of life. The teachers and students countered with an indictment of the priesthood in general. Their spokesmen complained that candour had been useless – indeed, positively detrimental to them. In many cases, things which genuine concern had prompted them to tell bishops or parish priests in confidence had later been used in disciplinary proceedings against them, and they suspected that something similar would happen after the present series of discussions. At one stage there was a debate on the necessity for changing the face of Conciencia by revolutionary means, also on the question of whether other priests would follow Valencia's lead and declare their solidarity. Bruce was alarmed by the extreme violence of the official reaction to this. The Cardinal's representative, who was also known to be the ghost-writer of his pastoral letters, called out: 'Christians must yield to legally constituted authority. That applies even more so to priests, whose duties are exclusively spiritual.'

The first public condemnation of Valencia, Bruce thought, and vaguely recalled the Biblical injunction to beware of the scribes and pharisees with their love of long robes, respectful greetings in the market-place, chief seats at feasts, and lengthy prayers. The rebel named Jesus had not minced his words where those people were concerned. Bruce studied the unctuous, self-satisfied faces of the latter-day scribes. It was obvious that they had long ago forgotten the warnings of the man they claimed to serve. Then he was jerked back into the present by a torrent of impassioned words. A foreign missionary who happened to be present was so incensed by what the Cardinal's representative had said that he vehemently denounced conditions in Conciencia and wondered aloud whether revolution was not the only way of curing them. After the meeting the Cardinal's representative took the missionary aside and informed him that his remarks were a disservice to Conciencia. He was wrong if he thought otherwise – quite how wrong he would soon find out. Two days later Bruce accompanied the same missionary to Cielo airport. He had been expelled at the Cardinal's personal instigation. The meetings continued, Vermeer told Bruce, but without the participation of teachers, students, or Vermeer himself. The earlier meetings had already taken their toll. A group of young Catholics – devout but highly nonconformist youngsters with whom Vermeer had spent several days in retreat – were officially pronounced Communistic and a danger to the faith of the common people. The Church authorities began to wage a near-hysterical campaign against foreign priests, crypto-heretics and people with Communist leanings, whereas the atmosphere in the other camp became reminiscent of the catacombs. And now, Bruce was on his way to sample that atmosphere . . .

He looked round. The man in dark glasses was clinging to his trail like a limpet. It struck him that the authorities must be really frightened of Valencia if they bothered to put a tail on a minor character like himself.

Half an hour later he met Esther, who was fresh from the hairdresser's and looked every inch a Conciencian. Like every Latin American girl, she spent a lot of time on her hair and clothes and abhorred the sight of women walking the streets in jeans. Bruce told her at once that he was being followed. She glanced quickly over her shoulder and smiled.

'I know him. One of García's bloodhounds, but not the worst of the lot. Let's take him for a ride.'

They strolled down the main street hand in hand, window-shopping, then dived into a noisy café for a cup of *tinto*. They grinned derisively as their tail sat down a few tables away. Being a true Latin American, he could not resist ordering himself a black coffee too. They seized the opportunity to pay quickly, jump into a taxi and drive off, leaving their pursuer behind.

'Let's eat somewhere outside the city,' Esther said. 'I'd like that. We can still get back to the University in time for Vermeer's meeting.'

'We?' Bruce raised his eyebrows. She nodded.

'You forget I'm Valencia's secretary now.'

'Forget?' he said a little harshly. 'The few times I do get to see you I hear of almost nobody else.'

She smiled.

'Sometimes I wonder if you'll ever understand, Bruce.'

He let go of her hand and sat there beside her like a stranger. And that was what he had become, Esther reflected. There were two men in her life now, Antonio Valencia and Bruce Cornell. Whenever she tried to analyse her feelings for them, as she had often done in recent weeks, she realized that her mind turned more often to Valencia than Bruce. But that might be because she had to protect Antonio from himself and his friends. There was no need to do that with Bruce. He was quite different. He would never destroy himself for the sake of his ideals, if any. On the other hand, Bruce compensated her for what she had to forgo in the case of Valencia. He was a passionate lover, and at this critical juncture she needed him more than he needed her. Valencia loomed larger in her life. Bruce always said what he thought, harshly and uncompromisingly. Valencia had a different approach. He could be sarcastic, but his sarcasm was mitigated by his sense of humour, his smile, his scholarship, his compliments. Valencia was a greyhound, Bruce an Alsatian which could turn and rend anyone who goaded it too far. Perhaps it was simply that Bruce was the man she liked to go to bed with and Valencia the man she liked listening to.

The taxi drew up and Bruce paid it off. In silence, they walked out on to a spacious terrace shaded by a flower-garden of striped umbrellas. It was hotter here than in Cielo, and the sun beat down out of a steel-blue sky. Every now and then peasants in wide-brimmed hats and yellow or dark grey ponchos trudged past, the inevitable machete at their side. Some of them rode nimble little horses and raised their hands in greeting.

'It's good to get away from it all,' Bruce said, 'just for once.' He sat down with an air of enjoyment which seemed to convey his determination not to spoil things.

'Away from what?' she asked sharply.

'The whole atmosphere of intrigue – clandestine meetings, dodging the secret police, brooding about someone who means a lot to me and spends all her time with someone else. I can breathe here, and fresh air is what I need.'

He stretched, lit a cigarette, and surveyed his surroundings with satisfaction.

'No bow can stay bent for ever, sweetheart,' he said. 'Try and relax for a couple of hours.'

Esther did not reply, but she could feel the tension easing. She knew he was right. On the other hand, she refused to betray Valencia or belittle him, even in abstract. Besides, in Conciencia the bow was permanently bent, and she knew something which Bruce had yet to learn. Valencia planned to announce his programme next day. The arrangements had been a monumental undertaking. Students from all over the country, trade union chiefs and leaders of various pressure-groups were already on their way to Cielo to attend to-morrow's mass meeting at the National University. She had been almost solely responsible for its organization, assisted by a team of helpers whom she knew to be Communists. She had taken phone calls for Valencia from people who wanted to sway him in one direction or another. She had made and cancelled appointments on his behalf. She was wholly identified – just as he was – with the revolution which he desired and she hoped for. She knew that she could act for him because he thought as she did but was too kind to hurt people who did not share his views. In this way, without his realizing it, she had so ordered his life that he spoke to some people and did not see others.

'You can't stop thinking about Valencia even when you're with me,' Bruce said. 'Never mind, there'll come a day when you need me – badly.'

He knew that his words were a challenge. More than that, he was hurting her, but he hardly cared any more. It was time she emerged from the rosy dream of herself and Valencia as twin em-bodiments of revolution. After all the days and weeks which he knew she had devoted to the cause, he realized that she was in love with revolution, not Valencia; that instead of a man she had, in a sense, found a child whom she wanted to protect at the expense of her own reputation and his.

'You're playing with fire, Esther. I don't have to tell you that.'

She stared at the view without speaking and took a sip from her small cup of black coffee.

Bruce was right again, but she was not obsessed with Antonio Valencia alone. It was his crystallization of the fight against poverty and her remembrance of the unspeakable suffering in the slums which bound her to him. The wounds in her heart would never heal unless she supported him wholeheartedly in every step he took. Bruce could not offer a solution. Only Valencia could do that, and that was why she backed him heart and soul. He was the personification of everything that animated Conciencia's millions of poor. He was their strength, their symbol, their very future. It would be many decades before another man arose with the same purity of motive, the same spiritual strength, the same devotion and ability to inspire love. Without him, yet another generation would succumb to poverty and despair.

Even though she half-knew what Bruce was driving at, she said: 'What do you mean, playing with fire?'

He stared at her in silence for a while. His eyes flickered over her breasts and thighs, and something inside her trembled as she thought of their times alone together.

'Priests are only human,' he said flatly.

She tried to remember if Valencia had ever conveyed that he felt anything for her as a woman, and recalled a conversation which they had had one evening shortly before she finished work for the day.

'Why are you doing all this for me?' he had asked.

'Because it has to be done.'

'What?'

'Your work.'

He stared at her for a moment and then said: 'I hope you never change your mind. I need you.'

When did people need each other? Only when they found it impossible to live without each other. The next evening Valencia recounted a bizarre and absurd dream which had come to him the night before.

'I was walking through the streets of Rome,' he told her. 'I crossed St Peter's Square and found myself in a maze of halls and passages. There were hundreds of priests to be seen, all apparently going somewhere fast. Every room I came to was crowded with senior dignitaries of the Church. Bishops armed with crook and mitre were haranguing priests of every rank. I heard snatches of every language I have any knowledge of. I couldn't understand what all the bustle was. There seemed to be a universal preoccupation with something that had little bearing on reality. Then I came to a hall where a bishop was lecturing in Spanish on the subject of celibacy. Every member of his audience had a printed form in front of him and was studying it avidly. The forms had to be filled out, for or against celibacy. I quickly wrote "Against" and hurried on, but as I did so I tripped over a cardinal's train. He kindly helped me to my feet, but it was a moment or two before I could disentangle myself from his cappa. Afterwards I stood all alone in

St Peter's Square while priests at every window hurled abuse at me. The only person who didn't join in was a beautiful woman who looked on silently as if she was surprised that the priests should make so much fuss.'

Esther had repeatedly wondered what his purpose was in telling her about this dream, but he had never referred to it again nor said anything which might have suggested that he regarded her as anything more than a true friend.

'Of course Valencia is a man,' she said. 'An exceptional one, that's all.'

Bruce leant towards her.

'Why don't you wake up, Esther? Can't you really see what your friendship will do to him?'

'What do you mean?'

She recognized the familiar look in his eyes which meant he was going over to the attack.

'You must be blind if you can't see it. What do you think his enemies in this priest-ridden country will do to turn him into a laughing-stock? They'll try to find a chink in his armour, and that's where you come in. They'll say he has a secretary-cum-mistress. A man who spends the whole time closeted with a pretty girl is bound to be sleeping with her – that's what they'll say. They'll tell smutty stories about you. Every man you meet at a party will leer at you because you've managed to seduce a priest. You'll . . .'

Her scornful laughter interrupted him.

'Oh, come on, Bruce! You don't have to lecture me on gossip in this country – I know the place better than you do. They'll always gossip about Valencia, and if I'm not there they'll find someone else. It's too easy. Stand outside any church door in Cielo after Mass and announce that I'm a whore who sells herself to the highest bidder. By tomorrow, everyone will know. No need to tell me how it's done. It won't matter if I'm still around or not. Valencia was engaged to someone once, he dances at parties, plays the guitar, pays women compliments – oh yes, of course he sleeps with them too! Well, I can assure you of this: he's never slept with me and never would, even if he wanted to. That man is more obedient in his disobedience than you could ever imagine.'

Bruce gave up.

'All right, let's eat,' he said quietly, 'and talk about us for a change.'

Professor Vermeer shut the diary containing his notes and deposited it in his desk drawer, which he carefully locked. As so often these days, he felt tired. He lay down on his bed and brooded about the meeting which he was due to attend that afternoon.

He realized that there were hard times ahead for Valencia. Anyone who had any connection with him was suspect in the eyes of the Church authorities. The atmosphere was tense in the extreme. It was rumoured that the Cardinal wished to retire but that the President had begged him to stay on. Rumour or not, it was quite symptomatic of prevailing conditions. Tomorrow, Valencia was going to set off the powder-keg. This afternoon's meeting was only concerned with arrangements. They were to discuss contingency plans in the event of a clash with the army. The time for formulating ideas was long past. They now had to face facts and gauge what would happen when Valencia and his supporters declared themselves in public.

Vermeer had watched the budding friendship between Valencia and Esther Graham with some concern. His own conversations with Valencia had grown rarer since her advent. Esther blockaded Valencia's telephone, as he had several times discovered when he tried to fix appointments with him. She was a determined young woman, and very left-wing. It was even whispered that, although her father ran a U.S. oil company, she was a Communist.

All in all, Vermeer was gradually becoming apprehensive about Valencia. Unless he was much mistaken, however, Valencia harboured no such fears on his own behalf.

After lunch, Bruce and Esther took a taxi back into town. It was a silent ride. They had chatted rather aimlessly over their meal, but Esther's thoughts had strayed so often that Bruce purposely stopped speaking until she reopened the conversation herself. There was a tension in her which he could not fathom. To him, the mass meeting scheduled for tomorrow was simply a newsworthy event which might provide him with copy and possibly form the prelude to a revolution. As for Valencia, he liked the man just as everyone liked him, even members of the ruling clique. In other respects, Conciencia was just one of a dozen countries where revolution was always brewing. It was also far smaller than Brazil, where men like Dom Helder Camara and Dom Jorge Marcus de Oliveira were doing the same as Valencia.

The same things happened everywhere – that was the trouble with journalism. The problem was how to convey to readers that facts mattered less than the human element – that it wasn't crucial whether a revolution occurred or not. What mattered was the people involved, people who went without sleep, who were wounded or killed, who lived in the mountains and were mercilessly hunted from one day to the next.

But how to convey all the suffering, the poverty and wretchedness, when all that one had at one's command was cold print?

The taxi drew up outside Bruce's hotel, and he invited Esther inside for a few minutes. Over a drink in the bar he asked her if the afternoon's meeting was important. She looked at him as if he had said something incomprehensible.

'Are we finished?' he asked eventually.

She shook her head.

'No, I need you. You know that.'

His voice became hard.

'I didn't say anything about needing. I'm asking you if you love me.'

'Why all these questions so suddenly?'

'I've always asked them. I remember a certain answer you gave me once, too.'

'How much did it mean to you?'

'A great deal.'

'Everything?'

'What do you mean, everything?'

'Precisely what I say. Didn't it ever strike you as odd that you calmly went off and left me afterwards?'

'It was a question of personal freedom . . .'

She interrupted him.

'I've never been petty, Bruce. I never encroached on your freedom and now you're trying to encroach on mine. Isn't that a bit unsporting, to put it mildly?'

'Are you talking about Valencia?'

'No, my freedom. The right to decide what I want to do without your sitting in judgement on me. The right to live my life the way I want and not the way you dictate. The right to pick my own friends, hold my own political convictions, go my own way as you've always done. That's what I mean by freedom. Now do you understand?'

He understood only too well. The Esther facing him was a different person from the girl he had known for so long. A resolute young woman who had taken charge of her own life and renounced weakness and sentimentality because she believed fanatically in the work she was doing.

'All right, Esther, have it your way, but I'll tell you something in advance. There'll come a day when you need me more than you ever did. That's when I'll have to make up my mind if I've still got any time for you. I'll decide then whether or not I'm prepared to play second fiddle.'

She smiled faintly.

'Are you trying to turn this into a straightforward row, Bruce?'

He controlled himself with an effort.

'No, trying to be honest with you even if it hurts. I'm annoyed because I don't mean much to you any more, and it wounds my vanity. I'm annoyed that you've thrown me over for an idea rather than a man – jilted me for a revolution. I'm annoyed because you're all I have in the world, my main source of tenderness and beauty. Everything else is emotional claptrap. Look, Esther, if Valencia dies in this revolution he'll be a man I knew and sympathized with, a man whose intentions I not only understood but approved – a sort of abstract hero, if you like. But if you die with him something of me will have died too, something I thought I possessed, literally and metaphorically. And as if that wasn't bad enough you tell me, loud and clear, that you've locked me out of your world, that you've turned the key and thrown it away. Well, I'm too vain to take it.'

She lit a cigarette and stared at him. He stared back at her, wrily now.

'So it's the same old Bruce Cornell,' she said. 'Full of sarcasm, full of self-reproach. The spurned lover getting drunk on his own sweet words. Those were the things that always worried me most about you, Bruce, don't you remember? You're a pragmatist, I'm an idealist. You're a sober fact-finder, I'm someone who can sympathize with the poor even when they're to blame for their poverty. You're a man who can become so engrossed in his work that he forgets me, I'm a woman who can get so absorbed in someone else that she forgets herself. But with your ideas of personal freedom you'll probably never grasp that. What is freedom, anyway? The art of roaming the world without ever committing yourself to anyone? Or is freedom what Valencia's doing? You'll have to answer that question for yourself, but freedom isn't an abstract concept to be juggled with. Asserting your freedom doesn't mean hopping a plane – it means staking your life. It doesn't mean writing, it means swapping your typewriter for a rifle.'

'And is Valencia doing that?'

She sighed.

'He may be forced to. He may have to do worse than that, but he's a man of action as well as words. He's taught me to think positively instead of negatively, and how many people can still do that?'

'Couldn't we talk about it upstairs in my room?'

She shook her head.

'No, Bruce, not now. You've had my body so often it's time you started thinking about my mind, and you don't need a bed to do that.'

He stood up.

'In that case I'll start now. You'd better go to this meeting without me. Maybe we'll see each other tomorrow at the University. So long, Esther.'

She stared after him as he left the bar. He walked slowly down the broad passage lined with placards and showcases proclaiming that Conciencia was the tourist paradise of the twentieth century, complete with jungle and mountains, white men and Indians, cities and swamps. Why hadn't he simply told her that he loved her, said the words that all human beings use when they feel they can't live without someone? Perhaps it was her talk of Valencia that had silenced him. He swore as he entered the lift because the thought of his lonely room smote him like a chill wind.

9

Arthuro Cuellar, editor-in-chief and proprietor of *El Minuto*, Conciencia's second-largest daily, had never been afflicted with worries of any kind, least of all financial. His father had been one of the country's foremost landowners and industrialists, and the fortune which he had shared with three brothers and two sisters was astronomically large.

Arthuro Cuellar lived on a vast estate outside Cielo. Few people ever set eyes on the house because it lay at the heart of an expanse of privately owned land to which no one but Cuellar and his guests had access. His newspaper, industrial concerns and plantations were all thriving, and his executives were so efficient that he could afford to devote several hours a day to his favourite recreation, which was riding. His stable was famous for the horses which he bred and raced at Cielo and other major tracks in Latin America, and which paid handsomely for their keep. It was almost impossible to imagine the *casa grande* without a swarm of house-guests. In the holiday season, all twenty guest-rooms were occupied by relatives and friends from home and abroad. Arthuro Cuellar was a contented man. Life had done well by him. His wife was a former school-friend, and both of them accepted their marriage as a matter of course because they had been constantly together from the age of twelve onwards.

There were few zeniths or nadirs in the story of Cuellar's life to date. He had been only a remote observer of the troubles of the past ten years. Besides, he considered himself a progressive land-owner because his agricultural labourers received higher wages than the workers on any other estate. Other people resented this and he knew it, but the Cuellar family characteristics included a certain cussedness. This may partly have accounted for his most recent venture, a model village of forty cottages for his labour force. Now, in the late afternoon, he was riding over to check on their progress. He was mounted on his favourite horse, Oro, a powerful golden chestnut with a long pale brown tail and a blaze on its forehead.

Beside Cuellar, calm and relaxed, rode Antonio Valencia on the magnificent black stallion which the landowner had given him. They spoke little. Valencia sensed intuitively that this might be his last day in the saddle for many months because he would have no spare time in the coming year.

'You won't do anything foolish, Antonio, will you?' Cuellar said suddenly.

'What's one more stupidity in a country like ours, Arthuro?'

Cuellar looked gravely at the vigorous young man riding beside him and wondered where his real strength lay. Was it his gentle sarcasm, his sense of humour, his education, or were they underlaid by something far greater?

'I'm afraid you'll go too far too fast, Antonio. The idea frightens me.'

'I didn't think fear was part of the Cuellar vocabulary.'

They rode on in silence across the sun-baked fields. Mountains loomed on the horizon and interminable coffee plantations stretched on either side of them. In the far distance could be seen the roofs of the village where the workers lived.

'I'm not afraid for myself, Antonio. It's you I'm worried about. We've known each other for years, after all, and I owe you a debt of gratitude. You helped me to open my eyes . . .'

Valencia turned his head abruptly.

'You owe me nothing, Arthuro. You formed your own conclusions because you couldn't stand by and watch the workers being bled white.'

Cuellar chuckled.

'You and your confounded modesty! Do you really think the paper which prints your articles only has an influence on its readers? What about its editor-in-chief?'

Valencia reined in his horse so unexpectedly that the animal snorted in protest.

'You honestly believe I have some influence on the readers of *El Minuto*?' he demanded.

The older man nodded.

'Of course. Nobody sends me any correspondence about you, but silence implies approval.'

'You think so? Discounting your own little empire, have any changes occurred in agriculture or industry? Has there been a single change in the field of social legislation?'

Cuellar frowned.

'Why pretend it can all be done in the space of a few months? Come down to earth for once. To make changes you first have to jolt public opinion. After that you need better news media, stronger trade unions, a decent parliament, and finally a president who's capable of grasping the whole picture. You can reverse the order if you like, but only if the jolt to public opinion takes priority.'

'And don't we have these things now?' said Valencia.

Cuellar ran a hand through his thick black hair.

'Of course not. You know that better than I do.'

'How do you suggest we get them?'

'I just told you. Jolt public opinion, which is what you're doing, and the rest will follow.'

'You think it's possible?'

'It'll have to be.'

They were approaching the site of the new village. Although it was late afternoon and long past siesta-time, there were no workers in sight. They rode past the almost completed houses, so lifeless that they resembled a Western film set.

Cuellar and Valencia dismounted, tethered their horses to a tree and strolled along the deserted street.

'See what I mean?' Cuellar said. 'You can't blame everything on the employers. I pay top wages, and the only result is that my men push off an hour before time.'

He led the way into one of the cottages.

'They're better than the ones I've seen in France and just as good as their German equivalents,' he said. 'What's more, every *campesino* gets a plot of his own. Anything he grows on it belongs to him. Take a look at that – not a sign of cultivation anywhere.'

Valencia surveyed the green landscape through one of the still unglazed windows. What a superb country Conciencia was, he reflected. God had given it everything that could gladden a man's heart, and only a few thousand people enjoyed what it had to offer.

There was a footfall outside. Cuellar went to see who it was, followed by Valencia. They found themselves confronted by a skinny little *campesino*. The man swept off his broad-brimmed straw hat when he recognized Cuellar.

'Where are the builders?' Cuellar demanded brusquely.

The man smiled and pointed vaguely into the distance.

'Today is the feast of St Anthony, the patron saint of the village,' he said. 'They went to Mass this morning and now they're probably drunk.'

'And you?'

'I, *patrón*? I came to do a little work on my plot of land.'

Cuellar dismissed the *campesino* with a gesture and turned to Valencia.

'Damn your feast-days,' he said. 'Why don't you abolish them? The saints of Conciencia are collectively responsible for the loss of at least thirty working days a year.'

Valencia laughed out loud.

'And the rich of Conciencia ensure that the poor make the most of them!'

They walked slowly down the street, occasionally stopping to examine the inside of a house.

Cuellar pointed out the shower, lavatory, small bedroom and patio.

'When they're finished I'll throw a party,' he said with an air of satisfaction.

Valencia, leaning against a door-post, eyed him levelly.

'Don't make a meal of it, Arthuro. Don't invite some minister who hasn't lifted a finger to help, and don't let any pompous bureaucrat give a speech. The people must be made to understand that decent living conditions are quite normal. I hope you're not planning to go into politics with a model village as your stake.'

Cuellar lit a cigarette.

'I'm up to my neck in politics as it is – thanks to you, my boy. Or don't you think it's politics, publishing articles written by someone like you?'

'Thank you for giving me a chance, Arthuro. I prostrate myself in the dust at your feet.'

'It's no laughing matter,' Cuellar retorted irritably. 'I don't always agree with you, but I'll go on publishing your stuff as long as you don't go too far. Preaching revolution is fine – I'm all in favour. At least it wakes people up. But grabbing a gun and taking part in a revolution is something else. You'd be mad to contemplate it.'

'That's your considered opinion?'

Cuellar went over to his horse and stroked the beast's muzzle.

'There's been more than enough bloodshed in this country,' he said bitterly. 'It's time we rolled up our sleeves and started building instead of tearing down. I've had enough of fear and hatred and bestiality. We're human beings, not animals.'

Valencia did not reply. They remounted and rode back through the quiet country-side, savouring the green fields spangled with butterflies, the birds under a blue sky, as if Conciencia were a heaven on earth.

Cuellar had invited some of his closest friends that evening, an amiable but rather vociferous set of people, most of them belonging to the families which had effectively ruled Conciencia for centuries. They loved music, so he had engaged some guitarists. Outside in the garden, servants had already lit the open fires on which sides of meat would be roasted later on.

Valencia enjoyed these *asado* parties. He felt at home among Cuellar's friends and knew that, in general, they liked him. They regarded him as an agreeable eccentric, a combination of priest and playboy, someone with whom it was impossible to be really angry even when he acted in a way which did not fit into their scheme of things. He was still the most sought-after officiator at christenings and weddings, and his gift of conversing man-to-man and man-to-woman had saved a number of tottering marriages over the years. This had invested him with a certain authority, and he knew that people enjoyed listening to him. Outside on the terrace he was soon the centre of an animated group. Half-mocking, half-sympathetic, they asked what he proposed to do now that he had lost his university chair.

'Do tell us, Padre Valencia,' Cuellar's seventeen-year-old daughter said teasingly, 'are you going to become a real revolutionary now?'

Valencia smiled.

'Yes, and the first person I deal with will be you. Pert little teenagers come top of my black list.'

She pouted.

'I was hoping you'd have some exciting news for us.'

'Why exciting?'

'Because nothing ever happens here. Cielo's a boring old dump. It's time somebody injected a bit of life into the place. Everything worthwhile happens hundreds of kilometres away in the mountains.'

An elderly lady extended her hand and Valencia kissed it.

'I donate ten thousand dollars a year to my orphanage,' she said. 'I'm happy to be able to do something for the poor creatures. Do you really think we're not doing enough, my dear boy?'

'You're a marvel, Dona Madalena,' he said, evading the question. If there were more people like you . . .'

She bridled.

'How charming of you to say so. Couldn't I persuade you to pay

136

us a visit sometime? My eighteen-year-old son can't leave the girls alone. Sooner or later I shall have trouble with him.'

Servants in white jackets adorned with gold braid circulated among the guests, ensuring that their needs were attended to. The atmosphere became even gayer and more animated.

A burly little man elbowed his way through the circle and thumped Valencia on the back.

'If it isn't our tame revolutionary! Good to see you again, my boy. You're looking the picture of health. I thought you'd deserted us.'

Valencia smiled.

'What gave you that idea, General?'

'Pah! I've been hearing the strangest stories about you lately. Some fool told me you were going off to join the guerilleros.'

'Antonio could never do that,' Dona Madalena said gravely. 'A priest with a machine-gun? I doubt if he could find the trigger!'

The general rocked with laughter, but Valencia looked him steadily in the eyes.

'The trigger is there for anyone to pull,' he said, more sharply than he had intended, 'even a priest.'

The general changed the subject.

'You have a girl secretary now – that's what the same fool told me. Well, well, our priests are getting more and more modern these days.'

Valencia kissed Dona Madalena's hand once more.

'And our womenfolk more and more beautiful, General.'

'What a dear delightful boy,' he heard the old lady say as he moved on to another group.

A waiter came up with a tray. Valencia took a glass and drank it quickly.

In the spacious library of the *casa grande*, Cuellar was deep in conversation with another of his guests, Monsignor Zasi.

'The Cardinal has asked me to give you a message, Arthuro,' Zasi said quietly. 'To be honest, I find it distasteful. He and the President are both panic-stricken. They're convinced that Valencia wants armed revolution. In short, I'm to ask you to stop publishing his articles and take a pro-government line. It's all rather mysterious and I haven't grasped the full picture, but for some reason they're in mortal terror of Valencia and want to silence him as quickly as possible. I'm to make it clear to you that this is a matter of supreme national importance.'

Cuellar poured himself a glass of white rum.

'You know I don't like Medina,' he said peevishly. 'He's more conservative than any medieval prince of the Church and he's been scared of his own shadow ever since he became cardinal. It's a mystery to me how Rome could have entrusted the local Church to someone so completely out of touch with reality.'

'You won't mind if I keep my own opinions to myself?' Zasi said.

'Not at all, Ariano, but I know the man considerably better than you do. I also know his family. Not to put too fine a point on it, they're a bunch of avaricious swine who've never invested a cent in this country. As for the President, he's a peacock with the brains of a cow and the perspicacity of a rhino.'

Monsignor Zasi permitted himself a faint smile.

'Well, Arthuro, what would you do about Valencia?'

Cuellar shrugged.

'It's obvious, I'd say. Let him have his head. Back him. Tell him he's absolutely right and accept his recommendations. Valencia isn't stupid, Ariano. He wants a dialogue with Marxism. Well, what's the matter with that? Discounting the theological aspect, there's no difference between Marxism and the sort of Christianity we so desperately need in Latin America. Take a look at Frei in Chile. For God's sake don't let's have a repetition of what they did to Galileo. Isn't it enough that we rejected Galileo and the whole of the exact sciences with him? Haven't we learnt anything from Europe? Communism only came into being because the Church had forgotten to carry out Christ's teachings on the subject of social justice. In the past we had a schism because we dismissed Luther as a heretic instead of accepting him as a man who was right.'

Monsignor Zasi sighed.

'I wish you could convince the Cardinal, Arthuro.'

'Of what?'

Zasi leant forward.

'He will present Valencia with a choice: either he gives up politics or, if he refuses, the Cardinal will forbid him to fulfil his priestly duties.'

The silence that followed was so intense that the murmur of voices drifted up to them from the garden.

Cuellar looked as if someone had hit him over the head, but his eyes were bright with anger.

'The stupid, arrogant old fool,' he said furiously.

Barbecuing steak was one of Valencia's specialities. While he was at work, Cuellar's daughter and a group of giggling girl-friends kept him company. Overcome by the heat, he stripped off his soutane to reveal khaki shorts and an open-necked shirt.

'Now you really do look like a guerillero,' Maria Cuellar said.

'Guerilleros don't light fires at night,' he retorted gaily.

'How would you know?'

'I know everything,' he said with a chuckle. 'You've no idea what an inspiration it is to be surrounded by pretty girls.'

Maria Cuellar eyed him provocatively.

'Priests shouldn't say things like that.'

'Priests shouldn't appreciate feminine beauty – is that what you mean?'

'I mean,' she said serenely, 'that when a man looks at a member of the opposite sex with more than casual interest it means he wants her.'

Valencia burst out laughing.

'You flatter yourself, my dear girl.'

While he busied himself with another steak, she said, not looking at him: 'You were engaged once, weren't you?'

'Yes.'

'They say you made the most of your time as a student.'

He did not reply. Memories flooded in on him suddenly, as vivid as if they were of yesterday. Bent over the glowing embers, he relived the highlights of his young existence.

Perhaps it had all begun when he realized that his parents' relationship was not what most people understood by the word marriage. This somehow cut the ground from under his feet, and as a student at Cielo University he flung himself into the pleasures of drinking and womanizing because they helped him to forget the tension that pervaded his home.

His parents had been sensible in one respect. They rarely quarrelled in front of him, though that might have been just what made life so intolerable. Sometimes he took his father's part, sometimes his mother's, but he realized even then that remarks taken out of context did not give a true picture of the whole situation. His mother was the exact contrary of his father. She would talk in a faintly mocking and often scathing way which her far more reserved and taciturn husband found deeply hurtful. On such occasions Antonio usually left the room and listened outside the door, simultaneously reproaching himself for doing so.

Sometimes months elapsed between outbursts, but the everlasting tension was worse than an open clash. One evening when his mother was out, some friends called on his father. He eavesdropped on the conversation. They were discussing the state of the country and making caustic remarks about the current President. His father said nothing for a while, then rounded on them.

'I'll tell you something. What's happening in this country has been going on for more than a century. Arm-chair critics get together and talk as if they had a lien on the wisdom of the ages. They say that the President is corrupt, that Congress is a cipher, that everything must be changed. When the conservatives are in power the liberals say it, when the liberals are in power the conservatives say it. But when it comes down to the real business of governing, nobody is ready to fight corruption or put officialdom in its place, nobody stands up and acts like a man. Men – that's what we need.'

A brooding silence fell, and in the hush he heard his father say:

'Our country is sick, *señores*. As a surgeon, I know what that means. One can operate on a human being. Countries are inoperable except by a man who can do the impossible.'

'Well,' someone said, 'don't we have one?'

'Not yet. One day, Conciencia may produce another Simon Bolívar, a real leader of men.'

'That's a dream.'

'Yes, an insane dream. I doubt if even Simon Bolívar would stand a chance here today. They'd cart him away before he could open his mouth.'

'What if he belonged to the Church, this leader of yours?'

'A priest?'

'Yes.'

'The right priest would be more powerful than all the rest, but you know as well as I do, they don't breed priests like that.'

A little while later Antonio tiptoed upstairs to his spacious attic bedroom, a frequent venue for parties and discussions with his fellow-students. As he crept up the stairs he heard his father's voice again: 'Sometimes I wonder what we are. Blind mice, scurrying for safety! Blind to life, afraid of death, terrified of ourselves, greedy for influence, power and money. Ugh!'

Half an hour later his father suddenly appeared in his room. He looked tired.

'Working?'

'No, just thinking.'

Professor Valencia sat down and gave him a long silent stare.

'Have we disappointed you as parents, Antonio?'

Antonio did not reply.

'I asked you a question, my boy.'

'The answer is no, Father. I can't pass judgement on your problems. I'm sorry, that's all.'

There was another silence.

'What's your real motive for studying sociology?'

'The country needs sociologists, Father.'

Professor Valencia nodded.

'A good enough reason. And what's your attitude towards Conciencia?'

'I'm proud of the place.'

'Why?'

'I can't explain. I was born here – it's my home.'

'How's the work going?'

'Pretty well. My tutors seem satisfied.'

'What about girls?'

'Girls?'

'Yes, and don't look so innocent. If I were you I'd take things a bit easier.'

'I'm not such a hell-raiser as all that.'

'Glad to hear it. Anyway, be careful and don't drink too much.'

His father rose with an effort and went out, pulling the door to behind him. Antonio did not move.

'One day, Conciencia may produce another Simon Bolívar, a real leader of men. A man . . . a man . . . a man . . .'

When Antonio was twenty-one he became friendly with a girl student named Ines, a gentle, serious-minded girl of good family with whom he often discussed the lack of harmony in his home. But his restlessness did not subside in spite of their intimate relationship. He sometimes broke dates with her to go gallivanting all night, and he was not strictly faithful to her.

One evening she looked at him gravely and asked if anything was wrong. He kissed her and told her not to be silly.

'Don't you love me any more?'

Antonio raised his eyebrows.

'What makes you think that?'

'It seems I'm not enough for you.'

He grinned.

'Everyone has to sow a few wild oats sometime.'

Ines went down extremely well with his family. She was quiet,

141

unassuming and cheerful, and her presence dispelled some of the shadows that had hung over the household for so long. Sometimes they were scarcely perceptible. Peace reigned and even his father's manner thawed. One evening he told them that the Cardinal had summoned him for a consultation and asked if he would operate on him. He agreed, and shortly before the operation the Cardinal paid a visit to the Valencia home. He asked Antonio a myriad questions about the university, and just as he was leaving he said: 'Your son has a good brain. What a shame he isn't reading theology.'

The operation was a success, and some days later his father observed wrily: 'To think that a brave man like Medina has to be Cardinal – the prisoner of all he surveys!'

The same evening Ines asked Antonio when they were going to become officially engaged. They agreed on a date three months ahead.

After Antonio had driven her home he was overwhelmed by the same feeling of restlessness which had given him no peace for months now.

Was this to be his life, marriage to Ines, further studies, more examinations, and possibly a lecturership? Part of his day would belong to the University, the rest to his family. Meanwhile, nothing in the country would change. His studies had familiarized him with Marx and Lenin. He and his fellow-students discussed them avidly and to some effect. One day Antonio proposed that they should carry out research into the shanty-towns and produce a sociological survey as a basis for future discussion. To his surprise, his tutors showed little interest in the project. While not exactly rejecting his proposal, they never referred to it again.

A few weeks later Ines told him flatly that, if his present state of mind persisted, she wanted to postpone their engagement. 'I'd sooner you made a retreat – a long one. It may help you to collect your thoughts.'

He reluctantly agreed. A few days later he retired to a Dominican monastery where, in complete seclusion, he awoke at long last.

He could not afterwards recall when the idea came to him, but one day he knew that he had not eavesdropped on his father in vain. 'A man . . . a man . . . a man!'

There was only one place where such a man could develop unhampered by externals, and that was within the Church itself. As a priest he would be granted authority. As a priest he could devote himself heart and soul to the gospel which his father had transmitted to him.

He ended the period of retreat with his mind made up. He went to Ines, and, as soon as they were alone together, informed her gravely that he intended to take holy orders.

She stared at him in dismay.

'When?'

'I shall present myself tomorrow.'

'But why, Antonio?'

Why? Impossible to explain in a few words. She would not have understood.

'Can't I do anything to stop you?' she asked.

'No, Ines, not even you.'

His parents greeted the news with equal incredulity.

'Think it over for a month or two,' his father advised.

He protested that there was no need.

'It's a rash decision, my boy. Surely even you can see that?'

'No, Father.'

'Well, I can. However, I won't try to dissuade you, much as I regret your decision.'

'Why should you regret it?'

'Because I thought you might have done something for this country.'

'Can't I do so as a priest?'

'I very much doubt it.'

'Then I'll have to prove you wrong.'

After completing his studies at the seminary in record time, Antonio Valencia was ordained. His father died soon afterwards, leaving Señora Valencia in straightened circumstances.

One day the Cardinal called at her apartment. Having inquired after her welfare, he said abruptly:

'Your late husband, with God's help, saved my life. Would you object if I repaid part of that debt?'

Señora Valencia shook her head wonderingly.

'I don't follow, Your Eminence.'

'I should like your son to pursue his studies.'

'But . . .'

'In Europe. I should be happy to finance him.'

'No, Your Eminence, I couldn't agree to that.'

The Cardinal laughed.

'There is another way. I can simply order him to go to Europe to study. Then he will have no choice.'

This time Señora Valencia joined in the laughter.

Next morning Antonio was summoned to the Cardinal's sanctum. Medina looked at him for a moment and then said: 'You're very like your father sometimes, Antonio. Why didn't you say anything yesterday?'

'Because you're always telling us to obey, Your Eminence. Did you wish me to dispute your orders?'

The Cardinal merely chuckled.

'You will continue to study sociology, Antonio. We need men like you in this country.'

'Why, Your Eminence?'

'I should have thought that was obvious. In years to come our chief enemy will be Communism. We must combat it, but how can we do so when we know so little about it? I look forward to a time when every bishop and every parish priest is better informed about Marxism than the Marxists themselves. That is the only way to fight it.'

Mice, thought Antonio, scurrying blind mice, and the thought helped him to hold his tongue.

'May success attend you, my son,' said the Cardinal.

His studies in Paris and Rome only brought confirmation of what his father had said.

Success did attend him, but not in the way Medina had meant. It really began when he delivered a letter from Medina to another cardinal in Rome.

The spectacle that met his eyes was pure Renaissance. Coming through the door, he espied the cardinal at the far end of a long throne-room. The cardinal did not rise, and Antonio supposed that it enabled him to weigh up his visitors from his chair as they diffidently traversed the huge chamber. The cardinal, who had to celebrate Mass in a factory on the outskirts of the city next day, invited Antonio to join him. The journey there and back gave them an opportunity to discuss numerous topics at their leisure. Antonio felt extremely honoured at first. Conversation soon turned to worker-priests, an institution of which the cardinal strongly disapproved. He listened benevolently to Antonio's arguments but contended that society was too fraught with dangers. The priesthood, he said, was a frail vessel and one which required careful shielding.

Antonio was puzzled. This particular cardinal came of humble parentage and had studied at other people's expense, yet his manner was unadulteratedly aristocratic. He seemed to have forgotten all about his original environment. When he spoke of social problems it was in purely theoretical terms. Antonio often noted, during his time in Italy, that the study of theology could sever a man's ties with his early background. Priests who claimed to be well versed in the problems of the poor because they themselves came from a poor family were usually labouring under a delusion. Childhood experiences were small guide to the needs of adults.

For all that, the cosmopolitan city made a profound impression on Antonio because it brought him into contact with all sorts of people, even intellectuals who lived completely outside the bounds of society.

He smiled as he remembered Professor Potosi, who had invited him to join a committee for social studies. Potosi offered him a generous retainer, and although the young priest could not imagine what form his duties would take he accepted the post.

The foundation over which Professor Potosi presided was financed by a number of big industrialists. Antonio had a preliminary discussion with Potosi over a lavish dinner at the professor's home, but he was never privileged to attend a meeting of the advisory committee because this consisted, on paper only, of a number of prominent personalities whose names the professor exploited for prestige purposes. Regularly, month after month, Antonio's generous salary cheque arrived. Patiently, month after month, he waited for the research assignment that never came. From time to time the professor invited him to drop in for another talk. Over yet another abundant repast Potosi recounted all the problems he had solved in the interim and thanked Antonio extravagantly for services rendered, his invaluable advice and fruitful suggestions. Then he drove him to the station, and that was the end of it until next time.

Antonio continued to wait for something important to turn up, but nothing ever did. It later transpired that the professor's mysterious institute possessed no real importance whatsoever. Potosi had aristocratic connections, a non-existent bank balance, and a number of acquaintances among the wealthy. It was the latter to whom he had turned for money to found his institute. The impressive advisory committee was set up, together with an office in which secretaries spent the entire day typing superfluous circulars and reports. Antonio summed the professor up as an idealist who wanted to do something useful but did not know what. Potosi did succeed in one respect at least. He managed to interest Communist workers in the establishment of discussion groups on social questions, and when these groups started work Antonio delivered a lecture on labour problems in South America. Before long, however, the whole scheme burst like a balloon and the professor had to seek fresh fields in the United States.

Rome, Paris and Louvain all represented milestones in Antonio's life, but he underwent most of his formative experiences while visiting Holland, Germany, Norway, Sweden and Denmark. He studied the social services that had been built up there. He got to know something about pension schemes for the elderly. He saw high living standards, workers' settlements, trade unions that achieved their aims without corruption, elections in which malpractice was unthinkable. He heard that Europeans regarded his country and continent merely as an area where hot-blooded people plunged from one revolution into another, whereas in reality these revolutions almost invariably started at the highest level. He found that people in Europe knew virtually nothing of conditions in Latin America and debated problems of which they were totally ignorant.

He had wondered if they looked on his country as the pearl of a distant continent, but the more he spoke to them the more evident it became that they were wholly uninterested in how things progressed there and how many lives were lost. The most they showed was a certain surprise that someone from Conciencia was not as corrupt and wealthy as all the rest, even if he was studying in Europe. They justified their lack of interest in his country by implying that it was futile to concern oneself with a continent where the birth-rate was soaring, where the rich continued to exploit the poor, and where military and civilian dictators held the people permanently in thrall. It was only when Fidel Castro almost sparked off a third world war that they woke up with a start and asked each other how things could have been allowed to go so far. Che Guevara's gospel of guerrilla revolution and his avowed intention of creating two new Vietnams in Latin America certainly raised some eyebrows, but even then it was not much more than curiosity – almost as if Conciencia were somewhere on Mars instead of half a day's jet flight from Europe and even less from the United States. There in Europe, Antonio had laid the foundations of what he was doing now. A man . . . a man . . . a man! That had become the watchword of his life, he reflected. Suddenly he noticed that the steak was charred to a cinder and that he was standing there alone, mesmerized by the incandescent charcoal.

A cough behind him made him look round.
'Ah, Monsignor Zasi, how nice to see you.'

'A mutual pleasure, Antonio.'

They eyed one another. Valencia was familiar with the bishop's almost peasant cunning, but he liked him all the same. He appreciated the difficulty of Zasi's position and admired the calm detachment with which he viewed matters at the cardinal's palace.

'You almost burnt your fingers, my son.'

Valencia smiled as he pulled on his soutane.

'We all do that sometimes, Monsignor.'

'Would it bore you to take a stroll with me? After sitting behind a desk all day I feel the need for a little exercise.'

'I should be delighted, Monsignor.'

Valencia's composure made a deep impression on the bishop. Nothing in his manner suggested that he was on the eve of an ordeal by fire. Zasi sensed the vitality which flowed from the young priest and felt a pang of envy that anyone could show such confidence in the face of so many problems.

It almost seemed to Zasi that Valencia was the superior and he the subordinate. One sometimes met living reminders of qualities which had long been suppressed in oneself, rather like the occasional breath of spring enjoyed by old men in the autumn of their days. People like Valencia were armed with inward certainty and the knowledge that they were fighting for others, not themselves. They were men who soared above ephemeral things and mundane cares, men who had within them all that one had ever dreamed of possessing. They had something which transcended time and eternity. Their conscience was a mirror which gave an undistorted image of self, their strength elemental in its purity.

Cuellar's grounds were lit by coloured lanterns suspended from the trees. The terrace where his guests were enjoying themselves lay in a pool of light, and above and beyond it could be seen the turrets and crenellations of the *casa grande*, a miniature Latin American Versailles.

'Cuellar tells me you plan to announce your political programme at Cielo University tomorrow. Is that true, Antonio?'

'Your Grace is well informed,' Valencia replied curtly.

The bishop hesitated. He knew from confidential reports that the man beside him had already formed hundreds of cells throughout the country and was backed by all the minority parties, even the Communists.

'This National Revolutionary Front of yours – the Cardinal won't like it. You realize that, of course?'

Valencia nodded and glanced up at the house.

147

'I do, Monsignor.'

Zasi studied Valencia's face. The young man's dark eyes stared back at him coolly.

'Have you given any thought to the steps which His Eminence may take?'

Valencia restrained his annoyance with difficulty.

'Is this a conversation between the two of us, Monsignor, or are you speaking on His Eminence's behalf?'

Zasi smiled.

'I am your bishop, Antonio. I can think of no better reason for talking to you. What do you intend to say tomorrow?'

'I shall appeal to the country.'

'Which section of the country?' Zasi's tone was a trifle chill.

'All sections, Monsignor.'

'You propose to speak in your capacity as a priest?'

'Of course.'

'What if His Eminence should forbid you to do so?'

'I have to act, Monsignor, because I feel that we of the Church share responsibility for conditions which we shall never change until we open our eyes to them. The authorities believe that conferences can stop the rot. Personally, Monsignor, I abominate conferences and committees. They don't give value for money. It's talk, talk, talk, but nothing ever changes except the number of committee members, which goes up and up. I've always found it easier to understand Christian principles than to lay down firm rules. Modelling oneself on Christ means modelling oneself on goodness, truth and beauty.'

Zasi nodded.

'Of course, but if you act on your own initiative you'll have three groups to contend with – the rich, the army and the Church.'

'Perhaps, but that won't matter as long as the common people are behind me.'

'You're playing a dangerous game, my son. More than that I can't say.'

Valencia's brow remained unclouded.

'To me, the essence of priesthood is communion, union with Christ. When I administer the Eucharist to people who exploit their neighbours and claim to be Christians on the strength of a few donations which do nothing effective to help matters, I feel like an accomplice.'

'There are many good things too . . .' Zasi broke in, but Valencia did not seem to hear.

'I love this life, Monsignor. I'm obsessed with it. What am I to do, ensconce myself behind a desk and feign indifference to the sufferings of my fellow-men? Am I to let them die like animals without lifting a finger to prevent it? If I do, I shall not have justified the existence which God gave me. Surely you wouldn't wish me to adopt such an attitude, Monsignor?'

The bishop gazed across at the illuminated terrace with its ring of charcoal braziers, and sighed.

'My only thought was to warn you, Antonio.'

'Thank you, Monsignor,' Valencia replied quietly. 'Believe me, I can't turn back now.'

'I realize that, my son, but I'm worried about you. That was why I had to speak.'

Zasi turned away and walked off across the broad expanse of green lawn, into Cuellar's house. He could not do more than he had done. Valencia's will was stronger than his own, stronger than the Cardinal's. People would certainly listen to him, but for how long?

Valencia stared after the bishop's small departing figure and wondered what he had meant to convey. How much did he know? What was being whispered in the corridors of power? What plot was being hatched against him at that very minute?

And suddenly he realized how alone he was. A hundred yards away, people were enjoying themselves. They had no problems that money couldn't solve. They were the repositories of power. Many of them lived in mansions even more imposing than Cuellar's, some of them in palaces. They were still at one with him. They found him entertaining, probably sincere as well. They liked him because he was one of them. But if he repudiated them, if he announced that he must dispense with them, if he advocated confiscation of their property and threatened their way of life, how much longer would they continue to regard him as one of their own?

The general popped up beside him so unexpectedly that for a moment he thought he was under physical attack.

'Antonio, I'd like a word with you.'

'By all means.'

'I was joking earlier, but now we're alone I'd like to talk seriously. As you know, I was a good friend of your father's and I'm a great admirer of your mother.'

'What is it, General?'

'Not so fast, my boy, not so fast. I've a proposition to put to you.'

'I'm listening.'

'I've just had a long chat with Don Ignacio Fierro. We've come to the conclusion that you'd be invaluable to us as a sociological adviser attached to our various enterprises – factories, plantations, newspapers and so on. How does the idea appeal to you?'

'A new department, you mean?'

'A brand-new approach to labour relations, and vital to our future plans. You can pick your own team, and don't worry about the money side of things – we value your advice far too highly to quibble about a few pesos. You can name your own salary.'

'And what would my terms of reference be, General?

'You would undertake a comprehensive study of industrial and agricultural working conditions and we would put your recommendations into practice.'

'When would I have to submit my findings?'

The general flapped his hands jovially.

'No rush, my dear boy. I know how complex these things are. You can have a couple of years at least.'

Valencia smiled.

'An interesting proposition, General. May I think it over?'

The general shook his head.

'Preferably not. We were hoping you'd accept and start work tomorrow.'

'I'm due to speak at Cielo University tomorrow.'

'Call it off, Antonio.'

'You mean . . .'

The general nodded.

'Precisely. No arguments, no politics, just a free hand, plenty of finance, and a chance to improve living standards. What more do you want? It's exactly what you've been urging all along.'

It was indeed, thought Valencia. A sociological centre with adequate resources and himself in charge. A centre whose influence could be brought to bear through the medium of his published writings and reports. A centre which would influence the press. His thoughts ran away with him. It had always been his dearest wish. Freedom of action, freedom to write, enough money to allow him freedom of movement.

The general pressed his hand.

'Think it over and give us your answer tonight.'

His tread was less hesitant than Monsignor Zasi's, his figure more erect. He represented power and money. Recalling what Zasi had said, Valencia understood everything. It was a plot, probably the first of many. First the bishop with his appeal to the emotions, then the general with his appeal to social conscience. He wondered who would be next.

Slowly, he strolled back to the others. The garden was thronged with the people who ruled Conciencia with their money. He knew them all and they knew him. They were proud, cultivated and charming. They had style. He liked them. It was hard to see them as enemies of the people, oppressors of an entire nation.

Cuellar tugged at his sleeve.

'Did the general speak to you, Antonio?'

Valencia smiled.

'Are you part of the conspiracy too?'

'No, but it seems to have got around. What are you going to do?'

'What do you think?'

'Refuse, I imagine.'

'You imagine right. It's a peculiarly subtle form of bribery. I suppose I ought to admire it, in a way.'

Maria Cuellar came over to them.

'Are you going to accept, Padre?'

He shook his head.

'I don't think so.'

'Oh, how exciting! Why not?'

'Because I can't turn my back on the whole country for the sake of a cosy career. Conciencia needs men, Maria,' he said, quoting his father. 'Men, not blind mice.'

At the end of the evening Conciencia's most powerful industrialist, landowner and press tycoon, Ignacio Fierro, tried to force the issue. He called his fellow-guests together and surveyed them thoughtfully. Fierro was short and stout, with a rugged square-jowled face which conveyed that anyone who opposed him got short shrift. Raising his glass, he looked round the circle of expectant faces.

'*Señoras, señoritas* and *señores*, I drink to Padre Antonio Valencia, in the confident expectation that he has accepted our proposal to set up a sociological centre.'

He smiled and turned to Valencia.

'Padre, I also drink to your future career and thank you in advance for your efforts to improve the living conditions of our employees and the workers of the entire country.'

All eyes were on Valencia as he walked over to Fierro. It was so silent that his every footstep could be heard on the mosaic paving of the terrace. He gazed serenely round the gathering and gave a sudden smile which broke the tension.

'I accept,' he said evenly. Then, as applause burst forth and Fierro's face creased in a triumphant smile, he raised his han 'I shall take up the post in a year's time. That will give me a chan   to study the problem in depth.'

The general and Fierro looked as if they had just been slapped in the face, but they were too proud to admit defeat.

'To your new appointment, Padre Valencia!'

'To my new appointment,' he said, and then everyone started to talk at once. They sounded like a swarm of bees.

Valencia threaded his way through the crowd and strolled off across the lawn, but he had not gone ten paces when he felt Cuellar's hand on his shoulder.

'Straight between the eyes,' he said. 'They won't forgive you in a hurry, Antonio.'

'They asked for it.'

'I know they did, but you can't buck men like the general and Fierro and get away with it. They never forget an injury.'

'My first sworn enemies, eh?'

'I'm afraid so, and they've got a ready-made argument for public consumption. They'll say they tried to help you but you rejected them in favour of revolution.'

'What was Zasi's reaction?'

'He says that Fierro will inform the Cardinal tomorrow. It won't do you any good, believe me.'

'Where is Zasi?'

'He just left.'

'I see. So he's another . . .'

'I don't know, Antonio. He looked very old and tired and sad. He muttered something about "All this power will I give thee . . ." '

'St Luke,' Valencia said quietly. 'The temptation in the wilderness.'

10

Talmac clung to the mountainside so precariously that a distant observer might have fancied that the village was about to slide into the valley where Don Henrico's vast coffee plantation lay.

Discounting the village shop, Talmac's three focal points were the church, the inn, and the army post. Don Henrico Mendoza did not live in Talmac itself. His *casa grande* stood in its own grounds, which were surrounded by the small houses allotted to his private police force, a body of tough, impassive-looking men who earned between four and ten times as much as the *campesinos* who worked in the coffee fields. The army post had been established at Talmac in consequence of a visit which Don Henrico paid to Colonel Zambrano. The two men knew each other from Cielo, where they had both attended the same Jesuit school. Don Henrico had completed his education in the United States whereas Colonel Zambrano received his professional training at Conciencia's military academy. Their interests differed, but on the morning of their meeting Don Henrico said a number of things which Colonel Zambrano found extremely interesting.

Don Henrico reported that guerrilla units had stepped up their activities round Talmac in recent months. They usually operated in groups of ten to fifteen men who suddenly marched into villages and tried to win new recruits. Their conduct had been unobjectionable except in a few cases, when they shot supporters of Don Henrico and left their bodies on public display. A number of his workers had vanished into the mountains, though not too many as yet. However, his bodyguards had often noticed parties of *campesinos* setting off for unknown destinations at nightfall, and he suspected that they took part in raids on neighbouring villages. He had instructed his plantation manager to try and glean more details, but it was no use. Everyone was as silent as the grave. Don Henrico felt as if he were hemmed in by a wall of hostility. He confessed to Colonel Zambrano that he found it disagreeable. Running a plantation under these conditions was no joke. After all, he produced some of the finest coffee in Conciencia – why, it was even advertised abroad. He had discussed the situation with the parish priest, who only visited Talmac on Sundays. The priest had tried to set his mind at rest by promising to deliver a sermon on loyalty, but Don Henrico had only laughed at this. The men never went to church. However, they did send their families, so perhaps the womenfolk would pass on what the *cura* had said.

The strategist in Colonel Zambrano came to life. The fact that there were sizeable concentrations of guerilleros in the Talmac district might mean that Rodriguez Tobar had set up his headquarters somewhere near by. If a local *campesino* could be persuaded to talk, Zambrano would be well on the way to capturing one of the most dangerous rebels in Conciencia.

'I'll send a half-company to Talmac, Don Henrico,' he promised, and the landowner drove back to his plantation feeling well satisfied.

As soon as Don Henrico had gone Zambrano sent for Lieutenant Losano. He secretly detested Losano, but the man had more initiative than any other officer under his command.

Losano commanded a mobile unit equipped with modern weapons including Browning automatics and Madsen MG30s. The lieutenant was a brute who had been further brutalized by life in the army. His sang-froid was such that he could calmly place the muzzle of his pistol against a man's neck and pull the trigger if he refused to talk. Killing meant no more to him than food and drink, in fact food and drink were more important. Zambrano knew nothing of Losano's emotions and would not have been surprised to learn that he had none.

Losano had been to Panama, where anti-Castro Cuban, Haitian and Guatemalan instructors supervised by senior U.S. Army officers had trained him in the techniques of guerrilla warfare. They taught him to kill or be killed on the principle that murder was an instrument of policy and a form of self-defence. It all meant little to Losano. He was a tough, cold-blooded killer, a man of few words whose black-olive eyes seemed to scythe through his enemies as if they were thin air.

There was a knock at Zambrano's door.

'You sent for me, Colonel?'

The colonel left Losano standing at attention and studied him for a few moments. Losano was slim and well-built, with the almost square shoulders and slender waist of the born athlete. He had a small thin-lipped mouth, broad cheekbones and a low forehead.

The black wavy hair sprouted just above the eyebrows. His dark eyes had a permanently cold and watchful expression.

'What do you know of Rodriguez Tobar, Lieutenant?' asked Zambrano. 'Sit down and make yourself comfortable, by the way. Cigarette?'

Losano took a chair but politely declined the cigarette.

'I'm aware that he knows a hundred times more about guerrilla warfare than we do, Colonel.'

'Are you familiar with his previous history?'

Losano permitted himself a faint smirk.

'Of course. Wife and daughter raped, son shot. That was the work of the police, the damned fools.'

'Why fools, Lieutenant?'

'Because we might have been able to bribe him later on. A man who's tied to a tree and forced to watch his wife and daughter being raped doesn't take bribes, Colonel. God knows how many men we've lost over the years, just because those randy bastards couldn't control themselves. Any peasant-girl would have done, but they had to pick on the daughter of a man like Tobar. No sense of discrimination, to put it mildly.'

Zambrano eyed the man in silence. Callous he might be, but his words were testimony to his good judgement and common sense. Brutal he might be, but Zambrano was sure that he would use his brutality to good effect. He had his men well in hand, and if he were appointed commandant of Talmac the *campesinos* would tremble in their straw sandals. Authority would be restored there, and not before time, because Tobar was expanding the area under his control kilometre by square kilometre in spite of the weapons at the army's disposal. These included Browning 50mm. machine-guns, which were incredibly accurate, and M79 grenade-throwers. The latter resembled over-sized rifles but projected grenades which had already blown a number of guerilleros to pieces.

'I've decided to appoint you commandant of Talmac. You'll have a completely free hand.'

There was no change in Lieutenant Losano's expression apart from a slight tightening of the lips.

'Is that where Don Henrico Mendoza has his coffee plantation?' he asked.

Zambrano nodded.

'Yes, and now listen. Medium-sized guerrilla units have been sighted round Talmac in recent weeks, and Don Henrico thinks they're receiving help from the *campesinos*. It's the same old story

– they work on the plantation by day and fight with the guerilleros by night. Your job will be to stop them. Use any means you can think of – within reason. I won't breathe down your neck if you do something unwise, as you did recently, but don't push your luck. Understand?'

Zambrano paused and eyed the lieutenant again. He speculated on the depths of cruelty that lay behind Losano's inscrutable mask of a face. A few weeks ago he had detained some *campesinos* and found arms hidden in their huts. He asked where they had come from but the *campesinos* would not talk, so he had driven their women and children – ten in all – into one of the huts and trained a machine-gun on them. When the men tried to resist he had slit their throats.

The colonel wondered if it was right to use a man of Losano's calibre but came to the conclusion that it was necessary. Losano was reputed to be one of the best anti-guerrilla specialists in Conciencia and had been personally responsible for the annihilation of five guerrilla units. Besides, the guerilleros were not models of compassion themselves, and Zambrano often shuddered at the thought of falling into their hands.

'I understand, Colonel.'

'I don't want any outcries in the press, Losano. Whatever measures you adopt at Talmac, don't involve me, let alone Don Henrico. Operate alone and without witnesses – you follow me? That other business would have cost you your job if I hadn't bribed at least five people, and you can thank your lucky stars that John Wells wasn't here at the time. I don't want any repetitions, so watch it.'

Losano nodded.

'Certainly, Colonel. I'll be careful, but I wish you could suggest another way of getting the scum to talk. Fear is the only thing that works, and they wouldn't be afraid if I behaved like a father confessor.'

The man was right, Zambrano reflected. If you trained men to kill you could hardly take it amiss when they did so. If you turned human beings into animals you could hardly expect them to behave otherwise. And if you taught them that a guerillero was a mad dog they naturally treated him like one. It was fortunate, in the long run, or Tobar and his men would have massacred even more people than they had already.

'Very well, get your men ready to move out and leave tomorrow. Call on Don Henrico when you arrive and talk the whole thing over with him. Choose a good site for your headquarters. Post pickets at either end of the village and keep them on their toes. Try to buy information – I'll give you the necessary funds. One more thing: I don't know for certain, but I get the feeling that Talmac isn't too far from Tobar's headquarters. If you manage to catch him, don't kill him. I want him alive, or the secret police will give me hell. Understand?'

Losano stood up.

'Anything more, Colonel?'

Zambrano shook his head.

'No, just make sure that all goes well. Oh yes, there is one thing. Look in on Lieutenant Wells and tell him I'd like to see him.'

John Wells was a tall and lanky Texan who spoke Spanish with the fluency of a native. He was the complete antithesis of Losano in outward appearance but he had also received his specialized training at Southern Command. Although technically more skilful, he lacked the brutality of Losano, with whom he got on reasonably well. But then, John Wells got on with everyone. He had a disarmingly straightforward manner and a tremendous zest for life, which he regarded as one long adventure. He also lacked the hatred of guerilleros with which Losano had probably been inoculated as a child. That was why he took a more detached view of the situation and was slower to react emotionally. He looked on the guerilleros simply as enemies who had to be destroyed by military means. He did not share Losano's contemptuous view of the war in the mountains. His opponents were well-led men who knew how to shoot; consequently, the Conciencian army must be trained to perform with equal efficiency. To Wells, the enemy was neither liberal nor Marxist, simply a man with a gun who would blow your brains out if he beat you to the draw. The moral was, shoot first.

Wells saluted casually and sat down uninvited. He and Zambrano were on good terms.

'Our scheme to get Guillermo de la Cruz shot by Tobar's guerilleros didn't work, John,' Zambrano said. 'On the contrary, it looks as if de la Cruz has executed five of Tobar's men. Five rebels fewer without our having to lift a finger – that's something, at least.'

John Wells looked dubious.

'The bodies haven't been found,' he replied. 'Also our man has vanished without trace. To be honest, Colonel, I don't believe a word of the *cantinero*'s story.'

'How do you mean?'

157

Zambrano found it excessively warm in spite of the humming fan above his head.

'My guess is that Guillermo de la Cruz has outsmarted us again.'

'What makes you think so?'

'I've been trying to reconstruct what happened. It all looks a bit too neat. If de la Cruz had really shot Tobar's men we'd never have heard about it. It would only have meant trouble for him.'

'You mean the man we planted was made to talk?'

Wells nodded.

'Sure, and I reckon the worms are busy with his carcase right now. The guerilleros don't like traitors – you know that as well as I do.'

Zambrano heaved a sigh.

'I sometimes think I'm wasting my time here,' he said. 'There are moments when I doubt if it's worth it, John.'

'It's worth it, Colonel. You represent law and order round here. If it wasn't for you there'd be an even worse reign of terror.'

Zambrano stared at the American for some seconds. Then he said quietly: 'Are you fond of this country, John?'

Wells seemed to be puzzled by the question.

'What makes you ask?'

'Because I often wonder why you're here at all. Is it because your country wants to protect its investments or because, big and powerful as it is, it's afraid of the guerilleros?'

John Wells shrugged his shoulders and grinned.

'My country's intentions are high-level politics, Colonel, and if there's one thing I've never had anything to do with it's politics. I'm a soldier. I fight when and where I'm ordered to. I was posted to Southern Command without being consulted. I'm ready to serve anywhere the top brass sends me. It's part of the job.'

'So you don't feel any hatred?'

Wells stared at him in surprise.

'Why should I hate anyone, Colonel? A guy who's eaten up with hatred doesn't last long in a shooting war. You have to play it cool if you want to earn your pension. Hatred is for peace marchers.'

'And love?'

The lieutenant grinned.

'Plenty of pretty women in your country, Colonel.'

Zambrano waved the remark aside impatiently.

'I didn't mean that kind of love.'

Wells lit a cigarette and pondered. He was a member of the C.I.A. as well as an anti-guerrilla specialist, so he knew the statistics. There had been times in his career, in Vietnam, for example, when he knew for certain that three or four hundred American troops had been killed in a single engagement. The whole world had known it as well. But did the world also know that, in twenty years of the most ferocious civil war Latin America had ever witnessed, some four hundred thousand people had lost their lives? He leant towards Colonel Zambrano without answering his question.

'Losano just told me you're sending him to take over at Talmac. Is that right?'

Zambrano nodded.

Wells looked at the man behind the desk. He liked the colonel a great deal. Zambrano was an efficient officer and a skilled tactician. He was taller than the average Conciencian. Wells put him at about forty, though his greying hair made him look older. He was married and had five children who lived with his wife in Cielo. He visited them every fourteen days.

'Is that a good idea, Colonel?'

Something in his tone made Zambrano look up.

'What do you mean?'

'What I say. Is it a good idea to let him loose – give him an independent command?'

Zambrano's expression changed. His eyes narrowed and his mouth grew stern.

'That is my business, Lieutenant, not yours.'

'May I remind you, Colonel, that the United States is supplying you with arms, most of them free of charge?'

'That is a matter for President Colombo. It doesn't concern me. If you have any complaints to make about my orders, address them to him. I'm in command here. This is a fight between Conciencians, not a Yankee war. I hope I make myself clear.'

John Wells stood up and ambled to the door, but just before he reached it he swung round. 'Set one mad dog on another, Colonel, and you're liable to get bitten yourself. That's all I wanted to point out. Sorry we don't see eye to eye for once.'

He leant against the door and ground his cigarette out with his heel.

'You asked me about love and hatred, Colonel. Better leave them out of it. This kind of war should be fought without either. They only get in the way. Good morning, Colonel.'

Zambrano rose to his feet.

'John?'

'Yes, Colonel?'

'I asked you if you were fond of this country. You never gave me an answer.'

Wells shrugged.

'You know the trouble with Conciencia? Nobody can stand to hear the truth. If you really want an answer, *bueno*, okay. I know I'm a *gringo*, a damn *Yanqui*, and a few other complimentary terms in the same price-range. We aren't particularly respected here, Colonel, neither up top nor down below. At least the ordinary folk are honest – they call us capitalist bloodsuckers and neo-imperialists. The top brass share their opinion of us but they need our dollars. Could you love a country where you're not wanted? The guerilleros may be able to, but I can't. So long, Colonel.'

Wells closed the door quietly behind him, leaving the colonel alone at his desk. Zambrano picked up the framed photograph of his wife and children and told himself that he, at least, had something to fight for: his children, who would lose their freedom under Communism, the freedom for which Simon Bolívar had fought. He would not only continue the struggle for as long as he lived but do his best to destroy anyone who threatened that freedom, guerilleros first and foremost. Satisfied, he replaced the silver frame on his desk and resumed work on the report which he had begun just before Don Henrico arrived from Talmac.

The men of Losano's combat group, bristling with weapons, roared into Talmac trailing a cloud of dust behind their U.S. Army jeeps. The *campesinos* stared at the green paratroop uniforms and shivered.

Lieutenant Losano took stock of his surroundings. The village was built on a steep slope and presented the same time-honoured picture as any other mountain village. Tethered outside the huts, flea-bitten donkeys and skinny horses waited patiently in the broiling sun. The plaza was dominated by an equestrian statue of Simon Bolívar, and the church was painted a cloying shade of blue which hurt the eyes. The café with shop attached was called the *Santa Catalina*, and the hovels of the inhabitants jostled each other closely on both sides of the unpaved street. Dogs yapped and children raced along behind the jeeps as they drew up in the plaza, where Don Henrico and his bodyguards stood ready to greet them.

Losano jumped out, adjusted his holster, cast a distasteful glance at the dust on his gleaming boots, and saluted smartly. It was not entirely clear whether the compliment was directed at Don Henrico or Simon Bolívar.

'Welcome to Talmac, Lieutenant,' said Don Henrico, scrutinizing the newcomer with interest. He was satisfied with what he saw but had to admit that a sudden chill ran down his spine when he glimpsed the cold ferocity in the lieutenant's eyes.

'The house over there has already been cleared. There are two large rooms for you and your sergeant, storage space for weapons and accommodation for your men. Smaller houses are also available for the pickets at either end of the village, and I've found a few women to cook for you.'

Losano shook his head.

'No, no women. If my men want women they can get them in the village. Women gossip, and I don't want that.'

'Very well, I'll tell them their services aren't required. You've brought a cook of your own, I imagine?'

'Yes, we have to operate as a self-contained unit. If this place is the rat's nest you say it is, I must work on the assumption that nobody's to be trusted.'

They walked silently into the headquarters building and inspected it.

'Sergeant Gomez!'

'Yes, Lieutenant?'

'You take the room on the left, I'll take the one on the right. Get the men settled in quickly. I have to speak to Don Henrico.'

They drove to the *casa grande*. When they were seated comfortably in the patio, Losano said:

'Well, Don Henrico, how are things going?'

A shadow crossed the landowner's face.

'To be honest, from bad to worse. I don't have a moment's peace. I know what has happened to a number of my friends and associates on other plantations – abduction, torture and death, in spite of military protection and careful surveillance. I've already packed my wife and daughters off to Cielo, but I don't propose to leave myself. My own men are reliable. They keep watch day and night, but it's exhausting in the long run. I'm glad you've come.'

'What about your workers?'

Don Henrico's face became cold and arrogant.

'My workers? I've never trusted them in my life. They're stupid, lazy, and, when they're drunk, dangerous. I sometimes think they're animals, not human beings.'

Losano's lips twisted in a half-smile.

'Have you carried out any house-to-house checks?'

'No, it would only worsen the atmosphere.'

Don Henrico went inside and came back with a bottle of wine

and some glasses. He glanced at Losano as he poured, and in that instant the two men realized that they were kindred spirits.

'You're in charge here, Lieutenant. You must do whatever you think fit. If you have to lean on a couple of the swine – yes, even if you lean on them so hard you squash them – I shall look the other way. It's time somebody took this place in hand. I drink to the success of your new command.'

Losano swallowed the contents of his glass and said: 'Where do you suggest I start?'

The landowner understood at once.

'Try searching the hut of Jorge and Pablo. Anyone will tell you where they live.'

'Jorge and Pablo?'

'Yes, I don't know for sure, but at least they've got brains. Get rid of those two and the rest of the zombies that live here will come to heel. You don't know this district, Lieutenant, but it doesn't breed men, just a kind of two-legged animal which happens to have the power of speech. Liquor, sex and the occasional brawl – that's their life in a nutshell. I sometimes wonder how a civilized man like me has managed to endure living among these human cattle for so long. No, as far as I'm concerned you needn't waste any sympathy on them.'

'Are you being serious, Don Henrico?'

There was a brief silence. The landowner stared at Losano as though he doubted his sanity.

'What do you mean, serious?'

'Precisely what I say.'

Don Henrico took a small sip of wine, ran his tongue round his lips and then shrugged.

'But of course. Have you seen how they live? How they wallow in filth? How many children they have? Just consider how much of their wages goes on liquor. If I paid them more they'd drink more . . . And now some of them have got the idea that the guerilleros are their passport to salvation.'

'I can count on your full support, then?'

Don Henrico nodded.

'You certainly can. I give you a free hand. The only thing they've any respect for in that godforsaken village is the big stick. To me they're lower than slaves. At least slaves work, but these people don't know the meaning of the word. If I didn't have my overseers, nobody would do a hand's turn on this plantation.'

'Jorge and Pablo,' Losano repeated as he got up. 'They won't be expecting us to act at once. *Hasta la vista*, Don Henrico, and start looking the other way from now on. It's time the *campesinos* of Talmac learnt their first lesson.'

Jorge and Pablo were friends. They lived in a hut beside the main street and hid weapons in it. Their links with the guerilleros were of long standing and the information they provided was of great value to Tobar and his men.

A score of *campesinos* had joined them in the course of the years. They operated freely because the members of Don Henrico's private army never showed themselves in the village at night for fear of leaving the *casa grande* unguarded. The *campesinos* disappeared singly into the mountains for a few days at a time and took part in raids on other villages. They also supplied the guerilleros with food, for which they were generously paid.

Jorge was the more taciturn of the two, Pablo the tougher. The arms were concealed under the floor and the supplies of food in a chest buried in the garden. The two men looked on impassively as Lieutenant Losano's well-equipped unit moved into the village. They did not head for their hut until the soldiers were safely inside their billet.

'*Madre de Dios*,' said Jorge, his hands trembling, 'we must get rid of those guns.'

Pablo's brown face, with its traces of Indian blood, was a grim mask. He said:

'They won't come today, but I don't trust Don Henrico. He may have a plan of some kind. Did you see that lieutenant's face?'

Jorge sat down on an old crate and lit a cigarette.

'Yes, the face of a murderer. I know the type.'

They fell silent. Both of them sensed that fear had crept into the village on the heels of the soldiers. All down the street, other people would also be sitting in their huts, silently staring at the grimy and pitiful possessions which were the meagre legacy of a lifetime.

'Get in touch with the guerilleros,' Pablo said softly, as though to himself.

'Now, this minute? *Madre de Dios!* What about you?'

'Don't worry about me, I'll get away. I've had more than one brush with the army in my time. Anyway, they won't come today.'

'What if you're wrong?'

Pablo drew a deep breath.

'If I'm wrong they may walk through that door at any moment

163

and catch both of us instead of me alone. And now go, as fast as you can.'

Jorge stood up. He looked exactly like any other man in Talmac, just as poverty-stricken and, at first glance, just as apathetic, a brown-skinned peasant with a machete, a sombrero, and a ruana draped over his shoulder. He walked through the village, turned off up a narrow track leading into the mountains, and was out of sight in a few minutes.

He wondered why Pablo hadn't come with him. He shouldn't have stayed behind, but obstinacy had always been his long suit. Once Pablo made up his mind nobody could change it for him, not even Jorge. Perhaps that was why Tobar had put him in command of the village. He knew what he wanted and kept his mouth shut. Even if they took him prisoner they would never get anything out of him, however long they tortured him. Pablo was as tough as seasoned leather.

Still pondering, Jorge swiftly climbed the winding path that led to the area where he hoped to find Rodriguez Tobar's guerrilla unit. The mountains had turned an almost transparent shade of violet which contrasted strangely with the luxuriant green of the vegetation. The sun, now at its zenith, seemed to stab the granite-hard mountainside with a shower of fiery arrows.

Jorge soon felt rivulets of sweat trickling down his neck and chest, but he kept going. He had climbed this steep path often enough in the past, but never with a more important message. Losano would probably send out his first patrol next day, so the guerilleros must be warned.

Two hours later, shortly before Jorge reached the guerilleros' hide-out, a squad of Losano's men commanded by Sergeant Gomez came to search Pablo's hut. They appeared so suddenly that he had no chance of escape. Instead, he leant casually against the wall as they hurled his wretched furniture into the street and tore up the floor. Having unearthed four rifles and some ammunition, they bore them triumphantly to Losano. Pablo was also hauled off to the army post and into Losano's bedroom-cum-office, which was still in a state of disarray.

'Four rifles? What would you need rifles for, you dog of a traitor?'

Before Pablo could utter a word, Losano's riding-crop whistled through the air and bit into his cheek.

'Speak up!'

Red blotches appeared on Lieutenant Losano's face, a rare sign of emotion. Sergeant Gomez knew what they meant. Losano's anger was like the cold hard ferocity of a snake which sinks its fangs into human flesh.

'Sergeant, come here a minute!'

Gomez eyed the *campesino* dispassionately. His emotions were not aroused. This was his daily work, a mere formality in the life of a soldier. It had to be. Regulations and orders prescribed it, that was all. His conscience never troubled him afterwards, and nobody slept more soundly at night than the intrepid sergeant – even his men joked about it.

'Out with it, man,' he said quietly. 'Anyone would think you didn't know who we are. We'll torture you for as long as it takes to make you talk – or don't you believe me?'

'I use the guns for hunting, Excellency.'

Pablo gave an involuntary cry. This time the riding-crop laid his right cheek open so that blood dripped on to his grubby shirt.

'Yes, for hunting men, you dog! Tell me the truth or I'll slit your belly from top to bottom.'

Pablo did not reply. What was he to say? To confess that he was working with the guerilleros would earn him a bullet in the back – shot while attempting to escape, the green devils' favourite trick. If he denied it they would torture him. If he turned traitor the guerilleros would track him down and give him the treatment reserved for cowards and renegades – another bullet. He decided to say nothing at all.

'Strip him!' commanded Lieutenant Losano.

Sergeant Gomez tore the shirt from Pablo's thin body in one movement and then cut the string that held his trousers up so that they fell round his ankles. Naked, the wiry little *campesino* faced his persecutors.

'Give us the names of your guerillero friends!'

'I know no guerilleros, Excellency.'

The room fell silent. From outside came the barking of dogs and the heavy tramp of soldiers carrying weapons and straw palliasses into the house. The sun was almost white now, and the dome of the sky hung, quivering with heat, above the dusty village street. Pablo felt a strange calm descend on him. So this was the end: a tall, slim man with eyes like black olives, dressed in the green uniform of the army and wielding a riding-crop which pierced his skin like a shaft of lightning. It was strange, but he felt no fear. Perhaps he had been inwardly steeling himself against this moment for so many years that it was no more than a repetition of what his waking nightmares had led him to expect. A lieutenant and a sergeant who eyed him as if he were a bug, not a human being. So that's how it ends, thought Pablo, and sensed a certain irony in the situation. Everyone had to die sometime. One man died of a heart attack, another of malnutrition, another of leprosy or cancer or tuberculosis. He was going to die by torture.

Losano shrugged his shoulders and laughed.

'Very well, Sergeant, take him outside and tie him to a tree. I won't be long.'

Within a few minutes, the whole village knew that Pablo had been arrested. The rumour spread more swiftly than anyone would have thought possible. It was whispered that they had found rifles and machine-guns destined for the guerilleros in his hut. The plaza where the menfolk habitually lounged in the shade of Simon Bolívar, the Liberator, emptied. The sun spewed heat over the two slender towers of the church, and even the dogs ran off with their tails clamped between their legs. Here and there a man mounted his horse and furtively rode away. Women watched and waited anxiously for their husbands. Cursing soldiers searched a few more huts and, when they found nothing, compensated themselves with the women and girls who lived in them.

Everyone in Talmac knew Pablo just as Pablo knew everyone. He had actually been a student at one time, it was said, and that, in a village where more than seventy per cent were illiterate, was something quite exceptional. He sometimes wrote letters for people and kept the shopkeeper's accounts for him. Not that he occupied any official position, this made him in a certain sense a man of authority like his friend Jorge, who was even reputed to understand a foreign tongue. Both of them hated Don Henrico, and it was they who had brought it home to the villagers quite how miserably paid they were for picking coffee on his plantation. They all secretly abhorred the *patrón* but never dared to say so out loud. They swept off their straw hats and bowed when he passed by. Truth to tell, Don Henrico could seem quite amiable at times, especially when he patted a child's head or inquired after its parents' health. Perhaps Pablo and Jorge had stirred up too much trouble in the village – who could tell? They were used to their low wages. They knew what they could earn in a year. They drank their *aguardiente* and watched the mountains change from black to blue or mauve, the sky from brilliant blue to cloud-swept grey. Their children either survived or died at the whim of Almighty God, who presided over everything from on high and meted out certain damnation to those who refused to bow their heads in reverence. Their whole life was compounded of grief and suffering, but they were barely conscious of it. Grief and suffering were the inescapable norm. They even learned to smile at them. Some things were naturally beyond their reach – for instance, the sort of earthly paradise accessible only to the *patrón*, who drove around in a car, owned horses, had servants to wait on him and *campesinos* to work for him. No, the *patrón* was all right. He was friendly on occasions but he also had to be strict. Few people really resented this. The *patrón* was as much a part of their world as their starving children. He was sent by God. He reigned over them, and his word was law. Anyone who opposed him suffered accordingly. Those who broke the law had to bear the consequences.

It had been like that since time out of mind. How were they to know that their homes should have had water and sanitation or that their nights might have been brightened by electricity? They had never known these things. How were they to know that their children should go to school? There was a schoolhouse, in fact, but it had been empty for years in spite of the government's education programme. But what was Talmac, after all? A village which existed by the grace of Don Henrico. If he abandoned his coffee plantation every man in the village would be out of work, and what would become of them then? Accordingly, they gave thanks to God for the *patrón*'s continuing good health.

Pablo and Jorge had pointed out that they could grow coffee themselves if they set up a co-operative. The profits now garnered by Don Henrico would then flow into their own pockets. They had found the idea almost unimaginable at first. Money of their own and no more indebtedness to the *patrón*? It was a vision of infinite loveliness. They would be able to build better houses. Their women would no longer have to fetch water on foot and wash clothes in the icy mountain stream. They would have piped water and radio sets.

They often spoke of these things, even though they seemed more dreamlike than real.

But now Pablo had been arrested. The lieutenant would torture him, and Pablo's death would mean the end of their dream. No new houses, no piped water, no electric light, just terror.

Pablo was lashed to a tree so tightly that the ropes sank into his flesh. He felt the sun burning hot on his naked body and knew that he was seeing Talmac for the last time. He tried to pray. 'Hail Mary, full of grace . . .'

167

A bullet smacked into the tree above his head and another buried itself in the trunk close beside his neck.

'Make them hit me soon, Mother of God,' he prayed. 'Make them shoot straight. I do not know how long I can endure this. I only know that these men are capable of anything. They are wild beasts, not human beings.'

'The names of your guerillero friends, you treacherous dog!'

A kick in the stomach made him gasp, and he urinated.

Losano laughed loudly.

'Look at that, Sergeant! The man's wetting himself with fear. Fetch me a bottle of rum. I need something to take the taste away.'

Losano sauntered up to the tree with a cigarette dangling from his lips. He looked at the bound man as if he were a carcase of beef. Deliberately, he holstered his pistol and buttoned the flap. His voice sank to a whisper, and his hot breath caressed Pablo's cheek.

'Listen to me, *amigo*. Confess and we'll let you go, I give you my word as an officer. Tell me the names of your friends. You want a cigarette and a swig of rum? All right, but first you must talk. I don't understand your attitude. Why shield those traitors? They're wild animals – they live like the puma of the jungle. Turn your back on them and join us instead.'

Pablo knew what such a promise was worth when it came from a lieutenant who commanded the green devils of the national army. He would never keep his word. They did not speak the same language. It meant nothing if one promised an animal not to beat it any more. One did not keep one's word to an animal any more than one did to a guerillero. So Pablo spat full in Losano's face, right between the black-olive eyes. A blob of sputum was the only weapon he had. And when he had done it he thought: now let him draw his pistol and fire in blind rage. The ground will reel beneath my feet and turn into a huge red disk, spinning faster and faster until nothing remains but endless night and an utter silence which may – who knows? – lead to immortality.

But Losano did nothing of the kind. Calmly, he pulled out a handkerchief and wiped the spittle from his face as if it were an everyday occurrence that prisoners should treat him in this way. Then he removed the cigarette from his lips and, with quiet deliberation, pressed the glowing end against the prisoner's thin chest so that Pablo could smell his own scorched flesh.

'So you are one of the scum who shoot our soldiers in the back,' he said. 'That settles it. I shall show this village once and for all what we do to dirty rebels.'

168

He turned and shouted: 'Sergeant, where the hell's that rum? I said I was thirsty.'

Gomez came doubling up and Losano snatched the bottle from his hand. He removed the cork and drank, feeling the fiery spirit course down his throat and into his stomach. Then he turned to look at the naked figure lashed to the tree. Losano did not know him, had never seen him before. The man was skinny like all *campesinos* and close-mouthed like all who helped the guerilleros. In that respect they were all alike.

He drew his pistol.

'All right, Sergeant, untie him. He won't get far.'

Pablo swayed when he felt the ropes fall away. He tried to move, but it was no good. No one spoke. He stood there, breathing with difficulty, until he felt the blood start to flow again. Did freedom mean death after all? The body lying stiff in its six feet of ground, the spirit soaring like a bird above the beautiful mountainscape of Talmac, for ever beyond the reach of bullets, suffering, cruelty and despair? It was like a vision in which pain had ceased to play a part. *Amor, felicidad, belleza*, a land of liberty, equality and fraternity . . .

'Well, why don't you run for it, you dog?'

Two pistols were trained on him. Soon they would spit fire. He would feel a jolt, harder than the unexpected kick of a horse, and then he would join the hundreds of thousands who had died the same way. And suddenly he saw the sun again, beating down on the whitewashed hovels of Talmac. He must not die because his death would extinguish all hope in the village. The people would think it had all been in vain. They would again pray to the God who had not helped them and again listen to the priest who promised them a better life in heaven, not on earth. The great lie would triumph thanks to the *cura* and the *haciendero*, who forbade people even to dream. Don Henrico would laugh because it had all been so easy and drink a glass of wine with the coldblooded murderers who had quelled an entire village with the death of a single man. And from that moment onwards Pablo began to think feverishly. Only a diversion could save him now. They were bound to shoot soon. Then came a reprieve.

'Why not have some rum? Just a mouthful – you must be thirsty.'

Pablo was thirsty. The welts on his face were still dripping blood on to his chest.

They were so sure of themselves, he thought. Well armed, well fed, tough, merciless. That was how they held the country down. They must have come at Don Henrico's request. It was the eternal

Conciencian pattern. Landowner and priest, army and police. And there they stood now. Two men, minions of those who ruled in Cielo, bloodhounds sent by bloodhounds.

Suddenly he froze. He had heard a faint rustle in the tall undergrowth near the tree. He stood stock-still. Someone was there, but who? The guerilleros? Impossible, Jorge could never have reached them so quickly on foot. In that case, who was it? He must play for time, if only a few minutes. Hold their hands, *Dios!* Perhaps there was still a chance after all.

'What if I talk?' he asked.

'You get a cigarette.'

'And afterwards?'

'Afterwards you can go wherever you like.'

'No, you will shoot me just the same. That is the usual way.'

Losano holstered his pistol again. Only the sergeant was covering Pablo now.

The lieutenant's face twisted in a sardonic grin. Triumph shone in his eyes. It would not be the first time he had broken a prisoner's resistance. They were all cowards at heart. One good look at the great god death and they crumbled, almost to a man. This one would talk, name names. Others would be arrested and they would talk too. A chain reaction, and at the end of the chain Rodriguez Tobar, with a price on his head which would make him, Losano, a rich man overnight.

'Well, speak up!'

A shot broke the silence, but it did not come from Gomez or Losano. The sergeant's face registered dull amazement as he stared down at the patch of blood which was slowly staining his green shirt. Then he fell over backwards and lay still. Furiously, Losano drew his gun and emptied the magazine into the undergrowth at the spot where Pablo had disappeared. Soldiers came running up, firing their rifles. They combed the area behind the tree, but all they found was the bullet-riddled body of a boy who could not have been more than fourteen. There was a rifle on the ground beside him and a look of exaltation on his face. As for Pablo, he was already scrambling up the narrow path that led into the mountains, the path that Jorge had taken when he went in search of the guerilleros hours before.

He never saw the child who saved his life. A bare fifteen minutes after the first shot, the boy's body was thrown into a hastily dug hole in the ground, an anonymous memorial to the infamy of those who had killed him.

But that was the end of resistance in Talmac. Hearing nothing more from the guerilleros and subjected to a mounting reign of terror by Lieutenant Losano and Sergeant Gomez, who soon recovered from his wound, the villagers relapsed into torpor and bowed to military authority just as they had done to the landowner for centuries.

The guerrilla base from which Rodriguez Tobar was directing operations against the government troops lay high in the mountains about thirty kilometres from Talmac. It consisted of a command post, a radio station, an armoury, a small field hospital, and a store of weapons, ammunition and food. The track that led there, steep but just passable on horseback, was guarded day and night by heavily armed guerilleros. Concealed machine-gun nests had been installed at three different points, and outposts equipped with walkie-talkies reported any unusual movement in the valley below.

It had taken Tobar a long time to establish this base. His first headquarters, about forty kilometres away, had been detected by the army and completely destroyed. Large quantities of arms were lost, together with medical supplies, foodstuffs, and electrically detonated mines. It had been a blow from which the guerilleros took many months to recover, but it had taught Tobar a valuable lesson. Complete control of a large area was essential before one could afford to set up a permanent camp.

Colonel Zambrano, his anti-guerrilla experts and the C.I.A. specialists attached to his command had naturally laughed at this first fiasco, but their amusement waned when Tobar, with a hundred and sixty men divided into two combat groups, ambushed an entire army battalion as it was marching through the mountains and cut it to ribbons. The guerilleros recaptured their trucks, weapons, mines and ammunition, and Tobar was again able to conduct minor operations designed to persuade villagers that it was wiser to support the rebel cause.

The key to this policy was simple. One had only to make the *campesinos* feel that power rested with the guerilleros, not the army, and they came over of their own accord. People living in the shadow of the Andes and on the flanks of that massive mountain range had for centuries bowed to authority, whether exercised by landowners and their entourage of hired killers or by the army and police, who acceded to the *hacienderos*' every wish and asked no questions. This authority had been consistently upheld by brute force, and Tobar would have been quite mad to proceed upon the assumption that the *campesinos* would readily rise against people who had kept them on their knees for so many generations that subservience was in their blood. Finally, Tobar had realized that his only means of winning over the *campesinos* was a graphic demonstration that armed guerilleros were more than a match for all the soldiers, policemen and landowners put together, also that traitors could expect to die a horrible death. From then onwards, small guerrilla patrols of ten or fifteen men combed a different part of the region every night. They were trained at base camp and skilled in the art of ambush. Relentlessly, they shot down oppressors of the people and left their bodies where everyone would see them. Tobar assumed personal command during major attacks. He carefully worked out his tactics in advance, sometimes creating panic and confusion by isolating part of a column from the main body. Tobar fully realized that the guerilleros' life was a hard one and that his men must be in prime physical condition if they were to remain on the move day and night, toting their heavy packs through the jungle and traversing difficult and dangerous terrain without leaving tell-tale tracks behind. For that reason their training was quite as tough as any course at the Southern Command anti-guerrilla camp in Panama, compared with which the so-called 'hard' camps of the U.S. Marine Corps were holiday resorts.

The biggest initial problem had been that of food supplies, but this was solved with the co-operation of the *campesinos*, who bought food, hid it in their huts, and transported it to base camp under cover of darkness. Now that Lieutenant Losano had been placed in command at Talmac, other problems had arisen.

It was late afternoon, and Rodriguez Tobar was worried about Raoul Castillo, Emanuel, Pedro, Carlos and Armando. He already knew what had happened in Taloma from radio reports. He realized that they would make a detour and try to reach the guerilleros at Talmac, where he himself had been only a few days earlier. He also realized that he had fallen into a trap, and as soon as he learned the truth he abandoned the hide-out where he had interviewed the traitor whose false information had sent the five men to kill de la Cruz.

'*He*, Jorge!'

The fugitive guerillero from Talmac hurried up, saluted, and waited for orders. 'Yes, *Capitán*?'

Tobar was sitting with his back against a tree, watching the valley.

'When is Losano going on patrol from Talmac?'

'In two days' time, *Capitán*, if our information is correct.'

'Are your contacts to be trusted?'

'I don't know. Sometimes I doubt it. Their reports are becoming vague, to say the least.'

'What do the *campesinos* think of Losano?'

'They're mortally afraid of him, *Capitán*. They call him "*el Misántropo*" and his soldiers "the Green Devils". They're ruthless murderers, all of them.'

'Worse than us?'

Jorge shrugged his broad shoulders.

'It depends on your point of view.'

Rodriguez Tobar offered Jorge a cigarette.

'Sit down, Jorge, and stop looking so military. How are the men?'

'The usual trouble, *Capitán*. Friction between the intellectuals, the ex-*campesinos* and the veteran guerilleros.'

'It disappears as soon as they have to fight,' Tobar said curtly. 'Keep them at it, Jorge. Keep them so busy they don't have time to think, and make it clear to them why they're being knocked into shape.'

He stared pensively at the vast expanse of peaceful country-side spread out below him. The calm was deceptive.

'How is Pablo?' he asked, after a pause.

'That boy's death has shaken him. He broods all the time. He can't wait to see Losano hanging by his thumbs.'

'Send him to me.'

'Immediately, *Capitán*.'

Tobar was still staring down into the valley when Pablo appeared a minute later. His expression was grave and preoccupied on account of Castillo and his men, who had still not returned.

'Sit down, Pablo, I have to talk to you.'

'Certainly, *Capitán*.'

'Something on your mind?'

The scrawny little guerillero did not reply.

'Well? I expect a man to answer when I ask him a question. Are you worried about something?'

'Yes, *Capitán*.'

'What?'

'All this waiting. We ought to liberate Talmac at once.'

Tobar sighed.

'We can't liberate Talmac, *amigo* – we haven't reached that stage yet.'

'And meanwhile . . .'

'Yes, meanwhile Losano has a free hand.'

He leant forward and looked Pablo squarely in the eye.

'You don't understand yet, do you? Those people down there will have to feel a touch of the whip before they rally to our cause. After all, you didn't leave Talmac for the mountains until they tortured and almost shot you.'

Pablo's face stiffened.

'Is that why you're waiting so long?'

Tobar nodded. He gestured at the lowlands.

'The *hacienderos* and the *curas* have hammered it into their heads that we're a gang of dirty *bandoleros* and that only the authorities have right on their side. The *campesinos* must come to realize what scum the government soldiers are. They won't take us seriously until enough of them have been denounced and tortured and murdered in cold blood. You know as well as I do how many rumours they spread about us. We rape women and commit atrocities on children. What's more, the *curas* claim that we're all Communists and that God has banned Communism, so anyone who sides with us goes straight to hell.'

'So you're waiting on purpose, *Capitán* – just because of that?'

'No, not only that. Our training and equipment must be adequate before we take the offensive. Losano thinks he can retain control by terrorizing people. He's right in a sense, but he's going about it the wrong way. We must gain control, also by terrorizing people – a different set of people. I've changed my original plan for the attack on the army post. I don't think the first idea was a good one. I studied it very carefully, but there were too many weak points and we can't afford heavy casualties. In my opinion, we must concentrate on Losano and Don Henrico. Killing them would gain us a lot of popularity – probably a lot of new recruits as well.'

Pablo's gloomy face brightened a little.

'Can I take part?'

'I don't know yet. You hate Losano, and men who hate find it hard to think clearly. Hatred makes the hand tremble, my friend. An operation of this sort calls for a cool head and a steady hand. We have no use for hatred, however justified.'

'How would you feel, *Capitán*,' Pablo said, scowling, 'if Losano had stubbed his cigarette out on your chest?'

'Exactly as you do, *amigo*, but I lost dozens of men in the old days because all that inspired me was blind hatred. It wasn't until I controlled my hatred that our first successes came.'

'What are your plans, *Capitán*?'

Tobar stared at him keenly.

'I will tell you. First we hang Losano from the tree where he tortured you, and then we deal with Don Henrico.'

'What will you do with him?'

'Kidnap him.'

'When?'

'When everything has been worked out to the last detail. Are you in charge of food supplies?'

Pablo nodded.

'Good, then question every *campesino* you meet. We need a precise picture of Losano's daily routine, also Don Henrico's. Find out when they get up, when they go to bed, when they tour the area, when they meet. Neglect nothing, however trivial. Ask what guns they carry and how many guards escort them. I give you a week to discover everything. Be careful. Tell no one what we have in mind and make sure your informants keep their mouths shut. Only trust people you know well. You understand?'

Pablo beamed.

'Of course, *Capitán*.'

'In that case, you may go. Pool your information with Jorge. And above all, keep cool. Hatred never won a war yet.'

I I

The traffic in Cielo was heavier than usual. Mingling with the thousands of cars and buses were hundreds of jeeps and trucks filled with special police, scathingly referred to by the local inhabitants as '*los bandoleros de la ciudad*'. The jeeps and trucks – U.S. surplus stock and almost all of World War Two vintage – had been bought up in large quantities by the Ministry of the Interior, though it was common knowledge that some of them had been presented to the Conciencian government by the United States as a free contribution towards the maintenance of law and order. The special police were on their way to the National University, where Padre Valencia was scheduled to announce his political programme.

On the second floor of the massive United States embassy building in the Avenida Bolívar, two men stood watching the exceptional police activity. Their expressions were grim.

'I don't like the look of it,' said Thomas Cooper, the U.S. ambassador.

The man beside him, Don Ignacio Fierro, press tycoon, industrialist and landowner, gave a sidelong glance at Cooper's hawklike profile. He respected the ambassador's influence, power and political acumen. Above all, he respected the hard American dollars which he and the President had standing to their credit at a New York bank in grateful recognition of their good offices. In return, he and the President supported various North American business interests, among then the Star Oil Company, several major cocoa and coffee plantations, the capital's biggest hotel, and a number of other concerns which had set up shop in Conciencia. By arrangement, Ignacio Fierro regularly published sanguinary stories about the guerilleros, their atrocities, their attacks on buses and estates. He conveniently forgot to mention the atrocities committed by government troops and the police, let alone the secret police. In this way, his newspapers and periodicals had carefully erected a wall of odium round the guerilleros, and Thomas Cooper had grinned to himself when, during the last military parade, the anti-guerrilla units in their green paratroop uniforms were greeted with thunderous applause by the public.

Cooper was a relative newcomer to Conciencia, but in contrast to his predecessor he spoke fluent Spanish, was conversant with the literature and history of the country, and had managed to build up a good picture of what was happening there from the detailed reports compiled by his staff.

Shortly before his departure from Washington he had been summoned to the State Department and informed that he owed his selection for the post to his many years' experience as an ambassador behind the Iron Curtain.

The conversation had been an eye-opener to him. The senior State Department official had drawn his attention to the risk of social upheaval, to leaders like Fidel Castro and Che Guevara, to churchmen like Dom Helder Camara and Dom Jorge Marcus de Oliveira, and to the anti-Americanism which was steadily gaining ground in Conciencia. He had also been exhaustively briefed on key figures such as President Colombo, Cardinal Medina, Ignacio Fierro, Arturo Cuellar, Antonio Valencia, and others. Their dossiers had made fascinating reading.

Cooper turned to Fierro.

'Well, Don Ignacio, what do you think?'

The press tycoon frowned.

'I spoke to Valencia yesterday evening, at a party given by Cuellar. I offered him a sociological research job, but he refused.'

The ambassador did not speak for some moments. When he did, the reproof in his voice was faint but unmistakable.

'You were too late, Don Ignacio. You should have corralled him five years ago.'

That was the least he could say. Don Ignacio must be blind if he hadn't noticed that his fellow-countrymen were becoming sick of half-measures, sick of futile public relations exercises. Cooper was only too familiar with such propaganda campaigns and the blare of trumpets that attended their launching. Large-scale welfare projects, the founding of residential settlements for workers and *campesino* refugees from the mountains, radio courses designed to stamp out illiteracy, television appeals on behalf of those in dire need – all well-meant and occasionally successful ventures, but incapable of effecting any real changes in the country.

Left-wing groups had taken advantage of the situation to demand land reform, a thorough overhaul of the educational system, and radical administrative reorganization. They had also looked for a leader and found one in Antonio Valencia.

Understandable as he found it all, the ambassador's duty was to safeguard the heavy American investment in Latin America, which had already passed the 5 billion dollar mark. Above all, he had to prevent a growing concentration of power on the left which might endanger the interests of his own country. Cuba had proved that once and for all.

'What do the police plan to do if there's a strike at the National University?' asked Cooper.

Don Ignacio's fingers drummed impatiently on the window-sill. There were times when his dearest wish was to tell the ambassador that he was sick of economic tyranny and sweep out of the room, but that would have lost him his influence with the President. Colombo probably shared his opinion of the Americans but owed them too much, both personally and politically, to break with them. Not that Ignacio Fierro felt a hundred per cent convinced of this. It was a widely known fact that the United States had invested approximately 5 billion dollars between 1951 and 1961, but that profits during the same decade had exceeded 10 billions. Although these revenues might not have accrued directly to the U.S. Treasury, they did go to major business concerns which carried great weight with the State Department. But when all was said and done, it was safer to ingratiate oneself with Conciencia's mighty allies in the north than to alienate them, safer for oneself, safer for the big landowners and safer for the government. Apart from that, the United States was assisting the President in his campaign against the guerilleros. On balance, discretion was the best policy.

'We've done everything possible, Your Excellency,' Fierro said after a long pause. 'All units have been alerted and President Colombo will have no hesitation in proclaiming a state of national emergency if serious disturbances break out.'

The ambassador walked over to his imposing desk and stared with subdued pride at the Stars and Stripes and Presidential portrait that dominated it. Deep down, he disliked his posting to this Latin American country and the daily horse-trading that was part of an ambassador's job here. It had been different in Eastern Europe. There he had been dealing with reports on military and political matters, highly confidential reports which travelled to Washington by diplomatic courier with clockwork regularity. He could not restrain a smile at the thought of what would have happened if he had ventured to pronounce on the government's handling of affairs as he did here. He would have been expelled inside a month, with all the attendant repercussions on his career which such a scandal would have provoked. Cielo was no picnic, for all that. You had to be a tightrope-walker not to wound the sensibilities of Conciencian officialdom. On the one hand, the Conciencians suffered from a king-size inferiority complex instilled by permanent confrontation with the power of the United States; on the other, they regarded every *Norteamericano* as an uneducated boor who stomped around on Latin American culture as if he thought Conciencia was a glorified zoo instead of one of the most civilized countries in the continent, if not the entire world.

'The President is noted for his speed of decision. I'd appreciate it if you would convey my sincere respects. He's a brilliant man, as I always emphasize in my correspondence with the State Department.'

The ambassador was learning fast, Don Ignacio thought happily. He wondered what the quid pro quo would be.

Cooper sat down behind his desk and cleared his throat. Fierro realized that he was about to impart something of interest, possibly of State Department provenance. Cooper proceeded to open a folder containing press cuttings. Many of them were in English, others in French and German with neatly typed translations appended.

'Recently, Don Ignacio, reports have been appearing in the international press which did not come from our own press agencies and correspondents. They were written by Bruce Cornell, a British free-lance journalist who works for various European newspapers. Does the name mean anything to you?'

Fierro nodded.

'Yes, our security police have been watching him for some time. He's involved with Esther Graham, daughter of the Star Oil Company chief and currently employed as secretary to Padre Valencia.'

The ambassador eyed Don Ignacio keenly.

'Why don't you withdraw his visitor's permit?'

Fierro smiled.

'Colonel García declines to. His argument is that Cornell's articles will soon pay dividends.'

'In what way?'

'I can't say, but as far as I know the President has given him a free hand in the matter.'

The ambassador made no comment. He closed the file, stood up, and walked to the window again. Small groups of young people, presumably students, were making their way silently towards the National University. The streets were still thick with military vehicles, almost as though the state of emergency had already been proclaimed. Cooper debated whether to have a word with Graham sometime – perhaps it would be more advisable if his daughter continued her studies in the States. Graham needed careful handling, though.

'Could the President see me today?' he asked.

'It might be better if you called on him after Valencia's speech,' Fierro replied. 'He would welcome a talk with you, I'm sure. Thank you for sparing me so much of your valuable time, Your Excellency. I must go now. Today should be a newsworthy day.'

The ambassador shook hands with him.

'News is less important than the way it's presented,' he said. 'I know I can count on you, Don Ignacio.'

A sudden blanket of fatigue descended on Cooper as the door closed behind Fierro. He felt almost sickened by the conflict of interests that confronted him, the conflict that had robbed him of sleep for nights now and made him brusque and irritable at home. Not even the social whirl of Cielo could dispel his recent attacks of self-criticism. He was fifty-two, and what had he done with his life except play the role assigned him by the State Department? In his embassy he was constantly surrounded by people like his younger self, by up-and-comers who were never themselves and wore a social tuxedo over their street clothes, by people who were so remote from reality that they had no idea of the issues involved. He was rarely able to mix with people he liked because they were crowded out by the 'important figures' who needlessly monopolized his time and forced him to take decisions with which he privately disagreed. In such cases he had to choose between his own inclinations and the interests of his country. The latter always triumphed because he was his country's supreme representative wherever he went. He vacillated eternally between his ego and the State Department. His upbringing and education, career and ambition made the choice a fairly easy one, even though he was conscious that he all too often betrayed himself. If he had to choose between the President of Conciencia and Padre Valencia, for instance, his personal vote would go to the priest. On the other hand, Colombo presented no danger to the United States whereas the priest did. If he had to say which man he considered the more honest it would undoubtedly be Valencia, though if Valencia got his way there was a risk that

Conciencia would become a second Vietnam of the sort aspired to by Che Guevara, among others. Politically, the President was an ally of the United States and Valencia an enemy. Humanly, the President was a profiteer and Valencia a species of Latin American Christ. The ambassador studied his hands, ready to wash them like Pilate, who had once felt similar admiration for the man who was later nailed to the Cross.

He flicked the intercom. His personal secretary answered promptly.

'Yes, Your Excellency?'

Cooper smiled to himself at the sound of her calm and confident voice. It was a trifle husky, but alluringly so.

'Would you come in here a minute, Ellen?'

'Right away, Your Excellency.'

He could picture her patting her ash-blonde hair into place and freshening her lipstick a little before tip-tapping briskly down the short passage that linked their offices.

Her knock was gentle and discreet. He looked up as she entered. His eyes travelled swiftly over her body, then came to rest on her face.

'You look good, Ellen. How do you always manage to look so fresh in this climate?'

'Early nights and plenty of tennis, Your Excellency. Thank you for the compliment.'

'Sit down and put that shorthand pad away. I need to talk a little – think out loud.'

He was the loneliest man she had ever known, in spite of all his social contacts. His marriage was crumbling, though few people knew it, and his children were at college in the States. Ellen wondered why ships' captains were always painted as the loneliest men in the world. An ambassador was also surrounded by people whose future depended on him, but his loneliness was accentuated by decisions which he often had to make against his better judgement. A ship's captain steered his own course. He was the man who brought his ship through a storm, who bore sole responsibility and whose word was law. An ambassador might disagree with his government's decisions but he had to implement them just the same. It must be like dying a little every day.

'Do you know Esther Graham?' he asked.

She nodded.

'What sort of girl is she?'

Ellen pondered the question. It was hard to judge another woman from a man's standpoint. Men had different standards.

'Chic, pretty, intelligent, rather volatile, well developed mentally and physically. All in all, I'd say she had sex appeal, Your Excellency.'

He fidgeted with his tie as he felt her eyes on him, then met her gaze and held it. For the space of a second she had the strange sensation that his arms were round her.

'What about her political views?'

'They say she's a Communist, but I doubt it. Anyone round here who takes an interest in social problems is immediately branded that.'

It irked him to hear Ellen say out loud what he already knew, but she was right. Communist was the label applied to all opponents of the President, certainly those who advocated social reform. He offered his secretary a cigarette – not a familiarity which an ambassador should really have permitted himself, but it had happened quite often lately. Perhaps it had paved the way for the veiled intimacy that had grown up between them.

'Tell me, Ellen, do you know how much the United States has invested in this continent?'

She smiled.

'I typed the figures for you.'

'We have an interest in coffee, cotton, sugar, rice, tobacco, various major industries, and oil. Our shipping companies earn plenty, mainly on the tanker side. We can't afford any disruptions from men like Antonio Valencia.'

She sensed the insecurity behind his words but could find nothing reassuring to say.

'I know, Your Excellency.'

He rose and walked to the window. His figure outlined itself sharply against the sunlight as he leant against the sill.

'Poor Cuba, so far from God and so close to the United States – you know that catch-phrase, Ellen? You could apply it just as well to Conciencia. Equally, you could say: poor old States, so close to God and so far from Latin America. Some people think we've backed too many strong-men like Colombo. He co-operates most of the time, but sometimes I think he's too smart for me.'

She shook her head.

'Not smart, Your Excellency, just unscrupulous. We tend to be naive. It's part of our national character, and it isn't always pleasant to have to admit it. We invest five billion dollars in a continent where nobody can stand us – neither governments nor intellectuals nor the man in the street. We supply dictators with arms and money in the hope of imposing our democratic principles. It's illogical, in my opinion. We want peace in Conciencia, but our dollars may be buying just the opposite.'

Cooper swung round.

'Maybe,' he said quietly, 'but if they bring in a hundred per cent profit all your delicate considerations can go hang. This is a hardheaded, hard-boiled business operation. It's part of our job to see that raw materials are exported from here to the States so that they can be turned into finished products and shipped back here for the benefit of the American economy. Or didn't you realize that?'

She looked at him diffidently, blushing.

'I'm sorry, Your Excellency, I didn't mean to push my point of view.'

He stared at her in silence. Of course she didn't. She was only voicing what his colleagues seldom dared to imply, what he himself never admitted even to his immediate subordinates.

'Forget it, Ellen. I'm glad you said what you thought.'

She took the hint and got up. He followed her movements with his eyes, and once again she had the feeling that his look was an embrace.

'*Paciencia*, Ellen,' he called after her as she shut the door. She wondered what he was referring to, their own relationship or the political situation. Sitting down at her desk she rested her head on her hands for a minute or two. Their brief encounters were becoming more and more of an emotional strain. He said nothing and showed little, but the whole thing was so obvious.

Not for the first time, she thought of applying for a transfer and dismissed the idea as quickly as it came. However hopeless the future looked, he was the only thing that Conciencia had to offer her.

Valencia had asked Esther to meet him at 7 a.m. because he wanted to pay another visit to the shanty-town of El Futuro before he announced his political programme. He was already waiting outside in his car when her taxi drew up. He said little for the first few minutes and focused his whole attention on the traffic. His face was graver than she had ever seen it, the lines etched still deeper by the hard morning light and the tensions of the last few days.

'I couldn't sleep last night,' he said, and his voice sounded strained. 'From now on I shall be the prisoner of my own conscience. I feel that more strongly than I've ever done.'

She did not reply, just listened in silence because anything she had to say would have been too much. His invitation to accompany him had puzzled her a little. True, she was now his secretary and had helped him to deal with almost all his recent correspondence, but visits to El Futuro were hardly part of her normal duties.

'What about you?' he said. 'How are you feeling?'

Esther hesitated for a moment. She could have told him about her row with Bruce Cornell and retailed his comments on the subject of malicious gossip, but she banished the thought from her mind. She must not burden Valencia with trivialities on this day of all days, let alone divert his attention to herself.

'I feel fine,' she replied with a smile. 'Have you made any last-minute alterations to your speech?'

He reached for a cigarette and she lit it for him. His eyes met hers for an instant and then returned to the road ahead.

'No, not really. One of my main aims is to convey how much I love this country,' he said. 'I was thinking only last night how many people here go through life without loving or hating anything. They're the robots of the age. They can't summon up anger, even. They can't weep, almost as if weeping were prohibited. Can you weep, Esther?'

She laughed.

'A woman uses tears where a man would punch someone on the nose.'

He smiled at her.

'Frankly, I feel like the happiest man in the world today. I shall be fulfilling my vocation at last. I shall say *mea culpa*, loud and clear, on behalf of myself and every priest in the country. We've done too little, Esther. We've failed to reach the people, either through incompetence or disinclination. To be blunt, we've fallen down on the job. We haven't brought Christ any nearer, neither by word nor deed nor public example. That's why people regard us as men to be avoided rather than Christ's successors on earth. Well, I became a priest so as to be with people and do something for them. As soon as you grasp that you feel yourself drawn deep into the tragedy of human existence. You also feel the throb of life in the raw and realize how bad it is for any human being to live in permanent squalor.'

She glanced at the strong young hands lying loosely on the wheel, the angular masculine profile lit by the climbing sun. It was strange, but she simply couldn't imagine having an ordinary row with him as she could with Bruce, who said what he had to say in tough and unmistakable language. And yet this man was tougher than Bruce

– more courageous, too. He was doing something potentially lethal, but he had the composure of an experienced boxer leaning against the ropes before a big fight.

'The special police are out in force,' she said.

There was something like derision in his voice.

'They're frightened. Not the men themselves but the authorities who sent them. They know this is the moment of truth – our truth, not theirs.'

'Aren't you nervous?' she asked.

He shook his head.

'No, I know what I shall say. I know what I must say. Silence would be spiritual suicide.'

She nodded, and feminine curiosity prompted her to ask: 'Why are we going to the *barrio* now?'

He flicked his cigarette out of the window and grinned.

'You wouldn't be a woman if you hadn't asked that and I wouldn't be a man if I left you wondering. It's quite simple. As you know, some of my ex-students work there, living among the people and trying to sort out their problems. They phoned me last night to say that García was going to release his prisoners at dawn. I want to know what sort of time they had. I may refer to them in my speech.'

She was glad he had said that. So much better than telling her he needed a last dose of inspiration from the slums to arm his soul for the struggle to come.

He pulled up and pointed out of the window.

'This *barrio* is built on Cielo's oldest garbage-dump, did you know that? Thousands of people living on the refuse of centuries. It stinks. It teems with rats and flies, fleas and dogs, all drawn to the filth like pins to a magnet. After you've seen these hovels, try and imagine what it would be like to live in one all your life. I was forgetting, though. You're no stranger to the slums.'

He locked the car carefully.

'We'll have to walk the rest of the way. The car would never make it.'

A path had been cut through the mountain of garbage. They made their way along it, flanked on either side by walls of ancient refuse fifteen feet high. The stench was acrid and penetrating. They almost tripped over a young drunk who was sleeping it off in the lee of the mound. His clothes were torn and filthy and his feet shod with rags in place of shoes. Valencia bent over the man and tried to wake him, but failed. He stared at Esther and shook his head.

185

'You see how man distorts the image of God?' he murmured, and his shoulders seemed to droop. 'These people have no electricity, no sewers or water mains. No doctors ever visit the slums. Even if people could pay them they'd never raise enough money for the medicines they prescribe. Most of them are unemployed. Every morning they walk to the factories and stand in long queues, waiting apathetically for work, and every evening they trudge back here. Another long day gone, another rung on the ladder of degradation.'

He knocked at the door of a tumbledown hut, somewhat larger than its neighbours, and a young man opened it.

'Thank you for coming, Professor. We're all here.' He gestured over his shoulder at the other members of the student team.

Valencia shook hands with them, glancing as he did so at the camp-beds, the cigarette-butts on the floor and the grimy blankets.

'I see you believe in total identification,' he said drily.

Alfonso del Monte, the student who had let them in, joined in the general laughter.

'We're not much richer than the other inhabitants, Professor, you know that.'

Valencia nodded.

'When did they release the prisoners?'

'Just under two hours ago.'

'What are they doing?'

Del Monte grinned at his friends and shrugged.

'Getting drunk.'

'Where?'

'There's only one place in El Futuro where you can get drunk, Professor. Ricardo's.'

'Our ex-bandolero?'

'The same.'

'Have they told you anything yet?'

'No, they looked like a bunch of squashed bananas when the trucks dumped them. Nobody said a word at first. Then one of them began to swear horribly.'

'And Ricardo?'

'They hauled him out of bed. He didn't dare send them away because there were too many of them. The first one pushed him over and the second fell on top of him. He managed to take a punch at the third one. Then they calmed down, squatted on the ground and demanded a drink.'

'Did he give them one?'

'Of course.'

186

'Why of course? *Aguardiente* is a national disaster – you know that.'

'Like the stench in this *barrio*,' retorted del Monte.

Valencia shook his head.

'Spend years on a garbage-dump and you don't smell it any more. What's their mood like?'

'A mixture of apathy and resentment. I know these people, Professor. You have to be careful when they're like this. They're itching to take it out on someone for what García did to them.'

Valencia stared through the dirty window at the *barrio*. He knew its problems only too well. Those slum-dwellers who happened to be in work earned fourteen pesos a day, although his research indicated that they needed twenty-two to keep body and soul together. Many of them suffered from tuberculosis, the dreaded endemic disease which represented an even greater scourge than leprosy. Drunks fell into open sewers and drowned, unheeded by passers-by. Hundreds of children ran around with sunken eyes and bloated bellies of malnutrition. Almost worse was the fate of old people who could no longer fend for themselves. Unless their children or grand-children took them in, they were doomed to die a miserable death because the entire range of social legislation made no provision for them at all. Valencia knew what would happen to the people who had been released from prison that morning. By tomorrow they would be roaming the streets, begging. Some of them would deliberately add to their injuries and sprinkle them with sugar to make them look worse. And yet, despite all the misery which these people had to endure, one never encountered a trace of compassion or love. It was almost as if they had been sucked dry of all capacity for emotion.

And then there were the children, little vagabonds who ran wild like stray dogs because there was no one to care for them. You could recognize them by their bald heads and old men's faces. There were so many of them that the police no longer bothered to pick them up. Born in a doorway or a field, they were wrapped in a few rags by their mothers and abandoned somewhere. The lucky ones were reared in an orphanage until they were five or six, when they ran away and joined a *pandilla*, or gang. The *pandilleros* slept in corners and spent the day stealing and begging or simply looking for food to keep themselves alive. Many of them had 'wives' by the time they were eleven. When they were fourteen or so and their thefts became more productive, they would sleep twenty strong in a decrepit doss-house. At sixteen, many of them had already seen the inside of a gaol, where they were schooled in criminality and corrupted by the older prisoners. They died young, most of them under the age of thirty, if tuberculosis had not put an end to their wretched existence still earlier. And who was to blame? The government? The Church? Both, though in view of its calling the Church probably bore greater responsibility because it failed to recognize that the problem and its solution were the Church's concern.

Esther stared at Valencia. She knew him well enough to realize what he was thinking. These were the moments of self-torment, the moments of truth when he saw his country's open wounds through a magnifying-glass. She had worked on sociological surveys herself and was familiar with local conditions. She knew Alfonso del Monte and the other students, knew what they had to witness day after day. She recalled the woman who had given birth to a child and lay for forty days in a dark hut, every chink in its walls stuffed with newspaper. Her diet consisted solely of a few crusts, except when her husband managed to bring back an occasional bowl of soup. Esther had reproved her for lying there in the dark, but the woman replied that Mary had not emerged until forty days after Jesus' birth so it would be bad for the child if she did otherwise.

That was superstition, not Christianity, but there was no changing it. Esther had done her best. She had even tried to help dying women like the old cleaner who was confined to bed after a heart-attack. She went to the headmaster of the school where the woman worked and asked him to pay part of her wages while she was ill, but he merely replied: 'No, let her stay in bed till she's better. Of course she'll get her wages, but only when she starts work again.' She had stared at him wide-eyed, but her amazement was lost on him. Life was like that. If nobody else cared – and there were far too few charitable institutions – why should he be the one to redress the balance?

Valencia turned abruptly towards the door.

'May I come too?' Esther asked.

He looked at her. They stared deep into each other's eyes, groping for something and finding it. For a brief instant they were more than man and wife.

'Very well, you know them too – you worked here long enough. But don't speak. Leave the talking to me.'

The wine-shop lay three muddy, stinking lanes away. Ricardo was the most influential man in the *barrio*. He was thin and nervy, and the eyes which had seen so much rape and murder stared out of his brown face like the eyes of a wise but worried monkey.

Ricardo was a Communist, even though he had never read *Das Kapital* and would not have understood it if he had. He was a Communist because he believed that Communism was the only exit from a maze of suffering. He had written letters to Moscow but never received a reply, a disappointment from which he never recovered. As he pointed out, a man who wrote letters to Heaven knew in advance that they would never reach their destination, but Moscow was in this world. Occasionally, with all the fervour of his Latin temperament, he would write primitive poetry describing the time when he used to slaughter people like cattle as a guerillero in the mountains. The inhabitants of the quarter had a curious respect for him, and when he was speaking they fell silent and gazed at him as if he were their saviour. It was Ricardo who had first put Valencia in touch with Rodriguez Tobar.

Valencia noticed that something was wrong as soon as he and Esther entered the shop. Nobody greeted them. He pushed through the crowd until he was facing Ricardo, who stared at him in silence. The atmosphere was charged with hatred. He looked at the people in turn, but they did not respond. Suddenly he understood. He had underestimated García. Apart from the maltreatment which each of them had certainly undergone and the torture designed to wring a confession from them, something far more serious had occurred. García had turned them against him, possibly with threats, possibly by telling them that no *cura* could be trusted and pointing out that Padre Antonio Valencia still lived in his cosy apartment while their huts had been torn down. Valencia knew how inclined they were to hate anyone better off than themselves and how ready to knuckle under from one day to the next. García had evidently been too subtle for them.

His eyes fell on the man who had always been their spokesman in the past. He knew him well. It was through Valencia that he had found work in a small factory, and his hut was the neatest in the entire *barrio* – or had been until its destruction by García. Valencia scarcely recognized him now. The flesh round his eyes was puffy and his face covered in abrasions and crimson weals. He could only just sit upright, and even then he had to be supported. The two men who were propping him up also bore the marks of their enforced visit to the Seguridad Nacional. One of them had no teeth left and the other's arm was wrapped in a dirty cloth. Most of the others were in a similar state. Looking at them, Valencia felt a surge of fury. So that was García's technique. First break the body, then the spirit. Their leader had been mishandled worst of all, as an example to the rest. Afterwards, the police had probably treated them slightly better and emphasized the consequences of listening to Valencia and the accursed University students. Who would restore their homes now – Antonio Valencia, whose fault it was that their huts had been torn down and their wives beaten, if not raped? Valencia looked at the women. Many were as badly injured as the men. Others stared back at him with their dark eyes full of unspeakable suffering.

'Ricardo, give them all something to drink at my expense,' he said briskly. Taking a glass, he went to the figure slumped in the chair and bent over it. At that moment the man spat in his face. The spittle struck him with the force of a whip-lash and clung to his forehead, but he made no attempt to wipe it off.

'What did they do to you, Enrique?' was all he said.

My God, Esther thought, he's going to lose. What if they drove him out of the *barrio* and it became known that he had been half-lynched by the very people he was fighting for?

'The dirty bastards,' Enrique said.

'They are that,' Valencia said quietly. 'One night when you were in prison I went to García and asked him to release you. Weren't you told?'

Curiosity flickered in Enrique's eyes.

'You, at the Seguridad Nacional?' he said.

Valencia nodded, and for a minute they stared at each other. Suddenly Enrique produced a grubby handkerchief.

'Wipe that off,' he said with an effort. 'I can't stand the sight of my own spit.'

'Thank you, Enrique.'

Valencia could smell the man's sweat as he held the rag in his hand. He wiped the spittle away, slowly, and returned the handkerchief.

'What happens to us now?' asked one of the group.

'I came to tell you,' Valencia replied. 'I shall make it my personal concern to see that you get better houses than before. We start building tomorrow, but you'll have to lend a hand yourselves. Agreed?'

Strange, thought Esther, Valencia could say everything in a matter of seconds. Politicians took hours, and even then they never got to the heart of the matter. Their phrases were prettier than Valencia's, their Spanish had more elegance and their gestures conveyed burning enthusiasm, but nothing ever happened. Their promised land was a land of unfulfilled promises.

The faces of the people brightened. Enrique had been beaten to a pulp and his resistance broken. Hatred had been sown in their hearts, but García had forgotten one thing: even their hatred lacked stamina.

Valencia squatted down beside Enrique and repeated his original question, but this time it was Ricardo who spoke. He put his hand on Enrique's shoulder and shook him.

'These people want to help you!' he roared. 'Did the Padre beat you up? Did the students trample on you? Did I kick you in the balls? Forget about those swine of the Seguridad. Do you prefer to believe them instead of us? Do I have to beat you up too before you believe in my good intentions, or are you simply frightened to speak? If you want to lead these people in future you must tell everything, now rather than later and to Padre Valencia in person. Here, drink this, it'll help.'

Esther watched, fascinated. This was the language which people understood.

'*Bueno* . . . But only to the Padre and his friends. Not here.'

Valencia nodded.

'We'll go to the social centre. We won't be disturbed there. What about Ricardo?'

'I'll tell him later. He has too many customers at the moment.'

Back in the students' hut, Esther brewed coffee. A cup of *tinto* was put in front of Enrique and he began to speak with his head bowed. Altogether, he said, fifty men had been detained and taken to the headquarters of the Seguridad Nacional.

'Did they maltreat you on the way there?' Valencia asked.

Enrique shook his head.

'No, not on the way. Later. We were taken before an officer one by one. He removed everything, even the string that held our trousers up. Our names were taken and we were herded downstairs into the cells. Ten to a three-man cell.'

As Enrique told his story, a picture took shape in Valencia's mind. He could see the police in their white helmets, with white webbing and truncheons. They had surly faces and a single watchword: hit hard and hit them where it hurts. The prisoners had been packed tightly together in the closed vans. Afterwards they were driven with curses, kicks and blows from rifle-butts into a room where a police officer listed their names and confiscated their scanty personal effects.

'So you're the leader of this rabble, eh?' the officer asked Enrique. He did not deny it because his predecessors in the inter-

191

rogation-room were bound to have given him away long ago.

'Sí, Excelencia.'

Somebody hit him on the head.

'Then you're responsible for opening fire on the police. Who supplied you with the guns?'

He did not reply because he had no idea. Nobody had told him. He had not even known that many of the men possessed guns at all. One of the guards jabbed him in the back with a rifle-butt, so hard that he thought his spine was broken.

'Start talking, hombre. Then you can go.'

He didn't know what to tell them. If he had known, he might have talked.

'Who fired that shot?'

Somebody kicked him in the crutch. Tears came into his eyes and great beads of sweat erupted on his forehead.

'I know nothing . . . nada . . . nada . . . nada!' he screamed, then stopped abruptly when he saw the smile on the officer's face. It puzzled him. How could one man smile while he tortured another? Surely a smile was something beautiful and exalted? Suddenly his eyes hurt him. The white walls seemed to come alive and close in on him. He recoiled a step just as they were about to engulf him. A curse and a blow on the neck, and a fresh tide of agony surged through his tormented body. Then he was booted out of the room and down some steps.

The cell they threw him into was small and filthy. Other men had relieved themselves in there, and the pungent smell of human ordure and urine made him feel sick. His body ached all over, and pain shot through him like a knife when he vomited. His lips were parched and his eyes smarted. Painfully, he strove to keep his feet rather than collapse into the mess on the floor, scrabbling at the smooth walls for a handhold. But he slowly sank to his knees because his legs refused to carry him any longer. He squatted there for some minutes, panting, then pitched forward into the excrement.

He recovered consciousness when nine more prisoners were thrust into his cell. They cursed and dragged him to his feet. He could not fall down again because there was no room to do so. They were crammed together so tightly that they could scarcely move.

'The madman,' whispered one. 'If he hadn't opened fire this would never have happened.'

Enrique doubted it because the shot had been fired after the police began to tear down the huts.

'You're crazy,' he said hoarsely.

192

The breath of the man next him was hot on his face.

'And you stink, Enrique.'

'Of course I stink. I passed out and fell into that shit on the floor. What's so funny?'

It became very close in the cell. They all began to sweat profusely. One of them urinated in his trousers and started cursing the police.

'Shut up!' Enrique said. 'They may be listening outside.'

After several hours all ten of them felt near to madness. They hammered on the cell door and shouted, but nothing happened. There was no sign of the guards. The men in the other cells joined in the shouting until Enrique had had enough. 'Keep quiet!' he called. 'We aren't animals. Act like men, even if they don't treat us as such.'

Silence fell, and they could distinctly hear the sound of rain drumming outside. After another half-hour Enrique felt water beneath his feet. It rose over his ankles and he realized that a drain had broken somewhere. Now they would have to shout to attract the guards' attention.

'Make as much noise as you can!' he bellowed. 'The water's rising fast!'

This time their shouting bore fruit. They were herded out of their cells and into a large room on the ground floor. Most of them fell asleep at once, heedless of the guards.

They stayed in the room. Every now and then one of them was led away to be interrogated. It happened to Enrique every day, until he eventually learnt how to live with pain. On the last day a senior officer harangued them. They had never seen him before, but Enrique would never forget what he said until his dying day.

'You will now, after this brief acquaintanceship with the security police, be released. But we shall be watching you. I have persuaded some of you to keep me informed about your activities in future. Anyone who says anything about his stay here will be rearrested within twenty-four hours and made to curse the day he was born. Anyone who conceals weapons will be even more harshly dealt with. Anyone who consorts with agitators and Communists will spend the rest of his life as he has spent these last few days. You have been warned.'

After that they were loaded into trucks and driven back to El Futuro . . .

Enrique's voice died away. He raised his eyes and looked at Valencia, then at Esther and the four students.

'So I've been warned,' he said quietly. 'Once and for all. Nobody can count on me any more. Anything is better than that. You understand, Padre?'

'Yes,' Valencia repeated, 'anything is better than that. You couldn't have brought me better news, Enrique. If I had any doubts about the rightness of what I'm doing, you have dispelled them. I'm grateful to you.'

Enrique looked bewildered.

'What do you mean, Padre?'

'Forget it, Enrique. Stay here and sleep. Treat this place as your own. I'll come again tomorrow.'

He turned abruptly, nodded to the students and strode out, not even holding the door for Esther as he usually did. Outside he turned once more as if he wanted to imprint it all on his mind for ever: Enrique, battered and maltreated, locked up with nine men in a cell which was barely large enough for three. He experienced it all as if it had happened to him personally. A beaten man sinking unconscious into the excrement of others. No, that was no distortion of God's image in man, it was the rape of God's image *by* man. Anything was better than that, but to Enrique 'anything' meant an acceptance of the facts. To him, Valencia, it meant the opposite. It meant revolution, violence, and the ruthless extermination of an oligarchy which retained power by employing such methods. They had proved effective with Enrique and a hundred thousand others. All spiritual strength, all courage and resistance had been beaten out of their starving bodies. Many had been given work so that they belonged to the comfortable elect, only to say, as Enrique had said: 'Nobody can count on me any more.'

But didn't they say that merely because they felt they had no one to count on themselves? Didn't they accept their beating simply because all resistance was vain, quenched in the blood that flowed from their own excoriated bodies? Where was the image of God, anyway? Could it be found in these slums? Where was Christ, or had Enrique been a vision of the Christ who was tortured before being nailed to the cross? The cross? It stood in every slum, even this one.

Valencia hurried on. The people stared into his face, silent and dismayed. The cross . . . It hung in the hovels of the poor as well as the mansions of the rich, but the Christ who was nailed to it seemed dormant, not agonized. His face was serene, his beard smooth, and his eyes had a tranquillity which the real Christ could never have known.

Before the cross erected by the inhabitants of El Futuro he knelt down and tried to pray, but the words would not come. What would

Christ have said two thousand years ago? Would he, too, have cried out that he was giving up? Or would he have fought on like Peter, the erstwhile coward, like Paul and a host of others? And yet, to anyone who used his eyes, Christ seemed to have died for a crazy and contemptible world. His love was like a cream-cake on which the wealthy gorged themselves while the poor fought for crumbs. His courage had been degraded into theological treatises, his gospel was proclaimed by richly attired prelates who dared to wear the symbol of his pain and suffering – the cross – on their breasts in precious metal. Gold . . . A gold cross in a world expiring from poverty. *Ecce homo*, behold the man. Yes, Valencia told himself, behold the man. Behold Enrique, behold Ricardo and Rodriguez Tobar – behold them all! The most important part of Christ's own prayer went 'Give us this day our daily bread', and the Church of Conciencia had forgotten it. Didn't that make it a farce, this prayer which thousands of priests repeated daily?

The black wooden cross towered above him on its mountain of garbage. No, he thought, no Christ hangs from that cross. Christ did not die so that misery might persist. Even his sign, the cross, should really be wrested from this poisoned earth, from this dung-heap whose stench was an affront to the nostrils.

He rose to his feet, slowly, wearily. Esther came towards him, and he said: 'You must know that nothing can stop me after this. I must speak out at once, and I shall speak more emotionally than I had meant to. I must put a stop to these lies. We cannot allow the Enriques of this country to be terrorized any longer. They aren't dogs to be whipped for barking too loudly.'

Suddenly he noticed that she was weeping. They were the first tears he had seen that morning, and they moved him more than he could say. He gripped her by the arm and turned her to face the cross.

'Weep for me too,' he said softly. 'Weep for a country where people seldom weep. Weep for all the crosses to come.'

The National University of Conciencia occupied a strategic position on the outskirts of the capital. There were two entrances where minor disturbances often occurred and where, during strikes, passing cars were battered and burned. Traffic bound for the international airport had to skirt the campus, so a students' strike made it virtually impossible to leave Cielo by air.

Most of the University buildings were venerable reminders of the colonial era, but the faculties of sociology and law were new, and looked like gleaming white cubes surrounded by baroque churches.

Oscar Ramirez, Valencia's principal student organizer, was studying at the National University against the wishes of his father, a banker, who regarded the place as a breeding-ground for Communists and agitators. Oscar could hardly dispute this because he recognized that national universities throughout Latin America were centres of unrest. They dated from the period which followed the wars of independence, when the ideal of a new America lived on in the minds of a small independent élite, and could already look back on a century of activity by the time the first political parties came to be formed. Conciencia's National University had pursued a hand-to-mouth existence in the past because the ruling cliques showed little interest in university development. With the advent of a constitution, however, it acquired autonomy and managed to assert itself in the face of growing political corruption. As the years went by, its lecture-halls gradually filled with middle-class youngsters and others who refused to stand by and see the fate of an entire nation ruled by an arbitrary and unjust minority.

Oscar Ramirez had chosen to read sociology because he wanted to place science at the service of his fellow-countrymen. Valencia's lectures had made him painfully aware that his country lacked even the rudiments of social justice. The common people were destitute of almost everything that could make life tolerable and secure them an existence worthy of human beings. There were insufficient hospitals and doctors, except in a few isolated centres, and the position in regard to schools was even worse. In short, there was a dearth of all the social institutions which the country so desperately needed. But this, as Valencia had once pointed out, was not the most important factor. More important still was the responsibility of Church and State, also the fact that vast estates were an evil infringement of social justice and that the army swallowed up more than a quarter of government expenditure.

Oscar Ramirez sometimes asked himself why Professor Valencia's lectures left such a lasting and ineradicable impression. He could still remember, word for word, whole sentences which Valencia had flung at the students in the hushed auditorium.

'You students must be the strength of our country, the backbone of our thought, the wall behind which the timid can find shelter.'

But there had been other times when he attacked them sharply. He had reproached them for their instability, told them that they were frightened and that it was fear which made them resort to expedients beyond their power to control. The silence in the hall had deepened then because they all knew that his attack on them stemmed from love, not hatred.

The telephone rang, snapping the thread of Ramirez's thoughts. It was Ramón, a fellow student. He reported that his helpers were busy setting up the loudspeakers and putting the final touches to the speaker's platform. People were already arriving.

'Are the police taking an interest?'

'Not yet, but we've got stones ready. Petrol-bombs too.'

'Get rid of them.'

'But . . .'

'Get rid of them, I said. The Professor would be furious if he knew.'

'*Bueno*. We'll keep them for later.'

Ramirez put the phone down. He knew what Valencia wanted. He wanted to speak, that was all. No riot, no provocation, just the power of the spoken word. Above all, no sensation which would play into the hands of the other side. What he had to say was plain enough. He had made his intentions quite clear at the final briefing session: 'When the day comes, the University must not be dismissed as the *enfant terrible* of national politics. Nobody must be given an opportunity to accuse us of half-baked political views. There must be no doubt that the students are fully conscious of their important task, which is to labour in the furtherance of human knowledge. We must be able to measure ourselves against the universities of the rest of the world. We must demonstrate that our alma mater is acquainted with the problems of this country and continent, that our action is creative in respect of the future and revolutionary in respect of all the institutions and prejudices that have hampered the development of our people for hundreds of years.'

Oscar Ramirez smiled as he watched the sunlight beat down on the faculty of sociology.

Professor Vermeer got up that morning with an uneasy sensation at the pit of his stomach. The day would be a trial of strength for Antonio Valencia, not unlike the one which he himself had undergone as a result of his study of Protestantism in Chile, which had been commissioned by the archbishop there.

Vermeer had unobtrusively attended Protestant services, mostly those of the so-called modern charismatic sects, in order to gauge their popular appeal. To the horror of his superiors, he discovered that Santiago de Chile alone boasted over four hundred buildings devoted to Protestant worship, including churches with a total capacity of more than five thousand. Cool and dispassionate research convinced him that the modern sects offered the common people a religio-emotional compensation for the hardships of everyday life. Their services often led to frenzied and hysterical outbursts during which people screamed, sang and danced in the name of the Holy Spirit, but also to a form of mass hypnosis which resulted in some impressive conversions. Drunkards swore never to touch another drop and criminals became model citizens. Despite their previous history, Protestant converts proved to be highly reliable individuals, both socially and industrially. The spread of Protestantism was an appeal to the religious awareness of man and for many people their first genuine encounter with the Christ of the Gospel.

Vermeer paid dearly for writing, as he did later on, that in his view the success of the modern American sects was clearly indicative of a profound religious need among ordinary folk. Back in Rome, the bishop who held a watching brief on these matters greeted Vermeer's findings with fury. Protestants were heretics, nothing more, and Vermeer had totally underrated the superlative missionary work performed by the Spaniards in Latin America. The bishop duly became Vermeer's mortal enemy. He tried – unsuccessfully, as it turned out – to prejudice his standing with the archbishop of Chile and in Washington, and later, when Vermeer's report was published in Buenos Aires, the cardinal of that city approached the archbishop of Chile and the rector of Chile's national university and cordially drew their attention to the dangers inherent in such an undesirable publication. The Chilean archbishop defended Vermeer, whereupon the cardinal of Buenos Aires retorted that, despite the importance of such a survey and its fitness for circulation among a small group of responsible persons, it was wholly unsuitable for the broad mass of the people. The archbishop replied that the Chilean hierarchy could decide for itself what was, or was not, suitable, but the cardinal of Buenos Aires did not leave matters there. With the support of the Vatican bishop, a papal theologian was instructed to call Vermeer to order. This worthy – another Italian, of course – sent the nuncio in Chile a ten-page critique, five pages of commendation and five of condemnation, a model of diplomatic balance which additionally set forth the unacceptability of Protestantism. The nuncio passed it to Vermeer, who replied that his report passed no judgement whatsoever on the doctrinal aberrations of Protestantism, favourable or unfavourable, simply analysed what was currently taking place. The nuncio advised him to couch his apologia in precisely those terms.

Vermeer did so, but Rome seemed to have taken the blow hard. The Vatican bishop was so enraged that he delegated yet another theologian to act as his champion, also without success.

Meanwhile, one of the cardinals at the Vatican had become irritated by the presumption of the bishop who was waging war on Vermeer. In a letter to the nuncio in Chile he requested him, while reprimanding the author of the survey, to make it clear that the dispute was no reflection of the Vatican's attitude but a wholly private initiative on the part of the bishop in question, who had no authority to speak for the Holy See.

Despite this intervention, Vermeer came badly out of the whole affair. During the Vatican Council the cardinal of Buenos Aires publicly attacked him during a working session outside the aula, and the result was a rupture with the South American archiepiscopate to which Vermeer was attached. It had been one of the most disillusioning experiences in his life.

And now, today, Valencia was about to take a far more crucial step. Did he really believe that one cardinal was so different from another? Had he really reflected on the possible consequences? There was a pastorate of speech and a pastorate of silence. Christ had spoken and been crucified. Peter had spoken and been crucified. Now, almost twenty centuries later, Valencia . . .

Vermeer could not bring himself to pursue that line of thought. Only last night he had discussed the question with two students who were lodging with him. The students adored Valencia with all the fiery enthusiasm of their race. They had been suspicious of him when he first arrived because they distrusted any priest who taught at a non-denominational university, but his ideas, his experiences in Europe and his almost quixotic campaign against the established order quickly overcame their mistrust. His lectures drew capacity crowds. They found it miraculous that a priest should talk to them like a normal human being – even take off his soutane and box with them. An almost incredible aura surrounded him, they said. He had become one of them, probably with no undue effort on his part because he recognized that their demands were fair and reasonable. He also disciplined their nonconformism and taught them to channel it. He sent them to the slums and showed them how to render active help, not simply demonstrate or compile reports, useful as these might be.

'He once asked me to give up smoking,' one of the students told Vermeer. 'Not because I could help the poor better by doing so, but because it would give me some idea of just how tough self-sacrifice can be.'

Vermeer listened to the pair in silence. He probably knew Valencia better than either of them because, as his father confessor, he was even more familiar with his immense strength of character as well as his failings. That was why he feared for him more than the students did. Valencia would never allow himself to be steered into a backwater. He would fight on whatever the consequences, but there was no point in discussing these with the two boys. They knew that strong forces were at work against Valencia, but did they realize how fanatical the opposition was? Vermeer doubted it and dreaded to think what would happen if Valencia were taken from them.

Late that night the young men picked up their guitars and began to sing, nostalgically, dreamily. Their dreams were of one man, a man to whom they had given their trust, one man . . . Valencia.

'Are you in love with my daughter?' Graham asked, eyeing Bruce gravely.

Bruce nodded.

'You could call it that,' he said. 'Is that what you invited me here to ask me?'

Graham looked down at the small cup of *tinto* in front of him.

'No, I asked you to come because I've got a problem. Esther's friendship with this priest isn't doing her any good. She's making herself a laughing-stock, but that isn't all. I just had a note from Cooper. He wants to discuss the situation.'

Bruce frowned.

'I saw it coming.'

'What, precisely?' Graham's tone was brusque.

'The whole thing.'

A look of anger passed across the older man's face.

'This priest – what exactly does she see in him?'

'Her own shortcomings, maybe, but you've known her longer than I have. You should know.'

Graham shook his head sadly.

'No father knows his own daughter when the chips are down, Cornell. I'm beginning to think we live in two different worlds, Esther and me. She looks on me as the stooge of a set of people she abominates. I know that perfectly well, even if she's never brought herself to say so out loud. Sure, we talk together – we even enjoy arguing together. I may mean something to her as a father, but as the boss of an oil company I don't rate two bits' worth of respect.'

'What about me?' Bruce said. 'Do I rate anything?'

Graham shrugged his shoulders.

'Hard to say. Women are complicated creatures. Have you spoken to her lately?'

'Yes, we had a difference of opinion about Valencia, as a matter of fact.'

'Did you persuade her to drop him?'

'Does it look like it?'

Graham sighed.

'I hoped you might have been the man she was looking for. That would have settled this crazy business once and for all.'

'I hoped so too, but it didn't work out that way.'

John Graham rose to his feet and stood staring down at Bruce. There was a look in his eye which said that only the truth would do.

'Were you having an affair with her?' The question came like a pistol-shot.

Bruce did not flinch.

'Yes.'

Graham's face registered a faint grin.

'I was afraid you'd deny it,' he said.

'Where is she now?' Bruce asked.

'She called me to say she was visiting one of the slums with Valencia and then going on to the University with him for this afternoon's jamboree. Are you going too?'

Bruce nodded.

'Yes, the only reason I'm still here is to write about Valencia. That's the craziest feature of the whole situation.'

'Why don't you have a word with him about Esther? I'd have thought it was the natural thing to do, if you're in love with her.'

'It is, but you can't force a woman to love you. Besides, I admire the man as much as she does, even if I'm saner about it.'

'You admire him?' Graham sounded surprised.

'Yes. Valencia not only knows what he wants, he has the guts to go out and get it. Why do you think the ambassador wrote you about Esther?'

Graham looked at him sharply.

'You tell me.'

'Your daughter is mixed up with a man who's rated as a dangerous revolutionary round here. Well, revolutionaries are a danger to U.S. interests, your oil company included.'

Graham did not comment at once. He lit a cigarette and smoked in silence for a while. Then he walked across to the window which overlooked his carefully landscaped garden.

'Would it influence her if I pointed out that she was undermining my position here?'

Bruce shook his head.

'That isn't an argument you can use. You won't either, if I know anything about you.'

A look of sorrow came into Graham's eyes, sorrow and tenderness combined.

'My daughter is the only thing I have left, Cornell. At the risk of sounding over-dramatic, anyone who harms her will have me to reckon with, and in my opinion this man is abusing her good intentions.'

Bruce thought before he spoke. He wanted to agree with Graham, but the awareness of his own prejudice made him loath to jump to conclusions.

'I warned her,' he said. 'I put it a different way, though. Valencia would never take advantage of Esther, not if he's the man I think he is. He'd lose her the moment he did, even if he didn't realize it at the time. If that's what's worrying you, you can set your mind at rest.'

'You talk as if you approved of her behaviour.'

Bruce cut him short with an impatient gesture.

'I don't. What's more, I've told her so repeatedly. Her friendship with Valencia – and I use the word friendship advisedly – can only benefit his enemies. If they wanted to turn him into a social outcast they couldn't find a better weapon than his relationship with her, however innocent.'

'What do you plan to do now?' Graham asked.

'Drive to the National University. Valencia is going to announce his political programme and there's likely to be trouble. I may see Esther too.'

'I'll come with you. I'd like to hear the man speak. I only met him once, casually, at that party. If I have to make a decision – and God knows it'll be hard enough either way – I want to know why I'm making it and exactly who the opposition is.'

The traffic flowed along, turgid with police cars and army trucks. Esther stared silently at them, then at Valencia's face. She wondered yet again why he had asked her to accompany him that morning. They had barely exchanged a word.

At one stage while Valencia was talking to Enrique and the

students at El Futuro, she had gone outside. Half-horrified, half-curious, she watched the approach of a funeral procession. A funeral? The corpse was wrapped in an old sack and the legs hung out, scuffing the ground. The men carrying the body had sullen faces. Every now and then one of them swore as the man behind trod on his heels. Nobody looked up as the macabre procession passed by, but here and there a woman hurriedly made the sign of the cross and averted her eyes.

During the period when Esther was still working with the student research team at El Futuro she had once seen people carry a corpse swathed in old blankets into Ricardo's wine-shop, order some *aguardiente* and dump the mortal remains on the next table while they drank. It was part of their apathetic acceptance of everything, even death. In any case, why should death inspire terror when life meant so little, when mothers abandoned their new-born babies on garbage-dumps because they could not feed them?

The same misery reigned everywhere.

The road they were driving along was lined with factories, many of them built with North American capital. Outside, hundreds of people stood waiting for work. They left their slums at crack of dawn and stationed themselves at the factory gates, unspeaking, waiting, hoping. Every evening they returned, and Esther wondered how they had the courage to tread the same path of torment day after day.

'Those are the people I want to help,' said Valencia. 'Sometimes I feel they've been standing there for centuries, like living monuments of despair.'

The skyscrapers of the capital loomed up before them, and suddenly Valencia felt his courage ebb away. His hands trembled convulsively on the steering-wheel and a pain shot through his chest, momentary but dagger-sharp. Breathing heavily, he braked to a halt beside the avenida.

'Would you mind taking over, Esther? I can't drive any more.'

He climbed out and drew the crisp air of Cielo deep into his lungs. Some passers-by recognized him and waved, but he did not appear to see them.

'Shall I get you something from a chemist?' Esther asked.

He shook his head.

'No, I'm feeling better already. It was just a dizzy spell. I haven't been sleeping enough these past few weeks.'

Esther looked at him and saw that his face was waxen pale.

'Perhaps you'd sooner go home,' she said.

He gave a jerky laugh.

'No, my dear. God's strength reveals itself in human weakness – it pays to remember that.'

She took the wheel and he got in. She did not stop to wonder what he meant because she knew his moments of self-reproach only too well. They occurred rarely, but when they came it was as if a dam had burst inside him.

'You must take better care of yourself, Antonio,' she said softly. 'We need you.'

She kept her eyes on the road, not daring to glance at him as she said 'we' when she meant 'I'.

Some colour returned to his face and he lit his pipe, a sure sign that he was himself again.

'I can't do without you either,' he said quietly.

His words were cut short by the wail of sirens. Esther pulled over to the right and four cars raced by, filled with armed men wearing the white helmets of the Conciencian para-military police.

Valencia chuckled.

'My reception committee. I hope the youngsters keep their heads – I warned them not to do anything silly. No burning cars or tangling with the police, no smoke-bombs or petrol-bombs, otherwise I'll never get a chance to speak at all.'

'How many people are you expecting?' she asked.

'I don't know. Quite a few, from the look of it. The organizing committee has received telegrams from every university in the country. If they all send delegations there could be an audience of hundreds.'

Valencia was wrong. There were thousands. The ovation that greeted his appearance on the platform burst over the arena like a hurricane.

He waited until it had died away and then began to speak, and as he looked down on the serried ranks he saw Enrique's lacerated face, and his voice took on a note of suppressed anger.

'Conciencia's hour has struck. In this country, as dear to you as it is to me, power is claimed by a minority which rules the majority. This makes it essential to change the political structure so that, in future, decisions are taken by the majority, not the minority. The only way to achieve this is to form a National Revolutionary Front. It falls to me, at this historic moment, to proclaim its formation.'

In short, impassioned sentences he described the plight of the people, the appalling contrast between rich and poor. His voice grew harsh and his words staccato as he continued:

'On behalf of all who support me, I demand radical agrarian reform. In future, land must belong to those who cultivate it. The estates of the big landowners must be expropriated without compensation. Banks, hospitals and clinics, industries, insurance companies, public transport, radio and television networks must be nationalized.

'The State shall enable all Conciencian citizens to receive free education and parents shall be obliged to send their children to school. No more oil concessions will be granted to foreign oil companies unless the State's holding amounts to at least seventy per cent. The refining, production and distribution of all forms of fuel shall pass into the hands of the State within twenty-five years, by the expiry of which period all materials and installations shall have been transferred to public ownership. Conciencian employees shall be paid at least as much as foreign personnel of the same grade.

'In addition, we shall introduce a progressive and comprehensive programme of social security under which all members of the population will be guaranteed the right to medical treatment. Studies will be made of all questions relating to provision for the sick, the elderly, and the bereaved. Budget appropriations for the armed forces shall be commensurate with their real military role. It being the natural duty of all Conciencians to support the government of their country, women over the age of eighteen will also be employed in various projects beneficial to the public good.

'Women shall in future enjoy complete equality with men in every economic, political and social sphere.'

He bent over the lectern, and his hands knotted themselves into fists.

'These are not just high-sounding phrases. They are promises which we shall translate into reality. The people on whose behalf I stand here before you would have to be deaf and blind not to respond to this appeal. I am not a politician. I am a priest who has grasped that the Church must no longer acquiesce in the social injustices which are being perpetrated here by a tiny minority. Day in, day out, we see destitution in the streets, in the homes of workers both here and on the land. That is why I call for a dialogue with Marxism, because all of us, whether Communist, socialist, atheist or Christian, must try to make our native land a happy one.'

Valencia seemed to grow in stature. His voice rang out again: 'In view of all I have just said, I demand that power be given to the people. I demand political absolutism so that we can put an end to the inhuman conditions under which most of our fellow-countrymen live. I demand political and social pluralism. I am here to request your help. I am here in the name of justice. The time for apathy is past. Non-violent evolution has proved to be a mirage. That is why I summon you to revolution in the hope that, if I myself take the first step, you will follow my example. May we be the protectors of our people! Long live Conciencia!'

He started to say something more, but a thunder of applause cut him short. Fists were raised, voices roared and bellowed, faces shone with ecstasy and exultation. Some members of the crowd climbed on their neighbours' shoulders and brandished the flag of Conciencia high in the air. Bruce, who was standing near the front with Graham, could see how moved Valencia was. He looked very small now behind his lectern, the priest whom Communists, socialists, atheists and Christians acknowledged as their leader. The white dog-collar was seen, yet not seen, by all. There was no smile on Valencia's face. No one realized better than he did that a moment of triumph could herald utter defeat.

He stared down at the thousands of faces raised to him like those of worshippers. He knew that his listeners trusted him implicitly and would carry his words to the farthest corners of the country, but he also knew that not all of them possessed his inner strength. There were cowards and waverers among them, traitors like Judas, perhaps, or men who would deny him at the eleventh hour like Peter. He was well aware that the image of Gethsemane was changing with the image of the world. This university campus might prove to be his Gethsemane, with Peter's cock-crow replaced by the police sirens which every so often attempted to drown his words. How many of that exultant crowd would stand by him when the real storm broke? But he was happy for all that. He had waited too long for this moment of recognition and spent too many years in self-preparation not to feel a thrill of excitement. Life must offer the same chances to all, and the Church must be the first to acknowledge that because its banner was emblazoned with the symbol of love.

He stared down, straight into the face of his friend Vermeer, and recoiled. The Dutchman was taking no part in the general rejoicing – he was not even smiling. The eyes behind the heavy horn-rimmed glasses were stern and thoughtful. Would Vermeer be the first friend to desert him?

The shouting swelled, as if his audience were bent on prolonging the moment for ever. Valencia felt suddenly terrified of the noise. He feared for himself, for the friends and confederates whom he was exposing to hatred, persecution and imprisonment. But then, love was a sharp-edged instrument to be wielded as a surgeon wielded the scalpel. Was it wrong for them to devote themselves to the happiness and welfare of millions of their fellow-countrymen? No, because he had seen their wretchedness with his own eyes. He must not betray himself. He had stood in the hovels of the dying and been unable to recall them to life as Christ had once done. He had seen injustices committed in the name of love and lacked the strength to drive their perpetrators from the temple as Christ had done before him. Then, he had been a lone voice crying in the wilderness. He was no son of God. He could not call on his heavenly father like Christ, the first revolutionary. That was why he had chosen the path of violence. Every other road was closed. There were 'No Entry' signs everywhere, in the cardinal's palace, in the President's palace, the nuncio's palace, in the bishops' palaces, in the offices of the ecclesiastical authorities, in the mansions of the rich, even in the churches themselves. Look round, he told himself. The world was living on the verge of a nuclear war. One-third of it was rich, two-thirds were dying of starvation, and in Conciencia economic exploitation was tolerated with a smile.

He raised his arms and the noise died at once.

'I ask you to join me in the Pater Noster so that all who hear us or of us will know that, so far from attacking the hallowed principles of our native land, we are preaching social revolution only because every other door has been slammed in our face.'

And, while the sirens of police cars wailed in the distance, Christians and non-Christians alike joined in the prayer that resounded from every loudspeaker:

'Our Father, which art in Heaven, hallowed be Thy name. Thy will be done, in earth as it is in Heaven. Give us this day our daily bread. And forgive us our trespasses, as we forgive them that trespass against us. And lead us not into temptation; but deliver us from evil. Amen.'

The amen was like the death-knell of an era. An unbroken hush followed, almost as if it had suddenly dawned on everyone present that the revolution had been summoned into being by a prayer. At last, someone had burst the barriers of political impotence simply by stating the facts. And once more the cheers rang out because Valencia's audience sensed intuitively that Conciencia's moment of truth had come.

Graham turned to Bruce.

'So that's the guy who's giving me so much trouble.'

'Yes. What did you think of him?'

'Pretty impressive, not that I share his views.'

'Esther does. I wonder if we'll find her in this crush.'

'We can try. I overheard someone saying that the students are giving a sort of reception in Valencia's honour.'

'Good, let's head for the department of sociology.'

Everyone inside was drunk with enthusiasm except Vermeer, who topped the rest by a head. He had said a few friendly words to Valencia without commenting on his speech in detail. Esther was standing in the main entrance when Bruce and her father walked in. She seemed surprised to see them together.

'Everyone's going mad,' she said excitedly.

'Mad is the operative word,' Graham retorted. 'What did you expect?'

'I certainly didn't expect to see you, Daddy. What brings you here?'

'You mean you don't know? My daughter tags around after a man who's the talk of Conciencia. Seems to me a father ought to take a look for himself when the man happens to be a priest.'

'Well, what do you think of him?'

Graham looked at her a little warily.

'At least he knows what he's doing, which is more than I can say for you.'

'How do you mean?'

'Work it out for yourself. I'm going now – I've seen what I came to see. So long.'

'What about you?' Esther said to Bruce, staring after her father.

'No comment.'

'Aren't you even going to make a scene?'

'This isn't the place. Besides, you wouldn't listen to me. People drunk with triumph never do.'

'So you admit it's a triumph?'

'Drunk with it, I said, and if you don't believe me take a look at yourself in a mirror.'

'What do you think of his programme?'

'Sensational. I'm curious to know how it'll appeal to the gentlemen who run this country. My guess is, we won't have long to wait before we find out.'

'And that's all you can find to say?'

'What more can I say? You obviously feel happier in Valencia's company than mine.'

'Have you been discussing me with my father?'

'Yes, at his invitation. He seems to be rather puzzled by the whole affair.'

'Did he complain to you about me?'

'No. He isn't the complaining kind. He's worried about you, that's all. Also, strange as it may seem, he likes me.'

'Do you like him?'

'Very much.'

'And that's all there was to it?'

'Why keep pushing me? Is your conscience pinching you, or something? Your father formed a good impression of Valencia, even if he wasn't too happy with his remarks about foreign oil companies. He didn't agree with a lot of other things either.'

'What was your reaction?'

'It was the most serious-minded speech I ever heard anyone make in Latin America. I doubt if we've heard the last of it.'

'You really think so?'

Bruce turned and found himself face to face with Valencia.

'I do, Padre, and I've listened to plenty of speeches in my time, I can assure you.'

Esther looked at the two men. There was no sign of impatience in either face, just questions that remained unanswered because neither ventured to ask them.

'Here are a few more details, Señor Cornell. The campus is surrounded by troops and police. As of now, the students are on strike, but I've asked them not to use violence. Violence requires organization to make it effective, and we haven't reached that stage yet. In future, nobody will stop me from making my programme known throughout the country. The students will help me.'

'And the press, Padre.'

'I shan't know that till I've read tomorrow's editions.'

Valencia's face remained grave in spite of the general jubilation.

'The hardest part comes later, I realize that perfectly well.'

'Let's hope the students realize it too,' Bruce said tersely.

'I'm sure they do.'

'At least you can rely on Esther.' There was a hint of mockery in Bruce's voice.

'I can indeed. She hasn't seen much of you lately, I gather. A pity. We all need friends at a time like this.'

The first smile crossed his face and he extended his hand.

'We must get together sometime. Mutual confessions clear the air. I shall hope to see you again very soon. *Hasta la vista.*'

Esther had disappeared by the time Bruce turned round. The applause took on a steady rhythm. Bruce sighed and elbowed his way through the vociferous, jubilant students as they lifted Antonio Valencia, priest and revolutionary, on to their shoulders.

Cheering and jubilation . . . The applause lapped over the old man like a flood tide, constricting his chest and threatening to engulf him, but he deliberately left the radio on because he wanted to feel the full extent of the thing that had overwhelmed him.

Esperanza Cardinal Medina was curious to know how long he could endure it before anger fought its way to the surface. He felt as if he were shackled to his chair with fetters of steel. People had warned him about Valencia, but what were warnings compared with all the evil nonsense he had just heard? He wondered if he were envious of the acclamation he had never known. The faithful occasionally applauded him, true, but only from a sense of duty and in deference to his position, not to the man he was. He could see, in his mind's eye, a crowd of young people with radiant faces, taking Valencia to their heart.

He felt pains in his back, searing pains which bound him still more firmly to his chair.

Had he lacked enthusiasm, he wondered, the sort of enthusiasm which now boomed from the radio on his desk? Should he have committed himself to something positive, cherished a dream and fought to fulfil it? Was that what he lacked, for all his assurance, all his devotion to the truth, all his love for those who did not return that love?

And then he recoiled. History was littered with the bones of fools who had striven to change the face of the world by violent means, called down unspeakable suffering on mankind and savaged consciences without number. A priest named Valencia, a representative of Christ the non-violent, had resorted to the weapon of violence and thereby committed a public rape on love. It was written: 'He that is not with me is against me; and he that gathereth not with me scattereth abroad.' It was lack of faith which made Valencia act as he did. God was not to be defied by violent means.

Coming to an abrupt decision, he picked up the phone and called Monsignor Zasi.

'Did you hear Valencia's speech, Monsignor?' His voice was harsh with fatigue.

'Yes, Your Eminence.'

'Good. I should appreciate a few minutes of your time. Immediately, if you would be so good.'

'But of course, Your Eminence.'

Bishop Zasi took off his loose and comfortable Franciscan habit but left the radio to blare out excited commentaries until he had donned his soutane, tied the sash round his waist and hung the gold cross round his neck. He knew that the Cardinal set great store by the outward signs of ecclesiastical dignity, whatever that might be. He turned off the radio with some reluctance and closed the door behind him feeling like a soldier bound for the front.

He walked along the main corridor of the palace, crossed the vast hall lined with the grilles which always reminded him of a post office, and opened the door which led to the Cardinal's chambers.

It smelt stuffy in there, a sort of old man's air redolent of mildewed paper, as if it were years since the windows had been opened to admit the fresh air of Cielo.

He knocked. Even before the Cardinal called 'Come in' he could hear the sound of the radio. It was switched off as the door opened.

Medina silently indicated a chair. His gout was troubling him now as well as his liver, and tongues of fire played over his ageing body.

'Well,' he said, fixing his eyes on Zasi's rather bucolic face, then glancing at his feet, which the bishop could never keep still, 'were you impressed?'

Zasi did not reply at once. He was thinking of his time among the bandoleros of Taloma and of his friend Pablo Boterro, professor of music and director of the Cielo conservatoire. He could still remember, almost word for word, a student's account of his death.

'We left Cielo at two o'clock in the afternoon, planning to attend a concert in the club-house at Camarco that evening. We stopped for fifteen minutes on the way and then continued our bus-journey to Taloma. We had just passed the provincial border a few minutes short of seven o'clock when we came upon a road-block. At first we thought the men were soldiers. There must have been about fifteen of them, dressed in army uniforms. The coach halted and one of the bandoleros told us to get out. He immediately confiscated all articles of jewellery, wallets and watches. The bandits surrounding us were all armed to the teeth and had their rifles trained on four other vehicles close by. There were several shots. Then the leader of the gang told us to split up into two groups, liberals and conservatives. It was obvious what he meant to do.

Anyone who admitted being a conservative would have been shot on the spot. Nobody budged, of course. We all stayed put while they asked us, one by one, which party we supported. The sixteen girls in the group were also questioned.

'Professor Boterro, who had organized the trip, explained that we were music students from Cielo and that he was head of the conservatoire. The leader of the bandoleros seemed satisfied and told us to get back into the coach. Professor Boterro waited until last, but when he tried to get in they punched him in the face so that he fell over backwards into the road. Our driver put his foot down and drove off as fast as he could, but we all saw the bandoleros aim their rifles at the Professor and fire. There was panic inside the coach but the driver refused to stop and drove even faster. Later, government troops found Professor Boterro and twelve other people lying dead in the road.'

The massacre unleashed such a wave of anger among the conservatives of Taloma that Zasi, the local priest, had no hope of checking it. Three weeks later some soldiers of the Conciencian army found a bandolero camp. The bandits were summarily dragged before a firing-squad and shot. The women and children who had been found with them were driven into a hut, which was duly soaked with petrol and set on fire. An army communiqué stated laconically: *'Government troops yesterday attacked a bandolero camp. The bandits fell after a brief engagement.'*

The soldiers were fêted as national heroes, but Padre Zasi, as he then was, knew better. And so it had gone on, year after year, not only between troops and bandoleros but between liberals and conservatives ...

Zasi became aware that the Cardinal was awaiting an answer to his question. He drew a deep breath.

'Valencia certainly made an appeal to violence, Your Eminence, but haven't we all been witnessing violence for years? Hundreds of thousands of people have died in an insane struggle between two political parties, yet as far as the population of this country is concerned, nothing has changed for the better.'

The Cardinal interrupted him impatiently.

'That is beside the point. Would you, as a priest, dare to assume responsibility for all Valencia's demands?'

Zasi drew another deep breath.

'I don't know, Your Eminence. Perhaps you could summon Valencia to explain his views – in fact a dialogue might be the answer, under the circumstances.'

'A dialogue?' The Cardinal looked aghast. 'Are you suggesting that I converse with this rebel on equal terms?'

Zasi nodded.

'It would be a mark of historic far-sightedness, Your Eminence.'

Medina felt anger gaining the upper hand. What in God's name was he thinking of, this peasant from Taloma? Historic far-sightedness, indeed! He detested such phrases on principle.

'He that is not for me is against me,' he retorted brusquely.

Zasi bent his clear gaze on the Cardinal.

'You can't be serious, Your Eminence. That summarizes man's relationship to God, not the relationship of one man to another. People who fight for the same cause can always find common ground.'

'Am I fighting for the same cause?' Medina's voice shook with rage, and Zasi sensed that he must tread carefully. The conflict was not simply between subordinate and superior but between youth and the conservatism of age, a clash between generations.

The Cardinal was certainly unaware of one thing, Zasi reflected, and that was the almost hopeless economic position of the country. The former colonial exploitation of poor countries by rich had been replaced by economic domination. Conciencia exported almost nothing but raw materials, and it was in the interest of North American buyers to keep the price of raw materials low. As long as Latin America confined itself to the production of raw materials there was no prospect of an improvement in real wages. However extensive, relief projects could never solve the crisis as long as all finished products had to be imported, principally from North America, whose high wage-rates and equally high transportation charges made them doubly expensive.

Zasi agreed that the country's only real hope of economic salvation lay in the development of local industries which would themselves make use of its rich deposits of iron ore, coal and oil. The United States granted Conciencia economic aid, it was true, but this achieved nothing because the same United States, alarmed by the Cold War, seemed to nourish quite as hysterical a fear of a Communist take-over in Latin America as the government and ruling circles of Conciencia itself. Instead of furthering social progress the government allotted an ever-increasing percentage of the budget to the armed forces and security police, thus squandering resources which might otherwise have been used for economic development. With the press safely in their pocket, the ruling circles fomented the hysterical fear of Communism and, ostensibly in the name of private enterprise, a phrase which always found favour with the United States, blocked all democratic reforms.

And now, Conciencian politics had become dominated by this reactionary approach to economics. The population was growing out of all proportion to any increase in national income. Commerce was falling back on an instalment-plan system which made a mockery of good faith. Schools were closing for lack of funds even though parents were demanding more of them. Tax receipts were falling instead of rising. The government talked big but were making cuts in every department of social welfare. The only commodity in ample supply was tension. Was it surprising that agitators came forward with utopian promises when, in spite of everything, the income of the ruling classes still continued to increase, matched by a corresponding flight of capital abroad? Tension provoked uncertainty and confusion on both sides, among rich and poor alike. Who could wonder if the call for dictatorship was heard? The rich demanded a military dictatorship, the poor a socialist or Communist one. Any democratic government could be toppled during an economic crisis, even a government more democratic and less prone to blunders than that of Conciencia. Meanwhile, real wages plummeted and the military were in the ascendant.

If it came to a showdown, Zasi reflected, the army would worst the Communists in most Latin American countries simply because North America was too close not to protect its investments and sources of raw materials. Russia was far away. Military dictatorships would come into being and the way would be paved for fascism. And the enemies of parliamentary democracy, having done everything in their power to impoverish the common people, would loudly proclaim 'I told you so!' and dismiss democracy as a luxury which Latin America could ill afford.

Bishop Zasi smiled. These ideas did not come from him. They appeared in an article by Professor Vermeer which he had read and re-read because it presented such a razor-sharp picture of the country's present position.

The Cardinal leant forward as if to read what was in Zasi's mind.

'I have been thinking too,' he said. 'You may speak to Valencia once more, in my name. Offer him a post here at the chancellery and tell him that his university salary will be maintained at the same level – after all, he has his mother to support.'

Medina winced at the thought that he was bargaining with Valencia as if he, not Medina himself, were head of the Conciencian Church.

'My one proviso is that he ceases this agitation forthwith . . .' He could not bring himself to continue.

The two prelates fell silent. The Cardinal yearned to discuss the whole matter with the Nuncio, who was a high-handed man but had shown himself to be a good tactician. But still he hesitated. The sound of public acclamation had taught him that he must be careful. Not too careful, though, because behind the acclamation lay defiance.

Bishop Zasi experienced a peculiar wave of compassion for the old man who was seeing the activities of one individual shatter so many of the values in which he had irrevocably believed. Obedience had proved to be an illusion and authority was trickling through his fingers like sand.

'Your Eminence,' Zasi said, and there was so much genuine concern in his voice that the Cardinal glanced at him in surprise. 'I would urge you once more, with all the force at my command, to speak to Valencia yourself. Summon him here. Give him a hearing. He is one of your priests. If you believe him to be in spiritual distress you should not withhold your fatherly help and guidance.'

Medina shook his head.

'You did not understand his speech properly if you think that. If he were really in a state of spiritual distress he would have come and asked my advice before he delivered it. Now that he has gone his own way I cannot help him. The most I can do is to place him in curatel.'

Zasi gave up. He should have known that the Cardinal would never summon up the forbearance to welcome a prodigal son. His flock was more important to him than one stray sheep.

'Very well, Your Eminence,' Zasi said, rising, 'I shall convey your message to him.'

He glanced back as he closed the door behind him. The old man's head had sunk forward on his chest and his hands were gripping the pectoral cross so tightly that the knuckles showed white.

1 2

Raoul Castillo felt as helpless as a hobbled horse. He knew that Zambrano's men might have been trailing him from the time he left Guillermo de la Cruz to rejoin Rodriguez Tobar, so he hid by day and continued his devious journey by night. In an hour's time he would reach the spot where he had arranged to meet his four companions. Their rendezvous was Gomez Ocampo's hut, where they had slept on the first night of their outward journey. Castillo sat motionless in a tree with his knees drawn up. He was hungry because all that had passed his lips for two days was sugar-water, diluted sticks of pale brown *canela*. Anxiety gnawed at him as well as hunger. He wondered if Pedro, Emanuel, Carlos and Armando had been as careful as he. Carlos, 'the Manager', worried him most of all. He tended to be garrulous and was less mindful than the others of the time-honoured guerrilla maxim: 'always on the move, always alert, always suspicious'. Besides, it was unusual for them to operate singly. Their strength lay in the team, a group of tough, strong, well-armed men who always attacked in concert, nobody knew from where.

Castillo looked round for his horse, which he had christened Ardiente and taught to stand motionless in the undergrowth when danger threatened or when he was resting after hours in the saddle.

Darkness was falling. The track led past his tree, and ten kilometres farther on lay the hut where they planned to meet. The night was cool, cold even, and Castillo was shivering. His vantage-point commanded a good view of the track, which disappeared into the jungle far below him in a series of hair-pin bends. Years of training had made Castillo's ears sensitive to the slightest sound: the unexpected snap of a twig, a man's breathing, the sudden whir of a bird taking wing. He wondered if he would always live as he did now. Towns and even villages were out of bounds to him. Their dangers were so real and immediate that he would at once have been

216

arrested by the 'green devils', who had been hunting him for years.

Behind him, Castillo heard his horse stop munching and raise its head. He stiffened. He could detect nothing, but there must be something close at hand. Ardiente's sharp ears had saved his life before now. He sat there for a moment longer, very still, then slipped quietly to the ground and crept into the undergrowth, leading his horse by the bridle. He halted every few paces to listen, and then he heard it: a dull thud of hoofs on the track some distance away. There must be more than two riders. He drew his pistol, gave Ardiente a soothing pat on the hind quarters and concealed himself in the branches of another tree. There he removed his safety-catch and waited. It was ten minutes before he heard voices. As the party rode by he recognized Gomez Ocampo, lashed to his horse, and round him, rifles in hand, a number of Zambrano's green-uniformed soldiers.

He weighed the odds. His four companions would also use this track to reach Ocampo's hut. He doubted if they were there already because he had travelled fast. Gomez Ocampo must have ridden into an ambush, as he would have done himself if fate had not decreed otherwise. What if Zambrano's soldiers had been covering the first part of the route as well? The risk was not great because his companions would only use this last stretch.

Half an hour after the soldiers had passed he heard more horses' hoofs. He waited tensely until he saw four familiar figures come trotting along the mountain path, then breathed a sigh of relief. The others were as weary as he was, and their faces darkened when he told them what he had just seen.

'No hot meal this time,' Emanuel said with a sigh.

Armando's cadaverous face was as inscrutable as ever.

'Do you know exactly how many there were?' he asked.

Castillo shook his head.

'A fair-sized patrol. I only know this: Gomez is in trouble and we must get him out of it.'

'Why? Let him die. Why should we risk our necks for Gomez? He gave us food and let us sleep in his hut, I grant you, but it would be worse if they caught us.'

The speaker was Pedro, 'the Monkey', who was lolling there in the gloom with his arm round a sapling.

'What if Gomez talks?' Castillo demanded. 'What if he gives the soldiers some idea of where we've come from? They may torture him until he betrays us. What then? Are you prepared to make a present of information to that swine Losano?'

'Who cares about Losano? We'll be back in our own territory by the time Gomez cracks. Nobody will find us there.'

In the silence that followed these words they heard Armando draw a deep breath. He went over to Pedro.

'Zambrano's men have been foolish enough to leave their home ground. Are you going to miss this chance of exterminating some vermin?'

Pedro laughed.

'I'm all for taking chances, but we still don't know how many we're up against. If Raoul is so keen to attack, let him go and find out.'

Castillo cut the conversation short.

'We'll all go.'

They rode in single file down the narrow track until they were half a mile from their destination. Then they dismounted and tethered the horses. A few hundred yards farther on they turned off down an even narrower path, invisible from the main track, which led straight to Ocampo's hut. They crept along it with drawn pistols and tense faces until they heard screams in the distance.

'They must be working on him already,' Castillo whispered. 'They won't be expecting us.'

The edge of the jungle was only five yards from the hut. Castillo remembered how he had stood there, not many nights ago, and envied Ocampo his little wooden shack, his yucca, maize and coffee, his chickens and cows. He no longer envied him. Ocampo had been set upon and tortured in his own home, and nobody would have heard his cries if they had not happened to select this supposedly safe refuge as their rendezvous.

The five guerilleros stood there without moving. To judge by the horses tethered outside, there were seven soldiers in all. They obviously felt safe because they had posted no sentries. Castillo smiled grimly but reminded himself not to underestimate the enemy. Incredible as it was that such a small group should operate independently at night, the soldiers must be well trained, well armed, and as ruthless as all the green devils.

Castillo peered through the window. Gomez Ocampo was being interrogated by a sergeant, a burly man of about thirty. He was evidently free with his fists, because blood was dripping from Ocampo's nose and mouth.

'I know nothing of any guerilleros,' he was saying in a tremulous voice, '– nothing. Why ill-treat me when you should be protecting me? *Madre de Dios!*'

The sergeant slammed him in the face with the heel of his palm and another man jabbed him in the stomach. Ocampo doubled up like a jack-knife.

'We were given your name by a man who's tired of working with dirty traitors. The man is not lying. He knows you, and he knows that you've been helping Rodriguez Tobar and his bandoleros.'

Castillo nudged Emanuel.

'You stay here,' he whispered. 'I want to hear some more. I want to hear what the sergeant says and find out if Gomez gives anything away. If I get into difficulties, don't wait. Shoot to kill, and shoot me if they capture me. Understand?'

He stole past the hen-house to the side wall of the hut, where he could catch every word. Tougher men than Ocampo had turned traitor under such treatment. Too much pain and humiliation could make people take the first step towards the enemy. The acceptance of money was the second step, and almost before they knew it they were working for the other side. Anyway, why should Ocampo keep his mouth shut for the sake of a handful of under-nourished, ill-clad guerilleros? Not because he was politically well indoctrinated or distrusted the President – Gomez Ocampo knew nothing of politics or the President. If he kept quiet, it might be because he vaguely felt that the guerilleros could do something to change the appalling conditions which prevailed in his country. Alternatively, he might be frightened of Rodriguez Tobar, who seemed to have eyes and ears everywhere.

The sergeant was seated now, as Castillo could see through the little window on the far side of the hut. He had draped his arms over the back of his chair and was studying Ocampo closely.

'Tell us who you've been in contact with these last few weeks and we'll give you money, Ocampo. You could use some money.'

Castillo counted the rifles. Seven U.S. Army models, good ones. He also counted the pistols. As far as he could see there were seven of them too. He would not leave Ocampo to suffer much longer, but first he had to make sure that there were no stray soldiers outside the hut. Meanwhile, Ocampo had slid to the floor. The sergeant booted him furiously in the face. Castillo saw it happen and was surprised at his own lack of emotion. The sergeant would be dead soon, but not before he had tasted a dose of his own medicine. He would see his men gunned down, one by one, and then he would tell them the name of the man who had betrayed Ocampo. They would see if he held out longer than his victim, if his hard shell of brutality cracked before he died.

Castillo crept round behind the horses, skirted the far wall of the hut, and returned to his original hiding-place.

He raised his arm in a signal to fan out. His men closed in on the hut. Their faces were grim, perhaps grimmer than Castillo's. His only thought was to discover the traitor's name. Nothing was more dangerous to the guerilleros than treachery from within.

The first shot struck the sergeant in the forearm, robbing him of any chance to draw his pistol. Aiming calmly, Emanuel shot three of the other six men in quick succession. Their faces registered nothing as they died, not even surprise. The others raised their hands and lined up silently against the wall. One of them made a sudden dash for the door, and Pedro shot him at point-blank range.

Covered by the rest of the party, Castillo advanced on the remaining two soldiers, drew his pistol and shot them in the head. Their bodies fell at the sergeant's feet and sprawled across the unconscious form of Gomez Ocampo.

'Emanuel, go outside and keep watch. Somebody may have heard the shots. You, Pedro, fetch our horses and be quick about it. Carlos, see if you can bring Gomez round. Saddle one of the army horses and tie him on as best you can. Gomez must be with us when they find the bodies tomorrow or they'll hack him to pieces. Now you, Sergeant. Who put the finger on Ocampo?'

The sergeant was braver than Castillo had expected.

'Go fuck yourself, you dirty bandolero,' he said.

Castillo was unmoved. Leisurely, he drove his pistol-butt into the sergeant's face, breaking his nose.

'Start talking.'

The sergeant said nothing. It was easy to see what he thought of Castillo and the others. They had shot his men in cold blood, ruthlessly, like dogs.

'Go to hell, where you belong,' he said with an effort.

Castillo thought for a moment. The man did not look as if he would talk, but it was worth a try before Pedro returned with the horses.

'Stupid as well as arrogant, eh?' he said. 'Only a fool would venture into this area at night with a handful of men. Couldn't you have done it by day, or were you afraid Gomez would escape at the last minute?'

'He did. I brought him back.'

The sergeant looked down at the bodies of his men. Their lifeless faces were blank, all except the last two to die, who wore a grimace of terror.

'The man's name!' Castillo said crisply.

The sergeant started to bellow with laughter. He might have been standing in a *cantina*, not in a peasant hut littered with the corpses of his men. The laughter was so contemptuous, so patently that of the stronger, that Castillo had a momentary vision of more soldiers standing in the doorway with their rifles trained on him.

'Filthy scum, son of a whore,' spat the sergeant as a fist smashed his teeth.

'Armando, collect the guns. Hurry! We move out in five minutes.' Castillo could hear the sound of horses' hoofs and the subdued voices of Pedro and Emanuel. He weighed his pistol in his hand, staring at the sergeant.

'So you won't talk. Don't you have anything to say?'

'To rebels like you? To a murderer like you? Shoot, *hombre*, it'll be a relief to see the last of your ugly face.'

Castillo nodded dispassionately.

He pulled the trigger and saw the sergeant fold up, slowly, as if he were making a last effort to keep his feet. Castillo turned away with admiration in his eyes, and when Emanuel came in and gave the sergeant's body a kick he snapped at him to stop it.

They shared out the rifles and pistols, mounted their horses, and set off on the final stretch of their journey to the thickly wooded mountains above Talmac.

Early next morning they arrived and pitched a temporary camp. Leaving his men to rest, Castillo went alone up a narrow track which led in the general direction of Tobar's base camp. He left his horse behind because it would have made him more conspicuous and given him less chance to hide in an emergency, although, being familiar with the track, he knew that government troops seldom used it for fear of ambush. High above the trees he could see the first light of morning rend the clouds, which were scudding low over the hillside like great white birds in search of prey.

The deaths of the sergeant and his six men did not weigh heavily on Castillo's conscience. He only felt admiration for the man he had shot down last of all. If he had to die some day he wanted to die as the sergeant had, arrogant and unmoved, defiant to the last. The enemy knew how to die as well as fight, there was no denying it.

Gomez Ocampo had ridden with them. He had not spoken on the way, but just before Castillo set out for base camp he came to him, shaking his head sadly.

'I know something now,' he said. 'When you saved my life last night you sentenced me to life imprisonment, here in the jungle.'

Castillo nodded.

'The alternative was death, Gomez. And if you ever lose heart and try to go back it will mean the same. If the soldiers don't catch you and torture you to death, we will shoot you. All or nothing, Gomez, that's our rule.'

'At least I know where I stand, Raoul.'

Raoul Castillo laid his hands on Ocampo's shoulders and stared into his eyes. 'Let me tell you something, Gomez. Last week when I slept in your hut I was envious. Envious of your home, your chickens, your maize, your yucca. I dreamt of living like you one day. I don't have to envy you any more. From now on you will fight beside me to regain your home. It's a healthy ambition, my friend, to fight for one's home.'

Ocampo did not reply because they both knew that words were superfluous. There was no going back for either of them. Death would dog Ocampo every day, teaching him what it meant to be hunted day by day, hour by hour.

Poor country, Castillo thought as he plodded along, poor Conciencia, where men were forced to take such decisions. The sun climbed slowly. A strong wind bore down on the mountains and swirled about them, sweeping away the clouds which clung to their flanks as though seeking to escape the force of the gale. Foliage was plucked from the trees, gathered up by a huge invisible hand and suddenly released, so that individual leaves exploded into the sky like jet fighters, then sank in wide spirals to the barren ground and formed a carpet there.

Birds took wing and soared high above the leaves, manoeuvring skilfully between gusts, or hopped along the ground, heads darting to right and left, tails bobbing convulsively, before spreading their wings and shooting upwards like arrows from a bow, their powerful wing-beats conquering the expanses of the sky. Sometimes, a dozen or more would peck at the ground one moment and rise in a body the next.

Nature was the one redeeming feature of life, Castillo reflected, the one thing which God could not take away. On days like this he forgot about human beings who were lower than the beasts. He yearned to be an animal himself, perhaps a horse, which could graze in peace for weeks, or a thick-fleeced sheep which comfortably survived the coldest Andean nights and defied the wind that plucked at its wool.

And so he trudged onwards and upwards with his captured rifle in his hand and his captured pistol at his belt. He glanced at the number of his rifle, 4558808 – an American M.I.30, of course. The whole of the national army was equipped with United States weapons just as the guerilleros carried Czech, Belgian or Chinese guns. He smiled as he envisaged Tobar's reaction to his story. It was undoubtedly one of the heaviest losses inflicted on government troops in recent weeks. He wondered what irresponsible fool had taken it into his head to operate at night with such a small patrol.

Castillo was now approaching the vicinity of the base camp. He had to be careful because the guerilleros tended to kill first and ask questions afterwards. He slowed his steps. The location of the outposts often changed. One day they might be here, another day a kilometre farther on, but outposts there undoubtedly were, and any attempt at concealment on his part would mean certain death. One gap in a ring of defences had been enough to spell annihilation for an entire guerrilla base, not only here but in Guatemala and even in Cuba during those first arduous months in the Sierra Maestra. There was something intimidating about the silence that hung over the forest when the wind dropped. It was a silence which said: kill or be killed, shoot first or die.

'*Quién va?*'

The voice came from the trees, but Castillo could see no sign of life.

'Raoul Castillo.'

'Password?'

'Mexico.'

'Drop your gun and stand in the middle of the path. Be quick!'

He did as he was told and was relieved, a moment later, to find himself surrounded by familiar faces.

'Jorge!'

'Raoul! We were afraid you hadn't made it.'

'All's well. The other four are back too. How are things here?'

'The *Capitán* has a good plan.'

'I know.'

'No, he abandoned the original idea. We are going to execute Lieutenant Losano and kidnap Don Henrico.'

'Why not destroy the whole rat's nest?'

'The *Capitán* will tell you. I'll escort you through the other outposts – it'll be easier.'

Castillo did not tell Jorge what had happened the night before. Rodriguez Tobar must be the first to hear. Besides, it still irked him that he had no idea of the traitor's identity, if indeed he existed at all. It was quite possible that the sergeant had invented him as a means of getting Ocampo to talk. Intimidation, bribery, treachery, that was the sequence. Castillo had used the same methods himself. The end justified the means, however reprehensible.

'And how are you, Jorge? I didn't expect to see you up here.'

The other man did not reply. How should he be? All he wanted was revenge for himself and his friend Pablo, and that had yet to come. Preparations for the raid on Talmac were proceeding slowly because Tobar had insisted that information should only be gathered from the most reliable sources. Jorge's nights in camp were made restless by the desire for a woman – any woman. Differences of opinion raged between the guerilleros from the city and those from the villages. Sometimes Jorge's nostalgia for Talmac grew so intense that it was all he could do not to go berserk. Guerrilla warfare might seem romantic to an outsider, and violence could be a sublimation of the aggressive urge, but there was much more to it than that. The danger of death was almost omnipresent. The mind became blunted, eaten up with envy of all who led a comparatively normal life. An unexpected voice or snapping twig struck terror into the heart. There was danger latent in everything – trees, bushes, even the sudden flight of a bird.

'Homesick, Jorge?' Castillo asked.

He knew in advance that Jorge would deny it. Recruits quickly became adept at hiding their feelings. This made them seem far harder than they actually were. It took them about five years to change. After that they became firmly rooted in their adopted environment.

Silence they were slower to learn, but silence was their only salvation, and once they had learned it only doubts remained to plague them – doubts about their strength and ability to win. One had only to look at Colonel Zambrano's men. They were better armed and equipped, had more supplies and better communications. At first sight, they seemed invincible. Castillo wondered how long it would be before the guerilleros realized that lessons could be learned from defeat, that a long succession of bitter reverses could demonstrate that the only way to win a guerrilla war was to accept one's inferiority and so gain superiority in the long run. The quality of perseverance meant more in guerrilla warfare than anything else. Outwardly, everything was against one, even the word guerillero itself, which was tantamount to bandolero, or dirty bandit.

They passed a number of heavily armed sentries and eventually reached base camp. Well concealed behind a belt of dense trees and undergrowth, it was a small village which no one was permitted to leave without the personal consent of Rodriguez Tobar. All the rules of guerrilla warfare were observed there, and not even those who knew the camp's location could have told from a distance that it was occupied by hundreds of people living in close proximity. This was where Tobar kept his horses, trucks, and even a couple of armoured vehicles captured from units of the national army. This was also where his armourers toiled night and day in their well-guarded workshop and where he maintained his ammunition dumps and long-range radio installation. There were even some light anti-aircraft guns for defence against a possible air strike.

Castillo thanked Jorge and went on alone to the commander's hut. Rodriguez Tobar, who was seated at his map-table, glanced up in surprise as he walked in, then sprang to his feet and embraced him.

'I was beginning to worry about you, Raoul. Where are the others? Sit down, a glass of wine will do you good. You look all in.'

Castillo smiled.

'Wait till you hear my news, *Capitán*.'

'Some of it I know already,' Tobar said. 'But tell me yourself.'

He listened without interruption or change of expression, his eyes fixed on the other man's face. The only time he showed any emotion was when Castillo came to the attack on Ocampo's hut.

'Was it necessary to kill them, Raoul? Wouldn't it have been better to take their guns and leave them tied up?'

'I think not. They knew too much.'

Tobar nodded.

'Do you believe the sergeant's story about a traitor?'

'I don't know, but I think we should act on the assumption that he was telling the truth.'

'I suppose so,' Tobar said. 'The trouble is, your little massacre will mean increased activity on the part of the army. Colonel Zambrano won't take this lying down.'

'No doubt about it, *Capitán*.'

Tobar pondered in silence. Then he said: 'You stay in camp for the time being. I need you for my new plan. Go and get some sleep now – I'll see you're not disturbed.'

Tobar frowned when Castillo had left the command post. He made a few more notes and debated whether or not to postpone the abduction of Don Henrico and the liquidation of Lieutenant Losano. The information collected by Pablo and Jorge was scanty. The *campesinos* they had questioned were in no position to follow the movements of their prospective prey. No one had any contact with members of Don Henrico's household staff, and information about what went on inside the army post was still harder to obtain. The inhabitants of Talmac were frightened. Everyone knew Losano's violent temper and many had suffered from its effects. Tobar was reluctant to make a move until the prospects of success were reasonably well assured. It might be an over-cautious attitude, but he had too few men to be able to afford risks. On the other hand, he could not afford to wait too long. The death of the seven-man patrol had no connection with Talmac, and Talmac was the place where accounts must be settled first. Besides, he could sympathize with his men's impatience. Losano's reign of terror must be brought to an end.

He returned to the map-table and continued to work on his plans.

Nearly two hundred kilometres away Colonel Zambrano and Lieutenant Wells were also bent over a map-table. The colonel's forefinger tapped the mountains round Talmac.

'In my opinion, John, that's where the main concentration of guerilleros is. How did your visit go?'

John Wells grinned.

'Much as I expected, Colonel. Losano runs the place like a penitentiary. It's so quiet there mightn't be a guerillero for a hundred kilometres around. On the other hand, I wouldn't be surprised if Tobar attacked tomorrow.'

Zambrano nodded impatiently.

'Couldn't you be a little more explicit, John? I appreciate your businesslike American approach, but I'd like a general summary of your impressions.'

'You mean that?'

'Why not?'

'Because you mightn't like what I have to say. It wouldn't be the first time.'

Zambrano shrugged.

'I thought I was the touchy one. Perhaps I was mistaken.'

'Okay, if you want the truth you can have it. Let's start with your old buddy Don Henrico. A complete egomaniac who never spares a thought for anyone else, least of all his *campesinos*. His estate may be the finest coffee plantation in the whole of Conciencia, but good coffee seems to go with a bad conscience – except that he doesn't have one. What beats me is how his workers have put up with it all these years. He exploits them. They're scarcely human to him. If somebody could invent a machine with arms and legs, a sort of self-propelled computer which didn't cost anything, he'd treat it just the same or even better. A field-hand who gets acute appendicitis or something equally curable is as good as dead. Don Henrico thinks doctors are a luxury. He runs a little dispensary, sure, but the drugs are fifty per cent more expensive there than anywhere else in Conciencia, so he even makes a good thing out of his sick peasants. We may be capitalists, Colonel, but take a good look at your home-grown variety first. Our financial tycoons are archangels compared to him.'

Zambrano interrupted him.

'I asked for a summary of local conditions, not a political analysis.'

Wells crossed his legs and gave Zambrano a quizzical stare.

'Now who's being touchy, Colonel. Okay, I'm sorry. Losano seems to have the situation well under control, certainly at first sight. Discipline is tight, morale good. He keeps his men on their toes. There have been almost no incidents lately. The local inhabitants are so scared of Losano they treat him like God Almighty. He's already on close terms with Don Henrico, and they spend a lot of time together. Talmac is a model of co-operation between the army and local business interests. Guerrilla activity has fallen off and so have attacks on outlying villages. Seems Losano has a couple of tame informers on his books but they can't deliver the goods because they never make more than one contact with the guerilleros. He tried to intercept consignments of supplies once or twice, but it wasn't any use.'

Zambrano drummed impatiently on his desk.

'Something's worrying you, though. Come on, let's have it.'

Wells lit a cigarette and stared thoughtfully out of the window. There was a rhythmical tramp of boots as a squad of green-uniformed soldiers marched across the barrack square.

'I don't know, exactly. It's too quiet, like some hick town in the mid-West, but appearances are deceptive and Losano doesn't seem to grasp that. He's too convinced of his own cleverness and the strength of his command. He's too easily misled by the docility of the *campesinos*. To be frank, his complacency gave me the creeps.'

'Losano is an efficient and experienced soldier, John, you know that.'

'Sure, but he's too self-confident, under the circumstances.'

At that moment the telephone rang. Wells watched Zambrano's expression change as he listened. It became hard and grim.

'What? Say that again, man. A sergeant and six men? Where? Send me the fellow who found them – at once, do you understand?'

Zambrano looked bitter as he replaced the receiver.

'A sergeant and six men shot near Monton. They were found in the hut of a *campesino* named Gomez Ocampo, out in the wilds. No sign of any weapons or horses. *Madre de Dios*, those damned bandoleros!'

Wells digested the news in silence. Then he asked: 'Were they Losano's men?'

Zambrano shook his head.

'No, Monton is outside his area.'

He walked over to the map.

'Here, more or less. Hilly country, though it lies on the highland plateau. The killers disappeared into the mountains, of course, but it should be possible to pick up their trail. Radio Losano and tell him to get to Monton fast.'

The *campesino* who had gone to visit his friend Gomez Ocampo that morning was brought into Zambrano's office four hours later. He was still completely bewildered by the turn of events. The furrowed face with the broad Indian cheek-bones twitched nervously beneath its thatch of blue-black hair. He looked as if suspicion attached to him, not the guerilleros, and John Wells deduced that the local troops did not treat the inhabitants of the area as gently as Colonel Zambrano seemed to imagine.

'What time was it when you reached Ocampo's *finca*?' asked Zambrano.

'About eight o'clock this morning, Excellency.'

'Why did you go there?'

'I wanted to buy some eggs from him. My wife has been nagging me for days.'

'Well, what happened?'

'I opened the door and looked inside. It was like a slaughterhouse. A sergeant and six men . . . A terrible thing, Excellency.'

'What did you do then?'

'I took my horse and rode to the army post at Monton. The sergeant there did not believe me at first, but he came with me in the end.'

John Wells, who had been listening in silence, forestalled Zambrano with a question of his own.

'How far is it from your hut to Ocampo's?'

The *campesino* thought for a moment.

'I don't know, Excellency. Two kilometres, perhaps more.'

'And you heard no shots?'

'No, Excellency, no shots. Nothing but the wind. It was blowing a gale last night.'

'No horsemen either?'

'No, I was asleep. I heard nothing. Nothing much happens down our way. The bandoleros are up in the mountains. They never come down to the plateau – that is to say, not as a rule.'

'So you've never seen any guerilleros?'

'No. I wouldn't know one if I saw one.'

The man's face was inscrutable, but Wells had the impression that he was lying.

'Have you ever seen strangers at Ocampo's *finca*?'

The *campesino* stared at him woodenly as if he had not heard the question.

'If you're lying I'll have you shot on the spot, so think again.'

Fear stirred in the man's eyes. Wells went and stood over him.

'Think well before you answer, *hombre*. Seven of our men have been shot, so we're not in the best of tempers. I'll try once more. Have you ever seen strangers at Ocampo's *finca*?'

Colonel Zambrano gave Wells a nod. He took the hint.

'You're hiding something. Very well, what's one man more or less?'

He beckoned to the escorting soldiers.

'Take him away and shoot him. It may loosen a few tongues.'

The American's voice was as calm as if he had asked them to fetch him a pack of cigarettes. The *campesino* shrank back.

'Last week I saw five men riding away from his hut, Excellency. I had never seen them before.'

'How did they look?'

'Like this,' the *campesino* replied simply, pointing to his ragged trousers and ruana.

'Were they armed?'

The man shook his head.

'They had no guns, Excellency, only machetes.'

Colonel Zambrano cut the interrogation short.

'Had the bodies been maltreated?'

'No, Excellency, not the soldiers. Only the sergeant. It looked as if they had hit him in the face.'

'Very well, you may go. Return to your home and stay there until further notice. We may need you again.'

Ten minutes later Zambrano and Wells left by helicopter for Monton. The two men stared silently at the country-side below them. It looked peaceful enough – deceptively so. Above their heads the slender rotor-blades thrashed the air in a steady rhythm. Zambrano frowned to himself. Everything was in their favour. They had the best weapons, the best-trained and best-fed men. They could call on helicopters, strike aircraft, ultra-modern equipment – all that an army needed. And yet, despite everything, the guerilleros inspired more fear than they did. They were quicker and more flexible. They struck here today, there tomorrow, vanishing into the mountains which were their permanent sanctuary. The army controlled the highland plateau, the guerilleros the mountains. The army could not drive them out because it was courting death to venture into their domain.

Zambrano glanced at Wells's calm face. Things were easier for him. He was not personally involved. If the rebels ever won he would be on the next plane home. For Zambrano himself, his family, friends and relations, their victory would mean death. Not at once, perhaps, but later on, when the leaders who now operated in the mountains seized power. That was why they had to be exterminated before their gospel of violence engulfed the country like a tidal wave of hatred.

A jeep was waiting for them when the helicopter landed, ready to take them to the scene of the massacre. Zambrano climbed out when they reached the hut and pushed the door open. He looked down at the bodies of his men. The sergeant's face was badly knocked about but the others looked as if they had fallen asleep from exhaustion. Zambrano picked his way between the corpses, stiff-faced, but John Wells showed more interest in an open space on the floor beside an overturned chair.

'Blood,' he said aloud. 'Quite a lot of blood.'

Zambrano looked up.

He stepped over the intervening bodies and followed the direction of Wells's finger, then stared into the American lieutenant's blue eyes.

'Are you thinking what I'm thinking?' he said.

Wells nodded.

'Yes, Ocampo must have been one of the guerilleros' contact-men. The patrol worked him over but dropped their guard while the interrogation was in progress. I wouldn't mind betting they didn't even post a sentry.'

'And Ocampo kept his mouth shut.'

'What else could he do? If one side didn't get him the other would.'

Zambrano leant against the wall of the hut and surveyed the interior. No carpets, no paintwork, just planks papered with old newsprint. The furniture consisted of a table and three rickety chairs and the floor was hard-packed mud.

'The same old story,' Wells said. 'Know who did this, Colonel? The men who were sent to kill Guillermo de la Cruz.'

Zambrano nodded.

'I know I make mistakes, John, but give me time. I'll outwit these bandoleros in the end.'

'I hope so, Colonel, for your country's sake.'

'Have the bodies transported back to base. We'll bury them with full military honours. Make a list of their personal effects, check the list in Monton, and inform the press what has happened. I read that madman Valencia's speech this morning. Let's give him a fitting reply.'

John Wells grinned sardonically.

'While we're on the subject of politics, Colonel . . .'

Zambrano stepped across the bodies and out into the open air. His face was sterner than ever. Without another word he climbed into the jeep and drove back to Monton, where the helicopter had attracted a silent, awestruck crowd.

'You wait here for Losano, John. On second thoughts, I'd prefer to draft that communiqué myself. I think it would be more appropriate. I'll send the helicopter to pick you up later this afternoon.'

13

It was the same everywhere. Acclamation greeted Antonio Valencia in every province and at every university he visited. The newspapers, even those controlled by Fierro, reported his speeches almost without comment. His friend Cuellar had ranged himself behind the new movement and published leading articles designed to show that the priest's aim was to rouse the country and government from their torpor. Fierro promised, editorially, to revert to Valencia's original declaration once its text had been carefully studied. Only Vermeer preserved a disconcerting silence on the subject. Vermeer must have his reasons for not endorsing the programme and Valencia wondered what they were.

But he did not have much time for reflection. In every town he visited his speeches provoked a furious response from members of the local establishment, who sometimes prevailed on the police to detain him for a few hours in the building where he had just spoken. He was never formally arrested, however, merely warned by various provincial governors that entry would be denied him in future. In his own circle in Cielo Valencia began to sense exasperation on the part of families with whom he had previously been on friendly terms. His telephone rang less often. He received fewer invitations to parties, and every now and then one of his former friends would phone him to ask, more in sorrow than in anger, if he didn't think he'd overstepped the mark at last.

One day Valencia asked Bruce Cornell to accompany him to a meeting with some trade union leaders. It soon struck Bruce that they were less enraptured by Valencia's remarks than the students and intellectuals who attended his public speeches. Discreetly, they reproached him for oversimplifying the situation and working too closely with the Communists, especially those who had been invited to join the editorial board of his new weekly paper. After the meeting Valencia decided to call on Vermeer and ask him outright what he thought of the current position. He couldn't quite define why he asked Bruce to come with him. Perhaps it was an almost subconscious wish to thwart the rumour-mongers who implied or openly stated that he was having an affair with Esther Graham.

Sitting in the car on the way to see Vermeer, he resolved to broach the subject of Esther because he somehow felt that Bruce had a right to know how matters stood. He did not find it easy, but his entire life had been such an unremitting struggle for honesty and sincerity that he could not keep silent. Without any preamble, he said: 'Do you also think I'm having an affair with Esther, Cornell?'

Bruce shrugged.

'Does it matter what I think, Padre? You may care but Esther doesn't, not any more. Strictly speaking, you're the one who's keeping me here in this country. My papers want me to stay here and await the outcome of your campaign against the establishment. If I didn't have this assignment to cover I'd probably have moved on weeks ago and washed my hands of the whole affair. Besides, you don't owe me any explanations.'

Valencia shot him a sidelong glance.

'Is that genuine indifference, or are you feeling hurt and trying not to show it?'

They pulled up at one of the numerous traffic lights in the main avenida. The pavements were thronged with pedestrians. Cielo was as beautiful as many other big Latin American cities, a friendly place with countless shops, swarms of shoe-shine boys, beggars who stared after well-dressed women with an interest which momentarily put them on a par with their more prosperous fellow-citizens. No one ever looked twice at the men and women dressed in rags. They were as much a part of the avenidas as the lamp-posts. They mattered less than a whimpering dog or a cat that snatches a morsel of meat from the table and makes off with it. People had simply ceased to see poverty for what it was. Many of them actually found it romantic, especially the camera-hung tourists avid for pictorial souvenirs of a fleeting visit.

'Would you be offended if I asked you to regard the subject of Esther and me as a personal matter – something between the two of us?' Bruce said.

Another traffic light turned red and Valencia braked.

'Of course not.'

His voice was so low that Bruce could barely hear it above the hum of the engine.

'But I'm a priest, Cornell, and priests are entitled to give advice. Esther is an excellent secretary and I should be sorry if her job led to a break between you and her. On the other hand, she has a will of her own.'

'So I've noticed.'

The note of sarcasm was stronger than Bruce had intended. He tried to compensate for it.

'To answer your question: no, I don't think you're having an affair with Esther, but I'm not convinced that she wouldn't prefer it that way.'

Anything but convinced, he thought. Something had happened to Esther in the weeks that had gone by since their latest reunion. He had enough experience of women to know what sudden elusiveness could mean.

'Would you like me to speak to her?'

Bruce shook his head.

'No, please don't, you'd only make matters worse. Better leave well alone. Everyone has to decide what happens in his own life.'

'Unless other people decide for him,' Valencia replied, and he was not thinking of Esther.

They drew up outside the block where Valencia and Vermeer lived. It overlooked one of the finest parks in the city, with the skyscrapers of Cielo towering on the left and the mountains on the right. They rode up in the lift and rang Vermeer's bell. The Dutchman opened the door himself, and Valencia could see his eyes light up at the sight of them.

'Antonio! Come in! How are you, Cornell? No, no, don't say a word until you're safely in a chair with a glass beside you.'

Nothing much had changed since Bruce's last visit. The room was still littered with books and gramophone records, but Vermeer himself looked more ascetic, his face graver and more transparent.

Bruce glanced at Valencia. He had a relaxed air and his eyes shone as if he had found complete peace at last. Vermeer's expression contrasted strongly with Valencia's. It was as if he were trying to gauge the effect of his nationwide tour, examine him for signs of complacency or doubt, detect any loss of vitality.

But Valencia puffed quietly at his pipe, took an occasional sip of whisky, and seemed quite content to sit there in snug seclusion, drawing on the spiritual strength of his friend and mentor.

'You came here to discuss something, Antonio?' Vermeer asked at length.

'I came for some private reassurance, though I realize I may be asking too much.'

Vermeer shook his head.

234

'My guess is, you came to ask what I really think. Am I right?'
Valencia laughed.

'*Bueno.* I came to ask your opinion, find out what your misgivings are, if any, and benefit from your experience and ideas.'

'My ideas?' Vermeer said, leaning towards him. 'Very well, Antonio, if that's what you want, but we'll have to approach the question from a theoretical angle, not a personal one. Any objections?'

Bruce Cornell studied the two friends. They could not have been more dissimilar, at least outwardly. Antonio Valencia with his athlete's build and Don Juanesque looks, bursting with health and vitality, and Vermeer, tall, spindly, and every inch a priest in spite of his slacks and open-necked shirt.

'All right, Antonio, let's begin at the beginning. You want the people to assume power at the earliest possible moment. You plan to wage war on the oligarchy and the ruling class. But why not operate vertically instead of horizontally? You surely wouldn't claim that there isn't a single man of goodwill in the whole of the upper classes? In my opinion, you won't create a new Conciencia overnight without drawing on the experience and ability of those upper classes, however much it goes against the grain. You must realize as well as I do that the people are totally unprepared to pick up the reins of government. The existing electoral system makes it virtually impossible for them to do so legally, that's to say, by exercising their right to vote. On the other hand, an illegal seizure of power will result in revolution and bloodshed.'

Valencia nodded.

'You admit it yourself. We can't achieve anything legally, so violence is the only answer. I'm amazed that you're still in any doubt.'

Vermeer smiled.

'Very well, let's proceed to the next point – to your practical objectives: political and social pluralism, equal rights and protection for minorities which have hitherto been persecuted. In my view, Antonio – and you mustn't take it amiss if I say so frankly in Cornell's presence – you're tackling this in a very naive way. You can't simply extend unconditional protection to minorities and incorporate them in society on an equal footing. It could be that one minority rejects pluralism on principle and cynically exploits it in order to gain power. For instance, the Communists have no prospect of succeeding here on their own, but they're only too happy to back you for the time being. You must also concede that they're

235

almost the only people – apart from Esther, of course – who really work hard on your behalf. Take the staff of that weekly of yours, or the people who accompany you on your lecture tours. The Communist press extols you for your pastoral and Christian virtues – all the more so because your programme will lend itself perfectly to Communist reinterpretation at a later stage. Don't you realize the risk you run by incorporating Communists in your movement?'

Valencia puffed at his pipe until he was swathed in a cloud of blue smoke. He shook his head.

'The Communists want revolution as much as I do, and that's a good enough reason for working with them. You may be perceptive, Francisco, but you're a foreigner. As a Conciencian, I know only too well what's going on here. The rich will never introduce any radical reforms. The most they'll ever do is step up their contributions to charity. They're prisoners of the dollar, United States trusties who bleed the poor to guarantee their own economic survival. No, Francisco, the rich won't work with me unless we make insane concessions, and we aren't prepared to – none of us. The land of promises must turn into á promised land, and we won't achieve that by enlisting the help of the ruling clique.'

Vermeer refilled the glasses. His face seemed even paler and his eyes, which were still more translucent than they had been at the start of the conversation, held a look of passionate disquiet and suppressed agitation which was echoed by the tremor in his hands.

'But Antonio, don't you see that if fighting broke out you'd only have part of the army on your side – not the whole of it, believe me. And that wouldn't be enough to secure power for the people if every legal avenue proved to be closed. If it did come to an armed conflict you could only count on material assistance from the Communist bloc, even though the avowed Communists in your movement constitute a minority. That sort of foreign aid would destroy you and all your plans. Power would fall neatly into the waiting hands of the Communists. Having exploited your Christian, democratic and pluralist principles to the full, they'd thrust you aside. Their new regime would not tolerate Christian concern for minorities or democratic pluralist principles. Haven't you grasped that yet? The whole of your well-meant revolution would turn into the opposite of what you intend.'

Valencia shook his head again. 'You exaggerate,' he said firmly. 'I'm prepared to make use of anything in Communism that has universal and practical value, but I dissociate myself from the system as such. I repudiate its materialist ideology and its acceptance that a specific end justifies any means under the sun. You're too pessimistic, Francisco. The people will help me to put my ideas into practice. What is more, I consider the revolutionary awakening of the inhabitants of this country to be more important than my personal basis of action, which I'll come to in a minute. Come what may, my policy will be founded on transcendental Christian principles. People who fail to understand that fail to understand me, even if you're among them.'

A faint smile crossed Vermeer's face.

'I'm almost tempted to applaud you, Antonio, but you're making a crucial psychological blunder when you call for unlimited State control – control of education and earnings, compulsory investment of surplus income in government enterprises, and so on. Limitation of private incomes might seem attractive at first glance because excess funds could be used to create fresh employment and earnings opportunities for the poor, but careful study convinces me that levelling down private incomes destroys personal initiative. Russia has tried a similar experiment and failed. Why repeat the process all over again? Do you know what would happen if you imposed such a system? In the long run, everyone would restrict his activities to a minimum – unless, of course, your new State intends to wield the big stick.'

Vermeer paused and looked at Valencia.

'Shall I continue, or have you had enough criticism for one day?'

'No, please go on. At least it's friendly criticism.'

Vermeer removed his glasses and polished the lenses carefully.

'Very well. You also call for the expropriation of all buildings and land surplus to personal requirements. That strikes me as utterly utopian, quite apart from being a source of unnecessary conflict. What do you hope to achieve – greater communal prosperity or greater communal poverty? Won't popular emancipation be accompanied by the creation of a political system which will devour the fruits of personal endeavour like a Moloch, transforming Conciencia into a colourless society of State planners and protectionists? I fully agree with you that it's impossible to create a new society without vigorous but temporary State intervention. In my view, however, it ought to be stressed that your programme has temporary application only. You should not only respect personal endeavour but reward it as well. The abolition of extreme contrasts need not be effected with the aid of extreme socialization. And what I'm saying now has nothing to do with orthodoxy or heterodoxy. It's simply a question of understanding the psychological forces at work in our society.'

'So you're in total disagreement?'

There was a note of impatience in Valencia's voice. A strange gleam came into his eyes. His hands were clenched and his whole body had gone taut.

Vermeer shook his head.

'I wouldn't say that. I agree with you but not your programme. In my opinion, your ultimate objectives in no way conflict with Church doctrine. I share your belief that the transformation of countries with sharp social and economic contrasts calls for a procedure of its own, and one in which revolution may conceivably have a place. Beware of oversimplification, that's all I ask. If your opponents accuse you of anything – and they soon will, if they aren't doing so already – that will be their first line of attack.'

'What point do you object to most?'

Valencia's voice was hoarse with emotion, but he controlled himself and studiously refilled his pipe.

'Political absolutism, as I've already said. It isn't hard to foment revolution in this country, thanks to the appalling conditions under which people live here. They have nothing to lose, materially speaking, but your projected form of government embodies such an element of State control that it's almost bound to end in dictatorship. Temporary dictatorship may be inevitable, I concede that, but who is to guarantee that it won't last? Dictatorship persists in Communist countries and the people are rebelling against it. I realize that a revolutionary has to simplify things because no revolution can take every factor into account. Also, the unsophisticated masses are incapable of grasping complex grounds for action. But take care. One day the masses may come of age and hold you responsible for the Communist menace. If they do, I wouldn't give a peso for your chances of success – and I thoroughly approve of your basic ideas even if I disagree with your methods.'

Valencia drew a deep breath.

'I've lost faith in the ruling class. At the risk of repeating myself, I know them too well. What if I co-operated with them? In a year's time they'd still be fobbing me off with the same old empty promises, and the situation would be what it is now. You're a European, Francisco. Could the French Revolution have dispensed with violence? Will the coming revolutions in Spain and Portugal dispense with violence? Didn't it happen that way in Russia? Well, here, a few dozen families control an entire country, and as long as power remains in

238

their hands nothing will ever change. I know them personally, don't forget. I know their strength as well as their weaknesses.'

Vermeer nodded.

'Yes,' he said, 'their strength,' and suddenly Bruce felt the menace that hung in the air, as if death were already winding its toils about Valencia's strong young body.

Valencia rose to his feet.

'There's no point in discussing this further, Francisco, not for the moment. I'm going to my room now. I'll let you have my views in writing tomorrow morning.'

'By all means, Antonio,' Vermeer said, 'but don't stay up all night. You need rest.'

Valencia did not hear the last words. He had already closed the door behind him.

'Was he angry?' Bruce asked.

Vermeer shook his head.

'No, not at all. Our talks often end like that. He gets an urge to commit his ideas to paper.'

Valencia paced up and down his study for a long time. Then he went over to the bookcase, picked out a volume by Pierre Teilhard de Chardin, and opened it at a marked passage.

The principle of development assumes an extraordinary dimension in the dynamic conception of the cosmos, the world and man. If man is the centre towards which the totality of cosmic evolution turns, then his absolute development as a human being forms part of this progress. A poor people and an underdeveloped society are offences in the eyes of God and contrary to the plans of creation.

Valencia sat down at his desk and stared into space for some minutes, pulling quietly at his pipe. At last, with sudden decision, he began to write.

We find ourselves, not in a perfect world within a completed cosmos, but in the midst of a cosmic evolutionary process. Far from having attained the plenitude of his earthly destiny, man is, as it were, on the road to fulfilment.

The man who is born into this world finds everything he needs within the cosmic order. If man really finds everything he needs, and if he is compelled to satisfy his needs in this way alone, then all men without exception must share in the world's natural resources. Anyone who erects a barrier between resources and unfulfilled needs is violently infringing the order created by God. A social order must correspond exactly to this cosmic order in such a way that all members of society share in the sources of the goods and services that are indispensable to their own fundamental needs.

Valencia put down his pen and walked to the window. He stared at the shimmering lights of the big skyscrapers, listened to the muffled roar of traffic and the sporadic blare of horns, then returned to his desk.

The present order of Conciencian society reflects situations which are diametrically opposed to the cosmic order created by God. First and foremost, social organization is utterly incapable of satisfying the basic needs of the members of our society, with the result that the overwhelming majority of the Conciencian people suffers from a lack of everything. Secondly, the structures of this social organization derive their rigidity and adamantine resistance to change of any kind – and this is especially true of the political power structure – to the fact that they are deliberately and categorically perpetuated so as to form a barrier between resources and unfulfilled needs.

The main features of our agricultural system are a high concentration of landed property and its control by a tiny minority. 61% of the land is owned by 3.6% of the population, whereas 56% of peasants farm only 4.2% of the land.

Conciencia's economic system is also distinguished by a high concentration of minority-owned capital because 4.6% of the population receive 40.6% of the national income whereas 95.4%, or the vast majority, share only 59.4%. The educational system displays similar anomalies: 41% of the population are illiterate, 51% have never gone beyond primary school level, 7% are receiving secondary education, and only 0.9% attend university.

Meanwhile, the labour force increases annually by 150,000, of whom only 30,000 find work on the land and the remaining 120,000 have to seek employment in the cities. Industry can accommodate only 12,000 of these, so the luckless 108,000 remain unemployed and thus swell the urban sub-proletariat, which in some Conciencian cities already amounts to 30–40% of the total population. We are all acquainted with the pitiable conditions under which the inhabitants of the invasiones *and other outlying urban districts are forced to live. Statistics indicate a steady increase in the number of crimes against the person, most of them committed by desperate parents whose fear of seeing their children die of starvation impels them to do what is forbidden by law.*

The result of these conditions is that our country has a great deficiency of everything, a deficiency which manifests itself in a very low standard of living.

The wages paid to agricultural workers in almost every part of the country vary between U.S. $1 and U.S. $1.70 per day. 92.6% of rural dwellings have no piped water, 88.7% no sanitary installations, 95.8% no electricity, and 68% have mud floors. The mortality rate among children aged four and under exceeds 40% and the most frequent cause of death is malnutrition. It should not be forgotten that the average food intake per head of the popula-

tion in this country contains only 78.4% of the calories, 59.4% of the proteins and 55% of the fats essential to healthy physical development. There is one doctor to every 4,000 inhabitants and one hospital bed to every 4,500.

Squandering of public funds on a vast scale, successive devaluations designed to enrich the few, mortgaging of the country's labour force and natural resources, intervention by foreign economic interests and the growing concentration of capital and property in the hands of a tiny minority – all these factors have very considerably boosted the cost of living for wage- and salary-earners.

Once more Valencia rose and walked to the window. Looking up at the dark mountains on the right, he saw the single pin-point of light which marked the site of the shrine of Our Lady of the Mountains. The very act of enumerating his people's hardships, accurately and in concrete terms, had drained him of energy. Statistics made the whole situation seem even more lurid, alarming and abhorrent. The figures stood there like stone obelisks, beyond the power of man to assail. They were crosses in a cemetery containing millions who had died because no one had summoned up the courage to inscribe their headstones with the statistics of reality. Quickly, he sat down again and began to write.

The privileged classes have no conception of the significance of Conciencia's global structure within the context of international relations. Instead of embarking on a homogeneous process of development which would primarily benefit the humblest sections of the population, they construe the steady growth of their personal incomes as evidence of development and further this misguided process by means of national or international loans.

Then there is the political regime. This is directed and controlled by pressure-groups opposed to political development. They ensure that the Conciencian people remain divided into two parties. Having embroiled the people, for all their poverty, in the horrors of a civil war which cost the lives of approximately 300,000 citizens, they founded the so-called National Front and now represent it as the party which can lead the country to democracy.

But the minority groups who wield political power actually dictate, forcibly and with specious legality, the 'juridical norms' which enable them to consolidate the system and perpetuate prevailing injustices.

The class favoured by the present social order is not interested in changing it; on the contrary, redoubled efforts are being made to reinforce it. 'Legitimate' opportunities for reform have been progressively curtailed. The groups which enjoy privileged status control the media of communication and attribute all dissent to the influence of foreign ideologies.

And what are the results? A growing danger of revolution among the poor, intensified reaction and repression on the part of the privileged. But the most striking feature is that such a situation can exist within a political and legal framework which is sustained by the statute book, the army and the courts, and can thus presume to 'mediate' between the haves and the have-nots.

The army is closely linked with the minority groups which unjustly wield political power. Economic power, too, is intimately dependent on the armed forces, which claim 25% of the budget. Because of this, power is consolidated and injustice perpetuated. The army is manifestly controlled by men who, so far from propagating patriotism and loyalty to the Conciencian people, impose obedience and subordination to the ruling clique.

Ecclesiastical structures are likewise closely linked with political and economic power. Dissociation from the material world, acceptance of social injustice, recognition of the prevailing order as the will of God, and a duty to participate in reinforcing the political hegemony of the privileged class – these are the points which the Church rams home. In this oecumenical age, with its receptiveness to all things human and rebirth of interest in a universal Church, the Conciencian hierarchy rejects any dialogue with the world at large, defends the established order and status quo as if they were sacrosanct and inviolable, and condemns certain members of the clergy for the evangelical attitude which prompts them to interpret the Church's social teachings and put them into practice.

The privileged minority strives to persuade the people that their poverty has its roots in the country's own poverty and lack of resources, in the unproductiveness of their labour and the population explosion, and camouflages the prevailing chaos with euphemisms such as 'democracy' and 'values of Christian civilization'. Alternatively, it seeks to prove that the established 'order' exists by divine command.

What this minority forgets, however, is that wherever deprived masses are confronted by social structures which favour the privileged few, there comes into being a nucleus of power which is capable of successful revolution. Under these circumstances, Christianity should range itself behind those who suffer and oppose the institutional structures responsible for their suffering. Neither the indifferent nor the complacent will be able to defer such an upheaval indefinitely, however much it may appear that the establishment is temporarily succeeding in its attempt to embellish bourgeois self-interest with Christian ideals . . .

Even as Valencia wrote the last words he realized that they came straight out of Ignacio Fernandes de Castro's *Theory of Revolution*. The man was right, though. He could subscribe wholeheartedly to the final paragraph, just as he could to every word on the sheets of paper in front of him.

He stared at them reflectively, wondering if he had left Vermeer's room in too much of a hurry. Perhaps he had given the impression that he was no match for the Dutchman's arguments or that anger had got the better of him.

242

Valencia felt a sudden craving for a man-sized Scotch. He stood up and went to the drinks cupboard, but half-way there he turned. Why shouldn't he see if Vermeer was still up? Just for the sake of company, not because he wanted to pursue the discussion. Now that he had unburdened himself he felt unendurably lonely. He picked up the handwritten sheets and made his way to Vermeer's apartment. The door opened sooner than he expected, though he knew that Vermeer was a poor sleeper. The Dutchman's face betrayed no surprise.

'I hoped you'd drop in again,' he said. 'Cornell was rather disconcerted when you walked out like that.'

'I don't much care what Cornell thinks,' Valencia retorted, unintentionally abrupt. 'Here, you might like to run your eye over this. It's a written answer to the points you raised.'

He handed the manuscript to Vermeer, who began to read.

Valencia made an effort to relax. Nothing had really changed yet, not at least where he was concerned. The press had been friendly so far, even Fierro's powerful syndicate. He had heard nothing from the Cardinal, and although some of his friends in high places had repudiated him he had acquired a large number of supporters, both inside and outside the universities. Colonel García had neither summoned him nor sent minions to fetch him, and his new weekly, *La Libertad*, already boasted a five-figure circulation. Invitations to lecture were still pouring in from all over the country.

On the other hand, he could not deny that a certain silence had grown up around him. There was a steady decrease in his social encounters with the upper crust, whose representatives had ceased to regard him as a playboy in a soutane, slightly unbalanced by his student days at Louvain but amusing company for all that. They no longer laughed at his revolutionary ideas, which they had dismissed as innocuous or, at most, a piquant addition to their social circle. They took him seriously now.

Idly studying Vermeer's tall spare frame, Valencia wondered how long it would be before his enemies went over to the offensive. It had to happen sometime, he felt sure of that.

'Interesting,' Vermeer murmured, still reading. 'Interesting and dangerous . . .'

The last word seemed to hang in the air for a long time, floating in the almost unbroken stillness of the room. Valencia poured himself a whisky. His eyes travelled from Vermeer's aquiline face, tense and earnest, to his long bony fingers, to the slippers which loosely encased his stockinged feet. Vermeer looked tired, but Valencia had never seen him look otherwise. Tired but forceful – a combination which he had never found in anyone else.

At last Vermeer put the manuscript on the table and reached for his glass.

'You intend to publish this?'

'Yes, as an article in *La Libertad*.'

'My God.'

'What do you mean?'

'Publish it and they'll cut you to ribbons.'

Valencia shrugged.

'If they do, they do.'

'But why not make sure you're strong enough before launching such an attack?'

'What else would you propose?'

'I told you. Wait until you're so sure of your political strength that no one will dare to raise a hand against you. Men have been assassinated for less. Nobody ought to sign his own death-warrant.'

Valencia smiled.

'You're on the wrong track, Francisco. Of course I'm attached to life, but not enough to be deterred by threats. If that's what you think, you don't know me.'

Silence fell once more. Not everything could find expression at this nocturnal hour, not all the friendship which Vermeer felt for the younger priest, not all the criticism he would have liked to voice despite his admiration, not all the doubts and fears which both of them left unspoken.

'What are your plans tomorrow?'

'I'm flying to Fuente to address a rally of young Christian progressives. Just another group of people who are sick of the present situation.'

'What time do you leave?'

'Shortly after lunch.'

'Then come and eat with me first, about midday. It would give me great pleasure.'

Valencia stood up. He felt empty and infinitely tired, a frequent sensation in recent weeks and one which overcame him even when he was with a crowd of people. He would fall asleep, pipe in hand, hearing the murmur of his friends' voices in the background.

'*Buenas noches*,' he said. 'It's time you went to bed too.'

Vermeer nodded and saw him out. Alone again, he stood there and looked round the room. Only a few days ago, someone in his Order had said: 'We must learn to live as frugally as St Francis.

There's no other way of getting close to the people or bringing them closer to God. If, in poverty, you ask something of the poor in the name of Christ, they may curse and slam the door in your face or tell you to work instead of begging. But afterwards they come to realize that they've refused something which was asked them in the name of Christ. In that way, men draw closer to God of their own accord.'

Vermeer climbed into bed, took a pill and tried to sleep, but sleep refused to come. Images flooded in on him, images of Europe and North America, memories of what somebody there had once told him. 'The Catholics of the United States want to be good Catholics just as every American wants to be a good American and a good businessman. Individually, all Americans aspire to a grand design of some sort. Many Catholics here would gladly die for their beliefs if only they knew what they were.'

More and more ideas came to Vermeer as he lay staring at the darkness. One day, in a plane, he had sat next to a journalist who told him that he had stopped believing in anything. Scepticism could become a vogue, he reflected, or a symptom of cultural over-indulgence. It could also be that life was stronger than dogma and that people no longer knew what to do with their faith. Usually, however, they were governed by a mixture of sentiments. The journalist had gone on to speak of a personal problem. He had just become a father for the first time and was flying home to see the child, still undecided whether or not to have it baptized. Vermeer told him that baptism would be futile if he intended to rear it in his own lack of belief. The man was very surprised at this, presumably because he thought that all priests recommended baptism on principle. As they were disembarking he said: 'On second thoughts, perhaps I will have him baptized after all.'

Vermeer took another sleeping pill, but it was no use. In spite of himself, he dredged his brain for other memories. Strolling through a small town in Southern Chile he had been pinioned from behind, so suddenly and effectively that he was unable to turn round. Shock gave way to relief when he heard a familiar voice say: 'Hello, buddy, what are you doing here?' It was some friends from the States who were spending their summer holidays in Latin America. Like most American tourists, they lived royally. Money was no problem. They were planning to make a fishing-trip next day and invited him along. It developed into a positively feudal occasion. Each member of the party was allotted a rowing-boat and a crew of two, one to ply the oars and the other to bait hooks and remove fish, in this case prime salmon. Leaving the lake where they had embarked, they set off down a river dotted with rapids which the oarsmen negotiated with great skill. They caught one salmon after another, but there was no need to soil their hands on this sort of fishing-trip. At about midday they reached a clearing on the bank and were greeted by a party of riders, friends of Vermeer's friends who had organized a picnic. Vermeer reclined in the grass like an Oriental potentate while food was served to him on a damask tablecloth. It must have been an expensive outing, all in all, because the boats could not be rowed back upstream and had to be loaded on to trucks.

Another time Vermeer had been invited to visit a huge plantation of 120,000 acres as the guest of one of the managers. He came of a wealthy family, lived alone, and had until recently been waited on by a large staff. A young man of somewhat revolutionary tendencies, he claimed that the present government was only pseudo-democratic. This did not prevent him from retaining a number of Latin American habits, among them the acceptance of slavish subservience from his staff. Vermeer and his well-meaning but rather self-opinionated young host had discussed the problem of rural emancipation, which was even more fraught with difficulty than he had supposed. It appeared that the manager had invited his workers to call on him one evening for a discussion of outstanding problems. He couched the invitation in cordial and informal terms, but the workers excused themselves on the grounds that they were unworthy to set foot in the house of their *patrón* – who was, be it noted, a youngster of twenty-two. They respectfully requested that the meeting should be held in the house of an overseer, which it duly was. The manager took advantage of the occasion to declare his solidarity with them and begged them to speak frankly, but a centuries-old pattern of life could not be broken in a single evening, and the manager admitted that the awakening of the individual was an extremely time-consuming process. The workers simply waited for orders and obeyed them unquestioningly. They never knew what to say if asked for their opinion.

Vermeer switched on the light, reached for a cigarette and lit it. He blew the smoke far across the room, remembering the hopeless apathy of the workers he had known in the days when he lived among them and shared their way of life. He wondered if Antonio Valencia felt the same, if he sensed their utter hopelessness, their inability to express their feelings, even, perhaps, the mistrust concealed beneath a mask of respect.

Four o'clock struck and still Vermeer lay awake, thinking of the man in the next apartment and his attempt to shoulder all these problems, the burden of an entire nation.

El Temporal, Conciencia's most prestigious daily, had its head-quarters in a skyscraper office block in Cielo. The same building housed the executive offices of the Fierro Organization, which controlled most of the country's newspapers with the exception of Cuellar's and one or two small left-wing organs. These were permitted to survive partly for the sake of democratic appearances and partly as a barometer from which the ruling clique could gauge the intensity of threats to its supremacy and the identity of those responsible for them.

On this particular morning Ignacio Fierro was holding an editorial conference. Provincial editors had been summoned to the capital from all over the country. Having arrived there, some by plane and others by car, they were now sitting rather apprehensively round the big table in the board-room, swapping journalistic gossip. The only man who showed no signs of nervousness was Alejandro Herrera, deputy editor and senior political commentator of the Fierro Organization and *El Temporal* in particular. He was not unduly popular with his colleagues, but the political pressure-group which retained him valued his keenly analytical articles, the biting scorn which he poured on his opponents, and his outstanding knowledge of Conciencia and its people, especially from the psychological angle.

Alejandro Herrera did not like his fellow-men; he only liked to manipulate them. He ruled Conciencia from his oversized desk almost as if he were President. Alternatively, he could have been regarded as an extension of the President's own pen. Like Fierro, Herrera came of a wealthy family and practised journalism as a hobby, which coincidentally earned him a fat income. He enjoyed great prestige among the ruling class, and his tall stature, jet-black hair, long saturnine face and sombre style of dress made him look the diplomat which, fundamentally, he was. If it suited him – after consultation with Fierro – publicly to demolish some minister who had incurred his displeasure, he did so with a relish and enthusiasm worthy of a better cause. This often created the impression that *El Temporal* was a champion of the oppressed, but the discriminating reader soon spotted that this was only partly true because the paper seldom sided with people who opposed the ruling clique. Individual abuses were occasionally exposed to the glare of publicity, mainly for propaganda purposes, as when Herrera launched a sensational attack on a police inspector who had roughed up a beggar immediately outside the newspaper offices. The man had been invited inside, given food and offered a job. Next day *El Temporal* demanded the inspector's dismissal and got it. Herrera also indulged in a little anti-American propaganda every now and then because he knew that it always went down well with the readers, but the vast majority of his columns were taken up with lurid accounts of beatings, parents who murdered their children, men who hanged their wives, and, needless to say, with reports about the heroes of the national army, who, heedless of blood, sweat and tears, were fighting so gallantly amid impenetrable forest and on inhospitable mountainside against the knavish bandoleros, alias guerilleros.

El Temporal was a stern taskmaster, as any newspaperman who earned his pay-cheque there knew. Herrera liked sensational stories, not exposés. Those he took care of personally when the moment seemed opportune. That was his colleagues' main complaint. On the surface, Herrera appeared to be as powerful as Fierro – in fact some people speculated that he was the one who steered things in the direction he deemed appropriate.

As an academic – he had studied political economy – Herrera tended to look down on those who surrounded him. They were competent enough to collect copy, but the rest he did himself. His reporters regarded him as a man with few human qualities, more like a calculating machine than a creature of flesh and blood.

Herrera knew this and was amused by it. That was why, at meetings like today's, he showed no flicker of emotion but sat there toying idly with his ball-point and noting every tiny detail for future reference. Hear all, see all, say plenty on paper – that was his motto, and his long front-page column proved it every day.

Fierro appeared at last. He shook each editor by the hand in his jovial way and sat down with a sigh. There was a certain tension noticeable in the faces turned to him like sun-flowers to the sun. He knew them all, having engaged their owners personally after instituting an exhaustive check on their previous history and background. It was they who moulded public opinion in Conciencia. He smiled at the thought that some of them were at least as influential as Herrera, not that he would ever have told them so. They were less suited to the niche occupied by Herrera because they were too independent and less unscrupulous. Herrera could write a man into a ministerial chair one month and banish him to the political wilderness the next. The other editors were less set in their ideas than Herrera, but they might sometimes have jibbed at performing services which he, Fierro, thought nothing of demanding from his deputy. That was one of his motives for convening the present meeting. The point at issue was a crucial one, and the more he had thought about it in recent days the more crucial it seemed.

Fierro debated how to begin, listening to the distant roar of the rotary presses situated several floors below. He lit a cigar with huge deliberation, nodded his approval when it was burning properly, and blew the smoke towards his subordinates. His voice seemed to burst on them from a blue cloud as he said: 'The main item on our agenda is the Valencia problem.'

Herrera's lips twitched in a grimace of satisfaction. It was high time. So far, they had reproduced the man's speeches uncritically because the Fierro Organization would have been ill-advised to fly at a revolutionary who championed the rights of workers throughout the country. That would have lost the paper thousands of readers and damaged the reputation which had been acquired and nurtured by years of careful publicity. He, Herrera, would have tackled the Valencia case less cautiously, but Fierro had restrained him. 'Never attack a man while he's riding high. Give him enough rope and he'll hang himself in due course. Politics is a waiting game, Alejandro. Publish straight accounts of his lecture tours. Stick his picture in the paper every day. The higher he climbs the smaller his chances of survival when we knock him off his perch.'

A stir ran round the board-room at Fierro's opening words. The word 'problem', in particular, was greeted with discreetly raised eyebrows. For most of those present, Valencia had never been a problem. They had been instructed by Fierro to publish every word he uttered – publish without comment, admittedly, but publish for all that. The directive had been couched in terms which defied them to omit a single word of Valencia's public pronouncements, and they had supposed that they were – for what dark reasons soever – doing Fierro a favour.

The editor of one provincial newspaper gave vent to the surprise which they all felt.

'Problem?'

Fierro nodded.

'Yes. Think calmly about it for a moment. Not only a problem but a menace.'

The dull throb of the rotary presses seemed to increase in volume.

'This is how I see the situation,' Fierro went on. 'The army is currently mopping up centres of resistance. In a few years' time there won't be any more guerilleros or bandoleros, whichever. The rebels have lost control of all but a few areas, one exception being the general vicinity of Talmac. I need hardly remind you of the seven soldiers who were shot the other day, probably by Rodriguez Tobar's men. If these bandoleros are still able to pursue their nefarious activities it's only because they enjoy the backing of the university students, led by a priest whose name you all know – Antonio Valencia. We've left him alone until now, but his speeches are causing such a ferment that fresh atrocities have been committed at isolated points. We uphold law and order whereas he preaches the gospel of revolution, the cult of violence. It's time he was stopped. If individuals like Valencia abuse our democratic system we must crush them. In a few days' time our syndicate will expose him publicly. I'll tell you what that means in practice. Each of you will try to ferret out Valencia's less favourable aspects. Interview people who disagree with him. Study his speeches and draw attention to the weak points in his arguments. Explain to our readers that his ideas are bound to lead to Communism and a situation in which the prisons will be fuller than ever. Publish articles on Stalin's purges in Russia, on the fact that Khrushchev nearly sparked off a third world war by trying to erect missile bases in Cuba, get hold of copy on Soviet concentration camps, on the dictatorships of Eastern Europe, arrange interviews with trade union leaders and make them look foolish if they come down on Valencia's side. Encourage correspondence with sociologically-inclined priests who disagree with Valencia's programme, investigate his private life and compare notes. You might consider ending every article with a hint that you're writing in the national interest. I trust I've made myself clear?'

No one spoke. It was an order, not a pious hope. Besides, it was not customary to comment on Fierro's instructions. Some of those present thought a written directive would have served the purpose until they realized that the meeting was strictly confidential. Fierro looked round the circle of faces. He detected hesitancy, even disapproval, but that was no matter. They were his lackeys. He paid them so well that they could never hope to earn as much elsewhere.

'Gather material,' he said, so softly that his voice was almost inaudible above the hum of the rotaries. 'Employ correspondents all over the country to do the same. The press has beheaded more men than the guillotine ever did. We may have trouble with Cuellar, but don't let that worry you. One more thing: this meeting never happened. Anyone who thinks otherwise had better tender his resignation immediately. Is that clear?'

There was no need to ask. Everyone had understood. Fierro nodded to Herrera.

'I'd like a word with you afterwards. *Señores*, there are some refreshments waiting for you downstairs. No discussions please, not even there. Thank you for coming. *Au revoir* and good hunting.'

He rose and left the board-room followed by his deputy editor, shaking hands with some of his minions and leaving the rest plunged in gloom.

Once in his own office, Fierro relaxed.

'Make yourself comfortable, Alejandro, we've got things to discuss.'

Herrera broke his silence at last.

'Short and sweet,' he said with a thin smile. 'I told you it would be better for you to handle that kind of meeting. Now they know what they've got to do.'

Fierro nodded.

'They took it hard. A lot of them seemed to think I really intended to support Valencia's despicable Communist ideas.'

He went to the bar beside his desk.

'A cognac, Alejandro?'

'With pleasure, Don Ignacio.'

Fierro felt warm inside at the thought that his scheme was proceeding on schedule. He knew that Valencia was to be summoned for an interview by the Cardinal next day. Little that went on in Cielo escaped him, and he had his regular informants inside the chancellery itself.

He poured two glasses of brandy and cradled one of them in his hands.

'Cuellar's workers moved into their cottages a few days ago,' he said. 'Did you know?'

Herrera glanced up in surprise.

'No. Are you sure?'

Fierro nodded and took a careful sip of brandy, swilling it lingeringly round his mouth.

'He kept it dark.'

'Why?'

'Oh, you know Cuellar. He's a good friend of Valencia's and he can't endure me – to put it mildly. It isn't just professional rivalry. I suspect there's a personal element involved. Our in-laws have been at daggers drawn for years.'

'Do you want me to do a piece on the cottages?'

Herrera guessed that Fierro had not invited him into his inner sanctum for nothing.

Fierro took another sip of brandy and offered his lieutenant a cigarette. He was amused, to judge by the faintly sardonic smile on his face.

'No, not you. Our Communist colleagues at *El Aurora*. Tip them off to the fact that people are living twenty to a house in Cuellar's model village. I know exactly what'll happen – in fact I'd bet a million pesos on it. Tomorrow morning *El Aurora* will be plastered with banner headlines to the effect that our philanthropic landowner has crammed twenty people into one tiny little house, and that it's an outrage against society.'

'But they'll check . . .'

Fierro cut him short.

'Let them – it's true. Our friend Cuellar forgot that his beloved *campesinos* don't know how to live decently. As soon as they were presented with their nice little houses they invited a horde of relations to move in with them.'

Herrera laughed aloud, but it was only when he started laughing that he saw precisely what Fierro meant.

'But will *El Aurora* bite? After all, they must know that Cuellar is a friend of Valencia's.'

Fierro wagged his head.

'I thought you were quicker on the uptake, Alejandro. From an objective point of view we've done exactly the same as Cuellar's papers. We've given Valencia a hearing – for different reasons, perhaps, but the editor of *El Aurora* can't be expected to know that. Cuellar is just another plutocrat to the Communists – in fact they may even resent his friendship with Valencia. They want Valencia to themselves. Apart from that, they distrust the whole of the establishment on principle, even if the odd individual does take sides with a man like Valencia. My information cost me a peso or two, believe me, but it's all bona fide.'

He regarded Herrera with complacent good humour and slowly drained his glass.

'Excellent cognac, don't you think? If we manage to neutralize Valencia and drive a wedge between him and Cuellar we'll split a whole bottle between us. I know, incidentally, that even Cuellar is beginning to have his doubts. He isn't the sort of man who lets himself be manipulated by others – he's too shrewd for that.'

Herrera sniffed his brandy. He had known Valencia since his student days, when the young priest-to-be was already the centre of a large circle of friends of both sexes. Academic life had come easier to him than Valencia. Herrera was reputed to have the keenest mind on the campus, and even some of his teachers had quailed before his acute and probing questions. But none of this altered the fact that people seldom had time for him when Valencia was around. There was something else, too. Valencia had made such an impression on a girl-friend of Herrera's at a party that she completely lost interest in him. Years had gone by since then, but the incident still rankled.

'Leave it to me, Don Ignacio. Cuellar will be suffering from apoplexy by this time tomorrow.' A sudden thought struck him. 'What if he gets rid of his unwanted tenants?'

Fierro bellowed with laughter.

'Simple! Two days hence *El Aurora* will be squawking that it shows a pretty feudal approach when a landowner turns hard-working people out of their homes. I hope he does kick them out.'

Herrera took a discreet sip of brandy.

'He will. Cuellar always jumps in with both feet when he wants to straighten things out in a hurry. All the better for us.'

Fierro replaced the bottle in the small but well-stocked bar and sat down behind his desk.

'*Bueno*, Alejandro. Now to business. Go easy with your leaders. You'll have to keep the first one slightly vague. We shall know more after Valencia has seen the Cardinal. Oh yes, and slip in another reference to the massacre of that patrol. Send people to interview their wives and families and publish a piece on them tomorrow morning.'

'It'll be a pleasure,' Herrera replied, and padded silently from the room like a long, lean beast of prey.

Esperanza Cardinal Medina was celebrating Mass in his private chapel. He used Latin because he found it abhorrent to worship the Creator in Conciencian Spanish, particularly at the moment of God's supreme communion with man.

The private chapel was where Medina felt most humbly conscious of the infinite love which manifested itself in bread and wine, where he prayed for all the poor of his country, for the relief of their needs and afflictions, for the banishment of all injustice from Conciencia and the world at large, for all sinners and recalcitrants. And today he offered up a special prayer for Antonio Valencia, whom he had summoned to his presence. He did not hate him. Cardinal Medina scarcely knew what hatred meant. In his view, faith implied love of mankind, always provided that mankind refrained from violating the love of the Christ who had been crucified for mankind's sake.

The Cardinal seemed to be saying Mass more slowly than usual. His face shone with a more than customary fervour and devotion, and his secretary, who was acting as server, had the impression that Medina was wholly and utterly at one with the supreme deity whose name so often passed his lips. In fact, the Cardinal was struggling to ignore the pains in his back and side, which had attained a pitch of razor-sharp intensity as the moment of consecration approached. Doggedly, he strove to concentrate on the agonies which Christ must have endured when his executioners drove the nails through his palms.

Medina reflected on how many people clung, in their hour of utmost need, to the foot of the Cross in quest of help and support from the God-made-man. He refused to accept that millions were unable or unwilling to fold their hands *in extremis* because they had been persuaded that such pious myths were only put about to keep them quiet and docile. He knew for a certainty that this was untrue. Man could not conceive of a life without God. Even when the conservatives and liberals were locked in battle, most of them had prayed to God for victory.

The Cardinal, who cherished a particular reverence for Our Lady of Perpetual Succour, offered up a special prayer to her to strengthen him in the decisions which he had to take that day. He asked the Mother of God to curb his temper, keep his judgement unimpaired by physical pain, and make him indulgent towards those who were set under his authority. He prayed above all that he might partake of the love which he had so sadly lacked throughout his life and which he had so seldom bestowed on others, perhaps because they had bestowed none on him. He recalled his first conversation with the Nuncio, who had said very little, merely advising him to be prudent at this critical juncture and avoid making enemies of potential friends. The Nuncio shared his conviction that discipline must be maintained and showed a surprisingly intimate knowledge of Antonio Valencia's speeches and articles. He had recommended him to allow Valencia to speak unchecked so that public reaction to his political programme might be assessed. Well, now the time had come. Still acting on the Nuncio's advice, he would make every effort to meet Valencia half way but compel him to renounce his political activities and break with his new-found friends, some of whom were nonconformists, atheists and Communists.

Medina wished that he possessed the papal diplomat's patience and tact. The two churchmen were very close by virtue of their aristocratic upbringing, erudition, and determination to preserve Christianity at all costs. They had dined well that evening, and it was one of the few occasions on which Medina felt he had met his equal.

The secretary cleared his throat because Medina had paused too long in the middle of the Preface. Glancing impatiently over his shoulder, the Cardinal proceeded with Mass.

Now and again, odd items from his daily list of engagements flitted through his mind. Interviews with bishops from all over the country, with prominent laymen, with cabinet ministers, with the committee on liturgical reform, with parish priests who had got into difficulties, usually of a financial nature, with directors of charitable institutions who requested support or asked him to become their patron. Sometimes the problems were more serious – relationships between priests and female parishioners, for example, or the difficulties of priests whose parishes were situated in rebel-held territory, or requests to hold yet another ecclesiastical conference of some kind. Many cases he passed to Monsignor Zasi, but the really momentous decisions he reserved for himself. If a man's office entailed responsibility he must shoulder it, infinitely hard though it might sometimes be.

Mass over, the Cardinal withdrew to the sacristy and removed his chasuble, stole and alb, mutely assisted by his secretary. Then he walked through the palace to his chambers, pausing occasionally when someone knelt to kiss his ring. He never refused anyone because it was one of the outward and visible signs of faith, but he never uttered a word of greeting or encouragement because it might have involved him in conversation. Those who wanted an interview with him had to make an appointment weeks in advance, and even then it was far from certain that he would receive them. People with mundane problems, large or small, could always consult their parish priest, whose duty it was to hear them in the presbytery or confessional. He, the Cardinal, had to direct the Church, and directing the Church did not mean listening to trivial complaints.

The Cardinal breakfasted simply on a glass of chilled orange-juice, two slices of toast thinly spread with butter, a boiled egg, and a cup of white coffee. An elderly woman who worked in the offices of the chancellery during the day ensured that he was served swiftly and in silence. Meanwhile, the secretary had already laid out the day's mail beside his plate. Medina liked to spend breakfast-time absorbing the main newspaper reports and skimming through his letters, which he re-read later on.

Glancing at *El Aurora*, the Communist daily, he saw that Cuellar was accused of unprincipled behaviour because he had crammed twenty or more peasants into one of his new houses. Photographs vividly illustrated the extent of the overcrowding. Medina caught himself reading this report with a certain glee. Cuellar had not only spurned his request to stop publishing pro-Valencia propaganda but failed to account for his refusal. Now Cuellar himself was under fire, and from a wholly unexpected quarter.

The Cardinal said grace, rose from table and made his way slowly to his study, escorted by his secretary, who respectfully held the door for him. With a sigh, he sat down at his desk and began to dictate replies to the most important of the letters which he had just received. But even as he did so his thoughts returned to the prospect of his interview with Valencia that afternoon.

It was still early when the Bishop of Cielo presented himself at Valencia's door. He breathed a sigh of relief when he found him in.

'It may seem unconventional, but I thought it better to visit you at home,' Zasi said, sitting down. Valencia poured two small cups of black coffee and asked if he might smoke a pipe.

Zasi felt slightly uncomfortable and looked it. His decision to call on Valencia was the product of long deliberation. He knew the Cardinal would never understand if he learned of the visit later, but he could hardly summon Valencia to the chancellery twice in a single day, once in the morning for a talk with him and again in the afternoon for an interview with the Cardinal. Characteristically, he took the bull by the horns.

'I have a message from the Cardinal. He wishes to see you this afternoon.'

The somewhat bald announcement seemed to affront the stillness of the book-lined room.

'I have to catch a plane this afternoon, Monsignor.'

Zasi shook his head.

'You will have to postpone your trip. A request from the Cardinal amounts to a command, Antonio. Not even you would wish to ignore such a summons, I'm sure. You must know better than I do what it's about.'

'Very well, Monsignor, at what time?'

'Half-past two precisely.'

Conversation languished. Zasi had come to Valencia to prepare

256

him for the interview. He sensed that a trial of strength was imminent and wanted to prevent it. There was a note of hesitation in his voice when he finally broke the silence.

'Whatever your personal feelings, my son, I beg you to remember that the Cardinal is well disposed towards you in his own way.'

'What way is that, Monsignor?'

Zasi's expression became stern.

'His Eminence contends that you have infringed a number of important doctrinal and theological principles which are central to the teachings of the Church. Do you really find it impossible to sympathize with his inability to support a priest who preaches violence?'

'Did the Church support Simon Bolívar when he preached violence, Monsignor? No, but that doesn't prevent us from holding annual services of thanksgiving and singing the Te Deum in celebration of our independence, even though we won it by force of arms.'

'Simon Bolívar was not a priest, my son.'

Valencia drew a deep breath.

'I decline to discuss the matter further, Monsignor. I did so yesterday evening with Vermeer, and last night I wrote an article refuting his arguments. And now you come here with the intention of broaching the whole subject again. You have read enough of my articles to know what my views are, Monsignor. I have nothing to add to them.'

'And you will say the same to His Eminence this afternoon?'

'Of course. Neither more nor less.'

'I must warn you, Antonio, the Cardinal's patience is exhausted.'

Valencia could not repress a faint smile.

'And the people's patience, Monsignor?'

The little bishop did not reply. It was not his first conversation with Valencia but he feared that it would be his last.

'I assume,' he said slowly, 'that His Eminence will command you to withdraw from public life. If you refuse you will be forbidden to exercise your priestly duties.'

He watched Valencia closely as he spoke, but there was no perceptible reaction.

'I'm obliged to you, Monsignor. At least I know where I stand.'

Zasi would gladly have tempered the official flavour of his visit with an informal word, but he had neither the courage nor the strength to do so. It seemed to him that the man sitting opposite him was no longer a priest, that he had ceased to comprehend the miracle of Christ Crucified. Or did he misjudge him after all? The hallowed and ancient traditions battled fiercely within him against Valencia's new ideology, but he knew that he must ultimately range himself behind the Cardinal. Religion had suffered wherever the Communists were in control, and Zasi was as much a guardian of Christianity as the Cardinal himself. Apart from that, there was the episcopal council, which was bound to speak out against Valencia's theories, especially if he continued to espouse them as a priest and thereby gave the impression that he was speaking in the name of the Church.

Zasi rose.

'I trust, my son, that you will show humility, wisdom and obedience. Resort to extremes and you will accomplish far less than you would by gentler means. Fierro's newspapers would have been at your disposal if you had accepted his original proposition. You can still say yes, even now. Nobody wishes to deprive you of the right to champion the underprivileged except when you threaten violence. Think it over calmly once more. It may be that you will discover a compromise solution – one that will enable you to reach agreement with His Eminence this afternoon.'

Valencia made a move to kneel out of respect for Zasi's good intentions, but the bishop shook his head. 'No, my son,' he said quietly, 'go down on your knees afterwards to the first rebel of Christendom and ask him why he suffered himself to be nailed to the Cross, saying "Father, forgive them; for they know not what they do." Goodbye, and God be with you.'

Slowly, Valencia shut the door behind him. He understood. The counter-attack was to be launched at half-past two that afternoon.

14

Since the death of the seven soldiers Zambrano had been sending out aircraft to reconnoitre the area at tree-top level. Rodriguez Tobar was reluctantly compelled to ban the cooking of meals over open fires, which made life more difficult for his guerilleros and lowered their morale. The proposal to use aircraft had come from Lieutenant Losano, who was convinced that Tobar's headquarters must be located somewhere in the jungle round Talmac and that the guerilleros would throw caution to the winds if only they were harassed for long enough.

Meanwhile, he kept the villagers under strict surveillance and once or twice managed to intercept consignments of food destined for the rebels. The carriers were summarily executed. Although Losano realized that he was becoming a target for reprisals by the clandestine fighters in the mountains, he lost no sleep in consequence. Death held few terrors for him and he demanded the same attitude from his men, who felt the effects of his merciless treatment but prized him as a superior because he always took the lead and never shirked a dangerous assignment. Despite this, Losano's patrols had so far achieved little. He had never once cornered a party of guerilleros although he sometimes knew perfectly well that they were almost within spitting distance. They were so much at home in the jungle that he felt like a tourist beside them, but he never lost heart. He was determined to hunt the bandoleros until he ran them to earth, then exterminate them.

Gomez, his sergeant, felt just as he did about the situation and sometimes discussed it with him in Talmac's only *cantina*, not far from the church.

This evening, as usual, the villagers slunk out timidly when they entered as though fearful of being arrested on the spot. The two men did not sit down but propped their elbows on the bar and exchanged laconic remarks which scarcely amounted to a conversation.

'Did you check the sentries, Sergeant? They're idle bastards, you know that.'

'Of course, Lieutenant. All the same, it's their own necks they're risking as well as ours.'

'Time we sent a patrol to the east. I wouldn't be surprised if we found something there. Hé, señorita, where's that goddamn bottle?'

They both stared at Maria, the barmaid, whose breasts were clearly visible under her thin blouse. Losano had slept with her a number of times. He liked her in his own way, more so than the other village girls because she surrendered herself completely when they made love and never played coy or asked him to marry her. In fact, the locals were very broadminded in these matters. Losano had discovered that many couples simply cohabited despite the priest's efforts to stamp out relationships unconsecrated by the Church. The villagers' sex-life was straightforward, uncomplicated, primitive, and distinguished by an almost animal sensuality which blinded them to much of the misery in their lives.

Losano was barely conscious of this misery. He was only interested in the young girls. The older women and men did not exist for him. He distrusted the men because he had come to the conclusion that they were all in some way connected with the guerilleros.

'Are you free tonight, Maria?' he asked.

She just nodded.

Losano smiled. She knew what he wanted, what they both wanted. They needed each other.

'You heard that, Sergeant?' he said. 'Don't get me out of bed unless it's urgent. I'll be busy.'

Gomez leant towards Maria and leered at her, but she avoided his eye.

'Tougher than a night patrol but more fun,' Losano said with a wink. 'Any time you get the urge, Sergeant, pick someone else. There are plenty around. See you later, Maria.'

They drank up and left. She gazed round the shabby bar. The guerilleros had come here in the old days, usually late at night when Don Henrico's bodyguards were on duty at the casa grande. She had borne three children, two of them by Pablo. Now the guerilleros had gone and Losano had taken their place. What Losano did not know was that she passed information to one of the villagers, who came in for a drink every Tuesday evening. She betrayed Losano one moment and gave him her body the next, making him believe that his charms were irresistible.

The man came in at the same time as usual, rough and uncouth, with all the indifference to externals which poverty imprints upon a man's appearance. His name was Martin.

He too stared at Maria's breasts, then at his hands as if wondering why he had not long ago thrust them inside her blouse and felt the warmth of her body.

'*Aguardiente*,' he said in his slow ponderous voice. He threw back his ruana, laid his sombrero on the counter and looked round cautiously for possible eavesdroppers.

'They're planning to send a patrol to the east,' whispered Maria.

He nodded impassively.

'The sentries have been inspected.'

She found it exciting to tell him these things, even more exciting than the touch of Losano's hands. Like all the villagers, she knew that Talmac was surrounded by guerilleros who were patiently waiting for the hour to strike. Every scrap of information, however small, was important, but she knew only what she heard from Losano. She reported it to Martin, who in his turn reported it to someone else. Nobody knew the name of the man who eventually conveyed the information to the guerilleros, so the system functioned smoothly and Losano and his men had no grounds for suspicion.

'Has Don Henrico been here?'

Maria shook her mane of long black hair.

'No. He comes to the plaza very seldom now. They say he almost never leaves the *casa grande*.'

'Is he afraid?'

She smiled.

'Who isn't? Some people fear the army, others the guerilleros, others the prospect of a battle here in the village. I know families who want to move out, especially since the aeroplanes came. The aeroplanes are what they fear most of all.'

'Where do they plan to go?'

'To Cielo.'

'What for?'

'More money and a better life. That's what they think, at least.'

'They'll be homesick,' Martin said firmly. 'Homesick for the trees and the sky, homesick for the silence – even for the sound of the wind in the mountains.'

Homesickness . . . Rodriguez Tobar was thinking of it as he slowly toured the camp on foot to satisfy himself that it could not be spotted from the air. The chief sufferers from homesickness were the women who lived here with their menfolk in huts beneath the trees, but their homesickness was outweighed by fear of the soldiers who would rape and kill them if they fell into their hands. Colonel Zambrano no doubt itched to drop paratroops on the dense forest, but he probably realized that it would mean certain death. Either they would lose themselves among the trees and lianas of this inhospitable region or they would be attacked and killed before they had a chance to get their bearings.

Tobar continued his tour of inspection. Turning a corner, he ran into Pablo.

'We're not receiving enough information about Talmac. Think you could pay the place a visit without getting caught?'

Pablo's eyes lit up.

'With how many men, *Capitán*?'

'Two others. You and Jorge with Raoul Castillo in command.'

'Tonight?'

'Yes. Find the others and bring them to me. There's a storm in the offing, so the sentries won't be too much on their guard. Don't forget, though – no attack on the post, just information.'

His ears detected the hum of an aircraft in the distance. It was slowly circling the area in a wide arc. Tobar knew that the observer on board would be scanning the ground with his powerful binoculars. If he found the slightest trace of their presence the pilot would radio for other aircraft armed with cannon and napalm. No more base camp, no more equipment or supplies . . .

The plane drew nearer, swooped low over the trees in a final run and then veered off to the south, presumably bound for its landing strip.

'Zambrano seems to be growing impatient,' Tobar said with a shrug. 'We shall have to move the supply dumps deeper into the jungle, also the women and children. I've been wondering whether to establish a temporary camp for them five kilometres away.'

Pablo made no comment. The perpetual fear of a sudden air attack, the eternal dodging from place to place, the minor patrol activity . . . Sometimes he felt as if he had been sentenced to life imprisonment in a jungle-green stockade.

Tobar eyed him thoughtfully.

'Feeling low, Pablo?'

Pablo nodded.

'Yes, *Capitán*. Is it so surprising?'

Tobar paused before he replied.

'No, not surprising. Not good either. Find Raoul and Jorge and come to my hut, all three of you.'

He strode briskly off down the forest path which wound through the makeshift village inhabited by his guerilleros. Now and then he paused to exchange a few words with the women and children. The men were not there. One group was out hunting, another training and a third manning the outposts. Tobar's hut contained the radio transmitter whose aerial only just topped the surrounding trees and was additionally camouflaged with foliage and creepers. He called up the group near Talmac and received confirmation that all was quiet. He asked if the man had seen any newspapers. Yes, he was told, *El Temporal* had devoted an entire page to interviews with the dependents of the sergeant and six men who had been killed near Monton. Tobar swore and signed off. He turned to see Raoul Castillo standing behind him.

'Was it really necessary to kill them?' he asked.

Castillo shrugged.

'I told you, *Capitán*, they knew too much. The sergeant may have been bluffing but I couldn't take the chance. Sparing their lives might have put us all in jeopardy.'

'Very well, Raoul. Tonight, go to Talmac and wait until Maria comes back from Losano. We don't hear much these days. Martin's reports aren't getting through and I want to know why.'

Castillo eyed him calmly.

'The sergeant spoke of a traitor. You think Martin . . .'

Tobar met his gaze.

'If so, Maria will be useless to us from now on. Martin may have passed all his information to Losano, who's sitting there waiting to spring the trap. Don't underestimate the man, Raoul.'

'Martin . . .' Castillo mused. 'He could be playing a double game. He could be passing himself off as an informer and gathering information for us at the same time. We mustn't jump to conclusions.'

Pablo and Jorge entered silently, their faces sombre and inscrutable. When they had received their orders they turned, still silently, and left the command post.

It was nearly midnight when Maria returned to her tumbledown shack behind the *cantina*. As usual, Losano had sent her away after their love-making. He thought it dangerous to keep women in his room all night and had told her so more than once. Besides, she knew him well enough to know that he would send for her again if the mood took him.

Slowly, she walked back through the deserted village. The storm was at its height, and the wind piped and whistled along the street, shaking the trees so that they seemed to crane after her with nodding heads. The villagers never ventured outside at this hour because drunken soldiers might beat them up or, worse still, haul them off to headquarters on suspicion. That meant being interrogated with the aid of a rifle-butt and eventually hurled, more dead than alive, into the darkened street.

Maria thought of the news she had passed to Martin that evening and wondered who Martin's contact was. There must be a long chain of informants between her and the guerilleros. The order to make friends with Losano and seduce him if necessary had come from Pablo via Martin. All she knew of Martin was that he worked as a *campesino* on Don Henrico's estate.

She opened the door of her hut, went inside, lit the oil-lamp, and saw Martin sitting on the edge of her bed, obviously drunk. He was sweating like a pig and his eyes roamed hungrily over her legs and breasts.

'What do you want?'

Maria looked at the ragged clothes, the calloused hands, the dark, avid eyes, the unbuttoned trousers.

'You,' he said hoarsely. 'I want you here, on this bed.'

She tried to sound calm.

'You've no business here. What do you think would happen if I reported you to Lieutenant Losano?'

He lit a cigarette and reached for a bottle on the floor beside him. He drank from it and suddenly burst out laughing.

'Threats, eh? Well, I can make threats too. What if I told Losano you're working for the guerilleros? Just think what would happen then, *querida*. First he'd have you raped by twenty of his men and then he'd shoot you. Not a nice thought, last thing at night.'

Maria made a dash for the door but he reached it first. He hurled her on to the bed with a single jerk of his arms and stood staring down at her.

'You aren't Losano's only friend, you know. I've been friendly with him ever since he came here. That surprises you, doesn't it? Every little thing you've told me I've passed back to him, except that I didn't say where it came from. That's to say, I never told him it was you. You remember the day Marcos disappeared? They shot him because I pretended the information came from him. Since then I've told them I collect it myself. *Astuto*, eh? And all the time I've been protecting you. Well, now I want my reward.'

The wind howled round the hut. Maria heard something fall outside. Martin heard it too, but he took no notice.

He bent down and groped for her breasts with his rough peasant's hands. She endured it, just as she did with Losano. She saw the spittle gather in the corner of his mouth and closed her eyes as his hands slid further down her body.

'Stop it!' she screamed with sudden fury and pushed him away.

At that moment the door opened and Martin found himself covered by three rifles. Raoul Castillo quietly closed the door, walked over to the *campesino* and struck him in the face with the back of his hand.

'Filthy traitor! Son of a whore!'

He pulled a handkerchief from his pocket, screwed it up and stuffed it into Martin's mouth.

'No need to say any more, we heard everything. What else do you know about him, Maria?'

He spoke casually, as if the appearance of three heavily armed guerilleros in the heart of Talmac were nothing out of the ordinary.

Maria shrugged.

'Only that he comes to the *cantina* regularly and collects what information I have to give him.'

'So he's been betraying us the whole time – that explains why we heard nothing. Do you think Losano suspects you, Maria?'

She laughed.

'No, he's only interested in my body and the fact that I can satisfy him. Losano has no feelings above the waist.'

Her eyes met Pablo's for an instant, but that was all. Castillo turned to the other two.

'Jorge, Pablo, stick him up against the wall and ungag him. You know what to do if he yells. A knife is worth more than a gun in this place.'

Martin broke into a torrent of speech, but he had little to add to what he had already told Maria.

Castillo gave a snort of impatience.

'Maria, wait outside.'

The dull thud of blows came to her ears as she stood outside in the storm. Then the door opened and she saw them carry Martin out and drag him along the path that led from her hut to the mountains.

Pablo paused beside her for a moment.

'Maria?'

She shook her head.

'We have nothing to say to each other, Pablo. This is not the time.'

'May the Mother of God protect you,' he said. He turned and

trotted off after the others, and they vanished into the surrounding forest.

Next morning Losano's men found Martin's body hanging from a tree. It swung to and fro in the wind, which was still blowing hard.

Losano drove to the scene at once. He stared at the corpse for a long time, as if he relished the sight of death. Then he strolled back to his jeep.

'Cut him down and bury him. I know the man. He used to bring me information.'

Savagely, he let in the clutch and drove off. It was a while before his face betrayed the uneasiness he felt. So the guerilleros had come to Talmac at last, taking advantage of the storm. What with the wind howling round the *campesinos'* huts, the rustling leaves and creaking branches, it had been an ideal night for a raid. Fortunately, only his soldiers had seen the body, and they could be instructed to keep their mouths shut. However, by the time he drove into the village little knots of people had already gathered in the plaza, evidently to discuss Martin's death. Losano wondered how they could have known, but they scattered at his approach and left him sitting there alone in his jeep.

He drove to the *casa grande*, fuming. Don Henrico turned pale when he heard what had happened.

'So they came in spite of all your precautions.'

Losano nodded.

'Yes, in spite of my security measures, in spite of yours, in spite of Colonel Zambrano's efforts – in spite of everything. I must say, I congratulate them.'

Don Henrico passed a hand slowly over his greying hair. There was little to be seen of his customary self-assurance. His lips trembled.

'What went wrong, Lieutenant?'

'Nothing specific. The storm helped them. They executed one of my informers, that's all.'

Don Henrico threw up his hands.

'What do you mean, that's all? Think for a moment, Lieutenant. In the first place, no one in Talmac will dare to side with us from now on. In the second place, you and your men have lost the initiative to the guerilleros. If the same thing happens again I shall have no authority left.'

Losano eyed the landowner coldly.

'It won't happen again, Don Henrico.'

'How can you be so sure? You have no idea of their numbers, even. If they really attack in earnest . . .'

He broke off and stared out of the window.

'Do you know why I refuse to leave here? Because I love this place, that's why. I was born here – it's part of my life. *Dios*, Lieutenant, can't you see what it all means to me?'

Losano shook his head.

'Our reasons for being here are different. I don't come from this part of the world and I don't like it. I'm here on the orders of Colonel Zambrano. The whole place revolts me, so do the guerilleros and the *campesinos*. I fight the guerilleros because they'd murder my family as well as yours if they ever gained control. That's why I do my job – as a soldier, as a Conciencian, as . . . But why should I make speeches? Everything about this place sticks in my craw.'

Don Henrico rounded on him. The fear had receded from his eyes and given way to passionate contempt.

'You know your trouble, Lieutenant?' he said slowly. 'You've no time for anything or anyone but yourself, and if it came to it you'd spit on me too.'

Losano turned on his heel.

'*Buenos dias*, Don Henrico,' he said over his shoulder. 'I suggest we save the compliments until tonight, when things get dangerous again. We can dispense with them at present.'

He stalked out, climbed into his jeep and drove off. Don Henrico watched the vehicle until it disappeared round a bend in the road. Then he went back into the house.

There was nothing to be heard but the servants. A distant murmur of voices, the odd footstep, the rattle of crockery. Don Henrico drew his pistols and checked for the umpteenth time to see that they were loaded. So the guerilleros had made an incursion into Talmac without being spotted by Losano's men. It frightened him, he had to admit. At first, fear had been no more than an incentive to redouble his precautions. He had armed his bodyguards better and given them an occasional present of money. Things were different now. He wondered if it was only pig-headedness that kept him on his estate or whether there were other reasons why he stayed. Was it possible that he found the tension stimulating? Could it be that he was just as frightened of the big city with its futile noise and bustle? He turned the question over in his mind, vainly, and as he did so he was smitten with a sudden restless urge to do something positive. He decided to drive to Colonel Zambrano's headquarters and request reinforcements on the grounds that the rebels' strength had been underestimated.

He ordered his men to prepare the specially equipped truck which he used for longer trips. There was a machine-gun mounted on the roof of the cab and the members of his escort were armed with tommy-guns. The guerilleros might be anywhere, and he knew now that he would not escape with a few bruises if he fell into their hands. The truck left just before nine. A few hours later it drew up at Zambrano's headquarters. Don Henrico was ushered into his office at once. There was something about the way the two men greeted one another which conveyed relief that neither had met with an accident, or worse.

'How are things, Henrico?'

They exchanged a searching stare, each coming to the conclusion that the other looked older and greyer – less confident too, perhaps.

'I don't imagine this is a purely social call,' Zambrano went on.

Don Henrico gave a wan smile.

'No, the plantation leaves me no time to pay social calls. I came to ask you for reinforcements.'

'Reinforcements?'

'Last night the guerilleros . . .'

'I know,' Zambrano cut in. 'Losano radioed me. They hanged a man named Martin just outside the village.'

'You're well informed.'

'It's my job to be.'

Don Henrico leant forward and involuntarily dropped his voice.

'If you want my opinion, we can expect more such raids at any time – tonight, even. Apart from that, my *campesinos* are growing restive. Many of them are already planning to move out. I don't know if it's deliberate policy on the part of the guerilleros, but if that happens Tobar will be able to take over the whole district without firing a shot. Everybody is afraid.'

Zambrano fixed his eyes on Don Henrico's face.

'You too?'

The landowner nodded. 'Frankly, yes.'

'What are you driving at?' Zambrano sounded irritable.

'Simply that I'm debating whether it wouldn't be wiser if I retired to Cielo and left my manager in charge. I sometimes wonder what I'm still doing in Talmac. All my contemporaries moved to the capital years ago – if they ever lived on their plantations at all. I've had enough. You should sympathize, knowing the area.'

Colonel Zambrano shrugged his shoulders.

'What makes you think I don't sympathize?' He toyed with a ruler. 'By the way, do you still get on with Losano?'

'I did until this morning, but I'm afraid I was rather blunt with him.'

'So he told me. Don't worry, though, Losano has a hide like an elephant.'

There was a pause. The two men stared gloomily out at the muddy barrack square and watched the rain lashing the window-panes. The strong winds had been followed by a torrential down-pour. On days like this the mountains loomed over the valleys like black giants sleeping under a coverlet of cloud. The roads became perilous and whole districts could be cut off for days by sudden landslides.

'A *tinto*?'

'With pleasure.'

A soldier brought in two small cups of black coffee. Don Henrico sniffed the aroma. Coffee was part of his life, perhaps the most important part. His wife knew this as well as he did. She had been reluctant to exchange the dangers of Talmac for life in the capital, but when he insisted she took the children and went quietly, never even asking if he would come too. She urged him to be careful, but that was all.

'Perhaps you're right about going to Cielo,' Zambrano said. 'It's time your wife saw something of you.'

Don Henrico sipped his coffee pensively. Would the plantation and the *casa grande* be safe if he left? Would his manager take suffi-cient care to guard the estate against intruders? Were the guerilleros only waiting for his departure? He asked himself these questions without daring to answer them. There was something in the air at Talmac. He couldn't say exactly what it was. He had taken to scrutinizing the faces of the peasants. In the old days they had seemed to him like dogs to be fed and given an occasional kick when they stepped out of line. A change had come over them, but he found it hard to define. They still did their work, received the same pay and lived in the same hovels, but it sometimes struck him that they were a little less subservient, as if they knew something was going to happen. They never said anything, but Don Henrico had lived too long in Talmac not to sense the difference.

'I can't send you any reinforcements, Henrico,' Zambrano said abruptly.

Don Henrico raised his eyebrows.

'Why not?'

'Because I can't spare the men. Talmac isn't the only trouble-spot, you know.'

Zambrano rose and went over to the wall-map. Little flags marked the points where government troops had clashed with rebel units.

Don Henrico's frown deepened as Zambrano, ruler in hand, pointed to one centre of guerrilla activity after another.

'See the red shading? That's where the guerilleros are in control of entire areas. We're just getting ready to launch an operation in Guillermo de la Cruz's territory – I was instructed to do so at the latest general staff conference. Apart from that, there are five more areas where terrorist activity has to be stopped.'

'But Rodriguez Tobar is in command of all the guerilleros.'

Zambrano shook his head.

'Yes and no. In general, the various groups operate independently. I very much doubt, for instance, whether a man like de la Cruz pays much attention to what Tobar says. That's their weakness, but it's a great source of strength as well.'

Don Henrico felt a resurgence of fear.

'Are their activities on the increase?'

The colonel's face darkened.

'Yes. What's more, the foreign press is starting to applaud them. Lieutenant Wells recently brought me some translations of leading articles from European newspapers. Public opinion is swinging in favour of the bastards. That's why we're stepping up the pressure too. The guerilleros may be motivated by similar considerations, though I doubt if they often get to see a European paper.'

'So Losano will also be launching a new operation?'

'Yes, with air support. We can't spare Talmac much in the way of ground forces, but aircraft will comb the area tree by tree until they find Tobar's base camp. No need to tell you what'll happen then. We'll blast it out of existence.'

'I'd give a lot to meet the man face to face,' Don Henrico said.

'Tobar? Only when he's behind bars, I hope!'

They both laughed. Strange, Don Henrico thought. His plantation had an outward tranquillity and peace which no other place on earth could match. The country-side was breathtakingly beautiful, yet behind its smiling face lurked the guerilleros, devils in human shape who struck terror even into him.

'How were things in Cielo on your last visit?' he asked.

Zambrano smiled.

'Much as usual. There was a bit of an uproar at the National University on account of an ex-professor – Antonio Valencia, if the name means anything to you. He made a speech in favour of armed revolution.'

'Oh, that crank.'

'The papers are full of him and his new party. He's touring the country.'

'And the authorities permit it?'

'Of course. We live in a democracy, Henrico. Anyone can express his opinions, even a priest.'

The landowner was uninterested in priests who preached revolution. Priests were fools, well-meaning fools, and that included the one who sporadically celebrated Mass at Talmac. It went without saying that he was on Don Henrico's side because Don Henrico had the power and money and had several times repaired the local church at his own expense. Out in the backwoods, women and children could not dispense with religious faith, with sugary little tales about the good Lord Jesus who was kind enough to have himself nailed to a cross between two murderers. Don Henrico thoroughly approved of these tales. The *curas* brought their flocks a certain contentment by aiming their forefingers skywards at the ostensible location of heaven, not that anyone had ever seen the place. You could prove a lot of things, but not the existence of heaven: that you had to take on trust, whether it was true or not. As for Don Henrico himself, he knew better. Happiness had to be sought here on earth . . .

Happiness? A peculiar form of happiness, he thought wrily, to be surrounded by guerilleros whose dearest ambition was to slit his throat if they got the chance. And yet he was reluctant to run away. His forebears the conquistadors had not turned tail when the Indians barred their path.

'The landing-strip is ready,' he told Zambrano. 'You would be very welcome if you paid an occasional visit. I should appreciate it immensely.'

The colonel nodded.

'Not a bad idea. I'll come and take a look at Talmac in the near future. Losano would like it too, no doubt.'

'Losano's likes and dislikes are a mystery to me,' Don Henrico retorted. 'A few hours ago he told me outright that Talmac and everyone in it made him want to vomit.'

Zambrano smiled faintly.

'Losano takes a straightforward view of the world. It consists of black and white. He's on the side of white. Everything else is dark, dirty and dangerous, a nest of vermin for him to vent his spleen on.'

Don Henrico rose.

'I enjoyed our talk. Next time you're in Cielo, please call my wife and give her my love. By the way, I brought a few sacks of coffee for you and your men. *Hasta la vista.*'

Engine roaring, the heavy truck lumbered through the gateway and headed back to Talmac.

Zambrano picked up the phone.

'John, come in here for a minute. I'd like a word with you.'

Lieutenant Wells ambled in and sat down with his usual lack of ceremony. He waited, digesting the concern on Zambrano's face.

'I don't like the look of things at Talmac, John. Some time last night the guerilleros infiltrated the village and hanged one of Losano's informers. Losano didn't say much, but I'm worried all the same. I'd like you to fly over there and take a look for yourself.'

Wells stared moodily into space and shrugged his shoulders, a habit which always irritated Zambrano.

'Did you hear what I said, John?'

'Sure, Colonel, but I did warn you. You wouldn't act on my earlier report.'

'How I assess reports is my business.'

'Of course.'

'I should appreciate it if you'd fly there today.'

'To do what?'

'Keep your eyes open and report back to me.'

'You don't want me to go by road?'

'No, take the helicopter. You can keep it for a day or two. I'd like you to make a few reconnaissance flights over that godforsaken jungle. Perhaps you'll spot something the others missed.'

'What about Losano?'

'Find out exactly what he's up to. Keep your ears open and see if you can't get wind of something from those damned *campesinos*. And check on security. I want to know if it's up to standard.'

Wells sighed.

'Losano's a fine officer. Maybe I do have some reservations about him, but they don't have any bearing on his military competence.'

Zambrano eyed the American silently for some moments.

'There's something far more important going on than you think, John,' he said quietly. 'A change of tactics, to be precise. For my taste, the guerilleros are being much too quick to give up areas which they've controlled completely until now. I discussed it with some of our top brass at the staff conference. According to them, the rebels have received instructions from Cuba to concentrate in trength and take the offensive. Talmac would be an ideal spot to put the new policy into practice. That's why I want you to take a good look. Any lessons you learn may be useful in other parts of the country. If we don't put a stop to the guerilleros now we never shall.'

Wells lit a cigarette.

'They'll always have the advantage of you, Colonel.'

'Why?'

'Because the *campesinos* are on their side, not ours.'

'What makes you so sure?'

'Well, these are more like police actions than military operations, and any cop except a traffic cop is everybody's enemy. Apart from that, the peasants are gradually beginning to sit up and take notice, thanks to newspapers, transistor sets and news from their relations in the big cities. And now they've found a leader in this dog-collar revolutionary, Antonio Valencia.'

'They can't read his speeches.'

'No, but they hear rumours and they think he represents the Church. Word-of-mouth reports carry far more weight with them, in any case.'

Zambrano made a gesture of dismissal.

'*Bien está.* Take the helicopter and fly over there this afternoon. The pilot will be at your disposal all day every day. Bring back some good news, John. I'm counting on you.'

John Wells rose to his feet. Don Henrico, Losano. Soldiers versus guerilleros. Violence. His world . . .

15

Cardinal Medina was resting on the sofa after his morning appointments. No one, not even his secretary, was permitted to disturb him during this half-hour of repose, which was in any case far shorter than the average Conciencian siesta. Today, however, the Cardinal did not sleep but lay staring up at the gilt-and-blue baroque angels which stared back at him from the ceiling, trumpets in mouth. Before long his eyes strayed to the painting of Our Lady of Perpetual Succour, with whom he had so often communed in the course of his arduous life.

Medina had never felt as exhausted as he did this afternoon. His chest seemed to be labouring under the weight of a gigantic millstone. The doctor had warned him against excessive tension because it might one day prove too much for his heart. The time had come for self-appraisal. He wondered if he were not too old to rule this troublesome province of the Church. There were times when he was so short of breath that he gasped for air, and when he coughed his head threatened to explode and the world lurched so wildly that everything went black before his eyes. His siesta had become a time of anguish. He had often considered the possibility of retirement, of tending his garden and spending the years that remained to him in the tranquillity of his villa. Then, almost simultaneously, he would castigate himself for his cowardice in wanting to put aside the burdens of office just when the hardest years lay ahead.

He wondered what he ought to say to Valencia that afternoon. He wanted to be lenient with him, but leniency might be misconstrued as a sign that he supported the irresponsible young priest's doctrine of violence. His advisers had told him that he should stand firm, that any symptom of weakness would be interpreted by Valencia's Communist entourage as an invitation to go still further. The Cardinal believed his advisers to be right. They were all men of erudition and wide experience, and he had often had reason to be grateful for their advice in the past. The Church would adapt itself to the social encyclicals in due course, they said, but care must be taken to see that the Communists did not use these encyclicals for their own purposes and interpret the written words of John XXIII and Paul VI as a defence of their own godless doctrines. They drew his attention to the new generation of priests now growing up, men who shared Valencia's concern about social conditions but would never dream of preaching violence. It would have a traumatic effect on these young priests if he gave Valencia even the smallest opportunity to expound his ideas publicly as a member of the priesthood.

Medina tried hard to gauge his own emotions and came to the conclusion that he was afraid. He had been afraid during his original conversation with the President. He had been still more afraid that morning, when Colombo phoned him to say that he intended to proclaim a state of emergency next day. Student disciples of Valencia's doctrine of violence had not only gone on strike but caused disturbances in all the major towns, and some of these had already claimed casualties among the police.

The Cardinal had done his best to soothe Colombo, but the President's voice grew so loud and agitated that Medina told his secretary to postpone the next interview for ten minutes and asked the visitor who was already with him to wait in a neighbouring room.

'Make it abundantly clear,' Colombo told him, 'that Valencia is speaking as a private individual, not a priest. You cannot keep silent any longer, Your Eminence. If the man continues in this vein we shall have a revolution on our hands. You are the only person who can persuade the people that Valencia does not speak in the name of the Church. You must compel him to take a public stand, for or against you. If you confront him with a choice between politics and the priesthood he will have to decide one way or the other.'

Having reluctantly conceded that the President was right, Medina continued his morning schedule. But he only half-heard what his visitors said to him. The forthcoming confrontation with Valencia loomed before him like a high wall. Despite his age, despite his misgivings, that wall would have to be surmounted.

Laboriously, he heaved himself to his feet and walked slowly to the window. He looked out at the plaza, where white pigeons were strutting round the equestrian statue of General Lopez. People sauntered by. He envied their lack of problems and tried to put himself in their place. They rose early and hurried to work on foot or by car and bus. Once there, they were told exactly what to do, and when the day's work was done they went home and relaxed. Medina wondered what they did with their evenings and whether they brooded on their country's problems as he did. Perhaps their only thought was how to survive, yet they sometimes looked so happy. They laughed, chattered, nudged each other, raced across the street or strolled idly past shop windows as if they had a whole century ahead of them instead of a day or a year.

Medina shook his head. How could one teach such people the meaning of responsibility, convince them that it was a ball and chain? Here in the solitude of his palace, which held him fast like a prisoner in a cell, he was seized with envy of these heedless passers-by. He did not know them. He had never seen them at close quarters but he felt they must be happier than he. The homes to which they returned at night might be pleasant or grim, but at least there was someone waiting for them. Nobody waited for him. There was only the secretary to whom he dictated his letters, a vicar-general who relieved him of minor responsibilities, Bishop Zasi, with whom he was seldom in accord, his housekeeper, and a handful of friends who had too often been a source of disappointment.

He turned away wearily and lay down on the sofa again. It was a full minute before he settled himself comfortably. The angelic trumpeters were still looking down at him. He wondered what had inspired the artist to paint them. Had he been thinking of the Gospel and of the night when Christ came into the world to redeem man-kind, or were the angels meant to be symbolic of himself and his predecessors in office, men whose duty it was to proclaim the victory of the Almighty throughout the length and breadth of the country?

Medina smiled wrily at his straying thoughts. Even he must have lost the courage to face reality if he allowed himself to be distracted by baroque angels whose trumpets had never been heard to sound.

He glanced at the clock above the ornate fireplace and saw that his siesta had another fifteen minutes to run. Then would come an hour's work, and after that he would receive Padre Valencia and command him to stop doing things which were intolerable in a priest. It was conceivable that Valencia would refuse. The Cardinal's expression changed at the very notion of such a possibility. His face became cold, hard, and suddenly devoid of humanity.

Valencia parked in the plaza with half an hour to spare and decided to go for a stroll along the main shopping street. He locked the car and looked round to see if he was still being followed. The man stared sullenly through him when he gave an amiable nod.

The centre of Cielo was alive with people. Everyone seemed to know him, even the beggars and shoe-shine boys. Now and again he shook someone by the hand, said a few friendly words and passed on. An old man selling lottery tickets pestered him until he gave in and bought one, and he stopped to have his shoes shined. The boy used three different brands of polish, and five minutes later Valencia's shoes were a mirror worthy of the Cardinal's own reflection. From time to time he paused in front of a shop and looked at the elaborate window-dressing. He wondered how the poor could endure the sight of all the luxury goods on display. They would never possess any of them. They were reserved for the country's small élite or for American and other tourists who took them home as souvenirs or presents, proudly boasting that they had bought them in exotic Conciencia.

Valencia decided to have a quick *tinto*. The espresso bars were crowded with people of all kinds, lawyers with their clients, businessmen haggling, clerks taking a fifteen-minute break from the office, lovers holding hands, students killing time now that they were on strike. His entrance caused something of a stir but he pretended not to notice just as, at home, he smilingly ignored anonymous letters even when they contained threats and obscenities. Suddenly he caught sight of Bruce Cornell. The Englishman threaded his way through the tables and joined him.

'Did you think I was angry last night when I left Vermeer's apartment?' Valencia asked quietly.

Bruce shook his head.

'I didn't quite know what to think. Anyway, Padre, how are things going?'

'Pretty well, thank you. I'm meeting more and more opposition in my own circle, but popular support for the movement seems to be almost universal. Have you seen Esther recently?'

'No. You keep her too busy.'

Looking round the tables, Valencia spotted the man who was following him.

'Tell me,' he said. 'If you found an opposition party in your country, do the secret police breathe down your neck?'

Bruce laughed.

'They don't breathe down your neck even if you're a newspaperman. That's a Conciencian custom.'

Valencia stared at him in surprise.

'You mean you're being followed too?'

Bruce nodded.

'In other words, there are two of them sitting here drinking coffee

277

at the tax-payer's expense. Quite an enviable job, really. This afternoon I'll find myself an empty bar and sit there for a couple of hours, just to see what happens.'

As he filled his pipe and lit it, Valencia made up his mind to tell Cornell about the Cardinal's summons. The fight had reached a stage where his enemies might do more than have him tailed. If Cornell knew where he was the authorities might be deterred from resorting to force by the prospect of unfavourable publicity in the international press. It was the first time that such a thought had crossed Valencia's mind – the first time he had felt a twinge of real fear.

'I have an interview with the Cardinal in ten minutes' time,' he said.

Bruce raised his head abruptly.

'Did he send for you?'

'Yes.'

'What sort of reception are you expecting?'

'The obvious one. Everybody knows where the Cardinal stands politically.'

Valencia looked at his watch and stood up.

'I have a suggestion. Wait for me here and we'll call on Vermeer afterwards.'

He shook hands and made his way out into the street, calm and unruffled, nodding and smiling to those who greeted him.

He enjoyed the short walk to the Cardinal's palace. People fascinated and obsessed him, even in the mass. He had an insatiable curiosity about the way they lived and worked and thought. Something inside him impelled him to explore the conditions under which they lived, talk with them for hours and console them in their daily tribulations. It was a priest's good fortune to know that he could help people in moments of stress, whether they were rich or poor in spirit, whether their lives were successful or disastrous. Man was the supreme miracle, he reflected, because he had been created in God's own image. That was why these people must not be allowed to persist in their morbid submission to the crime of exploitation. That was why the poor must be enabled to buy shoes, soap and other things which more fortunate people regarded as necessities of life. That was why villagers must drink no more impure water which blinded them with trachoma or rotted their intestines with dysentery.

He studied the faces of the passers-by, some of them identifiable as mountain folk by their ruanas and big black hats. They walked the streets as if Cielo were an enormous fair-ground where music dispelled suffering and they themselves were bathed in the reflected splendour of all that they would never possess.

Punctually to the minute, Valencia walked through the double doors of the chancellery and announced his presence to the Cardinal's secretary.

The secretary looked him up and down, a lean and colourless figure in his long black soutane and snow-white collar. Valencia thought how alike they must look outwardly. And yet, despite their common duty to preach brotherly love, they were separated by an unbridgeable chasm.

'Be good enough to follow me, Padre Valencia.'

The secretary's tone was cool and measured. He led the way with head erect, his broad gleaming sash making him look almost like a bishop.

Valencia inhaled the stuffy air that hung in the corridors and yearned for the feel of a fresh breeze on his cheek. The secretary knocked at a heavy oak door, keeping one eye on Valencia as if he expected the young priest to storm past him into the room.

'How old he is,' Valencia thought as he knelt to kiss the Cardinal's ring. 'How dry and wrinkled his hands are.'

Medina dismissed his secretary, gestured to an arm-chair and sat down opposite Valencia. For a moment the two men eyed each other as though gauging their respective strength. Then, speaking slowly and softly, Medina said:

'I have given you a certain amount of latitude, Padre Valencia, because I wished to know the precise nature of your aims. They are now clear to me. You preach the doctrine of violence, of revolution. Such a doctrine is incompatible with your priestly status and the cloth you wear. Can you not see that?'

Medina's eyes seemed to stare straight through Valencia as if he were thin air. Valencia retained his composure with an effort.

'I gather, Your Eminence, that it would be futile to defend myself.'

The Cardinal glanced up at the cherub-adorned ceiling.

'I have heard enough of your rantings as it is. Your duty is to listen with respect and obedience to what I have to say to you – unless, of course, you decline to do even that.'

This was not at all what Medina had meant to say, but someone else was speaking for him. The voice was one that had resounded through the Church for centuries, the voice of an authority that brooked no threat to its omnipotence.

'I am listening, Your Eminence.'

The Cardinal cleared his throat.

'Papal directives forbid priests to take part in political activities. You are not only cognizant of these directives but fully aware that I back them to the hilt. I give you a choice: either abandon your revolutionary activities and accept a post here in the chancellery, or request me to release you from your duties as a priest. Is that clear?'

The Cardinal knew, as he put the question, that he had done the right thing. Further discussion was useless. Love must cede to authority if he wanted to prevent this priest's recalcitrance from infecting others. If not, the edifice of the Catholic Church would soon lie in ruins.

He looked out of the window. Rain had started to fall and people were putting up their umbrellas. The city could change from one moment to the next, he reflected. When the sun shone Cielo became a microcosmic heaven and the crosses on tower and spire gleamed gold like those of the celestial city. When it rained, gloom descended on the capital as if some painter had instantaneously daubed it in grey wash.

'Quite clear, Your Eminence. Would you give me a little time to consider my decision?'

The Cardinal stared at Valencia in surprise. He sank into a momentary reverie at the sight of those clear eyes. Was the young bishop still stirring within him after all, urging him to treat his subordinate with indulgence? He seemed to hear a voice telling him that love, too, could be an obsession which drove men to extremes and set them at odds. 'Suppose ye that I am come to give peace on earth?' Christ had said. 'I tell you, Nay; but rather division: For from henceforth there shall be five in one house divided, three against two, and two against three. The father shall be divided against the son, and the son against the father; the mother against the daughter, and the daughter against the mother; the mother in law against her daughter in law, and the daughter in law against her mother in law.'

Division in the name of Christianity, yes, but not in that of Communism. With that, Medina commanded the young bishop within him to be silent, and Valencia, almost as if he guessed the Cardinal's thoughts, found himself recalling a different passage from the Gospel: 'If thou hadst known, even thou, at least in this thy day, the things which belong unto thy peace! But now they are hid from thine eyes. For the days shall come upon thee that thine enemies shall cast a trench about thee, and compass thee round, and keep thee in on every side, and shall lay thee even with the ground, and thy children within thee; and they shall not leave in thee one stone upon another because thou knewest not the time of thy visitation.'

Valencia looked at the Cardinal, the immaculate robe, the gold pectoral cross and the face above it. There were two deeply incised furrows above the eyes, like exclamation marks. The corners of the mouth curved downwards, a sign of discontent or chronic suffering.

The silence in the room was becoming oppressive. For a moment Valencia thought the Cardinal had forgotten his presence, but when he made a move to rise Medina curtly waved him back into his chair.

'By all means consider your decision,' Medina said brusquely. 'Consider it well, Padre Valencia. Above all, reflect on the harm you do the Church by persisting in your headstrong behaviour.'

He did not raise his voice as he spoke these words. They were too important to require emphasis. He merely gave Valencia a keen and searching stare to see if they, and the authority behind them, would produce any outward effect. He detected nothing. No humility emanated from the man facing him, simply a rocklike faith in his own convictions. It was not arrogance, but something more. What confronted Medina was youth gazing with compassion at an older generation faced by decisions which demanded too much of it. Clearly, Antonio Valencia had no doubts. He believed implicitly in his cause, yet the Cardinal knew full well that he was not motivated by self-interest or personal ambition. He was impelled by a fanaticism which made him dangerous.

Now it was Medina who felt the urge to make a move. He rose and walked to the window. The wind was lashing the rain along the streets, sweeping it round corners, driving it past the cathedral and diagonally across the plaza, where stooping figures scurried to find a haven from the storm. The Cardinal drew a deep breath.

'I will give you time. You know where I stand in this matter. Discuss it again with Bishop Zasi.'

As Valencia knelt to kiss his ring the Cardinal had a momentary urge to lay his hand on the young priest's head. Something inside him prompted him to do so, but something different and far stronger guided his hand towards the bell on his desk and signalled the beginning of the next interview. A committee on liturgical reform was waiting in the anteroom.

Valencia straightened up. There had been no dialogue. His hopes had not materialized. The Cardinal had barely allowed him to speak, and even before the heavy oak door swung to he knew that he had knelt before a cardinal for the last time, that the soutane he wore was no longer part of him because it had ceased to be a coat of mail and become an impediment. He felt naked and uncomfortable as he emerged from the palace, and could not wait to do what he had half-decided to do before his interview with Medina: remove his soutane but remain a priest for all time.

Forgetting all about Bruce Cornell, he returned to his parked car and drove slowly back to his apartment through the rain-swept streets of the capital. Preoccupied as he was, he did not omit to note that his tail was following him in a taxi. What a profession, he thought. What must it be like to trail one's fellow-creatures, to arrest, torture and kill them? What did such people think of, night and morning? He sighed. The worst of it was, they probably thought of nothing at all.

The door-bell rang just as Esther Graham was typing the last lines of a letter for Valencia to sign on his return. Irritably, she guessed that it was yet another student with news of latest developments at Cielo University.

She went to the door and opened it. The man outside was a stranger. He did not introduce himself.

'Professor Valencia is out,' she said.

The stranger nodded.

'All the better. You're the person I wanted to talk to.'

The man did not move as he spoke. He stood so still that for a moment she had a strange feeling that he was a dummy.

'What is it about?'

'You'll soon find out.'

She hurriedly tried to shut the door but the man wedged it open with his foot. Esther felt her forehead prickle with sweat.

'Stop pestering me or I'll call for help,' she said. She noticed his eyes for the first time. They were cold and unblinking, like a snake's.

'It wouldn't do you much good. Nobody would be unwise enough to interfere. Don't make any scenes, señorita. Seguridad Nacional.' She dropped her arms limply and he thrust his way inside, closing the door behind him.

Esther struggled to keep calm but her hands shook and a metallic taste came into her mouth.

'We'd better go to my office. Follow me.'

She led the way, feeling his eyes travel the length of her body from head to foot and back again.

'Sit down if you wish.'

He did so.

'That's more like it. I have a couple of things to tell you. Listen carefully and don't interrupt, is that clear?'

She nodded.

'*Bueno*. You're in an awkward position, *señorita*. You were born here but you're a United States citizen. We could simply deport you, but that would upset your father. We won't go to those lengths on one condition. You hand in your notice, leave this building at once, and take a job elsewhere. In other words, you turn over a new leaf.'

'What if I refuse?'

The man lit a cigarette and pulled the ashtray towards him.

'I wouldn't if I were you. It would be unhealthy.'

The words were uttered quietly and without emphasis, but Esther shivered.

'Is that a threat?'

'Of course.'

'But why? Won't you at least tell me why?' She almost shouted the question.

'Don't you know?'

'No. I thought this was a democratic country.'

'It is, and you're trying to turn it into a dictatorship – you and your friends under Valencia's leadership.'

She stared at him wide-eyed.

'Do you believe that?'

He sighed.

'Don't you, *señorita*?'

She looked round her makeshift office, the clutter of files, correspondence and press cuttings, the books and periodicals, the whole world into which she had thrown herself with such passionate enthusiasm.

'What if I make this conversation public?'

'I'm sure you won't.'

He said it meditatively but with such assurance that she stared at him in surprise.

'Are you really so sure?'

'Yes,' he replied. 'I forgot to mention one thing. You aren't to discuss this with anyone, not even Padre Valencia. If you do, the responsibility for what happens will be yours alone.'

'Is that another threat?'

'Call it what you like. We act quickly as a general rule. By the way, don't worry about all this waste-paper.' He indicated the correspondence on her desk. 'We aren't particularly interested in it.'

He stubbed out his cigarette with an air of finality.

'That's settled, then. You don't come here again after today. How you explain it is your affair. And don't forget, if I call again it won't be to warn you. We never repeat ourselves. I hope you'll be sensible, *señorita*.'

He rose and walked to the door. Before he opened it he turned to face her once more.

'Democracy must be safeguarded too, *señorita. Buenas tardes.*'

Reaction set in as soon as Esther heard the outer door close behind him. A violent fit of trembling overcame her and she felt faint. She went to the cupboard, poured herself a whisky and sipped it slowly, trying to collect her thoughts. After a few minutes she decided to call Bruce's hotel.

'No *señorita*, the *señor* is out, but he left word that he would be back later this afternoon. Can I give him a message?'

Esther hung up. She pulled on her coat, ran downstairs to her car and drove to the *Plaza*. Bruce was still out, the desk clerk informed her, so she left a note for him and went to the bar.

It was quiet in there at that time of day. The only customer was an American who regarded her with an inquisitive eye, clearly uncertain whether she was a prostitute on the make or a damsel in distress.

'Nice country,' he said affably.

'So they say,' she replied with a shrug.

He raised his eyebrows.

'Your English is good.'

'I'm an American,' she said, surprised at her readiness to admit the fact.

He sat down beside her as if their common nationality made it the natural thing to do, and she raised no objection because anything was preferable to being alone.

'What can I buy you?'

'A Scotch, please. Neat.'

The barman was new. Esther shivered again, wondering if his predecessor was languishing in the dungeons of the Seguridad.

'Bottoms up,' said the American. 'Scotch cures most things, in my experience. You live here in Cielo?'

'Yes.'

He looked like a businessman – a prosperous one, too, or he would not have been staying at the *Plaza*. He was pushing sixty, with grey hair and a pleasant tanned face.

'It must be great to live here. Beautiful city, Cielo. Nice quiet people, democratic government, healthy political set-up, free elections, lovely women, first-class hotels.'

He might have been reading from a travel brochure, she reflected. Her compatriots were so magnificently naive. They said what they thought, however crass it was. If she had told him someone from the secret police had paid her a visit half an hour before, he wouldn't have believed her.

'Here on business?' she asked.

He nodded. 'Export–import.'

Conversation lapsed, and at that moment Bruce walked in. She thanked the American and accompanied Bruce to the lift. They rode up side by side, unspeaking.

Still without a word, Bruce unlocked the door of his room and closed it quietly behind them. He pointed to a chair and sat down facing her.

'Has something happened to Valencia?'

She started.

'What makes you ask?'

'He was with the Cardinal this afternoon. Arranged to meet me afterwards and never turned up.'

'May I try his number?'

'Help yourself. He wasn't there five minutes ago.'

Valencia answered promptly. He sounded his usual self.

'I was expecting to find you here, Esther. Is anything wrong?'

'No. I wasn't feeling well so I went home.'

She avoided Bruce's eye as she spoke, resenting the lie.

'How did your interview with the Cardinal go?'

'Much as I expected. If I don't accept his proposal I shall be forbidden to exercise my priestly duties.'

'He didn't suspend you right away, then?'

'No, he gave me time to consider, but I know what my answer must be.'

She did not know what to say. In a few weeks' time he would cease to be a priest in the eyes of the world. She wondered how he would take it. Guessing what the prospect must mean to him, she longed to go to him and give him all the comfort she could.

'Has something happened, Esther?'

'No, no,' she replied hurriedly. 'I just wanted to know how you got on. I may come over tomorrow.'

She put down the receiver and turned to Bruce.

'I need your help,' she said simply.

He smiled.

'There's no one I'd rather help, you know that.'

Her face was deathly pale and he saw that her hands were trembling. He put his arms round her, and at that moment she started to cry. It was more than grief, he could tell by the way her body shook. It was an access of fear that had been suppressed for too long. He reached for his handkerchief and dabbed her eyes.

'He warned me not to tell anyone . . .' Her voice trailed away and she clung to him.

He led her back to her chair, thinking hard. Someone had threatened her. Suddenly he understood, and a claustrophobic sense of fear enveloped him too.

'Esther,' he said with deliberate calm, 'tell me the whole story. I don't care who threatened you. This room isn't bugged. Don't be afraid – tell me everything.'

'You don't understand.'

'I understand perfectly. You had a visit from someone in the Seguridad. Am I right?'

She nodded.

'And he warned you not to breathe a word to anyone.'

'Yes.'

'He advised you to leave Valencia or else.'

'How did you guess?'

'I don't have to be a mind-reader. Your father runs the Latin American division of a major U.S. oil company, one of the most important foreign firms in the country. His daughter teams up with a local revolutionary. The U.S. ambassador gets jumpy. He contacts your father. Your father tells him you're old enough to look after yourself and disclaims responsibility. The Conciencian authorities get to hear of the conversation. The boys at the Seguridad decide to put a stop to your activities and send an agent to warn you off, which he does in characteristic style. Either you say good-bye to Valencia, or . . .'

There was a long silence. Then Esther said:

'Has my father discussed this with you?'

'Not since that day at the National University.'

She closed her eyes.

'Bruce, what am I to do?'

He jingled the small change in his trouser-pocket, nervously.

'I'm not the ideal person to ask,' he said at length. 'I don't want to take advantage of your troubles. Any advice I gave you might sound prejudiced.'

She gave an exclamation of impatience.

'Leave us out of it, Bruce. Do I have to walk out on Antonio or don't I, yes or no?'

He looked at her.

'The answer is yes,' he replied quietly. 'You've no choice. Once the authorities run out of ideas they can be lethal. Valencia will find himself another secretary, no need to worry about that. If you stay with him to the bitter end you'll be doing it for personal reasons, not for the cause he represents, and I can't advise you there. One thing, though. Don't gamble your life away. Enough people are doing that already. Don't follow their example for your own sake – for my sake . . . Do you understand?'

She stared back at him with tears in her eyes.

'How can I leave him now, of all time? You want me to be that much of a coward?'

'You're not his mistress,' he replied gently. 'You're his secretary, remember?'

'I'm his friend. Too many of his friends have deserted him as it is.'

Bruce felt his composure ebbing away.

'What is this, Esther, a death-wish? If you play the martyr and something happens to you, Valencia will never forgive himself.'

She raised her head with a sudden air of decision.

'What else do you advise?'

He stood up and took her in his arms again.

'Get another job. Be my secretary for a while. There's plenty for you to do. Stay here with me. I'll book you a room in the hotel if you like.'

She drew a deep breath.

'Let me think it over, Bruce. I have to go home first. My father must be worried too. I don't know why, but it's only just dawned on me.'

'You hadn't noticed?'

'No, he hasn't said much since he heard Antonio speak.'

'Shall I go to Valencia and talk to him?'

'Isn't it risky?'

He smiled.

'The most they can do is cancel my visa. Foreign correspondents don't get themselves murdered very often.'

A little colour returned to her cheeks.

'Be patient with me, Bruce. Give me time to sort things out in my mind.'

'Don't do anything crazy, that's all. Don't chuck your life away. I'm still here.'

He escorted her to her car and stood looking after her as she drove off. Then he went back to his room and phoned Valencia.

'Could I speak to you, Padre? It's urgent.'

There was a momentary silence at the other end of the line.

'I'm just going across to see Vermeer. You'll find me there.'

It was late when Bruce got back to the hotel. He had told Valencia what had happened, and Valencia asked him to inform Esther that his heavy schedule of lecture tours would in any case allow him to dispense with her services for the time being. When the worst of the pressure had eased he hoped to thank her personally for all her hard work. Bruce went with him to collect her things. Then they returned to Vermeer's apartment.

They talked far into the night. Vermeer wanted Valencia to go and defend his doctoral thesis at Louvain and urged him to ask Bishop Zasi for leave of absence. Once in Louvain, he could elaborate and defend his revolutionary ideas in detail. In Vermeer's view, this was Valencia's only chance to regain his prestige with the ruling circles of Conciencia and banish damaging speculation about his aims. It would keep him out of the country for several months, admittedly, but passions might subside in the meantime and the threat of assassination recede. How, Vermeer asked, could he fight for a new system unless all Conciencians of good will co-operated in its establishment?

Valencia considered the proposal seriously. Tempted as he was to submit such a request to Zasi, he wondered how many of his supporters would be content with an academic vindication of his programme. They wanted to harness the spate of enthusiasm before it abated and rush him from one speaker's platform to the next.

Bruce was still not quite sure what Valencia intended to do when the party broke up. He had never seen him look so desperate. He drank more than was good for him and ended by giving a brief and rather disjointed account of his interview with the Cardinal.

'He looked so old,' Valencia concluded, 'old and weary and authoritarian. An accurate reflection of the Church, perhaps – who knows?'

After that he suddenly rose and embraced Vermeer, leaning his head on the Dutchman's bony shoulder like a child seeking comfort.

'Pray for me, Francisco. I need your prayers so much. I feel as if I'm bleeding to death inside and there's no one to give me a transfusion. Except you, possibly.'

He walked blindly out, leaving Bruce alone with Vermeer.

'I wish I could share his loneliness,' Vermeer said. 'I know him too well, though. He wants to work it out alone. Alone with God.'

'Why did the Cardinal take such a hard line?'

'It was predictable. The spiritual leaders of this continent are frightened of implicating themselves in revolutionary movements. A few priests, bishops and missionaries are doing wonders in the social field but there aren't enough of them. The Church as such is too remote from everyday life. It has stood aloof for centuries, lost its sense of reality, turned into a wholly spiritualized institution. Apart from that, it has become materially involved with the rich. Many churches are full on Sundays, full of friendly, Christian, civilized people who give generously to charity. They demonstrate their piety by taking part in public processions and making constant references to God and the saints, but nothing ever changes in the general scheme of things. One searches in vain for the specifically Christian type of spirituality which I've sometimes come across in Chile and parts of Brazil.'

Bruce listened, thinking of the man in the next apartment. He must by now be in the throes of the hardest battle which any man could wage, a battle with himself . . .

Valencia closed the door and leaned his back against it. So Esther had been compelled to abandon him like so many others. She would go back to Bruce Cornell, leaving a void behind her. He would have to cable his mother and ask her to return, though he hesitated to cut short her stay because she had performed such prodigies of hard work for him before her departure. What was more, much to his own surprise, she had defended him fiercely against all comers.

Suddenly his eyes fell on the crucifix which hung above his desk, a present from a fellow-student at Louvain. The artist had so steeped himself in the life and death of Christ that the face of the figure conveyed a nameless suffering, all the pain and solitude that any human being could experience. Valencia gazed at it for a long time. Revolution violated the teachings of the Church – such was the Cardinal's contention. But hadn't Christ also rebelled against authority? Hadn't men like Caiaphas wanted to seal his lips? All right, perhaps he might have acceded to Medina's command if he hadn't made such a close study of the appalling injustices that prevailed in his country. Knowing them as he did, was he not obliged to follow Christ's example?

He debated yet again whether to ask permission to go to Louvain. He could always try, but even Vermeer failed to grasp how crucial to the entire country the coming weeks would be.

Still gazing at the crucified Christ, he asked himself why things had had to go this far, and the tormented figure seemed to reply: Look at me, how far did I go? They seized me and nailed me to the cross. The disciples who stood by me at Golgotha were few. The others were deterred by pain, humiliation, imprisonment, the mockery of their friends . . . It was no cliché to say that Christ had died for *people* – he really had. He had fought not only against injustice, indifference and exploitation but also against pride, arrogance and hypocrisy. His enemies could not forgive him for that. He had consorted with the dregs of human society and lodged wherever people had extended their hospitality, however humble. His successors had built palaces and stocked them with innumerable treasures as though faith and salvation were purchasable commodities. They had become guardians of boundless wealth as well as custodians of a Church which proclaimed brotherly love in the name of a man who had been a pauper throughout his life. Christ's adherents had been poor fishermen, not rich men. His disciples had amassed souls, not gold, and helped them to partake of love and justice.

Valencia knelt down and tried to pray.

'God, your son has taught me that love must sometimes use force, as he did when he drove the money-changers from the Temple. The usurers of today are just as hard to dislodge. They sit there stubbornly on their chairs, deaf to the voice of justice. They use the Church as a refuge in time of need, and the Church disarms those who attack them as the Cardinal disarmed me today. If I lay aside my priest's clothing, it will be no denial of you, no denial of the true Church, no denial of Christian doctrine, but an assault on the Church here, on the vengeful God and perverted Christian doctrine which never formed part of your son's teachings . . .'

He sensed that his prayer was an attempt to justify himself, and, with him, all who would perish in a future revolution, all the families that would be rent asunder, all the hatred and cruelty, lovelessness and prejudice that would rise to the surface. But the force that impelled him to preach violence was stronger than he, even though doubt sometimes surged over him like a tidal wave, taller than the roof-tops.

He wrestled with himself for hours, weighing one argument against another. If the revolutionary in him triumphed in the end, it was because he could not bring himself to betray his people at the very moment when he had led them to the dawn of a new day.

16

Lieutenant Losano pointed to the east, where the flanks of the mountains were green with jungle.

'That's where they are, hidden by those damned trees. Every patrol we send out could be jumped. Tobar's men are ambush specialists. Our only chance is to turn the tables on them, but it's a slim one. They know the terrain better than we do. What's more, they always seem to have advance warning.'

John Wells nodded. They were sitting on the veranda behind the house which served as Losano's headquarters. Two sentries were posted with their tommy-guns covering the track which led straight towards them out of the jungle. In the far distance Wells could hear the hum of a reconnaissance plane, and horses' hoofs were clip-clopping on the caked mud of Talmac's single main street. It was seven o'clock in the morning. The sun was edging above the mountains, dispersing the dawn chill and painting long shadows in the dust. Talmac was at its best early in the morning. Even the villagers seemed better-humoured because another night had passed without gunfire and death.

The helicopter which Zambrano had put at Wells's disposal for the next few days stood like a giant grasshopper in the plaza in front of the church. The village children feasted their eyes on it all day long, waiting excitedly for the great rotor to turn.

John Wells was not sorry that Zambrano had given him the assignment. It had taught him for the first time that even a man like Losano harboured doubts about his ability to master the guerilleros. His patrols had so far achieved nothing, and the mestizo inhabitants of the smaller villages situated in a wide arc round Talmac seldom had anything to report. Relations between Losano and Don Henrico were still very strained. The landowner had been expecting too much. His original thought when the soldiers arrived was that the guerilleros would flee in terror to another district. Wells had done his best to correct this misapprehension. On the contrary, he told Don Henrico, the rebels would be attracted like wasps to a jam-jar by the soldiers' arms and equipment, for which they could find good use. What was more, they would one day try to eliminate the army post altogether. They probably had all the outlying villages under their control and were slowly tightening the noose because Tobar's only chance of acquiring more territory was to oust the army. If he had not tried to do so long before, it could only be because the guerilleros did not yet feel strong enough. That was why they limited themselves to small-scale raids whose aim was to spread panic among the people of Talmac or at least demonstrate that the guerilleros were on their doorstep.

It was a peculiar type of warfare designed to play upon the superstitions of the local inhabitants. Although not pure Indian, they had enough Indian blood in their veins to live in constant terror of the unseen. Rodriguez Tobar was gambling on this, and Wells had no doubt that the *campesinos* spoke his name with awe and veneration.

A strange experience, Wells thought, never to see the enemy himself, only what he left behind – like the seven bodies in the hut, for instance. Anyone who had successfully conducted such a campaign for years on end must be a tactician of the first order, a born leader who not only had his men well in hand but was shrewd enough to smell a trap a mile off.

'Ambush or no ambush,' he drawled, 'I reckon you ought to step up your patrols.'

Losano's black-olive eyes regarded him intently.

'Is that your personal advice, or does it come from Colonel Zambrano?'

Wells picked up a pair of powerful binoculars and trained them on the forest.

'Don't get me wrong, Lieutenant,' he said. 'I'm not here to keep tabs on you. You're in command here, not me. My orders are to look for Tobar's base camp in that goddamned helicopter and give you air support if you need it. That's the extent of my assignment.'

Losano did not believe him and showed it.

'Why can't you get away from the idea that this is a full-scale war?' he said bitterly. 'If we had the hardware, like your boys in Vietnam, I'd flatten the whole area with bombs and heavy artillery. That would flush the bastards out quick enough.'

The two men fell silent. It was going to be another long hot day. John Wells would take off in the helicopter. The pilot would follow his instructions to the letter, aware that there were three possibilities.

Either they would find nothing, or they would spot Tobar's camp, or they would be shot down.

Losano planned to take part of his command on another patrol. He would take the lead as usual, alert to any sudden ambush, and his bravery would turn into savagery as soon as he developed the slightest suspicion that one of the peasants was in touch with the rebels.

More peasants than rebels had been killed locally in recent weeks. John Wells knew this, although Losano disputed it and claimed that the peasants were rebels as well. They might not belong to regular guerrilla units – if that wasn't a contradiction in terms – but they were certainly auxiliaries. Interrogations were brutal and prolonged, and not much remained of a prisoner once they were over. Sometimes Losano left the corpse where it was as a graphic illustration of what happened to people who helped the rebels. Other victims of protracted torture were buried on the spot.

'What about driving over to Don Henrico's for breakfast?' Wells suggested.

Losano reluctantly agreed, if only because the landowner's food was better than army rations.

Climbing into the green jeep with its mounted machine-gun and two armed soldiers in the back, they drove slowly along the village street. The menfolk were already at work on the coffee plantation, but the women and children stared silently after them, terrified in case the jeep should come to a sudden halt. The prevailing atmosphere in the village was one of hostility and disguised hatred. Losano thought it was apathy. It might have been at first, but John Wells knew that it was the sullen expectancy of slaves who hear the bells of freedom ringing in the distance.

The sentries outside the *casa grande* waved them on without challenging them. They found Don Henrico on his patio, reading the latest batch of week-old newspapers. He looked weary and disgruntled, as if he had not slept much in recent nights.

'Are you going up again today?' he asked Wells. 'They seem to be well concealed, the swine.'

'What else do you expect?' Losano demanded brusquely. He might have been addressing one of his men.

Don Henrico shrugged. 'I don't expect much any more, Lieutenant,' he retorted in an acid tone.

Losano shook his head.

'You expect too much, that's the trouble. Things are quiet here – what more do you want?'

Even the steadiest nerves cracked under incessant strain, Wells reflected, but that was part of the rebels' tactics. You saw to it that your enemy got no sleep, began to lose faith in his own and others' efficiency. Then, when morale had reached rock bottom, you made a lightning attack which still further undermined his confidence – if he still had a chance to think about it at all.

'Any news?' he asked, pointing to the papers.

Don Henrico looked even more peevish.

'Yes, that clown Valencia seems to be going from strength to strength. If he ever has the effrontery to show his face round here I'll have him horsewhipped.'

'Why bother?' Losano said.

Valencia did not worry him. As long as there was an army, dreamers like Valencia could preach rebellion to their hearts' content. Their prospects of success were precisely nil. Government troops would drown any insurrection in blood because they had already had their fill of the guerilleros. The Valencias of this world were theorists, and theorists could be safely ignored.

Losano stood up.

'My patrol moves out in an hour's time. The rest of the men are staying here with Sergeant Gomez. If anything happens, contact him immediately.'

'Where are you going?'

'Cemento. Somebody reported seeing guerilleros there and I plan to take a look. You never know.'

Punctually at nine-thirty the helicopter rose from the plaza of Talmac in a huge cloud of dust. It circled the village once, insect-like, and then banked sharply to the east, where Colonel Zambrano guessed the rebels' main camp to be situated.

The pilot, Leon Martinez, was a quietly efficient flyer who did not mix with the villagers and showed no interest in politics. He had been trained in the United States and got on excellently with John Wells.

Wells was sceptical about the value of these reconnaissance flights and the likelihood of detecting anything at all. On the other hand, it was always on the cards that some unforeseen circumstance would come to their aid. A helicopter could fly even lower over the jungle than a spotter plane, and its ability to hover motionless made it possible to pick out almost every detail through binoculars.

In general, though, Wells enjoyed his daily routine. No other form of aircraft afforded a better view of the forest. He wondered how the guerilleros managed to live there at all and whether years of isolation and hopelessness might not have broken their spirit and bestialized them to such an extent that they would never be re-integrated in normal human society.

There was no audible report from below as the bullet struck. Martinez banked sharply and radioed his position to ground control, knowing that within a few minutes fighters would take off to cut a swathe of destruction through the jungle. John Wells winced when he saw the hole in the fuselage beside him. If the marksman on the ground had aimed a fraction of a degree to the right, or the helicopter had been flying one foot per second slower, he would be dead by how. Another bullet smacked into the plane.

'Let's get out of here!' he yelled, but Martinez did not respond. His head had slumped forwards on his chest and blood was streaming from his abdomen to the seat and from there to the floor. At the same instant Wells heard a frightful rending crash. Something dealt him a sledge-hammer blow an he lost consciousness.

He came to with the fierce chatter of machine-gun fire in his ears, so close that the bullets seemed to be ripping up the ground beside his head. He tried to sit up but collapsed with a groan. A moment or two later he managed to raise his head and look round. He must have been thrown from the helicopter on impact, because it was nesting in the trees twenty yards away. The rotor blades were smashed but the aircraft had not caught fire. Its crumpled aluminium skin glinted in the sunlight.

Wells could hear nothing apart from the rattle of gunfire and the roar of the fighters as they returned again and again; no sound of human voices, no movement among the trees. He felt as if his spine and legs had been shattered, and any attempt to turn round made him scream with agony.

Small black creatures crawled over his face, looming large as they skirted his eyes. Next time the planes receded he heard the twittering or birds and the humming of countless insects. He thought of Martinez, hanging in the trees. Was he dead, or had he just passed out? One of the planes made a final run, swooped, and sprayed the ground with bullets. The hail of steel tore holes in the forest floor and flayed bark from the trees. He tried to shout that the rebels had gone, that only he and Martinez were left, but no words came, only a jet of blood, and he knew that he had been hit. The trees seemed to fold inwards, the sky dwindled to a speck of light in a sea of darkness, and he died, machine-gunned to death by the planes that had come to his aid.

Simultaneously, a group of forty guerilleros led by Rodriguez Tobar launched an attack on Talmac. They overran the village with lightning speed, killing the sentries before they had a chance to identify the men in army uniforms. Sergeant Gomez was dispatched with a single bullet, but the rest of the men were disarmed and taken prisoner. Another guerrilla unit attacked the *casa grande* and carried Don Henrico off into the jungle.

The raid, which had been timed to the last minute by Tobar, lasted precisely a quarter of an hour. Most of the soldiers were in their billet, and surprise was so complete that none of them offered any resistance. Don Henrico's bodyguards thought the rebels were a new army unit and did not discover their mistake until too late. Three of them were shot and the rest surrendered. They were disarmed and tied up, like the soldiers, and left to lie in the broiling sun.

Exactly fifteen minutes later the guerilleros vanished into the jungle. Another half-hour, and whole families were fleeing from Talmac and the wrath to come – Losano's – on foot, on horseback and by mule-cart, bound for the anonymity of far-off Cielo. An hour after the raid Talmac was a ghost town. Even the dogs followed their masters. The *campesinos* had deserted the coffee plantation, the streets were empty, the huts abandoned, and Sergeant Gomez's body lay sprawled in the middle of the plaza.

In Cemento, Losano received a report that the helicopter had been shot down by guerilleros and tried to contact Talmac by radio. Nobody answered his call. He became uneasy and decided to start back at once. It was a three-hour trek through the jungle, and his misgivings increased at every step. He thought of John Wells and the taciturn helicopter pilot, both of whom would undoubtedly have been killed. He also thought of Colonel Zambrano. Perhaps this would persuade him to send reinforcements. Cursing, he drove his men to the limit of their endurance. They streamed with sweat as they forged a path through the trees, foliage and lianas, eyes darting nervously to and fro in constant expectation of an ambush.

If something had really happened he would have to lean on the villagers still harder. He was convinced that they were in touch with the guerilleros. All thought of fatigue vanished as ice-cold rage bubbled up inside him. His sole concern was to act, and act fast.

He checked the magazine of his submachine-gun and signalled to the patrol to halt. Then he personally inspected the weapons of his men, one by one, and warned them of the possible dangers that awaited them in and around Talmac.

Not far from the village he sent out three scouts. They returned with the news that all seemed quiet but that Don Henrico's plantation looked strangely deserted.

Ten minutes later Losano knew the truth. Condors were circling over the village, and that meant death. He strode into the plaza ahead of his men, to find Sergeant Gomez dead and the rest of the garrison tied up in their billet. Having questioned the men in turn, he realized that the attack must have been planned weeks in advance. Each guerillero seemed to have been assigned a victim of his own. The sentries on the outskirts of the village had been jumped by one group, the sentries posted behind and in front of the billet by another. The rebels must have operated in several small teams according to a precise time-table, because they had vacated the village in less than fifteen minutes.

The inhabitants had obviously fled. Losano sent a detachment to track them down, quell any resistance by force, and bring them back to the village. The corporal in charge, who had been man-handled by the rebels and was thirsting for revenge, took it upon himself to follow Losano's instructions to the letter.

Next, Losano went with thirty men to the *casa grande*, where he released Don Henrico's bodyguards. They told him that the land-owner had been abducted by a man who seemed to be a senior guerrilla commander. Boiling with rage, Losano returned to head-quarters and reported by radio to Colonel Zambrano that most of his men's lives had been spared but all the arms and ammunition were gone.

Zambrano at once radioed the news to Cielo and asked for a line to the Presidential palace. He got through after an hour. The President asked for a full report of what had happened. His voice was so indistinct that Zambrano could scarcely understand him and had to repeat every sentence three times. Eventually he got the main points over: the destruction of the helicopter complete with pilot and American adviser, the raid on Talmac while Losano was out on patrol, the death of the sergeant and sentries, the abduction of Don Henrico by another heavily armed guerrilla unit.

Less than an hour later President Colombo proclaimed a state of national emergency and announced over the radio that an army battalion was to be sent to Talmac with orders to eliminate the elusive and allegedly invincible Rodriguez Tobar once and for all. Tobar's name promptly became a byword throughout the country, which was hardly what the President had intended.

The same evening, an exhausted Don Henrico was led into the secondary camp which had been established an hour's march from Tobar's base. It was a hot and humid night, and moths were battering themselves against the paraffin lamps which illuminated the central tent. The men escorting Don Henrico were ragged and weary but well armed. The light glinted on bandoliers slung diagonally across their chests, and their eyes were almost invisible beneath their sombreros. Inquisitive women and children crowded round the tent.

The landowner's eyes widened when he realized who his captor was.

'Rodriguez Tobar?'

The muscular man with the short black beard gave a nod. There was no exultation in his face. He seemed calm, almost indifferent, and his voice was equally devoid of self-congratulation.

'If it interests you, we had been planning that raid for months, down to the last detail. Every man knew what he had to do.'

'Why have you brought me here?'

Tobar motioned to Don Henrico to sit down on a tree-stump. The tree must have been felled quite recently because the scent of fresh saw-dust still hung in the air.

'I can't offer you a chair. You will have to be content with that.'

'What do you want me to do?'

Tobar laughed.

'Nothing. Spend a couple of weeks in camp with us, that's all. We shall inform Zambrano that we're holding you as a hostage. Once you've had a taste of guerillero life we shall release you. Then you can tell the world about us. In addition, you will pay us a ransom, a big one. I'm sure your family will raise the money. I shall speak to you again tomorrow. A word of warning, though: don't try to escape. You wouldn't get far in this jungle. You can go now. My men will escort you to your hut.'

For more than a week, reports about Talmac dominated the front page of every newspaper in the country. Fierro's syndicate, with *El Temporal* in the lead, gave the incident particularly sensational coverage but played down the fact that the guerilleros had only killed a handful of soldiers and three of Don Henrico's bodyguards. Alejandro Herrera flew to Talmac in person, had the crashed helicopter and the solitary corpse in the plaza photographed from every angle, and published a heart-rending piece on the *campesinos* who had returned to the village, conveniently omitting to note that Losano had brought them back by force. Herrera also published a summary of the bandoleros' atrocities, a short biography of the doughty landowner Don Henrico Mendoza, famed throughout the country for his progressive approach to labour relations, and wrote a leader angrily demanding to know why the President did not intervene at once to put an end to the crimes of bloodthirsty bandits who regarded murder as a legitimate pastime.

The same evening, the President announced on radio and television that Colonel Zambrano would be taking personal command of the battalion assigned to Talmac. He informed the people of Conciencia that the guerilleros were receiving aid from China, Cuba and Russia, and could thus be described as fanatical mercenaries in the pay of foreign powers. Their policy, he said, was to disrupt peace and good order in Conciencia with the eventual aim of seizing power themselves. Eloquently, he predicted that a revolution fomented by the guerilleros would be bloodier than any the country had ever experienced, and declared that the rebels were inveterate criminals who killed with the regularity of machines. As he spoke, he wondered if the U.S. ambassador would be satisfied with his speech. Without actually mentioning Valencia by name, he admonished the country's intellectuals and assured them that anyone who preached armed revolution would rue the day. His patience was finally exhausted, and those who tried to subvert the established order must bear the consequences. 'We shall eliminate this Castroite-Communist threat,' he concluded, 'in order to preserve our people from dictatorship.'

The campaign against Valencia was launched next day. It opened with a public statement from the Cardinal Archbishop of Cielo which Herrera reproduced verbatim in all the Fierro newspapers. This statement, which did not attract much attention at first, ran as follows:

It is completely untrue that Antonio Valencia's visit to Louvain could not take place or was prevented by the Church authorities. Padre Valencia requested the Archbishop of Cielo for permission to leave the archdiocese in order to present his thesis at the University of Louvain. Permission was not only granted but later confirmed by Mgr Zasi in response to a renewed request from Padre Valencia.

Padre Valencia's political programme embodies various points which are incompatible with the teachings of the Church.

The statement was signed: *Esperanza Cardinal Medina, Archbishop of Cielo.*

Three days later Esther Graham clipped an open letter from the correspondence columns of *El Temporal.* It was signed by Antonio Valencia, and read:

Some days ago I was surprised to come across a statement by Your Eminence relating to my projected visit to Louvain, also to certain ideas which I have recently put forward.

I at once applied to the chancellery for a personal interview with Mgr Zasi. I thought it better to explain the situation to my bishop in person rather than through the medium of the press, having always felt that the relations between Christians in general, and a bishop and his priests in particular, are of a family nature and should be founded on mutual trust. Two days ago I had a long talk with Mgr Zasi in just such an atmosphere of trust. I told him very frankly of the difficulties which I have experienced since the publication of the programme which I helped to draft. It embodies a number of purely technical points which many Catholics would regard as essential to the common good.

As to the statement which Your Eminence released to the press, Mgr Zasi informed me that it represents Your Eminence's considered opinion. I am nevertheless bound to tell Your Eminence that I regard my programme as essential to my own peace of mind and that of those Conciencians who, caught up in the social changes which beset Conciencia itself, Latin America, and all countries commonly termed underdeveloped, are suffering from a sense of insecurity; essential, too, to the peace of mind of those who see the teachings of the Church as a reliable guide to social improvement. To set the minds of all these people at rest, I would entreat Your Eminence to answer at least two crucial questions:

To what socio-political programme does Your Eminence's statement refer?

Which of the points allegedly subscribed to or advocated by me does Your Eminence consider to be incompatible with the teachings of the Church?

Trusting that Your Eminence will view this request with paternal benevolence, I close with an assurance of total submission to the authority of the Church . . .'

The Cardinal's response, as Bruce Cornell remarked, came back with the speed of a boomerang. It appeared in all the Cielo newspapers and was printed in bold lettering by *El Temporal.*

To Antonio Valencia, priest of this city.

In your letter you ask me which of the points in your published programme conflict with the teachings of the Church. It is neither my wish nor intention to inquire into the motives which have prompted you to put such a question. You are well aware of the rulings of the Catholic Church in regard to the points raised by your programme, yet you have deliberately chosen to deviate from them. I say this in the belief that plain speaking is better than prevarication. I would add that, from the very outset of my life as a priest, I have been convinced of the wisdom of the papal directives which forbid priests to concern themselves with politics and with purely technical and practical questions relating to campaigns for social reform. In view of this belief, I have always striven throughout my long term of office to dissuade the clergy under my jurisdiction from meddling in such things.

This is the end of the matter. Rest assured, however, that my door remains open to you, should you wish to consult me.

Nothing happened for a while after the publication of this open letter. Valencia continued his lecture tours in an atmosphere compounded of hatred, admiration and speculation, and Alejandro Herrera waited tensely to see when the Cardinal would strip the rebel of his cloth. When the day came, Herrera splashed Medina's decree across six columns and sent telegrams bearing Fierro's signature to every paper in the organization, instructing their editors to open fire on Valencia at once.

The Cardinal's decree read as follows:

The Cardinal Archbishop of Cielo deems it his duty to inform Catholics that Padre Antonio Valencia has deliberately turned his back on the principles and directives of the Catholic Church. One has only to read the encyclicals of Holy Father to realize this deplorable fact, a fact which is all the more regrettable because Padre Valencia sanctions armed revolution as a means of seizing power at a juncture when the country is in the throes of a crisis occasioned in no small measure by the Opposition. Padre Valencia's activities are irreconcilable with his sacerdotal status and the cloth he wears. It is my wish to dissuade Catholics from accepting the false and pernicious principles which Padre Valencia espouses in his programme.

Esperanza Cardinal Medina, Archbishop of Cielo.

Valencia's response, which followed quickly on this decree, was also printed in Fierro's and Cuellar's newspapers.

Statement by Antonio Valencia.

When prevailing conditions are such as to prevent people from dedicating themselves to Christ, a priest must combat these conditions even if he is deprived of the right to celebrate Mass.

The present structure of the Church in Conciencia makes it impossible for me to perform my priestly duties in respect of the outward forms of divine worship. However, priesthood does not consist in saying Mass alone. Mass, whose celebration is one of the central tasks of a priest, is an essentially communal proceeding, but no Christian community can celebrate Mass unless it practises brotherly love.

I profess Christianity because I look upon it as the purest form of service to my fellow-men. I was called by Christ to become a priest for all time, eternally dedicated to my fellows. As a sociologist, I feel impelled to put brotherly love into practice. My study of Conciencian society has convinced me of the necessity for revolution as a means of feeding the hungry, clothing the naked, and promoting the welfare of the majority of our people.

I believe that the revolutionary struggle is a Christian and priestly struggle. Under the circumstances which prevail in our country today, that struggle is the only means of fulfilling the love which men must accord to their fellows. Ever since I took holy orders, I have tried in every conceivable way to encourage laymen, Catholics and non-Catholics to join the revolutionary struggle. In default of any vigorous popular response to the campaign conducted by certain laymen, I resolved to take action myself in the hope of bringing my fellow-citizens closer to God's love through the medium of brotherly love. I regard this decision as fundamental to my life as a Christian and a priest. My mission appears to conflict with the rulings of the ecclesiastical authorities. I have no wish to disobey Mother Church but, equally, I have no wish to betray my own conscience.

I have therefore asked the Cardinal to release me from my priestly duties in order to be able to serve my country on the secular plane. I am sacrificing a priestly right which is very dear to my heart: the right to celebrate Mass. I believe that it is incumbent on me to make this sacrifice because I have promised to obey the commandment of brotherly love in practice. Brotherly love must be the prime criterion on which any human decision is based. I am prepared to accept the dangers to which this attitude exposes me . . .'

The publication of this statement was the signal for a storm to break over Valencia's head. Unleashed by Alejandro Herrera with the smiling approbation of Fierro and his friends in the ruling clique, it eventually proved too much for men like Cuellar and the trade union leaders, who declined to keep faith with a man publicly accused of crypto-Communism, immorality, instability, arrogance and political naivety. Valencia was also rumoured to be a supporter of Fidel Castro and a friend of Che Guevara.

Vermeer, Bruce, Esther and other friends met several times to discuss the situation. The leaders who had been jointly responsible for the programme were deserting Valencia out of cowardice, and the masses who applauded him were forced to watch impotently as the man who now wore lay dress was driven into isolation. Public opinion trundled over him like a steamroller. Material for the campaign was procured from his wealthy former friends and from the chancellery itself. Pens dipped in vitriol accused the Catholics who continued to support him of being fellow-travellers. The accusations became more despicable with every day that passed. Herrera tore Valencia's speeches to ribbons, claimed that he had besmirched the cloth of his calling, declared that his presumption was unparalleled in the history of the Conciencian Church. With cruel cynicism, he painted Valencia as a deranged intellectual who identified himself with the bandits in the mountains and was perverse enough to act as spokesman for a gang of criminals who had committed murders and atrocities without number.

For Valencia's supporters, a catacomb era began. The slightest hint that they were on his side brought howls of execration from the establishment-controlled press. At the same time, his friends tried to persuade him to embark on a more moderate programme, but neither the Church authorities nor the ruling clique gave him any chance to defend his views. The army and police, who also opposed Valencia in his growing isolation, marched beneath the Cardinal's banner, and their ranks included Colonel García, who continued to submit reports to the President and lost no opportunity to blacken Valencia's name. The general public could no longer distinguish between truth and falsehood. Who was lying? The press, the priests, the President, the Cardinal?

Egged on by the press, government authorities took a tougher line in places where Valencia was due to speak. Sometimes they detained him for a few hours, sometimes they banned his appearance and persecuted those who supported him. The security police seemed to be everywhere, as did the journalists. The tide of abuse mounted. Among the milder words used were trickery, demagogy, insincerity, treason, mental instability, and megalomania.

It was whispered in the corridors of the chancellery that God would punish Valencia for his faithlessness, and this rumour, borne on the wings of calumny and disseminated from the pulpit itself, spread to every corner of the land. The Conciencian fear of divine retribution bordered on the pathological, and if God himself did not act with sufficient speed Colonel García would no doubt lend a helping hand.

Bruce and Esther saw no more of Valencia, who seemed to have avoided them since Esther's brush with the Seguridad. The only person he visited was Vermeer, who could see that the struggle had not weakened his resolve. On the contrary, the slanderous campaign in Fierro's newspapers and the silence of those owned by his old friend Cuellar had toughened him and strengthened his belief that only force could break the stranglehold of the oligarchy.

One night Valencia met the rebels' contact-man in Cielo. The conversation took place in his car, after he had lost his Seguridad shadow by dodging in and out of the heavy traffic. The unknown intermediary gave him all the information he needed. He was due to give a lecture at San Antonio, the nearest large town to Talmac. Men would be waiting there to take him by a devious route through the dense jungle to Rodriguez Tobar's base camp. Once there, he would do what the oligarchy had forced upon him. He would take up arms against those who had violated his ideals, who used their faith to cloak the exploitation of the people and were each day crucifying Christ anew. What he had failed to do by word or pen he would accomplish with the gun.

17

The sun hung vertically above him like the fiery eye of an angry god, but its scorching heat was tempered by the jungle foliage, a natural filter which robbed the rays of strength and let them fall like a shower of gold on the carpet of rotting vegetation.

Green-uniformed, with pistols, rifles, home-made grenades and fifty rounds per man, the party of guerilleros led by Raoul Castillo trudged through the jungle.

Antonio Valencia smiled in spite of his fatigue as he listened to the voices of the men ahead – Pedro, Emanuel, Carlos, Armando and Raoul Castillo, the inseparable quintet of whom he had come to admire Castillo in particular. They were uncomplicated people, ill-fed but indefatigable, with a toughness on patrol which made mock of the searing sun, the leeches and mosquitoes, the almost impassable tracks.

Rodriguez Tobar had summoned Valencia to his hut that first day. He was just briefing his men on the release of Don Henrico. His orders were succinct and to the point.

'Take him with you. Dump him near Talmac and keep him covered till he's out of sight.' He turned to the landowner. 'Keep your mouth shut, permanently. If we find out that you've talked, except in the most general terms, you will have signed your own death-warrant. The money has been paid and we shall keep our word.'

Don Henrico was led away and Tobar addressed himself to Valencia.

'I'm assigning you to Raoul Castillo's group. Obey his orders without question. We're a military organization – never forget that. Things are hotting up here. There's a whole battalion stationed round Talmac and in the village itself, and Losano has been promoted major. He owes it to himself and his career to shoot you down and take me prisoner. His men are out for blood.'

Pedro and Armando came to fetch Valencia next day. They

escorted him along densely overgrown jungle tracks to the place where he was to sleep among the trees with Castillo's twenty-five guerilleros. Valencia spent those first few weeks learning the rudiments of guerrilla warfare. He got to know the soldiers of the revolution, their sexual frustrations, their coarse language and the incredible adaptability which enabled them to live in the jungle more like jaguars than human beings. Many things repelled him at first. He was too accustomed to life in a comfortable apartment, to the plaudits of an enthusiastic audience. The jungle fighters sometimes reacted brusquely when he spoke to them, but his uncomplaining attitude and universal readiness to help soon won their confidence. At night, Valencia still dreamed of resuming the battle in university lecture-halls and the slums of the big cities, only to awaken with an even clearer realization that his place was with the guerilleros, the only people who were doing something positive to topple the establishment.

Even as Valencia's feet slipped in the rotting vegetation and sweat streamed down his back, he knew that he was sustained by something far stronger than himself. Conscience had brought him here, and no man could evade his conscience. He carried it with him always, stronger than his emotions, stronger than his dreams, stronger than the desire for repose.

Raoul Castillo turned and called a halt. The men sat down with their backs propped against tree-trunks and wiped the sweat from their faces.

'Listen,' Castillo said. 'Just before Cemento a path branches off towards the village. There are four huts at the junction. The *campesinos* have abandoned them and we're going to take their place. We move in tonight. An army patrol passes there regularly at about eight o'clock every morning. We let them go by and then slip into Cemento for supplies. Any questions?'

There were no questions. Castillo's word was law.

'Good, in that case we'll stop here for a siesta. You can have an hour.'

Valencia watched with a measure of envy as the others casually stretched out on the ground and fell asleep at once.

Raoul Castillo sat down beside him.

'How are you feeling? Nervous?'

Valencia considered the question in silence. Nervous? No, rather the opposite. He had sensed something strange taking place inside him in recent weeks. It came to him one night as he lay awake listening to the cicadas and the screech of the night-birds. He could feel every inch of his body. His muscles ached after the long day's march but his brain was clearer than it had ever been. Lying there in the darkness of the jungle, he reviewed his new way of life. He retired to his sleeping-bag at dusk and rose at dawn. He heard of guerilleros who had been shot, of successful patrols which had lured army columns into a trap. He came to realize that men like Rodriguez Tobar were obsessed by an ideal and admired their talent for crude but effective organization. During those early weeks he tended the wounded, often crouching beside a dying guerillero to hear his confession and grant him absolution so that he could die in peace and go to meet a God of love.

And then, that night, he had suddenly realized that life had ceased to be the most important thing. Only his death was important. Not until death had claimed him would eternal life be granted to his soul and, more especially, his ideals. His death could sow the seed of new ideas, kindle a flame which would burn ever more brightly until it shone like a beacon over all the countries of Latin America.

From that night onwards the thought of death had been as familiar to him as it was to every guerillero who greeted the dawn without knowing if he would live to see the setting sun.

'No, Raoul,' he said. 'I'm worth more dead than alive. Why should I be afraid of death?'

Castillo eyed the bronzed, muscular man beside him with keen interest.

'You're either a saint or an imbecile,' he mused. 'Whichever you are, you manage to fight imperialism and remain on good terms with God at the same time. That's quite an achievement.'

'You should read the papers, Raoul,' Valencia said wrily. 'I've been excommunicated ten times over.'

There was a lengthy silence.

'They're after us,' Castillo said. 'but it'll be a long time before they catch up with us. We're winning all along the line. It would take ten divisions to contain us.'

'They don't have ten divisions,' Valencia said. 'By the way, who actually shot that helicopter down?'

A broad smile appeared on Castillo's face.

'I did,' he said, almost gaily. 'We were well out of range by the time the fighters arrived. Cover, that's the best thing about this jungle.'

He stood up.

'We must get moving if we want to reach those huts by nightfall.'

Five minutes later the patrol was trudging along the narrow game-path in the direction of Cemento, unspeaking, rifles at the ready, last reserves of food and drink in the packs on their sweating backs . . .

The helicopter carrying Colonels Zambrano and García landed in the plaza at Talmac. A detachment of troops presented arms and stood there like statues until Major Losano had escorted the two senior officers into the headquarters building, which was heavily guarded. The conference took place in the room where Losano had spent so many nights with Maria. Its appearance had changed. Maps covered the walls, message forms lay on the desk, and the door was guarded by two green-helmeted sentries armed with submachine-guns. A small table and some chairs had been installed in the far corner of the room, and Losano politely invited the colonels to sit down.

An orderly brought coffee. The three men sipped in silence, but the atmosphere was tense and uneasy, and Colonel García's eyes reflected the impatience which was so evident in the President's abrupt directives to Colonel Zambrano.

Zambrano studied the other two over the rim of his coffee-cup. They were alike, he thought. They had almost the same expression, the same cold and unfeeling eyes, the same contempt for human life.

'According to my information,' García said, 'Antonio Valencia has gone to ground in this area. My men last saw him in San Antonio, where they lost him. San Antonio is within easy reach of here, so it seems almost certain that he has teamed up with his old friend Rodriguez Tobar. Have you anything to report, Major?'

Losano did not welcome the question. For some weeks now, patrol activity had been steadily increased. Hundreds of peasants had been interrogated in an ungentle fashion. Everyone even remotely suspected of being in touch with the guerilleros was hauled off to Talmac and screened by Losano in person. Many had failed to survive interrogation and were reported as having been shot while trying to escape, yet Losano's inquiries had yielded nothing save a suspicion that Valencia was somewhere in the vicinity. This suspicion had been half-confirmed by a *campesino* who thought that one of the guerilleros who recently raided his village for supplies was Antonio Valencia, or, if not, someone who closely resembled his picture in the newspapers. It was little enough to go on, but it did hold some element of certainty.

'Your professional survival depends on the elimination of Valencia,' García said curtly. Zambrano, thinking of John Wells, whose name had not been mentioned in the press when his helicopter was shot down, tried to mediate between the two men.

'It isn't as easy as you imagine, Colonel,' he said in his terse, rather abrupt way. 'There is a chance, but it's a slender one. Just after darkness, detachments will occupy the jungle round all the smaller villages. Their orders will be to lie low for forty-eight hours and keep the locals under surveillance. We've drawn up a list of the places where guerrilla units have most often replenished their supplies in the last two years. The villagers always plead ignorance when they're asked what the guerilleros say or do, but they're ready enough to admit having seen them. We often question the children, and children tend to be less discreet than their parents. Our records indicate that there are fifteen small hamlets which the rebels pass through once or twice a month. There have been seventy clashes between guerilleros and army units in the past two years. Hundreds of guerilleros and dozens of our own men have been killed as a result, discounting the one occasion when a major operational unit was lured into an ambush. I have given our new operation the code-name Sereno. Absolute secrecy has been preserved, but everything depends on whether our patrols manage to conceal themselves successfully. John Wells worked out the details just before he was killed.'

'Who will be leading these patrols?' asked García.

'Anti-guerrilla specialists. We have enough of them, now that the President has sent reinforcements.'

'What exactly do you hope to achieve, Colonel?'

Zambrano shrugged.

'We shall know that in a day or two.'

García nodded moodily, thinking of the President's fury at their last meeting. Major Losano's career was not the only one to hang by a thread. Zambrano's and his own were also in the balance, possibly the Defence Minister's too.

'Wipe them out – shoot to kill and take no prisoners,' he said harshly, echoing Colombo's shrill tone. 'Live guerilleros are a nuisance, even in captivity, and the trial of a man like Antonio Valencia would be a world sensation in the worst sense. Cornell and his fellow-journalists must be given nothing but the news of his death – you follow me, Colonel? One more thing: I propose to accompany Major Losano's patrol in person.'

Zambrano nodded. Nothing the chief of the security police had to say could surprise him. Losano gave a satisfied nod. García and he talked the same language.

Late that evening the guerrilla unit commanded by Raoul Castillo reached the four huts not far from Cemento. They stood on the edge of the forest near a bend in the track and had been uninhabited for so long that no patrol ever bothered to search them.

Valencia felt dog-tired. Rifle No. 4558805, passed on to him by Castillo, felt like a lead weight in his hand, and the cartridge-belts slung crosswise from his shoulders seemed to constrict his breathing. Absently, he chewed on a corn-cob and stared down at his sun-burned hands. His feet throbbed inside his boots and he thought ruefully of the bathroom in his Cielo apartment. He did not know if his mother had received his last letter to her in the United States. For a moment he could almost see her standing beside him and hear her voice. It grieved him to think of her and of the shock it must have given her to read the press reports about him. He pulled off his boots, scratched his short curly beard, and settled himself with his back to the wall of the hut. As he sat there looking round at the others, the full meaning of his predicament smote him for the first time. This would be his life from now on, the life of a hunted beast in the jungle round Talmac. Whenever he closed his eyes he could see the crowds who had hailed his programme at the National University, and he remembered what he had thought at that moment – that a moment of triumph could herald utter defeat.

Raoul Castillo stretched out beside him.

'At dawn tomorrow we pull back into the jungle. The patrol usually passes here at about eight, as I said. They're fresh troops from Cielo, not as well trained as Losano's original batch, about twenty of them to our twenty-five if it comes to a fight. You don't have to stand guard tonight. Better get some sleep.'

He indicated Valencia's rifle.

'Got the feel of it yet?'

Valencia nodded.

'One day you'll have to fire it, maybe kill a man. Doesn't the prospect worry you?'

He searched Valencia's face for signs of repugnance but found none.

'A man who preaches revolution can't stand aloof,' Valencia replied, slightly stung. 'I'm only putting my theories into practice, God forgive me.'

'God was murdered by the landowners,' Castillo retorted. 'God must be dead or we wouldn't be here now. He'd have punished us long ago.'

'Perhaps this revolution is our punishment.' Valencia spoke in a low, almost inaudible voice. He looked round at the faces of Armando, Carlos, Emanuel and Pedro, hard and impassive faces which conveyed almost nothing in the way of emotion.

He felt the unyielding wall of the hut against his head, and as he looked at the faces of his companions he saw other faces pass in review before his eyes: the pale, earnest face of Vermeer, whom he admired and in whom he had confided more freely than in anyone else on earth; the face of Bruce Cornell, who looked at him each time as if he were saying goodbye for ever; the peasant face of Bishop Zasi, vacillating between two worlds; the ancient face of the Cardinal, yellow and transparent as parchment; the face of Esther, more vivid and beautiful with every week and month that passed; his mother, whom he yearned for so constantly; and Arthuro Cuellar, whose expression at their last meeting had been as dismissive as that of Colonel García. Every sentence of their final conversation was engraved on his memory. 'I couldn't help it, Antonio. You want to destroy this country and bring the Communists to power. I'm scared. I trust you, yes, but not your friends. Do you know what will happen if you win? The Seguridad, which you detest in the person of Colonel García, I shall detest in the person of someone with a different name but the same functions. The Cardinal, who has expelled you from the Church, will be replaced by some weak-kneed nonentity who repeats government slogans like a ventriloquist's dummy. You'll exterminate people for the sake of your ideals. You'll kill without remorse on the assumption that you're killing in the cause of justice. Your ideas are becoming more and more extreme, less and less scientific. That's why I can't support you any longer.'

'You mustn't torment yourself,' Castillo said quietly. 'A lot of questions never get answered.'

Valencia slid forwards a little so that he lay at full length with his head pillowed on his pack. Darkness descended on him like a dusky veil, blurring the images in his mind.

He woke with a start, to hear Castillo addressing him in a subdued voice.

'We leave in five minutes. Get ready to move out, *rápido*.'

Valencia peered confusedly round the dim hut. He reached for his rifle and checked to see that it was loaded. Then he slowly straightened up, feeling the stiffness in his muscles. He buckled his cartridge-belts, pulled on his boots, shouldered his pack and went outside.

The others were waiting. Rifles at the ready, they disappeared one by one into the jungle behind the huts where they had spent the night.

Raoul Castillo looked at his watch.

'Half an hour to go. We'll eat in Cemento when the patrol has gone by. They never occupy the place, just check it before moving on to the next village. They won't be back before midday.'

Three-quarters of an hour passed without incident. Castillo became increasingly uneasy. Perhaps, contrary to latest reports, the soldiers had changed their schedule.

The forest was hushed. Now and then a *campesino* trotted by on horseback, shivering in the cool morning air despite his warm ruana. Then they heard the soldiers. They were trudging along in file, well spaced out, with their guns covering the track and the surrounding jungle. They did not speak. The faces beneath the green helmets were tense and strained. They could not have known that twenty-five rifles were trained on them, but Valencia got the impression that they increased their pace as they passed through the field of fire. They were young men with tanned faces, tough and well trained but sweating with fear.

Castillo breathed a sigh of relief when the patrol had rounded the bend.

'We'll wait another fifteen minutes and then head for Cemento. Just at present, food is more important to us than guns.'

The day awoke to joyful life as the sun rose blood-red above the mountains. Stirred by the morning breeze, the leaves seemed to wave to the birds as they took wing.

'Let's go.'

Raoul Castillo gave the order in a low, clear voice.

They marched in single file, hugging the edge of the forest so that they could dive for cover in an emergency. Half an hour later the huts of Cemento loomed up ahead of them. It was quiet, as usual. Just outside the village Castillo paused and turned to Valencia.

'This business is new to you, so be careful. Stay close to me the whole time. There's always the possibility of an ambush. *Cuidado!*'

The village had a single street, and its only shop was a provision store. The guerilleros assembled outside and waited for the proprietor to open up, but Castillo knocked in vain.

The first shots rang out just as he turned round. The guerilleros flung themselves to the ground and fired back, but it was no use. They had fallen into one of the simplest traps ever laid for them. The village square was entirely surrounded by government troops. From inside the shop came the voice of Colonel García.

'Surrender! Drop your guns!'

Castillo looked at Valencia.

'Start shooting,' he said softly. 'Pull the trigger and run. Keep firing and make sure you don't miss.'

There was a fusillade of shots from both sides. Firing from the hip, Valencia dashed for the nearest patch of jungle. A man reared up in front of him and fell over backwards with the breath rattling in his throat, and he knew that he had hit him. He felt a bullet smack into the ground beside him and ran on, gasping and retching, with his finger pumping the trigger.

Then the ground seemed to drop away beneath his feet as if rent apart by an earthquake, and he slowly keeled over on to his side. A strong brown hand tried to raise him.

'Raoul . . .' he whispered, but he got no further because before he could sit up Castillo collapsed across him. A searing pain shot through his arm, then through his leg. He looked up to see an officer with major's insignia reloading his automatic pistol with the dispassionate efficiency of an executioner. Castillo's body rolled sideways and came to rest beside him. His right hand groped its way along the ground and closed round Valencia's wrist.

Valencia tried to rise, but the pistol spat once more and pain spread to every corner of his body. Blood spurted from his mouth and cascaded over Castillo's hand. The officer's triumphant face began to gyrate, faster and faster, until it disappeared into a vortex. And when the firing ceased and it became so quiet that he could hear the breath rasping in his own throat, peace descended on him and he felt the infinite contentment that comes to those who dwell in a world where happiness belongs to all.

'That finishes one more of the scum,' said Major Losano. He sounded almost jovial.

The Life of Camilo Torres

3 February 1929
Born into a respected Colombian medical family. Visited Germany as a child and later attended the German College in Bogotá. Studied law for one semester after matriculating. Became engaged to the daughter of a family friend, also a doctor. After making a retreat, decided to enter the priesthood, initially against the wishes of his parents.

1954
Ordained after studying philosophy and theology for six years. Sent by Cardinal Luque of Bogotá to study sociology at the Catholic University of Louvain. This strongly influenced the course of his future activities.

1959
Returned to Bogotá and was appointed students' chaplain at the National University. Became joint founder of the faculty of sociology, where he was granted a professorial chair. His support of a students' strike brought him into conflict with Cardinal Concha, who called upon him to resign all his university appointments. Torres complied but persevered in his campaign for social reform.

17 March 1965
Publication of the basic programme of the *Frente Unido*, or United Front. Forbidden to preach.

26 June 1965
Laicization of Camilo Torres.

18 October 1965
Joined the National Liberation Front.

15 February 1966
According to an official communiqué, shot during an engagement with government troops. Accounts of his death vary but cannot be checked until government records are made public.

Statement by Camilo Torres

I think it important that my relationship to the Communist Party and its status within the Popular Front should be absolutely clear in the minds of the Colombian people.

I have said that I am a revolutionary, as a Colombian, as a sociologist, as a Christian and as a priest. Being aware that the Communist Party contains genuinely revolutionary elements, I cannot be anti-Communist.

I am not anti-Communist as a Colombian because anti-Communism tends to persecute nonconformist patriots of whom not all are Communist and most are poor.

I am not anti-Communist as a sociologist because Communist proposals for combating poverty, hunger, ignorance and lack of housing embody some effective and scientific solutions.

I am not anti-Communist as a Christian because I believe anti-Communism to be a wholesale condemnation of all that the Communists defend.

I am not anti-Communist as a priest because, even if the Communists do not realize it themselves, many of them may be genuine Christians. If they are of good faith they may possess sanctifying grace, and if they possess sanctifying grace and love their neighbours they will find salvation. My role as a priest, even though it does not accord with the conventional religious view, is to bring people into communion with God. The most effective way of achieving this is to encourage them to serve their neighbours in accordance with their conscience.

I am prepared to fight alongside the Communists for common aims: against one-man rule and United States domination; for the acquisition of power by the popular classes.

Not wishing public opinion to identify me solely with the Communists, I have always striven to consort not only with Communists but with all independent revolutionaries.

It is immaterial if the press continues to represent me as a Communist. I would sooner renounce my beliefs than yield to the pressure of dictatorship. I would sooner comply with the norms set by the Popes of the Church than with those laid down by the 'popes' of our ruling classes. John XXIII empowered me to join in concerted action with the Communists when he wrote, in his encyclical *Pacem in terris*:

'It is unjust simply to identify certain movements pertaining to economic and social conditions, spiritual development or appropriate systems of government, with certain philosophical dogmata pertaining to the nature, origin, aim and purpose of the world and mankind, even when such movements spring from, and are guided by, such ideologies. A scientific concept, once established, can no longer be changed, whereas these movements are necessarily subject to changes in the prevailing situation. Besides, who could deny that such movements, in so far as they accord with the laws of ordered reason and take account of the just demands of the human person, contain something good and commendable?'

The most important feature of Catholicism is brotherly love. 'He that loveth another hath fulfilled the law' (*Romans*, xiii, 8). If this love is sincere it must strive to be effective. If good works, the giving of alms, a few privately endowed schools, a few housing schemes – in short, all that is known as charity – fail to provide food for the hungry or educate the masses, we must seek ways of promoting the welfare of mankind.

The privileged minority, which is in power, makes no attempt to seek effective remedies because it would be obliged to curtail its privileges. It would, for example, be better for Colombia if capital were invested inside the country so as to create employment instead of taken out of it in the form of dollars. Because the Colombian peso is steadily depreciating, however, the possessors of affluence and power make no attempt to prevent the export of money.

This renders it necessary to wrest power from the privileged minority and give it to the underprivileged majority. To effect this transfer swiftly is the purpose of revolution. Revolution can proceed peacefully provided the minority does not offer fanatical resistance. Revolution is thus the way to establish a government which secures food for the hungry, clothing for the naked, education for the ignorant and fulfilment of the law of love, not by random or ephemeral means and not merely for some, but for the great mass of our fellow-men.

It follows that revolution is not only permissible but positively incumbent on all Christians who regard it as the only effective and sufficient means of realizing love for all men. It is true that all authority stems from God (*Romans*, xiii, 1), but St Thomas says that the concrete properties of authority come from the people. 'If authority be directed against the people, that authority is not justified and is called tyranny.' We Christians can and must fight tyranny. The present government is tyrannical because only 20 per cent of voters support it and its decisions stem from a privileged minority.

I have renounced the emoluments and prerogatives of the clergy but I have not ceased to be a priest. I believe that I have dedicated myself to revolution and brotherly love. I have ceased to celebrate Mass the better to realize this brotherly love in the temporal, economic and social domain. If my neighbour bears me no malice when the revolution is accomplished, I shall, if God so wills, celebrate Mass again.

I believe that in this way I am obeying Christ's commandment: 'Therefore if thou bring thy gift to the altar, and there rememberest that thy brother hath ought against thee; leave there thy gift before the altar, and go thy way; first be reconciled to thy brother, and then come and offer thy gift.'

After the revolution, Christians will come to realize that we have built a system based on brotherly love. The struggle is long. Let us begin!